Cold Dead Night

Brand of Justice
Book 1

Lisa Phillips

Two Dogs Publishing, LLC

eBook ISBN: 979-8-88552-135-2

Paperback ISBN: 979-8-88552-136-9

Large Print Hardback ISBN: 979-8-88552-139-0

Published by: Two Dogs Publishing, LLC. Idaho, USA

Cover Design by: Sasha Almazan and Gene Mollica, GS Cover Design Studio, LLC

Edited by: Jen Weiber

Chapter One

Friday, 10:37 pm.
Salt Lake City, Utah.

If Kenna didn't run fast enough, a child would die tonight.

Each breath puffed a visible cloud from her mouth and into the cold air as she raced down the alley past shoveled mounds of crusty gray snow that had fallen a week ago. On the street at the end, lanes of Friday night traffic buzzed in both directions. People blew through the city with the oppressive force of a blizzard.

She sprinted for the lone door that split the exterior wall.

Until a patrol car pulled into the alley.

Kenna slammed her shoulder into the brick and crouched beside a pile of pallets and soggy cardboard boxes.

The car eased by her.

She squeezed her eyes shut and stilled as if frozen solid. Encased in ice.

He couldn't know she was here. Not yet.

The second it passed her, she headed for the door. A minute thirty to pick the padlock and she was in.

The building was an abandoned theater where the rubber soles of her boots pounded the floor with a dense reverberation. Kenna continued her race through the lobby. The air of her movement curled up old show posters as she flew past torn velvet chairs to a door marked STAIRS. She twisted the handle, breathing hard, and flew inside the stairwell. Her clothing made no sound as she sprinted down the concrete steps.

All the way down.

Down.

She stopped on the basement landing. The schematics she'd found online showed a boiler room and laundry room just beyond the door. Storage rooms. Basically a labyrinth of hallways and chambers. Plenty of space for a killer to do his work without being disturbed.

She knew that all too well.

Everything within her investigation of the killer—and the kidnapping and murder of two little girls—pointed her to this place. Tonight, the killer had a third victim in his grasp, and Kenna wasn't going to let this life be extinguished the way the others had.

She couldn't. This was what she'd been born to do.

And yet, Kenna didn't move. Everything in her just... stopped. She'd faced down a killer before and it had all but destroyed her. Each time she confronted those heinous memories and fears, she wanted to be as far from it as possible.

She stood in that basement stairwell and the ice crept over her again. It always came over her the same way. First, the memories. Then, she'd become almost paralyzed. Not able to move or even breathe. After, the most frigid chill would swallow her whole until the hope of ever getting warm again seemed futile. One day, tomorrow or years from now, she would be found frozen to death somewhere. Whether that foreknowledge portended a peaceful end, or a horrific one, she didn't yet know.

Either way, the outcome would be the same. Time was going to run out, and Kenna would have to give an account for her life. What would they say about her? She'd faced her fears and done her best, or she'd let a sick man take everything away? Again.

In the distance, a child let out a short cry. Ellayna Feathers. Nine years old. The latest prey of the Seventh Day Killer.

Kenna pushed through to the hall. Beyond the heavy door was cold as a morgue. She had to ease it closed so it didn't slam, but nonetheless, air whistled down the corridor. A rush of wind that would alert anyone hiding down here.

Kenna flicked her baton and extended it to its full length. Sweat rolled down her temple. Cold moisture tracked like frozen fingers down her cheek. She didn't bother to swipe it away, just kept walking.

One foot. Then the other. The alternative of not continuing with each step wasn't something she wanted to see behind her eyelids when she tried to sleep tonight. There were enough lifeless gazes there. Kenna didn't want one more, least of all that of a child. Ellayna Feathers wasn't a body she wanted to find in the mountains the way she had with his other victims. Used and discarded. Tossed out like trash. No. This girl was going to live no matter what it took.

She headed for the source of the cry—a room at the end of the hall labeled within the building schematics as STOR-AGE. The whole place had been unoccupied, in disrepair and abandoned, since the theater company collapsed a few months back.

The killer needed to be in custody. Kenna would have to

involve the cops in order to hand over this guy. They would be forced to acknowledge her presence in their world, whether they liked it or not.

But Kenna's priority here was Ellayna. Not just because of the tears in the mother's eyes the day she'd hired Kenna, as she'd told the story of her daughter's disappearance six days ago. But because she knew how it felt to be taken. Violated.

The FBI hadn't been able to find Ellayna. Neither had the police. The mother had turned to Kenna, a private investigator *and* her last hope. Someone who'd lived in both worlds—as cop and victim—and now walked in neither. She wasn't an FBI agent anymore. And she certainly wasn't a victim.

She was a PI.

It was on the seventh day that this killer struck his final blow, giving him the moniker, "The Seventh Day Killer" in the news and online. But his name was Gerald Rickshire, and Kenna didn't care what everyone else thought or said about him. Or her, for that matter. Only that Ellayna made it home, and he never did this to anyone ever again.

Then she would go back to her solitary life, and the next case.

The storage room was bare except for a bloody, stained mattress in the middle. Ellayna Feathers huddled in the corner, her head turned away from the mattress. Kenna wouldn't have wanted to look at it either.

She took one glance at the hall—both directions. They needed to get out of here.

Then she stepped inside the room. Trapped with the girl. *No.* She couldn't allow her thoughts to coalesce like that. She wasn't a victim anymore.

Kenna moved left immediately so she could hug the wall. She had to do this in such a way the little girl didn't make a noise. Would she scream, or comply?

The little girl stiffened at the disturbance, her eyes squeezed shut.

Kenna crouched. She didn't want to appear big and intimidating like the man must've. She had to be far less imposing. She whispered, "Laynie." That was what her mother called her.

"Mama," the little girl whispered back.

Kenna nearly moaned. She choked back the lump in her throat. *This happened to me, too.* The trickle down her cheek was sweat, just like before. She didn't cry anymore. Why waste tears when the past remained unchanged?

Kenna heard no sound in the hall, so she dropped the whisper. "Ellayna, everything is going to be okay."

The little girl's eyes flew open.

Kenna tried a smile. "Hey." How did she tell the girl she knew exactly how she felt when they didn't have any moment to spare? How did she forge the bond they shared to find solidarity together? "I'm here to bring you back to your Mommy. She asked me to come get you."

Ellayna Feathers whispered, "I'm not supposed to go with strangers."

Kenna steadied herself and stood to slowly approach the little girl wearing the dirty dress. "Mommy said to tell you that Bubby loves you."

Ellayna's mother was currently seven months pregnant and confined to bed rest. It was a boy—something they hadn't told anyone else yet. A baby brother Ellayna called, "Bubby."

The little girl's eyes flickered. Kenna held out her hand. It would be cold to the touch, her fingers like ice. The way Ellayna's would be—until she recovered.

"I'm going to take you home, and we'll call your mom so you can talk to her, okay?"

Her eye flickered again, past Kenna's shoulder. The flicker turned to wide eyes. Terror.

Kenna heard nothing. But she knew instantly he was there.

She gripped the baton, now in her left hand, and spun. His hand was already coming down, and whatever he had clenched in his fist headed for her temple. She ducked her head to the side and swiped out to clip him across the legs.

He cried out and stumbled but didn't go down. A digital camera clattered across the floor.

Kenna launched up, knocked him off balance with a shove and rammed her heel into his stomach. His body bent as he tripped back two steps. Too quickly he shook it off. She switched her baton to the other hand and braced.

He ran at her, screaming a foul name.

Ellayna shrieked.

Kenna ducked. He connected with her shoulder in a jarring thud. Breath escaped his lungs as they grappled together. His fist hammered into her stomach. She coughed out the air and slammed the baton down on his thigh. An elbow clipped her forehead. Kenna gritted her teeth, dropped the baton, and reached for the holster on her leg.

She brought the stun gun up, her finger already on the button.

A crackle sounded. His body jerked. While he shuddered against her, she wondered if she would ever get that odor out of her nose. The second he dropped to the floor, Kenna spun him to his face, put a knee on his lower back, and reached into her side pocket. She secured his hands and feet behind him using the double cuffs, then stood. For good measure, she pulled out a third set and secured his hands to his feet.

Just in case.

The phone was tucked in her right back pocket. She

dialed 911 and waited for them to pick up. The second they did, she rattled off the FBI case number and the man's name.

"And your name?"

Kenna hung up and stowed the phone away. Gerald Rickshire glared at her from the floor. She turned to Ellayna. "You wanna go now, Laynie?"

The little girl just stared.

Kenna scooped her up, walked down the hall, and ascended the stairs. Two uniformed officers met her in the lobby, one younger and female and the other probably fifty. He wore the lines of years on the job—the training officer. Pierce and Meacham respectively, according to their name plates. They looked tired. Long shift, at the end of a long week.

"He's tied up downstairs." Kenna told them how to get to the storage room, then took a step back out of their space to put the cold air of the lobby between them and her—and Ellayna.

Meacham lifted one hand. "You're not leaving."

Pierce reached for her radio. "I'll call for an ambulance."

"The guy downstairs?" She hugged Ellayna closer, the girl now worryingly still. "It's the Seventh Day Killer."

Both cops flinched.

Pierce said, "How—"

Meacham cut her off. "Let's go." Their footsteps pounded the floor, belts squeaking and jingling as they headed for the stairs, calling back, "Don't leave!"

Kenna watched them race away. Before, she'd have been right there as well, doing the job of special agent for the FBI. At the same moment she thought that she realized she'd taken a step toward them. She turned on her heel and strode to the entrance instead, then out into the desolate alley where she belonged.

Her car was parked a street away, so she bypassed the black and white patrol car and headed in that direction. Blue and red lights flashed against the brick of the building, too bright of a contrast with the dark stage lights long since switched off.

The night sky hung thick with an inversion that obscured the stars over Salt Lake City. Mountains stood tall over this pocket of civilization, where business and religion were often one and the same. Great peaks arched above the lives below, as though standing guard. Or hemming them in.

She needed to leave. The pilgrimage home to pick up her mail—and find Ellayna—was done now. It was time to get back on the road.

Kenna climbed in the front seat of her Acura and held Ellayna on her lap as she drove slowly around the corner, back to the front entrance where the cop vehicle was parked. Those flashing lights lit up the interior of her car as she watched the officers walk out with Gerald Rickshire in cuffs.

She tightened her hold on Ellayna and managed to choke out a sentiment. "It will be okay." Was that even true?

Maybe for Ellayna it would be. She had a mother. She had friends and extended family. Caregivers. Support.

Kenna had none of those things, so what did she know?

The cops shut Gerald Rickshire in the back seat. An ambulance pulled in from the street. Kenna got out and carried Ellayna to the EMTs, handing the little girl off. "She's really quiet."

The EMT nodded, compassion softening her gaze as she turned to assess the girl. Ellayna didn't lie down. And she didn't take her gaze from Kenna, who lifted her phone to her ear and listened to it ring.

"Hello?" Ellayna's mother's voice shook, consumed with a motherly fear Kenna would never understand. But she knew what it felt like to lose someone—to know in her soul that she would always be alone.

"Ms. Feathers, it's Makenna Banbury."

The woman groaned, as though already in labor. Pregnant both with fear for her child *and* the baby she was about to have.

"Ellayna is safe. She'll be on her way to the hospital in a moment."

"Laynie..." Her daughter's name was a cry.

"She's right here." Kenna handed over the phone and made sure the little girl had a good grip on it.

Ellayna's hands trembled as she lifted it to her ear. "Mama?"

Kenna waited through the conversation while life buzzed around her. EMTs. The cops.

"You saved her."

The words came from her left. She glanced over at Officer Pierce. Words caught in her throat.

As soon as she had her phone back, Kenna walked away. The job was complete. There was certainly nothing else to stick around for.

Pierce called out to her. She waved the officer off, hardly able to even voice words when the adrenaline shuddered through her and the ice in her veins fought back. She strode to her car and slid in the front seat where she gripped the cold steering wheel and sucked in a handful of breaths. Life receded and the frost crept back in. Her body stilled; as good as dead once again.

A fist rapped on the window.

She jerked around, dropping one of her gloves before she could tug it on. Kenna rolled down the window.

Meacham held out a phone. "It's for you."

Her stomach lurched. Answering it meant connecting her

life here. She reached with shaky fingers and took hold of the phone. "Banbury."

Silence greeted her. Then his voice, deep and strong. "Makenna?"

A sharp pain jabbed through her chest. Probably just where the Seventh Day Killer's elbow had impacted.

"It's true then. Two years, and you're back?"

"I'm *not* back." She had to choke out the words.

Two hours, and she'd be gone again. Away from this frozen wasteland of memories. Where all the good she tried to do amounted to nothing. On the road, it was just her. She didn't have to deal with anyone else. Their emotions. Their expectations. What they thought she should think or feel.

She needed the silence.

Ryson spoke again. "And yet you're here."

He'd been her friend, once upon a time. Maybe even her best friend. Now he just sounded irritated and familiar in a way that made her chest ache, as though a part of her actually wanted to see him again.

She had to get out of the city. "Sarge—"

"It's Lieutenant Ryson now."

Kenna touched her fingers to her neck and let the cold seep into her skin. "What do you want?" She held the phone between her chin and shoulder and pulled both gloves on.

"More than you want to give." He was silent for a second. "But for starters, you can tell me why I'm looking at a dead body with your business card on him."

Chapter Two

Friday, 11:47 pm.

"Were you even gonna tell me you're back in town?" The low voice rumbled over to her from the other side of the yellow tape. Ryson was shorter but made up for it in bulk. Tonight, a beanie covered his thinning black hair, grayer than the last time she'd seen him. He lifted the police tape.

She stepped under. "It's been a long day."

"It's been two long *years*." Ryson grasped just above her elbow and tugged her around. She looked down at his hand on her arm, then back up. He let go.

At least there were no FBI agents here. As soon as her name popped up in the system, one would show. Kenna didn't want to see anyone from her former career as a fed.

That part of her life was as dead as her partner.

"You were first on scene?" She needed to get out of town

as soon as possible. Back on the road, with only solitude for company.

The way she needed it to be.

He folded his arms. "It's been a long time. You good?"

Kenna didn't really know how to answer that. Ryson wasn't a man she'd ever lied to before. "Just tell me about the dead guy." That's why she'd come.

Two years of living anonymously, keeping her head down. Did he even realize it was only loyalty to the friendship they'd had that made her come to the scene tonight, instead of disappearing again like she really wanted to do?

He didn't miss her glance as she, with feigned nonchalance, searched for her former colleagues. "After what the FBI did to you, you think I'd have called them here?"

He didn't know the half of it. "Well, you didn't call me. For all I know, you're glad I left."

"Is that what you tell yourself?"

"I'm tired." And sore. "Can we just get on with this?" Because it didn't matter whether Ryson tried to keep her name out of it, or not. The FBI would find out anyway. *He* would find out.

A muscle in Ryson's jaw flexed. "There's something you need to see."

He led her to where a body lay on the ground, surrounded by people. Investigators. Cops. EMTs. The medical examiner and his assistant.

People behind the tape and along the perimeter looked on. A cell phone camera flashed. A couple of other people held their phones up, probably live-streaming the highlight of a weekend that had barely started. Some local news van pulled up down the street and two people got out, a blonde and a tall man who reached back in for a camera.

More people than she'd seen in months.

It made the skin between her shoulder blades itch.

Kenna tried to look around the medical examiner to the dead guy on the ground. Tan slacks, denim jacket. Arms folded on his chest unnaturally, like they'd been positioned that way after the fact. She couldn't get close enough to see his face. "Who is he?"

"Don't know yet."

Kenna rolled her shoulders. "Start with what you do know."

Ryson took a breath that doubled his shirt size and blew it out slowly. The way his lips twitched almost looked like a smile. "You're back."

"I'm not back. Tell me, and then I'm gone." The sooner the better.

"Got a call about a dead guy, so we responded."

"We?"

"My partner, Officer Fauster." He motioned to the officer at the tape, recording everyone's names for the case file. "I'm his training officer."

"The body is fresh?"

He motioned at the medical examiner. "They tell me he's been dead a day, maybe more. But the temperature out here... it's just preliminary."

She nodded. "Cause of death?"

"Nothing obvious."

"So what was obvious?"

"No ID. No phone, no watch." He hesitated. "No hair on his body at all."

"Maybe he's a professional swimmer. Or a cancer patient."

Ryson held up a sealed evidence bag. Inside was a business card. "He had this on him."

Kenna didn't take the bag. *Makenna Banbury. Private*

Investigator. "So he got one of my business cards." She wanted to shrug it off, but if it was related to Ellayna Feathers somehow...she couldn't.

"We haven't seen each other in a while, but we've been friends a long time." Ryson folded his arms. "You really think blowing this off will work with me?"

If he hadn't been on the phone with Meacham, she wouldn't even have contacted him. She'd have simply left Salt Lake as soon as she picked up her mail. The way she always did.

He shook his head. "This means something."

Kenna pushed out a long breath. "Maybe."

"The way it was placed, he didn't just have it on him. It was positioned on his body. Probably by the person who killed him."

Since she would either recognize him, or she wouldn't, Kenna figured she may as well find out which it was. The only open spot to crouch beside him was by his shoes. A crime scene investigator clicked his camera like he was playing a first-person shooter and his fire team was under attack.

She peered at the soles and noted their condition. No scuffs or signs of wear. Brand new, or close to it. One pant leg hadn't been adjusted. The bare skin beneath was cracked and dry.

"I'll make sure you're kept in the loop, okay? You could even assist the detectives with their investigation."

Like Kenna was going to stick around long enough to investigate a murderer who'd left her a calling card? "I'm busy. I have...stuff going on."

She tried not to sound irritated with Ryson, but she was ready to collapse with exhaustion. After solving a serial killer case, what else was there to do? Her forearm still burned, and her ribs hurt more than she wanted to admit.

Ryson looked over his shoulder. "Time's up. The cavalry is here, and they sent the new guy." He moved away. "Special Agent Jaxton, good to see you."

Hands slapped together, a friendly shake. Had Ryson made friends with this FBI agent the way he had with her?

She didn't turn to greet this "Agent Jaxton"—whoever he was. Better that she get a handle on herself, otherwise she was going to wind up swimming in jealousy. The reality was that life in Salt Lake City had moved on without her, and she needed to get over it.

SAC Stairns had sent the new guy to look into something regarding Kenna. So what? The SAC likely figured he'd be the one with no bias. The rest of the team she used to work with at the FBI probably would've turned down the assignment. Not one of them had called her since she left. They'd rather not be reminded of the colleague they'd lost.

It was easier to let the past remain in the past.

Too bad for her, she had to walk around with it encased inside her. Like that flash of the camera. One second, frozen in time, followed by a hundred more all the same. Blood. Death.

The medical examiner gave her a side glance. Lieutenant Ryson and the special agent got into the details, basically a review of everything she and Ryson had just said to each other. A conversation she'd had with local cops a million times before.

Kenna kept her voice low and leaned over. "Cause of death?"

The medical examiner looked up at her. "I'll know more when I do the autopsy, but there are signs of asphyxiation."

Her throat closed out of empathy, and she took another glance at the body. The old man's skin was stark white, with pale lips. Eyes shut. Had she met him before?

"Can't tell yet if it was natural, or intentional."

"I know. Autopsies take time." She looked at the fingers, the way his arms and hands had been positioned. He hadn't fallen here like that. He had no coat. It was in the low thirties tonight.

A conversation went on in tandem behind her, and she heard her name whispered. A minute or so later, the agent's boots moved to her side. "What've we got, Collins?"

Collins was apparently the medical examiner. And he couldn't have missed the way she actually avoided looking at the FBI agent. Or maybe she simply was interested in a dead man. "A dead guy who has a date with my table."

Special Agent Jaxton said, "You can't give me anything?"

Collins rocked back on his heels and stood. "Like I said. I need to get him on my table."

"Who is—"

Kenna straightened and turned, locking eyes. She saw a flash of dark suit, white shirt. Dark tie. Heavy black wool over-coat. Dark hair. Same old, same old. A special agent like all the rest. "Excuse me, I was just leaving."

She stepped away, and he moved to cut her off. Lieu-tenant Ryson reached up and squeezed the back of his neck.

The new guy held out a hand. "Special Agent Oliver Jaxton. Most people call me Jax, but I'm guessing you're not most people. I'm guessing you're Makenna Banbury." He frowned. "SAC Stairns did not inform me you were currently in town."

Wasn't that why he was here? She turned to Ryson. "It was good to see you, Lieutenant."

He almost smiled as she spun to leave.

Jaxton called after her. "Your business card."

Ah. As she'd thought, this agent was here because her

name popped on the radar, not because the FBI knew she was back.

"I'm not back. Tell Stairns that." Kenna's stomach flipped over, and she walked faster. Jaxton caught up to her as she headed for the police tape. She glanced aside at him. "It's late. You don't need me here."

There were entirely too many people with eyes on her. She hadn't had this much attention since...

"Doesn't mean I won't ask why you're on scene."

"Ryson informed me there was a dead guy with my card on him." The lieutenant shouldn't get in trouble for that. "This guy's death has nothing to do with me."

"And yet you're here. Coincidentally, of course." He snagged her elbow and tugged. "Ms. Banbury."

She looked down at his hand. Then back up to glare at his face. What was with these law enforcement guys? She wasn't a suspect.

He didn't let go.

Ryson had wandered off to talk with a uniformed officer. *Traitor.*

"Why might a dead man be in possession of your business card?" He waved it in the bag like damning evidence.

"It's a business card." She tugged her arm from his grasp and folded both arms in front of her. Only because it was cold. "I have a thousand."

"Why would it show up tonight? And now you're here too, when my boss tells me you don't live in this city anymore. Why would that be?"

"Clearly I want my name back in the media because everyone's forgotten it by now. I like the attention." Kenna tried to shrug, but her shoulders weighed a hundred pounds each. "Heck, I probably killed that guy myself just so I can investigate just like the good old days."

He stared at her. "Should I write that in my report?"

"I had a job in town, and now it's done." She motioned to the coroner's van. "This guy will still be dead on Monday morning. You can call me then to ask your follow-up questions."

Not that she'd rather have this conversation later, she just wanted time to think it through and maybe do some work of her own. Then she planned to drive a thousand miles so there was no way she could get dragged into this. Time and space. Those were the only things that gave her peace. The good old days hadn't ended so well.

"Do you recognize him?"

Kenna stomped feeling back into her numb legs, all the way over to the stretcher the guy was now laid out on. Collins was in the process of zipping up the body bag. "One sec."

He gave a slight nod.

She had her phone ready. Kenna pulled it out, already swiping up with her thumb. She snapped a picture of the guy's face and then stowed it.

"Hey!"

Old man. Lined face, no visible differentiation in the skin tone between his forehead and where his eyebrows should have been. So they hadn't been shaved off recently. He'd had no hair on his body for a while.

"You can't take a photo of my vic."

Kenna stepped back, something niggling in her mind.

"Give me your phone."

"Get a warrant for it." She stowed the burner cell in her back pocket. "And he's not your vic."

"He will be." Boy, did that ever sound like a threat.

Collins finished zipping up the bag.

"I'll walk Ms. Banbury out." Ryson's comment jolted her from her thoughts.

Special Agent Jaxton frowned. He was going to need Botox if they kept running into each other. Good thing there was no way that would happen.

Kenna took a step back. "Nice to meet you."

The look on his face plainly said *liar*.

Ryson led the way back to the tape. "I can't believe you—"

"Thanks for calling me."

Never mind that she sounded completely sarcastic. That itch between her shoulders had morphed to a crawling sensation. As though a hundred bees flitted across her back.

"I didn't. You were just there." He sighed. "Did you really take a picture of the body?"

She pulled out her phone and sent the image to her email address so she could start the search as soon as she got home. After she made sure there definitely was nothing crawling on her skin, of course.

Ryson huffed. "This was a courtesy, nothing more. You're here and this involves you. It can't be a coincidence this happened tonight."

Except she'd been miles from here. How could the two be related? "It doesn't mean—"

"If I'd known you would get into it with—"

She spun to him. "You didn't even know I was here. It was happenstance you got the chance to have me come look at this."

She'd caught a serial killer tonight. Instead of celebrating by sleeping for nineteen hours, she was here in an ocean of people that threatened to drag her into the swell. Trying to figure out who this guy was, and why he had one of her business cards on him.

A muscle ticked in Ryson's jaw.

"I've gotta go." She stepped back. "It was good to see you."

"That's the first thing you've said that I actually believe." He sighed. "You're not gonna look into this case, are you?"

"I'm hitting the road tomorrow afternoon." Never mind that there was something about this victim, an idea she couldn't let go of. No hair at all on his body? Plus, the scene had definitely been staged. "I'll call you."

She left Ryson standing there.

"There you go, lying again."

Kenna kept walking. She'd worked hundreds of cases in her life. Her father had worked thousands during his career. That dead man could have been a mug shot she'd seen, or a sketch artist rendering. Someone she'd run into at a freeway rest stop, or on a city street. He could have been a photo in a case file left by her father on the coffee table while she watched Saturday morning cartoons and ate off-brand fruity cereal.

Officer Fauster looked up from his clipboard. "Private Investigator Makenna Banbury, whom I'm told is of the prestigious line of Banbury crime fighters. Checking out so soon? Was it something I said?"

"You'll just have to read the Yelp review I'm gonna write like everyone else."

Fauster held out his hand, his palm covered by fingerless gloves. Kenna took his hand and shook it, aware the Special Agent was watching.

"It's been a pleasure." Fauster let go. "And the lieutenant speaks highly of you. Says you saved his life during a bank robbery."

"Long time ago."

"All the good stuff was." The young officer seemed particularly perturbed about that.

"You'll get there. Just be careful because it might not look quite so glamorous when you do."

"Yes, ma'am."

Kenna clicked the fob for her car locks and climbed in. In the quiet, she took a breath. Inhaling solitude while she shrugged off the feeling of being hemmed in by so many people. She turned the key and cold air pumped out the vents. While it warmed, she looked at the image on her phone again.

Where had she seen this guy before?

The question lingered all the way back to her home. Even while she lay her head on her pillow, stared at the ceiling, and tried to fall asleep.

She knew the victim somehow.

Chapter Three

Two years ago.

The motion of the vehicle caused her body to sway. The whole world darkened, then car headlights illuminated the interior. Kenna rolled up against something solid. Warm. He smelled familiar.

"Pacer." She didn't know if she said his name aloud, or just in her head.

Her senses came back online like a computer rebooting.

Sounds crystalized—the hum of the road and the van's engine. Her vision cleared, and she found her face smashed up against Pacer's shirt. Headlights shone through the back windows, that LED glow against the frosted glass.

When she tried to move, all her nerve endings flooded with sensation at once. Freezing. Pain. Trapped, caught like a fish in a net.

Kenna cried out at the same time she tried to muffle her noise. She knew she shouldn't make a sound, but the pain was overwhelming. Panic tightened her chest like a hand squeezing a balloon. A scream escaped, loud and anguished.

Everything flashed white.

Pacer moaned. The van swayed. Kenna lifted her arms as much as she could—her elbows were bent, raised and hyper-extended at the joint. Twin slices bisected her forearms, her hands secured together by her own wrists. The tendons? She could barely move her fingers without them erupting in pain. There was blood everywhere. She had to get her emotions under control if she was going to be able to think clearly.

The van turned a corner and the unconscious body rolled into her. She grunted. "Pacer." Her voice was a barely audible whisper, her throat raw. "Wake up."

He moaned, low in his throat, though he was still unconscious. She twisted her neck and tried to breathe through the pain. Her hands were useless, her arms screamed with the slightest movement. She tried to see who the driver was, but there was a barrier between them and the front of the van.

Taking them to...

She cut off that thought. It wasn't going to get them out of there. "Pacer."

Kenna tried to nudge him. He only moaned. She tried to sit up but the van swayed again, and she fell back. Her head hit the floor of the van and pain ricocheted through her skull. She tried to breathe through it.

Tried to fight the fear.

Tried.

Tried.

Tears rolled from her eyes.

Pacer needed to wake up, but if she couldn't help herself, then she was as good as dead.

A sick feeling roiled in her stomach. She turned and heaved a couple of times, but nothing came out.

Kenna rolled back and stared up at the ceiling of the van. It was dark now. No headlights meant no cars behind them.

The van was alone on the road.

Her phone. Her gun. She didn't even have her belt on, and her shoes had been removed along with her coat and sweater. Shirt and pants were all he'd left her with. Even her hair-tie had been pulled out. Or it'd fallen out.

Pacer was the same. No belt or shoes. Left with just his undershirt and pants.

Cold skittered across her skin like frozen branches scratching a windowpane. She exhaled and her breath puffed white in front of her. She huddled closer to Pacer.

"You need to wake up." Her voice wavered with the pain. Her arms were on fire, slick with blood, useless.

The van rolled to a stop. They both shifted, and she had to wince as agony shot yet more fire up her forearms. It was an audible cry, the kind her best friend's daughter used to make when she was having a bad dream.

Red tail lights flashed on the back of the van. They were stopping.

A door slammed.

"Pacer, get up." She sucked a breath and nudged him as hard as she could with her shoulder as she rolled into him. "Get up. *Now*."

Her arms lay limp. She used her elbow to poke his side, no choice but to ignore the pain it caused. A frustrated tear rolled from her eye, down to touch the hair above her ear. She bent her legs and kicked at Pacer.

He moaned and shifted.

Thunder rolled outside the windows of the van. A huge wooden door moved right to left and a dark figure passed on the other side of the frosted-out back windows.

Fear tightened her stomach as though he'd taken hold of

it. Without even touching her. *The fear is in your head.* She had to get control. If she lost it, that meant he won. She would be okay with death as long as it didn't make him the victor.

"Ken." Pacer moaned her name. "What..?" He moved his legs and cried out.

She gritted her teeth and sat up. Her head swam. The inside of the van swirled around her. Bile rose and the burn of acid seared the back of her throat.

She reached for the leg of his jeans and cried out as well. It was all she could do. Her entire being swallowed in a whirlpool of fear and pain.

"Kenna? What is it?"

"You're bleeding."

"I can't move my legs that much." He shifted.

"I can't use my hands." Hearing it said out loud from her own lips caused terror to roll through her. She didn't want to think what the killer had already done to them. "We have to get out of here."

"I can't walk."

"That's what he's counting on." This guy wanted them incapacitated. Tendons sliced. Limbs useless.

Pacer pushed himself up. He winced and flashed gritted teeth. He choked out, "I don't know if I can walk." They both knew helplessness was more terrifying than pain.

She glanced at the back window. "He closed a door. Like a barn door." She knew she wasn't making sense, or at least wasn't being helpful. The killer was here. Somewhere. She shuddered, then forced her mind away from the worst that could happen.

"He'll be back soon." She turned back to Pacer. "I'll help you. Between the two of us—"

"No. Go." He didn't give her a chance to argue. Just lifted

his chin and gave her a resolute look. "I'll distract him. You get out of here."

"That's not gonna happen."

He bit off the words and shifted. "Just go, Kenna. Get out while you can."

"I'm not leaving you."

"Get help and come back."

He had no idea where they were, and neither did she. "We could be miles from anywhere. It could take hours for me to get to a phone. I'm not leaving you."

As if she would do that. Make a run for it, knowing he might die because she left him behind. Kenna would wind up hating him if he forced her to live with that.

"You get that chance, you take it." He gripped her shoulder and squeezed the tendon at the base of her neck. "I don't think I can walk. He cut the tendons in my legs, and I can't even move them. But you can save yourself. Tell everyone I died a heroic death."

She pressed her lips together because her arms were the same. Pacer leaned in and touched his to hers. His kiss was a momentary balm. A place she could be more alive than she'd ever been before. He would give his life for hers, because he knew he would slow her down. Maybe get them both killed.

"Go. Please." He kissed her again. "Go."

"Bradley." She moaned his name. Staying together was better, wasn't it?

She wanted to argue, but there was no time. They would only end up at odds instead of united to face whatever happened. She wasn't going to leave him. They would meet this together.

Pacer pulled away. Color bled from his face.

The van door rolled open.

Chapter Four

Saturday, 7:12 am.

Dawn broke while Kenna sat in the driver's seat of her car and watched the dead man's house. Waiting for the police to show up, or Agent Jaxton. She'd sipped from a paper cup of black gas station coffee while the early shift folks left for work.

It hadn't taken long for her to come up with the deceased's address, but if it took the cops much longer, she was going to enter the house and take a look around herself.

Beats doing nothing.

Anything was better than seeing the lost hope in her former partner's eyes every time she blinked. His terrified expression still lingered in her mind, but she still loved to see that face.

A therapist she met with on video chat called those night terrors. As if that made it all better. Whatever they were called, Kenna wanted to be rid of them as badly as she wanted to keep them. They were all she had left of Bradley.

What she needed was momentum—like solving the mystery of a dead guy, one with her business card on his body.

Doing nothing allowed the memories to seep back through the cracks into the present. Through the dissonant fragments of a life she held together by sheer force of will. The last thing she needed were more fissures.

The song on the radio changed. Kenna sipped the last few grainy mouthfuls of coffee. It was cold.

A silver four-door car, newer model, pulled up to the curb and a woman got out. Behind her, a black and white police car pulled to a stop and parked—that was Ryson. At the same time, a black SUV with government plates stopped across the street.

Why it warranted three cops, Kenna didn't know. She'd been working alone so long, backup was a distant memory. If she had a problem, she solved it. If she was in danger, she fought her way out. Failure meant death. Which was why she was still alive, and why she'd closed every case she'd worked since she left the FBI.

Special Agent Oliver Jaxton strode across the street. He was tall. Lean in build, the way they all seemed to be. As though the bureau stamped out suited agents on an assembly line—complete with a disapproving frown as standard. He'd probably gone to some Ivy League school his parents paid for. Meanwhile, her degree had been funded by a trust set up from her father's estate, and she'd been driving ten-year-old cars her whole life.

Today's tie was blue, like her Acura.

Jaxton huddled up at the end of the driveway with Ryson and the woman, clearly taking the lead. The name on the lease for the house was the name the dead guy had on his driver's license—Daniel Vaynes.

Kenna didn't need to participate in a search of the residence. But she did want to know if they found anything.

She murmured to herself in the quiet of her car, "Why are you still hanging around, Mr. Special Agent?"

Her former boss, Special Agent in Charge Stairns, had probably told him to find out if this case was something the FBI should know about. Her connection to a dead guy could mean a number of things these days. Maybe Jaxton was here to discover if she'd killed that old man.

Kenna had never met the woman with them, but from this distance it was clear she was a detective. She wore black slacks, low heels, and a brown wool coat. Probably early forties but it was hard to tell from her car. The woman's dark hair hung long and loose, and she had a shield on the lapel of her coat.

Jaxton and the woman moved from the huddle toward Daniel Vaynes's front door. Ryson headed for her. *Of course.* He'd probably seen her straight away.

Kenna grabbed her coat and climbed out into the chilly air.

"I thought you were leaving town."

She closed the door and shrugged on the coat, using those few seconds to figure out how to play this. "I still am."

She couldn't walk away when she didn't know what this was yet. It felt like being torn apart by the known/unknown. A rending inside her that meant she could do nothing, a self-imposed cessation of movement. To be stuck, rather than allow herself to go in two different directions. She both wanted to know and dreaded knowing at the same time. She wanted to stay, and she wanted to leave. She wanted her old life back, and she wanted the new life she'd carved for herself. Or she wanted none of those things.

Maybe she didn't know what she wanted.

"How about you go *after* you finish the investigation?"

"Maybe I'm only hanging around long enough to make sure you do it right."

Ryson nodded. "That's long enough you'll have time to go see my wife."

Kenna pressed her lips together.

He grabbed her arm and wound it through his. Her options were to go with him or fall on her face.

"I'm being hoodwinked."

He led her toward the house. "You know you want to look around in there."

Kenna groaned. "I work rescue scenarios, if possible. I find people—including killers—that no one else can find. I don't solve murders the police are perfectly capable of solving."

Not every case she took ended with a living victim like Ellayna Feathers, but that would always be her preference. She'd found plenty of killers without saving anyone except whatever future victims there would've been.

It wasn't a bad life they'd left her with.

"Stick around until we figure out what your connection is to this guy."

There was no connection, but she understood what he was saying since there was still the issue of her business card. "And then I'm *gone*."

"Sure."

"You don't believe me." They stepped together into the house, and she turned to him. "But I'm serious."

The last thing she wanted was to be stuck here indefinitely again. It wasn't her case.

"Ms. Banbury." Special Agent Jaxton nodded in her direction.

She tipped her head to the side and studied him in the light of day this time. "Notre Dame?"

"UCLA. What does that have to do with anything?" He glanced down to her lined boots, then back up her black skinny jeans and further up to her coat. She had on a short-sleeved shirt with snap buttons under which she wore a base layer. He shook his head. Confused or disappointed, she didn't know.

What did she care if he didn't like or approve of her, or her status as a civilian? Just because he was a fed, and she was only *formerly* an agent, didn't mean they needed a rapport. She could be professional, even if he'd decided to dislike private investigators. Or just her.

A flash of recognition crossed the detective's face before she glanced down at Kenna's forearms for a second, where the scars remained. *She knows what happened.* And she didn't bother to hide the wince. "You're Makenna Banbury."

Ryson took over. "This is Detective Suzanne Wilkern. The homicide is her case. You know Special Agent Oliver Jaxton."

The fed glanced between them. He probably only knew what the newspapers had reported about her, or the baloney that made up the incident report from two years ago. The company line they'd sold everyone. The official story was that she'd retired from the bureau. Given it had been two days after she and her partner were captured by a serial killer was something understood by most. The funeral had been covered by the press. The killer was in prison, and he'd died a few months later in a fight. She'd walked away from the bureau to live life on her own terms.

She pushed away errant thoughts to focus on the present.

Daniel Vaynes was dead. "Since homicide division is here, does that mean it's for sure a murder?"

"We don't have cause of death. Yet." Ryson stepped around her to survey the inside of the dead man's house.

"So we know why the police department is here, and why I'm here." She turned to Jaxton. "Why is the FBI here?"

Three of them with badges overwhelmed the space in this tiny entryway. It was beginning to get claustrophobic, and she didn't like feeling hemmed in. She'd handed her badge back to the FBI by choice. *Right.* Still, she liked being a private investigator. She made her own schedule and only took cases she wanted to work, not just the ones assigned to her.

Jaxton shrugged. "I've been ordered to assist the police department."

She'd followed orders, too. Where she wound up was somewhere far different. "Does Stairns even know I'm here, or did he just hear about my card?"

Ryson nudged her shoulder. "He probably neglected to tell the boss all about how you found that guy last night before jumping on this case."

Kenna bit the inside of her lip.

"I heard about that." Wilkern nodded. "Good work."

"Ellayna Feathers is back with her mother, that's the important thing."

"Thanks to you she's safe, and a dangerous man is in custody." Ryson grinned, not fooling anyone over the point he was trying to make.

The special agent twisted toward Ryson. "What are you talking about?"

"The Seventh Day Killer." The Lieutenant rocked back on his heels. "Kenna brought him in last night, before she met you. She saved his latest victim. A nine-year-old girl he was going to—"

"He didn't. That's the point." Kenna had seen enough of the Seventh Day Killer's work that she didn't need to relive it. She would rather look around at the bland interior of this rental house. "Besides, I heard two Salt Lake City police officers brought in that guy. Pierce and Meacham, right?" She stared Ryson down. He didn't need to go off on more of a tangent than he already had. "Now we're here. Ready to look around—"

"He's not the first psycho Kenna has caught since she left the FBI." Ryson shot the agent a side look. "Means you all were crazy to let her go."

Wilkern stuck her hand out, her eyes sad. "I'd just like to say, I'm sorry about your partner. I read about—"

Kenna turned away without shaking the detective's hand. "I'll take the bedroom."

She trailed down the hall and tried to convince herself she wasn't going to hurl on the carpet. It wasn't usually like this. She'd handed that guy over to the cops last night and made sure the little girl was safe. Usually no one knew what she'd done, and she preferred it that way.

Kenna had zero intention of doing more than satisfy her curiosity with this. To prove to herself there really was no connection to her card being on the victim.

Ryson followed her to the master. The whole place had threadbare carpet, except for the kitchen of the rental house. Vaynes had lived here just over a year, though the driver's license she'd looked up was probably a fake.

"At least it doesn't smell like old pizza."

"True." She stared at the unmade bed.

"I can't believe you're actually back, and we're working a case together."

"We're not working a case." She pulled on the gloves he

gave her and went to rummage through the sock drawer. "And you said that last night."

Her fingers searched the depths and found only underwear. Old, mismatched socks with holes and no partner. She would dump out the drawer on the bed and look again, except it really was nothing but clothing. No hidden gems to find here.

"We're just going to ignore the timing?" Ryson shot her a glance. His version of trying to be subtle closely resembled a fat tabby attempting to walk across the keys of a piano. "Kind of like the way you're ignoring my detective and that special agent? Here, but not *really* here. Catching the Seventh Day Killer, and then leaving town without even stopping by. Right? That was your plan."

"Does it matter?" Kenna pressed her lips together. "I just want to know why the dead guy had my business card on him. That's all." Then she would finally be gone again.

After the nightmare, she'd awoken to find her computer had run the dead man's photo through every database she had access to as a private investigator, and some she shouldn't. That was how she'd found the Utah driver's license, along with a rental agreement for this property.

A clean ID. No criminal record under the name Daniel Vaynes.

Kenna kept searching the clothes, then moved to the closet. The medicine cabinet and the cupboard under the sink. She came out of the bathroom to find Ryson standing in the same position in which she'd left him. Arms folded across his Texas-sized chest.

"It can't be a coincidence you're in Salt Lake working a case the same day a body shows up with your card on it. You haven't been back but a handful of times in the past two years."

"I needed to get the mail from my box." She tugged at the sleeves of her coat and pulled down the base layer she wore under the shirt to hook her thumbs in the holes. "And it *can* be a coincidence. It just probably *isn't*."

"So you're going to hang out in denial while you figure out what's going on?" Ryson went to the closet. It probably smelled like old man feet in there. "You think the FBI will let you investigate this case? They cut you loose once, they'll probably do it again whether you like it or not."

"I quit."

"You know what I mean. They could get you in trouble, and you'd wind up losing your license."

"My being in this house is nothing but curiosity. I'm sure your detective and Special Agent Jaxton are capable of figuring out whatever the connection is. They can send me an email when they do."

Ryson shot her a familiar look. "You can't ignore it. If you get in too deep, do you think Governor Pacer will let you skate out from under the spotlight again?"

Kenna smothered her reaction. To the governor, and the sound of that name. "I'm standing in the dead guy's house. How is that ignoring anything?"

The governor thing she wasn't even going to touch. Yes, they'd exchanged a favor two years ago. In return for giving up everything she'd ever wanted, she now had private investigator licenses for nine states. She hadn't asked what glad-handing accomplished that feat. They were square as far as both were concerned. It wasn't like she would bring bad publicity when she'd succeeded in not drawing attention to herself the past two years. That was what they wanted—the FBI and the governor. Was it her fault a business card ended up on some dead guy's body?

Ryson sighed. "Let's find the others, or they'll think we're doing nothing."

In the living room, Detective Wilkern crouched to look through the shelves under the TV lined with DVDs. Special Agent Jaxton was in the hall, his head in a coat closet.

She could feel Mr. Special Agent's gaze swing toward her, probably trying to figure her out. No way would she have waded in like he had without reading the file. Only now she wanted to know what her former boss had written about her.

How well it resembled the truth.

Detective Wilkern shifted a stack of DVDs aside and pulled out a shoe box. She lifted the lid and choked back a gasp. "Special Agent Jaxton!"

He squeezed between Kenna and Ryson. The detective tipped the box so they could see the contents. Mr. Special Agent took a step back. "Whoa."

Ryson said, "What is it?"

Kenna didn't want to take a step forward, but she did. Of course this day was only going to get worse. *Of course.*

Wilkern flipped through a pile of Ziploc bags. Inside each was a photo. Paper clipped to each one was a lock of hair. "Looks like mementos. They're all women." The detective lifted one. "She looks terrified."

Kenna swallowed. "How many?"

"There are nine in here."

Ryson watched from the doorway. "Our victim was a serial murderer?"

Chapter Five

Wilkern dropped the box. It caught the edge of the coffee table and tumbled to the floor where the contents spilled out.

Kenna stared at those plastic baggies. Nine victims. Missing persons, photographed so the killer could capture that final image and keep it forever. *She looks terrified.* Wilkern's words were what someone would have said about Kenna. If there had been a snapshot taken.

"A serial killer." Detective Wilkern breathed the words.

Special Agent Jaxton collected the contents back into the box, riffling through each one as though they belonged to the FBI. "None of them have names."

Kenna's stomach churned. She tried to fight the memories that lingered from her dream. "They do have names. You just don't know what they are yet."

"If this is what it appears to be, the killer is dead."

Ryson nodded. "We can put the victims to rest."

A handful of cold cases. The families not already resigned to what had happened to these victims would finally know the truth about their loved ones. As for Kenna's business card being on his body, that could mean nothing at all.

Or it could mean everything.

"This guy was good." Wilkern stepped back and ran a hand over her hair. "We had a serial murderer right under our noses and we never even knew. Now he's been murdered." She grinned, sloughing off the stress with humor. "That's some kind of comeuppance."

Kenna didn't have time for that. "Is the ME done with the autopsy?"

Ryson shook his head.

"So it might not even be murder. That's just a theory. He could've died naturally and been dumped there."

"With your calling card."

There was nothing light about this. "Maybe he was a fan." They didn't need to know how deeply her feelings ran. It was none of their business.

From the look of the three cops, they didn't believe it. If the old man had been murdered and her card left on his body on purpose, it could be an attempt to call her out. Or a gift. Either way someone wanted Kenna's attention.

She couldn't walk away without knowing the who and why of it.

Ryson shifted his stance. "A fan of you, or your dad?"

Kenna twisted to fully face the Lieutenant. "Who knows?" She spoke through gritted teeth, the expression on her face hot and probably thunderous. He actually swallowed. She bit out, "But it was *my* card. Not his."

Her father wasn't here. Not anymore. Why did Ryson feel the need to bring that up in front of two cops she didn't know?

Special Agent Jaxton rounded the coffee table. "I'll have to enter all this in as evidence. It widens the scope of the murder case, but we'll get some answers on what it means."

He moved to her. "Can you take a look right now and see if you recognize any of these women?"

The *victims*.

She lifted her chin. "Sure you don't want me to do that in an interrogation room?"

"Do I need to?"

Kenna didn't back down. "You're not going to rule me out from being the old man's killer." She waved a hand at the shoe box. "I know it crossed your mind that I might've killed these women and now I'm pinning it on the dead guy."

Ryson coughed. Wilkern braced to watch an impending explosion detonate.

Jaxton didn't react. "Did you?"

Before she could answer, Ryson got between them. "Of course she didn't. I can't believe you'd even ask that."

Kenna lifted a hand. "Lieutenant."

Ryson frowned at her. "Seriously?"

"If he didn't at least entertain the idea, then he shouldn't be working this case." Jaxton didn't know her. If he could be impartial, she might get a fair shake, which was more than she expected from any other FBI agent at the field office here.

From SAC Stairns all the way down to the admin assistant, Kenna would be treated with extreme prejudice. Justified or not, she had committed a cardinal sin. She'd gone up against an UNSUB and allowed her partner to die while she survived. No matter the circumstances, she had failed. A serial killer had won, even if he'd been imprisoned and later killed. The last thing any of them would do was trust her.

That had to be why Stairns sent Jaxton. When would that grace run out?

"Give me the box." Kenna held out her hand.

"Nope. Not gonna happen." Jaxton set it on the table and

laid out each memento. "This happens by the book, not because you waded in and took over."

Kenna pulled out her phone and swiped to the app that linked with the hard drive on her laptop just to make sure everything was okay on the home front.

Nothing had pinged on the surveillance she'd set up around her place. It was still secure, nothing to worry about.

Nothing to fear.

Yeah, right.

Jaxton gathered everything up and lifted the box. "Are we boring you, Ms. Banbury?"

"Ryson and I will go knock on the neighbor's doors." She headed for the front door. The air outside might be bracing, but it wasn't suffocating like in here. "We'll see if they knew the guy who lived here."

"Ms.—"

She didn't wait for him to finish. Kenna needed to breathe, not be railroaded. He was right. She did things *her* way.

"You okay?" Ryson hit the sidewalk right behind her.

She shot him a look.

"Fine, then answer why a killer would be hand delivered to us with your card on his body."

"I'm trying. Jaxton will have to check surviving family members. People with a reason to want this guy dead." She rolled her shoulders and stretched out her back as they headed for the neighbor's house. There was no one on the street watching. "I don't even know this Daniel Vaynes guy, and I have a grudge against him."

"You and me both."

Kenna stopped at the end of the drive. "Just because my card was on the body doesn't mean I'm gonna be drawn into this. I want to know who he is, and I'd like to know who those victims are. After that, I'm gone. If there's someone trying to drag me in, they'll be disappointed."

Kenna planned to find the person and get an answer. That was all. Whatever they thought they were going to get her to do wouldn't work, because for the past two years Kenna had accepted nothing less than case closed. If she failed now, she might as well have died with her partner.

"What kind of private eye doesn't need to set up shop somewhere and build a clientele? I thought it was all about hanging up a shingle."

"I'm not the normal kind of PI."

He shot her a look. "Yeah, duh. With the way you were raised—"

"Let's go." She didn't move, though. "After you confirm you won't bring up my father again."

"You don't want a promise?"

"Just give me your word." She lifted her chin. "I trust you, and that's better than any promise."

His expression softened. "Ken—"

"Now's not the time to grow an empathy bone. I want to know who this dead guy was. Then we can find out who murdered a serial killer."

"So we can shake his hand?"

"Or Jaxton can arrest him because it turns out he's even worse." She headed to the neighbor's house. "Like new blood, taking out the old guard."

Not a bad idea, but Special Agent Jaxton would work to rule out the victim's family members first. Simple revenge, with the added bonus they'd made sure to tell her about it. After that, Jaxton would close whatever cold cases sat in the shoe box Wilkern had found. Finding the person who killed a serial killer? She could see that not being super high on Detective Wilkern's priority list either. Kenna figured she had fifteen open cases of her own.

They were probably back at the house now, discussing the viability of the theory that Kenna was the one who had murdered the old man.

She lifted her fist and knocked on the neighbor's door. All the houses on this street were the same, barely a thousand square feet. Probably rentals. Chain link. Dirt yards.

The young woman pulled the door open and leaned on it. Unwashed brown hair had been secured in a bun on top of her head. She wore athletic leggings and an oversized sweater. Her makeup was perfect, though. Kenna heard a baby cry from the back room.

"Got a second?"

The woman shrugged one shoulder. Her sweater drooped to reveal a tattoo below her collar bone. "For what?"

"This is Lieutenant Ryson, and I'm Makenna Banbury. I'm a private investigator."

Ryson gave her his professional smile and pulled out his log book. "I'm sure you're busy, so we won't keep you long."

The young woman blinked at the big man in a suit and perked up.

Kenna used the distraction to ask. "What's your name?"

"Sandra." She shot Kenna an irritated look.

"We just want to ask you about your neighbor." Ryson pointed at the house with his stubby pencil.

"Did he do something?"

"Would it surprise you if he had?"

She scrunched up her nose. "I've never talked to him. So I don't even know if he 'keeps to himself' or whatever." She used air quotes. "Like some kind of psycho."

Interesting that was the first place she'd gone. "What makes you say that? This could be about a noise complaint."

"Middle-aged white guy?" Sandra shrugged her bare shoulder. "I watch cop shows."

Kenna said, "Do you have any idea what he did?"

"Like for work?"

Ryson nodded.

"Construction, maybe? He was always in dirty jeans and boots, and he drove a white pickup." The driveway was empty, so Wilkern would need to find that. Sandra continued, "Only it was never white, just always covered with dust. Or mud."

Kenna waited for Ryson to note all that in his book. "When was the last time you saw him?"

"Couple days, maybe."

"Thank you for your time." Ryson stepped back.

Sandra eyed the neighbor's house. The baby squalling ratcheted another notch. She rolled her eyes and shut the door.

"You think that kid ever stops crying?"

Ryson said, "They go through phases. Like if they're sick or having a growth spurt. Usually there's a hiatus between and you catch up about half the sleep lost."

Kenna stopped in the middle of the driveway.

"I've been reading parenting books and taking classes." He frowned. "I called you when we found out Valentina was pregnant. You sent a card, and another when Luci was born. I thought you were happy for me."

Kenna swallowed down the lump in her throat. "I am."

Life was moving on.

At least, everyone *else's* life was.

"Go visit Valentina. I'm sure she'd love to see you." He stared at her a little longer than necessary. "I'm serious."

"I know you are." Kenna turned toward the mountains, an itch between her shoulder blades.

She glanced from house to house for the ruffle of curtains in a window while the other two investigators came over.

"Ryson has notes," Kenna announced. Never mind that the detective hadn't asked a question. "Did you guys find anything else in the house?"

Wilkern shook her head. "Just that box of mementos from our dead guy. CSU is on their way."

Kenna had figured crime scene people would be called in. "And the medical examiner?"

Special Agent Jaxton lifted his chin. "Not done yet. I've already emailed my boss to fill him in on what we found here. Looks like I'll be identifying victims the rest of the day."

Wilkern looked like he'd just kicked her puppy. Apparently, she didn't want a division of labor. Kenna had no idea if her attitude was about working with the FBI, or this particular FBI agent.

Ryson nodded. "I'll wait here for forensics. See what else they can find."

"Great." Kenna thumbed at her car over her shoulder. "Sounds like you guys have it all covered."

All three of them looked like they wanted to say something to her. Wilkern was first off the line. "Maybe I could buy you a cup of coffee, or a burger?"

"I'm not sure what my plans are, but Ryson has my number." Kenna didn't look at the lieutenant. He knew she wouldn't call the detective back, whether he passed on Kenna's number or not.

"How about lunch. All of us?" Mr. Special Agent pulled out his cell. "That hamburger joint by the precinct. Say, one o'clock? We can brief each other on what we have." The phone buzzed, and he frowned down at it.

"Sounds great." Kenna headed for her car with a wave, a

smile pasted on her face. Mr. Special Agent didn't need to worry about her.

FBI shoes clipped the sidewalk behind her. "Ms. Banbury?"

She smiled over her shoulder, playing the helpful PI. "Yes?"

Jaxton stuck his phone in her face. She had to back up to read the text. The top of the thread said, *SAC Stairns.* Before she could read the message he said, "He knows about the mementos. I guess this means you're coming with me back to the office."

Tell her she comes in or I call the Governor.

She stiffened. "I'll follow you."

The skin around those blue eyes flexed. Yep, this guy was definitely going to need Botox by the close of this case. "You aren't going to argue?"

As much as Kenna wanted to simply drive back to her home, pull up stakes and leave town, she would only make things worse now that Stairns was issuing threats. "Might as well get it over with."

"After all, you've managed to insert yourself into every other part of this case. Why not do so at the office?"

Kenna glanced at the mountains that leered down at her from on high like Jaxton's beady blue-eyed gaze. "It's not like the place will feel the same after two years. Stairns probably just wants to see my face when he asks if I killed Daniel Vaynes."

This wasn't about reliving the old days. More like tearing

off the bandage to let the wound heal, exposed. Time certainly hadn't done the job.

Kenna left her gun and the other weapons she carried on her in the car because it wasn't worth the extra paperwork. Jaxton had her checked in through security, and she was issued a temporary pass for the floor where she had formerly worked. The office she'd spent so much time in.

There was no point dwelling on a past that was as dead as her partner.

Jax caught Kenna's gaze in the mirrored interior of the elevator. He gave her a polite smile, oblivious to anything except his own opinions. If she wore three-inch heels, she could match his height, but she didn't own any. The disparity between them didn't end there.

She stuck her hands in her jeans pockets. "So how long have you worked in Utah?"

"I've only been in Salt Lake for three months. I haven't gotten the lay of the land yet."

She was only half listening. Instead, her mind fabricated Stairns's reaction to finding out she was here. Two years ago, he'd told her in no uncertain terms to stay away. Now she was being summoned?

She felt a frown tug her dark brows together. "I didn't, by the way." She could put her two cents in, show him the real Kenna. At least try to persuade him why he should give her the benefit of the doubt.

"Didn't what?"

"Kill that guy, Daniel Vaynes."

"And I think...that you did?"

Kenna shrugged. "It isn't like I haven't thought about going vigilante so I can dispense justice in my own way."

Jaxton probably wished he'd set up to record their conversation, like she was going to confess or something.

"I couldn't do it." She studied her reflection in the mirror for a second. Would the nightmare come back as soon as she saw Pacer's desk?

"I came across a cold case pretty early on after I left the bureau. The victim's father called me. A missing girl from Ogden. I tracked the suspect all the way to Montana before I got the jump on him. She was long gone, cold in the ground. After I got him to tell me where she was, I took him to the local sheriff. Left the girl's killer tied up on a bench out front with a box of evidence on his lap. Watched the sheriff show up, realize what he had sitting right in front of him, and take the guy in."

"How many more times have you done that?"

She had to swallow down the lump in her throat. "Six."

"So it's a thing now, catching killers?"

"I guess."

As if she didn't know she was stuck in a loop, reliving the worst day of her life to try and get a different outcome. She was practically addicted to it at this point. Which meant her life was a bizarre mix of compulsion and fear she didn't understand. Every day, doing the one thing she never wanted to do again.

Probably because it was the only thing she knew how to do.

"And now one is hand-delivered to you, and I'm supposed to believe you had no influence on the perpetrator's actions?"

She swung around to face down his hard stare. He wanted all the attention on her. So that none was on him?

"Tell me, Special Agent Jaxton." She folded her arms. "Why exactly did you leave your last assignment and wind up transferred to Salt Lake City?"

His mouth shifted. "None of your business."

Something had happened. Whether that thing was his

fault, or he'd suffered, she figured he wasn't going to tell her before they finished this 8-second ride. Question was, which of them was the bucking bronco and who just hung on for dear life?

The elevator doors slid open. Murmurs dropped to nothing, until the only sound in the room was the drone of TV news on the wall. Jaxton shifted beside her. Whatever standing he had with the team, she could dissolve that in a second with whatever she decided to do next. Just to get back at him.

Instead, Kenna stepped off first, chin high. He followed as she headed for Stairns's office. Every agent in the room watched; distrust and hostility emanating from them.

"What..?" The word was quiet, an involuntary escape from Jaxton's mouth. He didn't finish his question.

Maybe she would explain. If she felt like it.

She stopped at the door to Stairns's office. Memories hit her like a wave, along with the smell of aftershave and coffee.

Stairns hung up the phone and waved her in from his standing position behind his desk. "Get in here."

Jaxton started to turn away.

"You too, Special Agent Jaxton. Shut the door behind you."

Wearing tan slacks and a button-down shirt, Stairns was nearly a foot shorter than her and forty pounds heavier than he looked—all of it in his shoulders. Topped with the flat hair of a Marine who had the Corps Flag on the wall in his office.

She figured there hadn't been much in the way of scenery in Brooklyn, where he'd grown up. During the Civil War.

Utah was about as far as Stairns could get from either military life, or the gang members who'd sniffed around his teenage daughters. One had married since, and the other was dating an Air Force second lieutenant. Stairns had almost convinced them he was fine with it.

It occurred to Kenna that his second daughter was probably married as well by now.

The way it also occurred to her that nothing in this place had changed. Being here birthed a familiar ache, like watching a beloved childhood movie but without the magic she remembered. Like reading one of her dad's notebooks. Or pulling out his quilt for the winter months.

Neither of them sat when Stairns did. "So. Dead guy, your business card." Stairns shrugged his squat shoulders and waved at the file open on his desk. "One of you talk."

That was it. No, "nice to see you" Or, "it's been a long time." Nothing about how he'd filed her retirement paperwork for her after he brought it to her in the hospital to sign. She'd always figured if he could've signed it himself, he would have.

How many times had she stood here and rattled off case details to get his opinion?

"You already know about the mementos." Jaxton glanced between them, his tone uncertain. "My next step is to run down any other aliases for the deceased, as well as follow up with the detective. Try to figure out where else, and who else, this guy has been. Then I'm going to visit families of the victims and let them know what we have. Find out what tied them all together. Why he might have picked them."

She shrugged off the nostalgia. "And the killer?"

Jaxton turned to her. "That's what I'm hoping for from the ME, something from the autopsy that will point to a suspect. Which the detective is taking point on."

"This is about you, as much as we'd all like to believe otherwise." Stairns waved a pen at her. "So we deal. Because you're here, and it turns out the dead guy was a serial. Special Agent Jaxton could use the help, and you're just the available consultant for the FBI to take on who can help us figure it out."

She took a step back. "No." He didn't think she'd done it. He wanted her to *investigate.* "You're out of your mind if you think I—"

"I don't need her help."

Stairns glanced between them. Despite how long it had taken her to get cleared through security just to come up here, she was ready to bolt.

Jaxton's phone buzzed in his suit jacket. "I should take this."

"The two of you are working this together." Stairns laid a weighty look on Jaxton, whose phone quit ringing before his boss released him to answer it.

As if Kenna didn't know that meant she was still very much a suspect. She would be on a short leash with no ability to manage the fallout if she signed up to work with Jaxton. As if. They were either banking on her making a mistake and implicating herself or they thought she could solve it for them.

"I'm not consulting for the FBI." She pinned Stairns with a look of her own. "You're the one who kicked me out." This place was an old stain she couldn't get rid of.

Kenna's phone rang. "It's Ryson." She didn't wait for Stairns's permission to answer the way Jaxton had. She swiped her thumb across the screen and put it to her ear. "Hey."

"It's Officer Pierce." Ryson's voice shook. "She's been taken."

Kenna frowned. "What does that have to do with—"

"Your business card was left at the scene."

Chapter Six

Saturday, 11:42 am.

Ryson was to meet them in the hallway outside the third-floor apartment. They rounded the corner and there he was. His pale face highlighted those dark brows and hair as he paced.

Kenna stopped in front of him, anchoring him to her. "Where is everyone?"

"We need to do this fast." Ryson glanced around, edginess in his gaze. "My captain isn't happy you're here."

"It was *my* business card."

"Just be quick."

Special Agent Jaxton stopped beside her. He'd been oddly quiet since they left the FBI office, though he'd offered to give her a ride over here. She didn't know what to make of it, so she'd just spent the time on her phone, running Pierce's name to get background on the officer. She knew he was probably just trying to figure her out—friend or foe—and she knew she shouldn't be offended. But she was.

Her business card at another scene—and a cop kidnapped? Stairns had probably ordered Jaxton to stay with her and make sure the loose-cannon private investigator didn't step on any toes, or make the bureau look bad.

Now the PD didn't want her here either? She should just go. Except that a woman had been taken, and Kenna was being implicated.

Ryson had lines around his mouth that hadn't been there this morning. "It's bad?" He nodded and closed the gap by pulling her in for a hug.

"Pierce got off work last night at the end of swing shift. Her husband got home half an hour ago. He's an EMT. The front door was open. There are signs of a struggle I'd like you to see, and blood on the wall."

"Evidence has been collected?" Officer Pierce could have been missing more than twelve hours already. This wasn't good.

"They're wrapping up now."

She thought about that young female cop last night who'd called the ambulance for Ellayna Feathers. Pierce, along with her partner, had gone after a vicious killer. Justice and compassion, with no room for stories of fame. Kenna probably could've made friends with the woman, and not just because Pierce hadn't known who she was. Kenna couldn't help that her father had been a legend, or that he'd embellished their lives into bestsellers.

In the world of law enforcement, cops like Pierce were few and far between. They were the reason Kenna had walked away from the FBI. She wanted to safeguard the work they did and its impact, not draw the wrong attention to everyone.

Kenna squeezed the Lieutenant's elbow. "She'll be all right."

She wasn't a cop. She could make whatever promises she wanted to.

"Why don't you just take a look? Wilkern should be here soon."

Jaxton said, "Isn't this more of an all-hands-on-deck type situation?"

Kenna nodded. "Special Agent Jaxton is right."

The agent leaned toward her a fraction. "Jax is fine."

As if she was actually going to call him that. He was probably only with her because it scored him points with Ryson and Stairns. She took a side-long glance at him. He wasn't exactly the FBI prototype. He didn't come off as chauvinistic or arrogant as the others. Two years ago, she'd have appreciated that he didn't quite fit in with the guys she used to work with. Now they were worlds apart, with zero point in trying to bridge the gap between federal and civilian.

This was about her business card and assisting the cops in finding one of their own. If they let her.

Kenna glanced around. "What about everyone else?"

"Come and gone. Now they're on the streets talking to neighbors and looking at surveillance footage from the parking lot. Meacham is leading the charge." Ryson blew out another breath. "Can you take a look at the scene? The card was on the kitchen counter."

Kenna wasn't going to tell him to calm down, but he needed to. "This didn't happen because of you."

"She was my responsibility."

"Run the timeline down for me." That was the first thing. Then they'd look at the scene, and after that they'd talk to the husband. She needed to see if she could pick up on something one of the cops might have overlooked. That unique perspective her friend, Lieutenant Ryson, was entitled to ask for. He would have if he wasn't pissed about the business card, or the fact that her deal now encompassed the abduction of one of *his* officers.

A killer might want to draw her in, but it wasn't a thread she was going to pull on. The police department probably didn't even want her help. They likely figured they didn't need it, either.

Ellayna Feathers was safe. Pierce had a precinct of men and women in blue, all hunting for one of their own. That would quickly stretch to every cop in the city. Everyone on the lookout for her.

Kenna would only get in the way. But she still might be able to help by giving them the perspective of two years working private investigation, mostly murder or kidnapping cases.

Ryson squeezed the bridge of his nose. "I can't believe I didn't realize earlier that something was wrong." He scratched both hands down his face. "I had breakfast with Valentina before her shift, and then met you at the house."

He hadn't even slept yet. Or if he had, it wasn't much.

"You need to get some rest."

Ryson shook his head. "Not until she's found."

"Valentina is working today?" His wife was a nurse practitioner for a family practice.

"Just this morning," Ryson said. "Her mom's watching Luci. She's supposed to take it easy."

"And Pierce? Walk me through the timeline." It might jog something, and then she'd be able to assist, even if it was in a small way.

"According to her husband, Officer Pierce hit the grocery store on her way home."

Jaxton said, "That would've been pretty late, right?"

Ryson nodded. "I've got two officers checking with the store to see if they have her coming or leaving on their cameras. See if she was followed home."

"Good idea," Kenna said.

"Meanwhile we were..." His voice cracked. "Please go and look."

She nodded and entered the apartment. The whole place looked like an IKEA show room, with a Hawaii beach feel to it. Light, breezy. She wanted an umbrella drink and a pair of flip flops.

The husband was on the couch. Slender and built like a mountain biker, he had neat, short blond hair and a tattoo of Polynesian swirls on his left bicep. He looked up when she entered, puffy-eyed. Tissue balled in his fist.

Kenna nodded and moved to the kitchen, where a bag of groceries had fallen off the counter. Milk pooled across the floor from a burst open half gallon, and several eggs had broken. Now it was mixed with footprints. Evidence markers. The dust left over from fingerprint powder.

Her business card had been left on the counter. Beside the now empty spot, another evidence marker.

A lone technician worked on a laptop at the table, with what looked like a diagram of the room pulled up on the screen.

On the wall was a smudge of blood and a dent. Kenna judged the height.

"You're thinking...her nose?"

She spun to find Jaxton right behind her and winced. "Ouch." If it had been a nose, and Pierce had made that dent, she'd have a serious headache right now.

"She fought him."

Kenna studied the room. "There was definitely a struggle,

even if he did take her by surprise. She gave him almost as good as she got, once she realized what was happening."

"Until he managed to subdue her, then haul her out of here," Jaxton said. "Or so I figure."

She wanted to ask if he'd worked many kidnappings wherever he'd been stationed before he came to Salt Lake. He might be the new guy here, but he wasn't a rookie.

Then again, if she asked personal questions about him, that also meant she cared about the answers. Which would lead to other things she had no interest in. Connection. Who had time for that?

Her life had been quiet and simple for two years. Something she'd desperately needed after everything that had happened. She worked when she chose to and didn't when she could use a break.

Kenna found people everyone else had given up on. She took down killers no one else could find.

"This isn't your case." Jax frowned. "The cops don't need our help, and even if they did, they still wouldn't want it."

"I'm not one of them." She glanced at Jaxton. "That's what you're saying?"

"This isn't about the great divide between law enforcement and private investigators."

"I know I'm not a cop anymore." She folded her arms, the familiar twinge in her forearms a solid reminder of all she'd lost. What had been cut away from her life seemed to hang around still. Like phantom pain. "If I can help—"

"The murder case from last night, the first card? That's how we help. Wilkern will be busy with this now, as will the rest of the police department."

"So we just leave them to it?"

"If someone is trying to draw you out, you can't be involved with the investigation."

"Because it's personal?" She took a step closer to him.

"That's the job."

"I'm not a cop. Every case I work is personal."

"Not this one."

She stared him down. He was right, but that didn't mean she would back down. Especially not if it cost Officer Pierce her life. "I need to talk to the spouse."

"Kenna—"

She moved across the hall to the living room, ignoring his attempt to make this personal by using her first name. He thought that was where this was headed?

The husband looked up as she settled on the edge of an armchair.

"Hi, Steven." She cleared her throat. "I'm Makenna Banbury. I'm a private investigator consulting with the FBI on a different case." Or, she might be, after she signed the paperwork. And probably they weren't different cases. *Ugh.* She didn't like complicated.

Kenna didn't bother to smile. "I actually met Officer Pierce last night. Nice woman. Good cop."

"Yes, she is." Nice enough that something like this shouldn't have happened. At least, that was the implication of both of their comments.

Kenna wasn't going to argue with it. "I can't investigate this. It's not my case, and I don't have a badge anymore. But I'm going to be breathing down the detective's necks. You can trust me on that."

He pinned her with a stare, bracing for something. "She told me about you."

"She did?" This wasn't going anywhere good.

He nodded. "Called me at work around midnight to give me the whole story. She thought you were some rando walking by and just happened to find that girl. Turned out you're this big-time investigator who used to be an FBI agent. Catching a killer. Saving a child."

Kenna's forearms flexed, flickering pain down to her fingertips. She clenched her teeth.

"She said she wanted to be you when she grew up." The echo of a smile moved over his face, before it was eclipsed by grief. Anger. "Where is she?"

"I wish I knew." Maybe if she was still an agent, she would.

"Your business card was here, right?" He shifted closer to her. The line of his shoulders tightened.

Kenna braced.

"That means you know something about what happened."

Lord. "I don't—"

"Makenna Banbury. You're here too?" Detective Wilkern strode in and crouched in front of Steven, as though she hadn't just thoroughly diffused the victim's anger. Wilkern laid her hand on Steven's, the one with the balled-up tissue in it. "I'm so sorry about what happened. We're all doing everything we can."

Steven said, "You'll find her?"

Wilkern couldn't promise that. Not that they would ever give up looking for a missing cop, it was just that some cases never had an answer. Even if they found Jessica Pierce, they might not find anything good.

"Everyone is looking. We won't stop until we have answers."

The husband nodded.

Ryson came in. "Let's take another look around, Steven. If she's been taken to the hospital, she'll need clean clothes."

Steven ambled toward him, and they moved down the hall to the bedroom, leaving Kenna standing with Wilkern. Kenna scanned the room, looking for Jaxton. He was talking with a suited man outside the apartment front door. Older, probably a captain.

"You're everywhere I turn today."

Kenna wasn't going to apologize to Wilkern. "I'm happy to get out of your hair."

Jaxton finished up and wandered over.

"Wilkern was just thanking me for offering my assistance."

The detective's smile for Jaxton was entirely different. "*Any* help you can offer. I mean *anything,* and I'll be eternally grateful."

Kenna nearly grinned, muffling a snort. "We'll do what we can."

"Special Agent Jaxton." Wilkern stuck her hand out and he shook it as she continued, "This might be a cop matter, but that doesn't mean we'll refuse assistance if it finds Pierce."

When he pulled back to let go, Wilkern covered his hand with her other one. Jaxton acted like he didn't notice.

Kenna had to resist an eye roll. "We're happy to take the investigation on the old guy. Since you all need to concentrate on Pierce."

"Agreed." He managed to get his hand free. "We'll work that, so you guys can focus on this."

At least he got what she was trying to do. Namely, to investigate what the cops didn't have time for. Their work on the other case might help find Pierce, and it might not. But what she did know was that she wasn't going to be sidelined or sit around doing nothing.

Not when Steven Pierce wanted answers for his wife's abduction.

Wilkern shot Kenna that smile again. "Thank you both."

"Like I said." Kenna lifted her chin as though she hadn't noticed any of their interplay. "Happy to help."

And help she would. By finding out who this guy was and why he thought she should be part of this. Maybe part of it was Wilkern's attempt to catch Jaxton's eye that rubbed her the wrong way, but Kenna suddenly wanted to work the old man's case until she found the killer. Just so Wilkern couldn't take any of the credit for finding out who he was and what he did to the nine women.

Hopefully Wilkern would be too busy finding Pierce to even notice they had solved the cases. She'd be able to dust off her hands and leave this town in her rearview. Where it was supposed to be.

Steven Pierce entered the living room again, along with Ryson. Both looked lost. Kenna moved to stand in front of the husband. "I do know what you're going through."

Loss was something she understood. Anger. Grief.

"You can trust Wilkern, and Lieutenant Ryson. They'll do everything they can." She would've handed Steven her business card, but right now that was a seriously bad idea. "Please let Ryson know if there's anything I can do. He'll pass the info along."

As soon as he nodded, she walked away. Jaxton followed, Ryson behind him. The three of them stood in a huddle in the hall.

Jaxton turned to Ryson. "We can drop the dead serial killer. Table it for a while and help look for Officer Pierce—"

She picked up where he left off. "—though that might be a mistake when the two are obviously connected. If we find the old man's killer, it could lead us to Pierce."

Jaxton spun to her. "I was going to say that."

Ryson turned to pin her with a stare. "I need you to find my officer, Kenna."

"And if I can't?"

"You really think you can't find her? It's what you *do* right?"

She tried to articulate but couldn't find the words. Anyone else, she'd have given them pat assurances. Ryson, and Jaxton for that matter, had to live with the unvarnished truth. It was who she was now.

Being overwhelmed with multiple cases at once wasn't a place she ever wanted to be again. Twenty-four hours back home, and she was already drowning. She hadn't worked more than one case at a time in two years. And she never moved onto the next one until she solved it.

Kenna sighed. "Are you going to take a nap until she's found?"

Ryson ignored that. "Let me know when you have something."

"Did you just give me an order?"

He shrugged. "I figure now that you're not a fed, I might have a better chance that you'll follow it."

"Have faith in your department." What else was she supposed to say? She'd seen the kind of woman Jessica Pierce was. The kind of cop all cops should be.

If being here saved Pierce's life, Kenna wasn't about to turn that down.

They descended the stairwell in the apartment building and Kenna checked the foyer. "Cameras?"

Jax looked around.

"This guy couldn't have gotten in and out without being seen. If Pierce was taken from inside her apartment, then the kidnapper had to have come up the elevator or stairwell after her."

Kenna would have taken Pierce on the street, but criminals didn't usually ask her opinion about what was best.

Jax said, "The parking lot is in the basement. Maybe he

didn't get the chance to take her before she got home. Or he broke into the apartment during the day so he'd be ready when Pierce arrived."

Meacham stood in the foyer. He held a paper cup of coffee and stared into space. Like he was lost. His partner was missing.

She knew how that felt.

Jax said, "This wasn't your fault."

Using her words against her? "I know."

What made him think she didn't know that? She wasn't responsible for every killer's actions, or for Jessica Pierce's safety. But that didn't stop her from wanting to fix it.

"You obviously are linked somehow, but there's no way you could've prevented whatever this guy has planned. Not unless you're a mind reader."

"Sadly, that isn't one of my many skills." She brushed imaginary dust from her shoulder.

Though Jax didn't buy her attempt to brush it off, he also didn't have time to comment before his phone buzzed as they walked outside. "Collins is ready for us."

"The autopsy is done?"

"I guess we have an appointment."

He drove to the medical examiner's office, located in a building neighboring city hall. It was in the basement of Salt Lake City's administrative annex. Jax's phone rang just as he was pulling into a parking space at the farthest corner of the lot.

Stairns flashed on the dash screen. Jax hit the button. "Yes, sir. I'm here with Banbury."

Hearing Stairns through car speakers brought back far too many memories. Kenna shifted to look out the window at the row of parked cars next to them. She'd rather have been the one driving today. Too much energy to burn off.

Back when she'd been an agent, she and Bradley had agreed to share the driving. They'd even gone so far as to establish an arrangement where whoever drove had to pay for the coffee. She had no idea how Jax figured out that stuff between him and whoever he normally rode with.

Jax gave Stairns a rundown of the officer's kidnapping. "We're headed to the medical examiner now to get his report in person."

"Good," Stairns barked. "I want these open cases from the shoe box wrapped up so we can give the families some peace about what happened to their loved ones."

That was what Jaxton should've been doing today—IDing each of the women from the collection of mementos. Instead, he'd accompanied her to the officer's apartment.

Kenna wanted to ignore whoever had made that move with the business card and just walk away. Too bad she'd spend the rest of her life wondering what the dead serial killer had been about. Maybe she should make some calls to a few of her old confidential informants. See if anyone had heard word about an abducted cop.

Resurrect old relationships.

Unanswered questions weren't her favorite thing. If someone had murdered a killer, then she wanted to know who and why. She'd rather help find Pierce directly, but outside Ryson's request, the police didn't need her interference. It wasn't good to get in the way when cops were finding one of their own, despite the fact everything in her wanted to.

"Yes, sir." Jax hung up and cracked his door open. "I think that went well, don't you?"

"What are you talking about? Stairns?"

He glanced at her. "He seems to be warming to the fact you're back."

She stared at him. "You have no clue how to read that man."

"What did I miss? I thought you weren't even listening to the call."

She got out the car and tried to shake off...she didn't even know what. Jax might think they were building a rapport, but they were *not*. There was only Kenna and her business cards. A dead old guy.

She shook her head. None of it was connected. Two different things, if not three. A serial killer, an attempt at getting her attention, and a missing cop. Two cases. She was *not* drowning.

Not again.

They headed for the lobby and went to the ME's basement offices where he was working on the autopsy. Jax waved through the window and the assistant buzzed them in. He turned back at the door. "Are you coming?"

Kenna just stood in the hall and inhaled a tangy chemical odor she had tried to forget over the past two years. It washed over her, in her, through her. Whether she wanted it to or not.

"Fine. Wait here."

The door shut, and he left her alone in the hallway.

She tried to exhale the tension and find relief. Kenna backed up to the wall, slid down until her forehead touched her knees and just breathed through it. Eventually the past would leave her alone.

She wasn't back.

Chapter Seven

J ust after nightfall, Kenna pulled open the door to the
corner building of a rundown strip mall. The place was
nearly black inside, except for the strobe effect of a room
full of eighties era arcade games.

Rhythmic whirs and chimes provided a soundtrack as she
weaved down the aisles and searched for him.

On her second pass through, she spotted her target. Two
years and he still wore jeans and a faded T-shirt, hair falling
over his forehead. His thumbs moved faster than she could see
in the low light and his body shifted as the game flashed colors
across his determined expression.

A second later he swore and stepped back.

"No new high score tonight?"

He spun. "No. No way."

Apparently two years wasn't long enough for him to get
over his grudge. "Come on, dude. It's not that bad."

"A missing cop?" He held up his hand. "I don't want
anything to do with that. You aren't dragging me back in."

"That's not exactly how I remember it."

"I'm clean now. Things are different."

"Congratulations."

"Whatever. I'm not getting into this."

"So you've got nothing for me?"

His jaw flexed. She thought she might've heard a low growl, but it was probably just one of the machines.

"Someone's been asking around about me, I'm guessing."

His gaze strayed over her shoulder. "Yeah." He lifted a finger and pointed past her. "That guy."

Kenna saw him straight away. "Jaxton." He spotted her. *Great.*

When she turned back to Billy, he was gone.

"You're here."

"Special Agent Jaxton." She pasted on a smile before turning to face him. "So good to see you."

"Have you tried the popcorn chicken? It's good."

He wasn't going to comment on the fact she hadn't stuck around the medical examiner's office? No, he was just going to give her a knowing look that made her want to shift her feet.

"Let's go." She led the way to the front door with no glance back to see if he followed.

"What are you thinking?"

"Someone has to know something." Of course, now that he'd found her, he was determined to be her shadow. "And I know that's so obvious it's redundant."

"Processing your thoughts out loud can be helpful."

She pushed her way outside. "I came back to Salt Lake in pursuit of the Seventh Day Killer. Maybe the old man was killed before I'd even found Gerald Rickshire. Did he have the guy on ice for such a time as this?"

Jaxton frowned.

Yeah, she knew full well what she was referencing. "Because otherwise, the timing is entirely too coincidental. The old man, murdered on the very night I come back for a job? I don't buy it. Did Pierce's kidnapper already know I was here, or did he find out somehow? And was that the plan all along, after he killed the old guy?"

"We need to talk to the Seventh Day Killer."

Kenna would rather go to the hospital and check on Ellayna Feathers—if she was still there. She was sure solving this case would actually get them a step closer to possibly finding Pierce.

"The ME won't confirm yet that the old man was murdered, though the autopsy is officially complete. He's still mulling over the paperwork." Jaxton worried two fingers against his jaw. "All we have is a link to nine unsolved murders to clear off. And a police officer to find."

Some of the mementos in the shoebox may be from decades ago, the height of the old man's career. Kenna might not have even been a cop yet. That meant the serial killer couldn't connect to her unless her father had investigated him at one time. And how could she find that out without reading his notebooks? She'd have to go back over a past she'd agreed a long time ago did not have a place in her present.

Jaxton blew out a breath. "So there's nothing recent enough to help us figure out what the deal is with this guy and your business card."

Us? She squeezed her eyes shut. "What's the latest from Ryson?"

Her gut churned just thinking about where Pierce might be. If knocking on every door in the city would help, she'd be out doing that. Kenna was running out of trees to shake. All to try and loosen a lead on whoever was interested enough in her to leave two business cards at crime scenes.

Jaxton scrolled on his phone screen. "Surveillance footage from the street where Pierce lives. Someone's home security that runs all the time, trying to catch who's letting their dog drop you-know-whats on the lawn."

"They caught something?"

"White van, single male driver. Looks like he hauled Officer Pierce out over his shoulder. Unconscious."

"And no one else who lives near her saw *anything*?" At least it hadn't been a woman in the footage, carrying the cop. They'd have been all over her then.

He shot her a look. "It's a downtown apartment building. Not exactly a tight knit community."

"What about plates on the van?"

"None. Generic make and model, plain clothes on the guy. He just looked like a regular guy."

"But they have his picture, though." They could put that out on the wires, get it posted to social media. Someone had to have seen him.

"Our best course of action is to keep doing exactly what we're doing and find out who's been looking into you." Jaxton shrugged one shoulder. "Ryson said most of the cops in the city are on the street looking. It's only a matter of time until they find her."

"Until then, Pierce is who knows where." Kenna understood how it felt to be powerless like that. Dragged into something out of her control.

"So, first we make sure this calling-you-out tactic is a mistake. We can ensure he won't like the consequences of this power play."

"You think he underestimated me?"

"I think he'll find out."

Kenna wasn't so sure. She was hardly the same FBI agent daughter of a famous investigator that she'd been. Once upon a time. "Now you think I'm going to contribute? Before you only thought I was this nuisance, right?" She folded her arms. "Why the change in your tune?"

"I decided to hold off on drawing a conclusion about you."

"So...it's not that you don't think I killed Daniel Vaynes. It's just that you can't prove it. Yet." She stared him down. "Right now, *you're* my chief suspect."

Jax sighed. "Coffee?"

She figured that was as good as, *Touché*. They would be at an impasse until they either learned to trust each other, or one of them was arrested. "We're not working together. So why would we get coffee?"

"If we're not working together, then of course you don't want to go and look at the case files for those nine missing women."

She jerked around and studied his expression.

"I'll grab food and meet you at the office. We can look over the case files."

She set off toward her car and called back over her shoulder. "*I'll* get the food and meet *you* there."

Chapter Eight

Two hours later she pushed the chair back from the conference room table and stood. Thankfully not many other agents were here so late. She didn't relish the moment she'd have to face them when even just being here in this room threw her off.

"You have nothing, either?" Mr. Special Agent sounded frustrated.

The food containers were empty, and she'd been reading yet another slim case file from the box of mementos. "Seventeen-year-old female listed as missing. She was taken sometime between leaving the fast food restaurant where she worked and the time she should've arrived home."

No trace.

No witnesses.

The victim had been described as "wild and carefree," and the investigating detective found a boyfriend the parents hadn't known about. The assumption was that she'd run off to be with him. Probably halfway to California by the time the parents reported her missing the next day, after she never came home from school.

"The skirt she'd been wearing was discovered by a hiker." Torn and bloody. "They got a DNA profile for the killer, but never matched it to anyone."

Jaxton nodded. "We should get the item tested against our dead guy."

She pulled up the form to request physical evidence on a case and started typing...then realized she had no authority to do that. Jaxton would have to sign off on it. "Anything in yours?"

"Witness sketch. I don't know how useful it's going to be, though."

She traded it for the laptop. Male, white. Trimmed mustache, thick brows. Tidy hair. Their dead guy was bald with no hair at all, and not because of a medical condition. Had he removed it so he wouldn't leave DNA at a scene?

"It's from a case that was twenty-two years ago."

Enough time that they had no idea if it was the dead guy. The techs would have to work some of that photo-aging magic if they were going to find out. "Longshot then, that this guy—" She waved the witness sketch. "—is the dead man down at the PD morgue."

"But he had the victim's pictures in his possession. If we can match the memento to the missing woman, we can close this case. The way we're going to close the rest of them."

She shut her eyes for a second. He'd been right that she needed to do something. Going through all this stuff was good work. There could be a lead in these files that pointed to the kidnapper.

Jax pulled over his laptop. "We'll find out." While he typed, he asked, "Have you talked to Ryson since earlier?"

"No."

"Don't bleed too much feeling, you'll make a mess on the files."

Like she felt nothing? Bleeding her feelings wasn't going to help. She'd learned that. "I'd much rather be the cold, silent type. Makes me smarter than someone caught up in their emotions, giving too much away."

He tipped his head to the side. "I noticed."

Her phone buzzed. She read the file.

"You're not even going to look at who's trying to get ahold of you?"

She angled her phone to see the lock screen. There were a couple of notifications from someone she followed on social media, the Bible verse of the day, and a few messages. "Wilkern is texting me nothing updates again so she feels like she's doing something." She knew how that went.

"You should call her back. Tell her you're doing everything you can."

As though this was her fault, and she needed to reassure everyone involved that former agent Banbury was on the case? "You call her."

"The cops might not ask for your help, but that doesn't mean they don't want or need it." So he'd read through her. Good for him.

"If they want something done, they should get out and find Pierce themselves." That was what she'd been doing for two years.

"I might believe you if it didn't look like you were about to throw up." Jax leaned back in his chair. "What if it was Ryson who was missing? Wouldn't you want to know everyone was on it? That they were all chipping in to find him?"

She lied. "I wouldn't micromanage."

"Because you'd find him yourself."

As if anyone would let her help with that investigation. She'd be told to leave town, which only meant she'd be free to search for him with no oversight. And no texting.

"I don't get you."

"You didn't read the file?" It wasn't like they were friends. He didn't need to understand her.

He said nothing. As much withholding his past as she was hers.

"For the sake of getting this conversation over with, I'll explain what is none of your business. I care about Ryson, his wife, and the baby they just had. Plus a couple of old friends I never see these days. That's literally it." She wasn't going to apologize for having a small circle of people she cared about. "I take the cases I want. I don't take ones that involve anyone I know. I go where I please, and I leave when the job is done."

The words tasted bitter on her tongue.

"What about me? You wouldn't even try to persuade Stairs that you'd help look for me if I went missing?"

"You aren't my partner."

The past two years had been about self-preservation and nothing else. He didn't need to know Kenna purposely chose to not feel emotions she couldn't handle. She preferred the ice approach after all she'd lost—a grief she didn't owe anyone, whether they felt entitled to it or not.

"I'm done talking about this." Kenna sank back in the chair and wished she'd asked for more coffee.

"So talk to me about the old man instead. Daniel Vaynes."

"The dead guy." She could do that.

"He got away with murdering for years. You think whoever took him out did it as a gift? Like a vigilante. Someone who thinks they're doing you a favor."

Kenna shivered. "I don't need that kind of help."

"The alternative is that the death was for their own gain. Whoever left your card on the body is now determined to maintain the legacy of this older man who was never caught. He wants to get away with more killings of his own."

She thought of Pierce then, unable to hold back her mind's insistence on showing her an image of the woman's face. Long blonde hair, light eyes. Not so different than Kenna had been, back in those days before the job meant she'd seen too much.

"The dead guy was dormant for years, right? Then, when he couldn't resist the urge, he took up his mission again. He moved around so as to never draw attention to himself." She wanted to shrug, but couldn't. "Now my card is left on his body. Someone wants me to play the game."

"There's one thing I do know for sure." Jaxton's expression turned dark. "Whatever way this shakes out, I'm not going to like it."

"That makes two of us."

"It did seem like Daniel Vaynes was presented to us."

Me. "A way to honor the old man's work. Or he's the solution to a problem we didn't know we had. The killer gets to tout his superior knowledge, and the old man's prowess, to the police and get my attention at the same time."

"Missing women, a serial killer under the radar." Jaxton nodded. "We'd want to know."

"So we match his DNA to these cases, the mementos. But it doesn't help find Pierce." Her throat closed up saying the name. "If someone is thinking of leaving a legacy that continues on where this dead killer left off, then we have bigger problems than just one missing police officer."

There would be disappointment on Jaxton's face. She knew, so she didn't look. There was no reason to internalize the truth when she needed her emotions clear to focus on the bigger picture, not just one missing woman the entire force was already out looking for.

Jaxton shifted papers on the table. "We've got kidnappings and murders spread over years. Across different states.

Different towns, which means different police departments. I've got state police, I've got marshals who investigated one. No one put it together."

"And they likely never would have." She got up just to stretch her legs and refill her coffee in the breakroom. Jaxton could update Stairns, and then they'd get back to it.

The smell of Stairns's brand of cigars hit her like nostalgia. Just walking to the door of the conference room, the way she'd done so many times. Only this one wasn't a fond remembrance. Nothing to do with her former partner ever was.

She expected to see Special Agent Pacer, but it was Jax surrounded by files, tugging at his tie. The two of them were nothing alike.

Home wasn't a place she'd ever wanted to be again. Not like this. Everything was so off-kilter. *How did I get back here?* Faith wasn't a comfortable subject for her, but long days and longer nights alone on the road, who else was she supposed to talk to?

If she explained it, they'd all call her crazy. And she'd had enough of that she didn't even want to go near it now.

Jaxton's phone buzzed. "Thomas, the lab tech, is coming up. He has something he says we need to see."

Kenna turned to the elevator, through the glass. As if on cue, the stairs door beside it opened and the tech raced out. Thomas was flushed, his skinny face damp.

She lifted a hand and waved so he knew where to find them.

The lab tech ran in, clutching his tablet. "I found Pierce online."

"You did?" She stood.

Thomas blinked. "Kenna. You're really here."

And that was the warmest welcome she'd expected, coming back here. "It's nice to see you, Tom."

Jaxton interrupted the reunion. "What did you find?"

Thomas looked at his screen. "It's a website on my list, one I monitor periodically along with several hundred others. I found this." He turned the tablet around.

On screen was an image of Officer Pierce, a headshot from her personnel file. Superimposed over her face was a red target. Kenna read the header. "Death Files?"

"It's mostly harmless. People who love true crime and Halloween, talking about murders made popular. Jack the Ripper. That kind of thing," Thomas explained. "Once in a while, someone will come on and brag about what they've done. I fill out a report, and it gets followed up on."

Jaxton looked about ready to barf. He wasn't going to last long as an agent, internalizing evil like that. "So the real killers want a pat on the back from the other sickos?"

"That's pretty much it," Thomas said. "There are legends in the chat forums of the website. People whose names get whispered around like myths."

"They're not myths," she said. "They're just men. And they're revered because they killed someone and got away with it?" She shook her head.

Thomas said, "Half an hour ago, Officer Pierce's picture got posted. She's gaining a lot of buzz. Mostly people commenting on why, and how, she should die."

Kenna gritted her teeth. "Who posted it?"

"The username isn't one I've seen before. I've got my team tracing it."

"Good. We need to know who." Then she would kick their door down, cuff whoever it was, and drag them in.

His Adam's apple bobbed. "There's more."

"Spit it out." Jaxton could have shifted closer but appeared to need only his tone to incite action. More would signal aggression.

Thomas sighed a shuddering breath. "There's a link on the page. It says, 'Class is in Session.'"

"Which means what?"

"I don't know. I haven't been able to get inside yet because it looks like its rerouted to a server that runs dark web sites. But we're working on it." He hesitated. "Recently I've been hearing chatter about a class. It's like 'How to Get Away With Murder,' or something like that." Just a rumor, or so I thought. It's been in my last two reports. Both were on different sites."

Someone wanted to teach others how to evade the police? How to leave no evidence on a body, or no trace of a crime at all.

Kenna stepped back, careful not to stumble into her chair. This was what Pierce had been dragged into? She found victims and took down killers. But an online, organized group headed by someone using Pierce as an object lesson? Not good.

She glanced at Thomas. "Send everything you have to the police department. Detective Wilkern. She's the one working on Officer Pierce's kidnapping. If you find anything that has to do with the dead old guy and my business card, by all means, forward it to Special Agent Jaxton."

Thomas left, already tapping away on his tablet.

Jaxton called after him, "I want copies of anything and everything you find."

Kenna grabbed her backpack, ready to get some air. "I have to go."

"Hold up."

She turned back to him.

"I'm guessing he wanted you to jump on that. You're here. He probably expected more than, 'send it to Wilkern.'"

"Because he's all excited, so I should be too? It's not my

case and I have plenty to do." Her voice shook, so she cleared her throat. "I'll be in my rig if you find anything else."

Jaxton's gaze darkened. "I guess now we know."

"That a killer wants me to look into this just so he can feel good because the daughter of a legend will be his opponent? Or he chose me because I failed so spectacularly the last time that he's convinced he can be sure of a victory." The killer wanted to prove he was better than her. And she was supposed to take the bait? "That's not going to happen."

She closed her eyes, only to see Pacer there. Life drained from his eyes as he bled out on the ground.

"If I wade in, it will only make things worse with all the media coverage this guy will get." More bitter taste coated her tongue. "You don't need me."

She strode over and hit the button for the elevator.

Jaxton stood at the conference room door. "Be back at eight on Monday, unless you find anything." She was in over her head, and he knew it.

At least he didn't know there was so much more to it than that.

Chapter Nine

Sunday, 9:42am.

"Thanks for getting back to me on a weekend. I appreciate it."

The man on the other end of the phone said, "No worries. Sounded important."

Kenna took her coffee to the tiny table in her motorhome and slid onto the bench seat. She'd mulled over the nine photos all night, then had gone for a run while her computer processed image searches online.

Now a Sunday sermon played on the dash radio as background noise while she determined to find someone who knew what had happened to at least one of the victims. She needed to be put to rest.

Kenna found the photo in a folder on her computer. She'd had Stairs order Jaxton to pass her a copy of the file after she left last night. Not that she wanted to get in the middle of the FBI's business, but she wasn't going to sit around and do nothing. This was a good distraction.

The cops were looking for their officer. Jax would be

working the old man's murder, once the autopsy paperwork was finished. She wanted to find these women.

Kenna tapped the speaker button on her phone and laid it on the table. "You took a look at the photo I sent?"

She didn't bother pulling up the image of Daniel Vaynes. That wasn't a face she wanted to see again, even if she hadn't figured out yet why she recognized him. It wasn't what this call was about.

Sarah Bestman had gone missing eighteen months ago. Recently enough someone had to remember *something*. Daniel Vaynes had been living in Salt Lake City and working construction.

"Yeah," the guy said. "I remember him."

Kenna sat up on the bench seat. "You do?"

"About a year and a half ago in the middle of summer. Sometimes I hire seasonal workers, and he showed up with a group. We had a huge contract that year, a massive office building. We needed extra guys because they wanted a fountain in the roundabout out front of the entrance."

"He worked for you?"

"Cash only, all those guys. There's no paperwork." Before she could respond, he continued, "But not this guy. He didn't stick around."

Kenna forced herself not to jump on his statement and demand answers. She glanced at the high shelf above the window where her father's books lined the wall from the kitchen to the driver's seat. Novels. Non-fiction. Notebooks full of his handwriting, case notes and random thoughts.

His Bible was on the table by her laptop, open to the passage the pastor on the radio taught from so she could read her father's handwritten notes in the lined margins. Sometimes she added her own.

"He worked a day or two, I think end of August."

"And you remember him?"

"Some guys just stick, you know?"

Kenna frowned. A guy whose life was designed to appear normal to the extent he'd blend in and be forgettable. That guy stuck out? It would've meant a break in his pattern. Possibly the point at which he'd made the kill. "What do you remember?"

"We were laying the foundation for the fountain. He was asking about our security, wanted to work after hours and get the concrete finished. I run a tight ship and everything is locked down at night. So I said no."

Her eyebrow rose. "He was belligerent?"

"More like...he asked too many questions. Wouldn't let go of the fact I have rules. I do high-end jobs, and there can be security involved. A night guard. He worked half a week, took his Friday pay, and I never saw him again. It happens sometimes. More than I'd like, actually."

"Did he seem unstable?"

"Not really. He did get agitated, yelled at a couple of my regular guys about how they were doing things. They complained to me."

Serial killers typically held themselves together well enough no one around them knew about their dark urges. They planned, and then executed that plan.

She tried to put herself in the mind of such a killer.

He's got Sarah Bestman. Or he knows her, and he's making plans for how it's going to go down. How he'll kidnap her, kill her, and get away with it for the ninth time.

Daniel Vaynes—or whatever his real name was—had finally succumbed to his urges. A man who'd reached the edge of his composure, looking for a place to dispose a body, somewhere no one would find it.

Like under a fountain.

But the crew and the boss didn't want to cooperate. There was too much security, so Daniel couldn't sneak back at night and bury the body.

Kenna put an X by this guy's name on her notepad. "Any idea where he went after he quit your crew?"

"There's a guy you can ask. He'll take on anyone. A real bleeding heart, you know? Told me he had this older man, cash only, nearly punched one of his journeymen. I figured it was the same guy."

Kenna made a note. "What's his name?"

She wrote down the name he gave her, and they ended the call.

Kenna typed it into her browser search bar and found the name of his company, noting all his information in case she needed to call him. After that, she went on social media to find out more about the guy.

Aaron Jimenez had a beard, three kids, and a wife with blonde hair perfectly curled in every photo. The wife had a thing for photoshoots with the family because it seemed they posed for every season, recording life in all its perfection, to be added to an album online that all her friends could gush over.

She scrolled to find his posts and saw he'd checked in at a local church to, "worship with the fam" for the ten o'clock service.

Kenna typed the church address into her maps app and closed the browser tab. Sarah Bestman's face—still open in the window behind it—filled her screen.

"I'm sorry." Her voice sounded strange in the empty motorhome. Rusty. Kenna took a sip of burned coffee and stared at the image from the website Sarah's mother had set up, calling for information about her missing daughter. "I'm going to find out what he did with you, and then you can go home."

Daniel Vaynes couldn't keep his secrets much longer. Wherever he'd buried Sarah, Kenna intended to find out. Construction was a good cover. He could sneak back to the job site late at night and hide her in a wall. In setting cement. Or bury her under a pipe laid in the ground.

An itinerant worker paid in cash. A guy with fake IDs who moved around to different states.

No wonder they hadn't caught him.

Kenna pulled on a down vest over her long sleeves, but decided a coat wasn't worth it. The vest covered her Glock, holstered at the small of her back. Winter clothing meant restricted movement. Summer meant fewer places to conceal a gun if the situation warranted it. Still, she was thinking about getting a Texas PI license so she could spend winters there, where it would be a balmy sixty, and she didn't have to deal with being frozen.

She grabbed keys to the car she towed behind the motorhome when she was on the road and locked up behind her. Before she stepped away from her rig, she used her phone to toggle on the security system that would notify her of an attempted break in.

She got a cup of coffee from a drive thru and headed for the church, the tail end of the sermon she'd been listening to in her motorhome now playing on the car stereo. Some local service they broadcast live over their radio station.

Service let out a little later than she'd figured. The crowd dispersed quickly through the lobby doors and headed to lunch. Others came out more slowly. Aaron Jimenez carried a hard-sided guitar case while the wife ushered the kids to their van.

Kenna approached just as he hit the button to lower the rear door. "Mr. Jimenez?"

He spun with a smile, which faltered quickly.

She held up the paper Utah private investigator license Governor Pacer had given her. But it wasn't given in the spirit of generosity. She'd figured it was partially to buy her silence, and partially just to get rid of her so he could keep tabs from a distance, but also because she'd be held to standards of procedure. And the law. That way he'd have plenty of ammo if he wanted her taken down at a later date. The license had been a ticket to a new life—a boon that could be taken away at any time. A way for her to hang herself if he decided she'd messed up.

"I'm Makenna Banbury, a private investigator."

"Aaron?" The blonde wife looked more tired than she did in her pictures, which translated to frustration.

"This won't take long."

Aaron scratched at the full beard on his chin. "A private investigator. Is this about the man found murdered on Friday?" Before she could ask, he said, "I saw it on the local news last night."

Kenna showed him the old man's photo on her phone. "This guy?"

Aaron nodded. "I was going to go to the police tomorrow morning and tell them."

"I can pass on any message. But if you need to make a statement you should still do that with them. I'm helping the cops with some of the legwork of the case."

He nodded.

"Anything you can tell me? I won't keep you long."

Aaron shrugged. "He worked for me for a couple of months, then one day just disappeared."

"When was that?"

"More than a year ago. I remember because it was the Alpine Community job."

Kenna swiped on her phone to the screenshot of Sarah

Bestman she'd captured from the website. "Have you ever seen this woman before?"

The wife strode to the end of the car. Probably to fully gauge his reaction to another woman's picture.

He studied the screen. "No. I don't think so. Who is she?"

"Someone I'm looking for." The news media hadn't reported the fact that Daniel Vaynes was a suspected serial killer, just the fact his body had been found. Eventually it would leak about her business card, and Officer Pierce's disappearance. Then she'd be hamstrung in her ability to ask questions.

Kenna needed to find this woman before that happened.

"Around the time Daniel Vaynes was working for you, did you ever have anything odd happen? Tools missing. Someone breaking in during the night. Anything strange like that?"

Aaron frowned. "Nothing criminal, so I didn't make a police report or anything, but I remember we had some work done off the clock and no one could tell me who did it."

"What happened?"

"We were laying a patio behind the building, an outdoor dining area. Someone came in after hours and poured the concrete."

"Were there security cameras?"

He shook his head. "The site was brand new, first building in the complex. We were the only ones there, and there was no security or anything."

"Can I get the address?"

"Because of a patio?"

Kenna didn't want to tell him she thought a missing girl was likely buried there. Mostly because she didn't want to deal with the wife's reaction. She didn't need this news on Instagram, and Aaron would wind up under suspicion until the police could confirm the woman was killed by Daniel Vaynes.

She shrugged. "It's just legwork the police don't have time for."

Aaron gave her an address, which she typed into the Notes app on her phone.

"Thanks, Mr. Jimenez. I—"

"Kenna?"

She spun to find Special Agent Jaxton on approach, a Bible in one hand. "Oh, hey." She glanced at the building. "You go to church here?"

"So far, yeah. It's only been a few months, but I'm liking it." He didn't seem convinced things were as light and breezy as she was making them out to be. He held out a hand to Aaron and they shook. "Good to see you."

Aaron headed to do damage control with his wife, and Kenna strode to her car.

Jaxton followed her. "What was that about?"

"I've got an address." She beeped the locks on her car. "If you can get some kind of ground penetrating radar, we can confirm."

"Confirm what?"

"The place Daniel Vaynes buried Sarah Bestman."

His brows rose. "You found her?"

"Maybe."

He pulled out his phone. "Give me the address. I'll put in a request." She rattled off the numbers and he entered the info.

"Want to get lunch somewhere?"

Kenna turned to her Acura. "Goodbye, Special Agent Jaxton."

"It's Jax. And I'll see you tomorrow at the office. Eight o'clock."

Chapter Ten

Monday, 8:09 am.

K enna poured coffee into a mug. The mug was swiped away before she could even carry it to her lips.

"Thanks. I needed a refill."

She gritted her teeth and poured another. Same thing, the mug was taken before she could even pick it up.

"Got any more of that? Sanchez needs some too."

She turned to the breakroom with the now almost-empty carafe in her hand and saw half a dozen former colleagues watching. Blue, gray, or black suits. Red ties, mostly. Practically the same haircut. Maybe that was her perception, given she was the outsider.

Two of the agents sipped from mugs she'd just poured. Maybe she shouldn't wish they burned their tongues on the hot brew, but she wasn't feeling super gracious at the moment.

She'd only come back this morning because, even despite yesterday's progress, she had nothing new. Though she was reluctant to admit it, working with Jax was better than sitting at her dining table twiddling her thumbs.

Miller sipped and stared at her.

She saw it in his eyes. Accusation. *You just let that guy kill Bradley?*

"This coffee isn't for civilians."

Kenna grabbed another mug anyway and held it in her hand while she poured. She replaced the carafe and turned on the sink faucet to put some cold water in her hot drink, then took a sip and stared right back. Face blank. Like their animosity didn't bother her.

Like the picture of Special Agent Bradley Pacer on the wall in the office didn't bother her.

"You shouldn't have come."

"The fact I did," she told Miller, "is only because I miss all you guys. So much."

No one laughed.

Miller's mustache shifted. "You probably killed that guy and left your card just so you could be the one to investigate."

She tipped her head to the side. "Because I want to be around dead bodies so bad? I could get a job at a funeral home and make up all kinds of theories about how they died. I'd never have to leave my office to solve any mystery that came across my desk."

She lifted her mug and took a sip. Still tasted terrible. Stairns called it Marine-strong.

A muscle flexed in Miller's jaw. One of the guys behind him snorted.

"What's going on?" Special Agent Jaxton stood in the doorway. His head practically reached the door jamb. He glanced around at the gathered crowd. "Let's go, Ms. Banbury."

She sipped her coffee and didn't move. "They were just welcoming me back. Since it's been two years and all."

Miller's gaze shifted to her grip on the cup, and the white

base layer shirt she had hooked over her thumb. He knew what she'd been through—he'd seen it himself. These guys were the ones who'd rescued her. Right before they arrested the serial murderer who'd destroyed her and her partner. They'd carried out the body of their friend and colleague while she sat in the ambulance and watched.

Miller lifted his chin. "*Civilians* aren't even supposed to be in the breakroom."

"Let's go, Banbury." He wasn't her superior, but Jaxton said it like it was an order.

She started between the guys. They'd never been her friends, per se, but she'd thought they had a rapport at least and the team had worked well together. Now she was an outsider.

Sickness swished in her stomach as she strode through the gathered throng.

Miller leaned close as she passed him. "Have fun in interrogation."

"We're going to the conference room." Jaxton turned sideways to let her pass him.

"I poured you a mug." She lifted her own a couple of inches and glanced back over her shoulder. "Miller is drinking it."

There didn't seem to be a whole lot of love lost between Miller, his "boys," and Special Agent Jaxton. But that wasn't the case she was here to solve.

"I don't drink coffee."

She stared at him. "You offered to take me to coffee before."

"Let's go."

She followed. "So it was a way to lure me somewhere? Or some other part of your evil plan to entrap me?"

Jaxton shut the conference room door behind her. "You know they're still just grieving their friend, right?"

She'd had this conversation in her head so many times last night, knowing she'd be back here to face their pointing fingers when the team was in. For two years it had been a constant refrain that kept her up at night.

"Sure. Right. They're grieving. Like I wouldn't know what that was all about. I'm only the one who actually watched Bradley die." She sat. "What do I care what they think? I'm not one of them."

She finished her drink while he set up the computer with a microphone he plugged into the USB port.

"So I really am being interrogated today?" After all, she was a *civilian.* "So much for helping you the last couple of days."

In the light of morning, she was little better than another suspect to them. An UNSUB, or what the FBI called an "unknown subject." Just a profile with no real identity.

His expression was irritatingly inscrutable. "If that were true, Kenna, we would be in an interrogation room. But we're not. This is just a formality for the sake of the file. You know that. And after, I'd like you to look at some things."

If he had information to share, then she would stick around to see it. He could fill in some gaps, which would move this thing along faster. She appreciated that enough to sit through whatever torture he had in mind when what she wanted to do was run out the door and forgo the elevator. Racing down flight after flight of stairwell would satisfy her need to flee.

He started the recording, explaining who he was and who she was, along with the date and time. His tone was clipped and professional, like someone who knew his boss would listen at some point. But she could see difference in his expression.

He knew just being here was hard for her. "Can you please tell me your whereabouts prior to the arrest of the Seventh Day Killer? Then, just to cover our bases, walk me through every move you made before us meeting at Daniel Vaynes's house."

"I wasn't aware I needed an alibi while I was catching Gerald Rickshire singlehandedly."

"Humor me."

She looked at her watch. "What did the ME say was his time of death? Because I spoke with Ryson on the phone just after eleven, and Daniel Vaynes was dead by then."

"I'll check my notes." He didn't move any papers around. "For now, tell me about the hours preceding that."

She only answered because the process of thinking it through aloud meant she might realize something about her business cards that would be lost otherwise. "I've been back in Salt Lake City for four days, since the day Ellayna Feathers's mom called me."

"Where were you before that?"

"St. George for a couple of nights. I was on my way back here anyway, though."

"Why return now?"

"I needed to check my mail." She set her cup on the table and leaned back in her chair. "It's in a mailbox. One of those mom-and-pop postal places. They keep my stuff for me, and when it gets full, I come home and empty it."

He gave her a slight nod. "And when you got here?"

"Drove to the RV place where I parked my rig. Checked in. Got it all hooked up, took the car and went to get groceries. Over the next couple of days, I met with Ellayna's mother. Tracked the killer." She shrugged. "Wound up finding him."

"Was anyone with you...in your *rig*?"

She shook her head, honestly surprised he hadn't followed her home yesterday to find out for himself.

Jaxton pointed to the microphone on the table between them. "For the tape."

Kenna leaned forward and spoke right into it. Her lips brushed the foam as she used an announcer's voice. "I was alone."

"Did you kill the man we have preliminarily identified as Daniel Vaynes?"

Kenna leaned over to brush her lips against the mic again. "No. I did not."

A flash of humor lit his eyes for a second. Kenna had to look away. She was old enough to know by now that she would never not find blue eyes attractive, no matter who they belonged to. It also didn't mean there was anything special about this guy.

"Did you tell anyone you were coming back?"

"No, I did not."

Jaxton slid a photo of the dead man across the table. The image from his fake driver's license. "This man has been identified as Daniel Vaynes, at least according to this ID, the one he rented the house under. Is it possible you may have met him before Friday night?"

Kenna studied the picture. The certainty she'd had about him being familiar was less now. "I don't recognize him, but that doesn't mean I've never met him."

"Why do you think your business card was found on his body?"

She fought the urge to sigh. "I've given out hundreds. Left them all over several states, with people I've talked to and on tables in coffee shops. With bank tellers." She shrugged. "Is it being tested for prints?"

Jaxton nodded. "Utah issued your official private investigator license. Yet you have licenses in other western states. How does that even work?"

Kenna wasn't interested in explaining her history, or how she came to leave the FBI. "The killer could be someone who's sure I'd be interested to know this guy is dead, even though I have no idea who he is. Might be he was left as a gift of sorts, someone who knew I'd be happy to learn he's gone now." She wanted to brush off the timing but couldn't. "If not for Pierce, I'd be inclined to believe it was random."

"Even though that would be little more than wishful thinking."

She ignored his implacable tone. The man was a brick wall. She wanted to poke and watch him crack. "He knew I was back in town. Or knew Lieutenant Ryson would get the call, since the body was left in his precinct, and know to call me."

"Either way, you hear about it."

Maybe she didn't need to talk with the Seventh Day Killer. He probably didn't know anything.

"And now Pierce has been taken."

She lifted her gaze from the seam on the leg of her black pants and tried to fight the sour feeling—left by the coffee, yeah that was it—in her stomach.

Not the idea of facing down a killer, even if only in an interrogation room.

"Your business card was left again."

"So it's not a coincidence." She sighed. "It's a pattern."

He asked her a few more questions, confirmed some details, and then wrapped up. When he shut off the recording, she leaned back and stretched her arms above her head, like she hadn't caught on that he'd rushed the end of the interview in order to ask whatever was on his mind.

Pain flared to life in her arms, shooting sparks to her fingertips. Damage left from her injuries that would never heal. She didn't manage to hide the wince, but Special Agent Jaxton said nothing. Did he know?

Kenna didn't need the conversation getting off track with whatever questions he decided to spin at her, so she stepped on the gas. "What do you have to show me?"

Jaxton twisted the laptop so she could see the screen. The picture on the left was the dead guy. On the right were...

"Two results?"

"This guy actually has three aliases that we've found. Daniel Vaynes, the name he rented the house under, and two others—Daniel Merks and Clive Burnette."

She clicked the mousepad to see the second result. Different name, with a Maryland license. The third was Idaho. All unique names, though they were still generic monikers that would draw little, if any, attention. "He looks like a fifty-year-old gas station attendant in all of these pictures."

"The neighbor said construction, right?"

Kenna nodded. What did his hands look like? Fingers and palms revealed many secrets. *Be careful little hands, what you touch.* "That's what I went with."

"And now you've likely discovered the last victim's body."

"We don't know that for sure." She never banked on a thing until she could be certain. After all, she only had herself to rely on. There was no one to run anything by.

"Should only take a couple of weeks for the crew to get out there and find out if she really is buried under the patio."

This guy had killed at least nine times that they knew of. That meant he'd been operating a while—a timeline of exact dates would be good the further back she went. Memories faded, which was why she'd chosen to investigate the most recent victim. The one who also happened to be geographically closest.

Jaxton clicked to a new picture. "Each of the licenses he had are less than five years old. So, they're all newer, and clearly fakes. As much as I'd like a correlation between his living all over, and your being licensed as a PI all over, there really isn't one."

Kenna wasn't surprised it had crossed his mind. "What was the cause of death?"

"Drug-induced heart attack."

Kenna pushed away from the table and stood. Her chair rolled back two feet and then stopped. "And the shoe box, with the mementos?"

Jaxton motioned to the stack of files.

"The rest are all missing persons?"

"Six missing persons, because you may have found one. Two were never reported. That makes all nine of our mementos. The cases we have are spread over the states that match his driver's licenses. Likely we'll be able to correlate the cases with times he used those IDs to travel around. I'd like your location for the last two years, so I can rule out a connection."

As if she was going to write all that down and hand it over to the FBI. "We'll never find a paper trail if he was paid under the table everywhere he went, not just here. Probably didn't file taxes either." She sighed. "And this guy never showed up as a suspect in any of the murders? Not even as a person of interest in one single disappearance?"

Jaxton shook his head. "I haven't read the case files, but he never even once popped on radar as *any* of these three identities. Not even a speeding ticket. Whether we'll find his real name by looking into the other eight women or not is something we'll have to find out."

All that would do was show how thoroughly the police

had failed these women. "What about his original identity? Cold cases where he left his DNA, but it was years ago so it was never tested. He could have killed countless times using a whole list of fake identities, or even his real name."

"I had the same thought." Jaxton's phone vibrated across the table, but he ignored it. "They're running his DNA, fingerprints. Dental records. We got nothing on the facial recognition but these three licenses. So now we wait for the ME."

She paced to the window, saw her old coworkers staring back at her, and spun the other way. She had enough trouble to deal with in this room without them adding to it.

Daniel had no ID.

Nothing distinguishing about him. Not even a watch. Probably no tattoos. The boots had been generic, the kind you can buy at Walmart. Off-brand versions of the good stuff they sold at the hardware store. He hadn't been undergoing medical treatment that explained his loss of hair.

But for those mementos, she might've believed it could be possible. Instead, he was a killer who'd taken extra steps to keep his DNA from the crime scenes.

"Hey." Jaxton interrupted her thoughts.

She spun, memories swirling in her mind. "What?"

"You were muttering." He filled a paper cup with water from the pitcher and brought it to her.

"Thanks." She swallowed down the sick feeling in her stomach. *Wrong killer.* For a moment she'd been trapped in her memories, remembering another time she had stood in this same exact room, but with a different agent. "Sorry, Special Agent Jaxton."

"Jax is fine, since we're going to be working together."

An olive branch. Not quite friendship.

She set the water down and pulled over the laptop. They

needed to solve this man's murder and put to rest the women he'd killed so she could go back to her normal life. This was nothing but an anomaly, and she planned on proving as much.

Kenna sat on the edge of the table. "We're assuming the old guy was murdered, but it could've been an accident. Maybe whoever left him there just tossed his body away to cover up something else and my card was placed there just to throw us all off. Could be he was on another construction job with Aaron Jimenez and his crew. It went bad, so they dumped him there instead of reporting it. Easier to walk away when you don't have to explain yourself to anyone."

"Did it seem like he knew who you were?"

She shook her head. So much for that theory. "Do you know him?"

"Not well, but he seems solid." Jaxton studied her, as though there was plenty more she should've realized. "Until we figure all this out, you need to be careful. Whoever left your card on that guy's body could be closer than you'd like. He hand-delivered one serial murderer to you. Could be he thinks you should thank him for getting rid of a dangerous man."

"You forgot the 'old' part. Dangerous *old* man. Not so dangerous these days. Maybe he was nothing but a has-been."

"If there's a killer, he purposely left your card on the body. If it was the construction crew, or a foreman, why would they leave your card? Why would it be there in the first place, when the whole point was for him to be anonymous and remain under the radar? We never even knew who he was."

She fisted her hands by her sides. "I don't need you to tell me that—"

"Kenna." Jaxton barked her name. "You've drawn attention to yourself. It's time to start being careful. And that means not being alone when there is a killer intent on drawing you out, thinking he's doing you a favor, which means he could kill again and deliver you another present."

That blonde face filled her mind. "Like Officer Pierce?"

He closed his mouth.

"I should write up a list of people I think should die for what they've done." She folded her arms. "Though, most of them I already put in prison. I'll leave it out for him. You know, in case he needs more ideas of who to kill. Like leaving cookies for Santa."

He came over to stand in front of her, his blue eyes narrowing. "This is serious."

She pushed off the wall. "I'm planning on being seriously out of here in about two seconds. We can catch up later."

As if she would still be hanging out in this city when that time came.

"You're just gonna run?" He tipped his head to the side. "I figured you had more courage in you than that."

"I'm fully capable of taking care of myself. You don't need to tell me to be careful." She tried to shrug but couldn't. "Seriously, can't I just leave and get back to my life? I don't actually want to be dragged into *anything*. Not now, and not ever again."

His gaze softened. "I'll do what I can to get you the information you need to put this to rest." There was a substance to his words she both liked and disliked at the same time. Like a weighted blanket on a sleepless night. "And I'll do my best to keep you out of it if that's what you need."

"I'm not responsible for what happens to Officer Pierce." Her voice sounded thick with the syrup of denial. *I know how it feels.* Jessica Pierce wasn't Ellayna Feathers. Pierce had a team of people looking for her.

Before he could respond, her phone buzzed. She dug it

out and swiped a button, wondering what Jaxton had picked up on to make his eyes look that way at her.

Kenna's hands shook as that familiar pain flickered down her forearms.

The phone fell from her hands and clattered to the floor.

"What is it?"

An image of Officer Pierce loaded. Tied up. Gagged and bleeding, she stared up from the floor.

At the bottom of the screen ticked a ten-minute countdown.

Chapter Eleven

"Whatever this is, it's loading now." Thomas lifted his gaze as the TV that hung on the wall in front of him flickered to life. Beside him, Wilkern and Ryson did the same. They'd come over as soon as she called to tell them about the text.

"It's directing me to a website forum. Looks like a video."

The TV screen flashed and dramatic music played in the background.

"Ladies and Gentlemen." The voice was distorted. Then, after another flicker, the image stilled and letters appeared: MURDER CLASS. "I hope you have your pencil and paper handy."

He sounded like a podcaster introducing the weekly episode and this week's special guest. As though this was nothing more than entertainment and not something so much more sinister.

Two faces appeared on the screen. Ryson gasped. "Pierce."

The officer looked to be secured to a chair—tied and gagged as she'd been in the photo. One of her eyes was swollen almost completely shut and her nose was broken. Blood had dried at the corner of her mouth and in her nostrils. She had on a white tank top, the kind of undershirt she might wear beneath her uniform. Jessica had blood and sweat on her face, and her blonde hair hung loose. Her nostrils flared as she sucked in deep breaths.

But it was the fear and pain in her eyes Kenna couldn't look away from.

I know how it feels.

The man over her shoulder had been pixelated, so it was impossible to make out features. The voice, also altered like the image, might have been male. He would be impossible to ID.

She turned to Thomas. "You can get something from this image, right?"

"Jessica Pierce," the distorted voice said. "Twenty-four years old and a police officer. Even with all her colleagues searching, no one has managed to find her." The kidnapper paused. "The van was spotted on surveillance, just as planned. However, no identifying elements of either the vehicle or myself have been helpful to the detectives."

Jax whispered, "How does he know this?"

The kidnapper continued, "I got in and out in broad daylight without incident, seen by no one." Kenna's mind buzzed as he continued to prattle on about how perfectly he had pulled off the abduction. The police would never be able to find Pierce. "But they will watch their officer die."

Pierce whimpered behind the gag and a single tear rolled down her face. Kenna saw Jessica fight back the urge to succumb to her tears and, in a show of solidarity, shoved her hands into her pockets. She squeezed them into tight fists, which made the scar tissue on her forearms ache.

Ryson shoved in front of her to get to Thomas. "Where are they?"

Thomas typed on his computer, then glanced up at the TV. "Looks like drywall in the background. No windows. Generic chair. They could be anywhere."

Wilkern said, "What about audio? Can we hear anything on the feed that might help us?"

"There's no..." Thomas stopped, typed, and then peered at the screen of his laptop and a bunch of code she didn't know how to read. "It's just their voices. Not even white noise. Like it was prerecorded and then edited so he could distort the image and clean up the audio."

It wasn't live. Pierce could already be dead.

"Get me what was removed," Ryson said. "I want facial recognition run. We need to know who this guy is. No excuses."

"That may not be possible, Lieutenant."

"Get me what was removed, or I'll put you in a world of hurt."

Wilkern set her hand on his arm, but he didn't back down. A cool head in a crisis wasn't necessarily an attainable ask when Ryson was about to combust. She knew enough about him to know that his frustration would come out sooner or later.

Kenna quietly said, "Lieutenant."

He spun to her. "This is on you."

Jax shifted, but she wasn't about to let him wade in. Before he could say anything, Kenna got in Ryson's face. "Back off."

He didn't. "Your tech needs to do his job."

Never mind that she wasn't FBI anymore. "The video is still playing. When it's done, we'll get what we can from it. We'll find her."

Ryson's eyes filled with tears. "You want me to watch her die, streaming live?"

"I want you to hold, so we can get as much from this as possible."

Thomas straightened. "This isn't a live stream."

"It's a recording?"

Kenna shot Wilkern a look. "Way to state the obvious. He already said that."

Jax started to speak, but Thomas interrupted. "The broadcast is happening now, but the video is definitely not live." He tapped his keyboard. "This transmission was definitely prerecorded."

In the background, the kidnapper droned on some more about how he'd managed to take Pierce and get away with it.

Ryson shifted. "Dig out the original file. I need to know if she's already dead."

"This isn't that easy." Thomas hammered on the keys. "Not like being a street cop."

Before Ryson could react, Jax said, "Lieutenant—"

He spun and got into Jax's face. "Let me guess. Your techs, so your case. Am I right?"

Kenna took a step toward the TV to watch the perpetrator's body language while the two continued to exchange words behind her.

She made a few notes on her phone, just so she could reference them later. He bragged about how he'd planned so well, and that was key to being a successful murderer. How he was the master now.

Now. He hadn't been the master before, but he was the master *now*. Because now he was free to take over since the old man was finally dead?

"We need to wait until the end." That was Jax.

Ryson said, "I can't just stand here and watch one of my people die."

"I know you're scared. No one wants—"

Ryson cut him off. "You think I give a rip about my own feelings right now?"

Kenna didn't turn, but she needed them to shush. "Guys."

"And so," the distorted voice said. "To the main event." He produced a knife.

She stepped forward, even closer to the screen. "He's gonna kill her."

"I will demonstrate the death blow."

"The video is on a website that connects back to a dark web server." Thomas's keyboard hammering got faster. "It was uploaded to be transmitted at a set time. I can tell you how many people are watching it. They're all logged in for the viewing." He blew out a breath. "This really is an actual class with actual students."

"For *what*?"

She moved to Ryson. "Maybe you want to step out and take a break. Tell Steven we have a new lead, and we're gathering information."

Ryson needed something to focus on so he could take a breath.

"We don't have information." The grief in his eyes nearly floored her. "We have nothing."

Kenna had to duck when he waved his arm at the screen.

"What are we gonna get from watching this but have to see her—" His voice broke.

Kenna got in his face. "You think Pierce needs this?" She might already be dead, but Kenna wasn't about to say that. "You have to focus and not lose it. You're a cop, Ryson."

"She's only been on the job just over a year." His eyes wet with tears. "She doesn't deserve this."

Kenna squeezed his arm. "I know." She of all people knew precisely what Pierce was going through right now.

Instead of acknowledging that, he turned on her, "You should've helped me."

In the background, Pierce cried out in pain. She watched the same agony register on Ryson's face as his officer went silent.

Kenna didn't take her focus off Ryson. She also didn't let go of his arm and tried to make eye contact. "We'll get her back."

"She's already dead. You heard it."

"Don't give in to that. Not until you have no other option. You *have* to keep fighting." She tried to tug him away, so they could talk. Get back to the friendship she'd always fallen back on. No way could she live through it if he lost hope.

Kenna couldn't go through that again.

"No." Ryson spun back to the TV. "I want to know."

Jax glanced at her. Kenna wanted to slump into a chair and give in to her emotions, but this wasn't the time for her feelings. Not when a woman's life was being extinguished.

A wound in Pierce's neck bled in a steady stream down over her shoulder. Breath hitched in her chest. Kenna watched each breath.

Please don't leave me.

She squeezed the bridge of her nose. She should be able to solve this, but instead there was nothing she could do. That was the real reason she'd gone after Sarah Bestman's body yesterday. There was nothing she could do to help Jessica. The helplessness was overwhelming.

She had to take the good with the bad. Or she would be the one with no hope.

"It's about the art," the killer intoned. "Death requires talent as well as medical knowledge. It requires time spent in practice so these skills are mastered. There can be no format. No certain way of doing it, or else each body discovered will be traced back to the killer, simply by the matter of the method used. This is unacceptable."

The pixelated image shifted, and she thought he might have smiled. "At the end of the day, it's about bringing your own individuality to the killing process. You will find more about how to attain this individuality and the keys to becoming a successful murderer in the downloadable PDF where I go into elaborate detail, using examples from our benefactor. This bonus PDF is only available for the next 24 hours. Upgrade to the Murder Plus package now."

Kenna scrubbed her cheeks, almost wishing she could cry. Then she wrote *benefactor* in her notes. Then PDF.

"Did he say a benefactor?"

She glanced at Wilkern. "That's what I heard."

Jax said, "The dead old guy, maybe?"

"We could find out if Vaynes communicated with anyone recently. Did we find a phone in his house?" Kenna hadn't heard. "Thomas, can we get our hands on that PDF?"

Wilkern shook her head, a sheen of tears in her eyes. "I don't think we found a phone but I'm waiting for the final report from the techs. They may have seen something we didn't."

"No-no-no-no..." Thomas banged keys as he typed furiously. Sweat poured off his brow.

On screen, the feed shut off.

Wilkern leaned over his shoulder. "Why did it stop?"

"They know we're accessing the link. They know we're on to them, watching, so they shut down the video."

Kenna shook her head. "They wanted us watching. They sent the link, so they know we're viewing it. Why cut us off before the end?"

"So we don't know if Pierce is dead or alive." Jax frowned at the black TV screen. "Because wondering is far worse torture than having to watch."

"Get it back," Ryson ordered.

"It's not that simple. I'm fighting off an attack right now. I can't do that and regain access to the video feed." Thomas glanced at Kenna. "That link you were sent was a fishing expedition to get access to our server. And no, I can't get the PDF."

Considering she had a sneaking suspicion the PDF would be about her, or her father, she didn't especially want to see it anyway, but it could still be useful.

Kenna said, "My phone and the FBI system aren't connected." Or, they hadn't been until she forwarded Thomas that link.

"It was all a trap?" Wilkern looked like she wanted to throw up. "Officer Pierce didn't mean anything to him. This is about Kenna and getting into the FBI system. But for what?"

She took a step back at the underlying tone of blame. An involuntary retreat. "I didn't ask for this. I came back to get my mail." And save Ellayna Feathers.

Jax touched her shoulder, but she shrugged him off.

"I *didn't* ask for this."

Jax said quietly, "No one thinks that." Louder he said, "This is a power trip. It doesn't matter who he's focused on. This is all about him, and what he believes he can get away with. Maybe he's throwing out a bunch of things to get us chasing our tails and then miss what will ultimately lead us to him."

"He's egging us on because of you, Kenna." Ryson stared down at her. "He took one of our officers, and he wants us to spin in circles trying to catch him." He turned to Thomas. "Get it back. Get *him* back."

"I'm trying. He didn't just shut me out of the video so we can't watch it. He's trying to plant a worm in our system."

A killer with technical know-how who posted a murder video like he was teaching a class. Kenna blew out a long breath. "That's a serious power trip." She turned to Jax. "There's no way we can let him get away with it."

"We won't."

Jax looked so certain. She wanted to believe, but how did she keep her hope intact when so much had gone so wrong in her past? The result of uncovering evil was never satisfying, even with a conviction or when the suspect ended up dead. People were indelibly changed. Victims suffered, and pain spread like ripples in water.

She rubbed at her eyes, balking at the way her mind conjured up those images she'd tried so hard to bury.

Was that pixelated man the same who killed and delivered that old man to her?

Dropped her business card. Twice. Dragged her into this, then pulled in the police by taking one of theirs. Pitted them against each other. Hit her in the place it hurt the most.

His voice—taunting and superior—rang in her ears. Fire burned in her for the way he was jerking them around. Thrown in their faces that he was hurting and using Pierce as part of some online class.

How to murder and get away with it.

"He probably *will* get away with it."

She turned to face Ryson. He looked haggard and enraged. She needed him to get it together. To keep fighting. She stepped toward him, staring him down. "You have something to say?"

Confronting him might backfire, but Kenna needed him to find the will to fight.

"You didn't want to be part of this investigation." Ryson folded his arms across his chest. "Why even ask us here when this is an FBI case now?"

"Back up." Jax got between them. "Everyone here is on edge. Just take a second."

Neither of them listened. Kenna wasn't going to let this go. "She's your officer, and your star detective didn't find anything. Right?"

"Guys—"

Ryson took a step closer, ignoring Jax's palm in front of his sternum. "We don't need your help. This is our case, and we'll find Pierce without you. You said this kidnapping had nothing to do with you. The big shot didn't want to help Officer Pierce. Neither of you have any business being here, as far as I'm concerned."

"Either I'm in the middle of this and it's my fault," Kenna said. "Or it has nothing to do with me. You can't have it both ways, Lieutenant."

"Things have changed."

She glanced at Jax. He knew exactly how that would go down with the cops.

"This is now—"

"It's not your case." Ryson shook his head so hard he probably gave himself a concussion. "No matter that you suddenly decide to feel bad and want to be the hero and save the day. All because now she's on a video and she's hurt. Or worse."

Kenna figured that wasn't what Jax had been about to say. Besides, he didn't need to ruin his relationship with the cops he had to work with just to stick up for her, so she decided to wade in. "You need our help, Ryson. We should all be working together to find this guy, right? Jax and I are starting with the dead man and any known associates. Approach it from that direction. Figure out who would want to kidnap Pierce. Right? We are on the same team."

Unless it was random and choosing her had been nothing but chance. So much had happened since last Friday night when Pierce responded to the scene and called an ambulance for Ellayna.

Now she was the abducted target of a killer and likely already dead.

Kenna couldn't help but think this might be at least partly her fault. She glanced at Wilkern, wondering if she might be the killer's next victim.

Ryson said, "You think I haven't done everything to try and explain this?"

That wasn't what she'd said. Or what she had implied. "Pierce will—"

"We don't need your help." Ryson's jaw flexed. "You can call if you get any more videos."

Kenna blew out a breath. "We can work together."

"You didn't want to." Ryson's expression hardened.

"We'll do it for Jessica Pierce." Her stomach clenched. "However we do it, this guy will be found. And stopped."

Ryson just shook his head, no consideration of old times or anything she'd been through. "We're leaving."

Wilkern headed to the door first. The detective had remained silent during the whole exchange, but it was clear from her expression that she felt the same way as Ryson. Deep grief over what had happened to Officer Pierce, directed at her in anger.

Like this was all her fault.

The room emptied. Even Thomas left, until she was alone with Jax. He took a step closer and started to speak.

She shook her head. "Don't."

"I'm not going to explain away their behavior. Just like they shouldn't explain away yours. Barbs were fired, and both sides should apologize. After Pierce is found."

"But it's my fault I was dragged into this?"

"I never said that." He shook his head, a placid look on his face. How was he so calm at a time like this? "We all hide our pain. But we lash out at the people we care about because we trust the deep feelings they have for us can weather whatever storm we bring. The problem is that we end up hurting those we're closest to."

"Misery loves company?" She shrugged one shoulder. "I have no company. All I have is me, so I guess that's why I didn't know that. Because no one has my back."

The elevator door opened, and Doctor Landstadt stepped out. Taylor's gaze flickered with tension around her green eyes. She was barely five-two and still slender even after having a child with her husband Ian. But she looked older. Two years and it was like she'd aged ten. "Kenna, I—"

"Are you kidding me?"

Jax moved beside her, his suit jacket in one hand. "Doctor Landstadt. How are you?"

Her professional smile appeared. Kenna didn't believe an ounce of it. "I'd heard Kenna was up here."

"So you came to apologize?" She set her hands on her hips and faced down the woman who'd been her best friend. Once upon a time. "Go ahead, Taylor. I'm listening."

The doctor's composure slipped. "Well, I—"

"Never mind. Please stop. There's nothing you can say that I wanna hear." Kenna slammed a hand out to hold the elevator doors open. "After what you did to me? I have no time for you."

Taylor was supposed to have been her friend. And with

one swipe of her pen, she'd taken away everything Kenna had left.

Jax started to follow. "I'll go with—"

"Don't follow me." He probably thought she would do something nuts, like *open up* to him. Kenna nearly laughed out loud. "I don't need anyone's help."

Chapter Twelve

Two years ago.

K enna twisted around and got her first look at him. Frozen in place, she took in his frame. Huge. Not tall, but wide. His chest was massive. Arms. Thighs. All of it, thick. Not overtly muscled but sturdy. Solid.

The hood of his sweater was down. His face could only be described as craggy. Stubble and hard angles. He could have been a fisherman on an old, crumbling boat on the coast by a tiny English village. Weathered. Worn.

Dead eyes.

"You kill us and a world of hurt descends on you."

He lifted his hand and pointed a stun gun at her. She flinched even though he had yet to fire. He'd ambushed them on the highway, while they'd been out for a run with Kenna's dog Bear. And when she'd been unconscious, he'd sliced the tendons on her arms, rendering them useless.

"Don't!" Pacer's yell caused another flinch she couldn't hold back.

Almatter saw it.

Everything in her wanted to rush the guy, tackle him and hope to subdue him, somehow, despite the fact her arms didn't work below the elbows. She gritted her teeth as her eyes swam. Brute force might feel good, but it wasn't likely to be successful.

He took in her features, enjoying her visible anguish.

He liked that she was scared but trying to be brave. Trying to figure a way out of this. He thought she was defeated and he had the upper hand. There was zero way she would allow that to happen.

Kenna needed to figure out an exit plan.

He kicked her in the thigh. "Get him out." His voice sounded like gravel being poured on the ground.

Fear froze her to where she sat.

"Get. Him. Out."

"I can't use my hands."

His left hand swiped up. She'd failed to take his other hand into account and realized her mistake when she saw the flash of a knife.

The tip touched her leg, and he slammed it down in one move, driving the knife clear through the muscle of her thigh. The pain reverberated down to her foot and up to her hip.

Kenna screamed. Pacer yelled.

He waited for her scream to diminish, then waited a few more seconds until even the silence was loud. He repeated himself. "Get. Him. Out."

Every breath from her lips was a moan. She shifted her body, crying out when she had to move her leg. Blood pooled under it, soaking her pant leg. She whimpered.

He stepped back. "Figure it out."

"Or you'll use the stun gun on us?" Pacer asked. "Just do it. Carry us yourself."

"Don't." Kenna pulled her hands up, the effect negated by

the fact she couldn't use them and could barely lift them. They hung limp. She turned to Pacer. "Come on."

"You can't carry me, and I can't stand."

"I know." She pushed out a breath. "Come on." He'd have to lean on her back so that she could carry him without using her arms. She hunched over as far as she could without toppling over. "Put your arms around my neck."

"You can't hold me up with your leg like that."

They both knew this was just another way for Almatter to torture them. The whole point was to mess with their minds, and it likely was only going to get worse.

Pacer huffed.

Kenna scooted to the edge of the van floor and set one foot outside. Their abductor backed up but was still close enough to shoot her point blank with the stun gun if he decided to.

She waited for Pacer to shift his body closer to her back. His arms came around her. She wanted to bask in the sensation of being enveloped by his strength. That bigger frame surrounding hers.

He gripped his one wrist with his other hand. Kenna lifted both their bodies with the strength of one leg. Pacer's feet touched the ground as he bit back a cry of his own. Her injured leg, causing the same misery, while the good one shook as if she'd just finished the worst CrossFit class in the world. She moaned through her jaw that now ached from being clenched so hard. Blood pounded through her temples.

"That way." He jerked the stun gun to the side, knife still in his other hand.

Kenna took one step. Pacer cried out.

The next one, she'd have to put weight on her injured leg. "Don't."

She had to. No matter what Pacer thought, there was no way it would end well to turn the tables on this guy. They weren't even fully functional at this point. Even if she twisted around and he somehow managed to launch himself at their murderer, one of them would get stabbed. The other would get stunned. Each. Both. Either way, they'd end up worse than they were now and without a guarantee they'd be able to take the guy down. Even working together.

Across what appeared to be a barn, there was a cellar door in the floor. Open.

Nothing more than an opening, and beyond it only darkness.

Death.

Her body shuddered and sweat rolled down her face.

"Move."

She took a step.

"Don't do it, Kenna. You can't hold us both up."

She braced their combined weight on her bad leg and took another quick step. Not more than a shuffle. She'd have to repeat it multiple times before they got anywhere near that opening.

"Set me down."

She took another step.

The longer they were here alive, the better chance for someone to find them. She had to believe that or she would give up hope. There would be no other reason to continue on. They weren't being hurt more right now. They weren't trapped. They would survive this.

Down in that cellar...no, she didn't want to go there.

Maybe he was right. Maybe this was the end.

Pacer's hands loosened.

She tried to grab for them but couldn't get purchase with the sliced tendons in her forearms. The pain overwhelmed her senses until black spots clouded her vision. Her head swam, and she began to topple over. Pacer, too.

Probably what he wanted.

Just in time, she twisted, planted the foot of her good leg down to hold them up and cried out all the pain and frustration that needed to get out.

And then she took another step.

They were getting closer. Their time was up, she couldn't wait out rescue anymore. Not if she was going to keep them from going down into that cellar.

Pacer wanted her to go. To leave him here. But what if she died, her back to the killer, because she'd made a run for it instead of waiting and surviving? Could she risk her life, knowing she might die quickly? She would be leaving Pacer to face a slow and even more painful death alone. Kenna didn't know if she could leave him like that.

Kenna started to turn back. They'd have to launch at him together so their combined weight could take him down. If she got stabbed again in the process, then it was what it was. Just another thing to deal with. At least they wouldn't be in the dark of that—

His boot kicked her leg. Her knee buckled and she started to fall, the weight of both her and Pacer too much for her injured leg to handle.

And then a final shove.

Pacer's weight overwhelmed her smaller frame, propelling her over. Together they hit the ground and their bodies, with no strength to change their trajectory, rolled toward the cellar.

Pacer dropped first. He didn't let go of her.

Together they fell.

Down into darkness.

And death.

Chapter Thirteen

Tuesday, 1:15am.

Kenna sat up in bed, mid-gasp. She shoved off the damp sheet and comforter and flopped back against the pillow to stare at the ceiling. A sob rose up into her throat.

Thank You.

The memories dissipated as wakefulness rose, relentless as the morning sun. She grasped for each tangent of reminiscence, even as they seemed to melt like snowflakes on the palm of her hand. The touch of his hand. Her fingers against his cheek.

She blew out a long breath and stared at the outline of the light fixture in the semi-dark. Two years, and she still didn't like pitch black.

But that didn't mean there, in the dark with Bradley, wasn't exactly where she wanted to be.

Thank You.

Without the nightmares, she would never see him

anymore. Those last hours with him were all she had now. One day time would steal them, the way a killer had stolen Pacer's hope at the very end. After that, she'd no longer be able to recall how he smelled, or the feel of his arms around her. The memories they'd shared would grow stale. Even the terror of those few hours would be muted. Gone.

Forever.

Kenna rolled and looked at her alarm clock. 01:17.

Decaf it was. After all, there was a chance she might be able to fall asleep again, and maybe she would dream about being with Bradley—but without the nightmare part this time. There was a chance she might get what she wanted, even if it was only for a little while.

She brewed the decaf in her French press and leaned against the opposite counter to check her phone while it steeped. Despite four texts and two calls, Ryson still hadn't touched base. They didn't know for sure that Pierce was dead. They hadn't seen her die. The killer might have said as much, but then he'd kicked them off the website. Who knew what'd happened?

If Ryson lost hope, there wasn't much she could do. Kenna could work the case, but she couldn't be someone's foundation. She'd learned the hard way that life didn't work like that.

Kenna slumped onto the bench seat at the table and wiggled her wireless mouse. She leaned back against the window, her legs straight along the seat while the laptop booted.

Two captain's chairs, one the driver's seat. A couch she never sat on. The table. A galley kitchen. A bathroom, and the bedroom she could separate from the rest of the motorhome with a partition. This was her domain. The space she could control. Where she shut out the world to be alone with her father's notebooks and the same blanket he'd used in the winter months.

They'd lived in an Airstream he towed with a diesel truck. Her life now was an upgrade from that, thanks in large part to the inheritance he'd left her, but she'd maintained the spirit of the life he led. After the FBI let her go—kicked her out, whatever—she'd wanted to go back to what she knew.

A life on the road.

Taking cases. Solving crimes the police couldn't, or didn't want to. Sometimes due to a lack of departmental budget. Often it was that they'd run out of leads and had too many other cases to afford a wild goose chase even if they wanted that more than anything.

Kenna had time, and she had the resources. What else would she do?

Her inbox had a handful of emails, one of which was from Thomas. The FBI tech had obtained permission from Stairns to provide her with a copy of the video so she could take a look. That was enough to allow the disquiet to creep in.

Working alone was much simpler. She didn't have to worry about the motives of guys like Stairns, who had one conversation with the governor and then pushed her out of the job she'd loved. The career she thought she'd have until she succumbed to death, like in the middle of a high-profile case, or perhaps from a giant bird knocking her off a cliff and causing her to tumble into a frozen river.

All of it. Gone.

Kenna sipped black coffee and stared at the still image Thomas sent of Pierce and her kidnapper. She tried not to think about her recurring nightmare.

She stared at the kidnapper's blurred eyes. Smart. Cunning. *Who are you?* This guy had a bigger plan than one murder, and it wasn't to simply kill again. It was more than that. He wanted to teach others to kill and get away with it.

He had to have killed before. Learning by experience, or taught by someone else? Trained. Groomed. The old man, Daniel Vaynes, maybe. The benefactor.

Now he had her attention.

Someone who'd been raised as she was, brought up to serve a higher purpose. He thought he could do whatever he wanted. While her purpose was to find justice, his was to kill.

As much as Kenna wanted to stay in her motorhome and hide out. Or get on the road and find some wide-open space not covered in snow right now, she couldn't leave until this was solved. He'd trapped her here by dropping her business cards.

Her phone vibrated across the table. She leaned over to look at the screen and saw it was Ellayna's mother. "Hello?"

"It's one in the morning. You weren't supposed to pick up!"

Kenna frowned into her coffee cup. "Can I help you with something Ms. Feathers?"

"She...it's just..."

God knew Kenna was well versed in the aftermath of trauma. She figured that was what this was. "Tell me."

Ellayna's mother blew an audible whimper across the phone's mic. "I just got her to lay back down. She's not sleeping. I thought being home would be better. I can't be stressed, I'm on bedrest."

Kenna bit her lip.

"She's *terrified* he'll come back and get her."

Her skin split and a bead of blood touched Kenna's tongue. "He's in prison, and he will *never* get out."

"I told her that. It's like she doesn't want to believe me. Nothing is working."

"They told you it takes time, right?" Surely she had access to a counselor who could talk Ellayna through what had happened.

"I know."

"Ah," understanding washed over Kenna. "You're afraid you don't have time, because the baby will be here soon." Kenna could imagine, but that didn't mean she knew what it felt like. All she had was the tendency to choke over the word, "baby."

"Meanwhile it's like she's…" She didn't finish.

Kenna said, "Stuck there."

She squeezed the bridge of her nose and lifted her knees to her chest on the seat. "I want to tell you it'll get better. And in a way, it will. But also, in some ways, Ellayna will always be stuck in that room in the basement of the theater. Terror like that? It's like it freezes you in time. You can walk away, but you leave a piece of yourself in that moment."

"I knew you would understand. I know what happened to you. I read about it in the papers. How that killer murdered your partner in front of you." She'd told Kenna when she hired her that it was in part because Kenna would understand the desperation she felt to get her daughter out of that man's hands. "What can I do?"

Kenna swallowed. "Stick with her. Be you. Have that baby. Draw her in with life and what's happening all around you. She wants to feel the joy. She wants to experience it with you, she just doesn't know how to do that and be the person she is now. The one who went through that."

Her exhale was audible. "Thank you. I didn't mean to wake you, if I did."

"I was up." She didn't tell Ellayna's mother it was because she was still, two years later, having the same kind of night as Ellayna. Reliving that night.

No one got that from her. Those memories belonged to Kenna, and she was going to cherish them until they were gone.

As dark and devastating as they were in the middle of the night, it was all she had left.

"Don't hesitate, if you need to—" Her laptop chimed. The notification mirrored a vibration from her phone against her cheek. "I have to go. Please call me if you need me."

Kenna hung up.

Whatever movement outside that triggered the motion sensor continued. And then it set off the next sensor, the one closer to the front door.

She retrieved the loaded Glock from the cupboard above the refrigerator and moved to the bedroom where she pulled back a corner of the carpet. Quietly, she opened the custom trapdoor she'd had installed to lower herself into the storage area underneath. Kenna closed it behind her, managing to grasp a few strands of the carpet to pull back over the door, just before it closed entirely. She then scooted to the outside door where she opened the latch from the inside.

She slid out and hissed at the cold air. Her arms were bare.

She nearly went back in for a sweater. It was dark, so it wasn't like anyone would see, but curiosity fueled her forward.

Kenna rounded the Class C motorhome to the front bumper. A man dressed in dark clothes approached slowly, creeping up on her front door. She stared at him. Beyond the intruder, another man followed silently on the heels of the first guy.

Oliver Jaxton. This was getting worse with every second.

Kenna rolled her eyes and stayed put behind the hood of her home. She opened her mouth to tell them both to get lost.

"Freeze! FBI!" Jaxton had his feet planted, gun up. "Hands where I can see them and turn around. Slowly."

The intruder stiffened and spun away from her. "FBI?"

"Don't move."

"I'm not doing anything."

"You're here. That's something." Jax took a step toward him, authority in every line of his body. "Tell me why you're here."

As though even he had a right to be here, watching her home. How else would he have seen an intruder approach unless he'd been spying on her? He had to have been camped out in his car across the RV park with his eyes peeled. Watching her, or watching out for her?

"I just want to talk to her."

Kenna stepped out from behind cover of the front of her rig. "About what?"

The intruder spun around, revealing his face. Steven Pierce.

She pressed her lips together and stood fast, though her legs wanted her to take a step. Meanwhile, Jax moved in an arc around to where he had a view of Steven's face. The light was dim enough neither would be able to see the ragged scars on her forearms.

Officer Pierce's husband. Did he know about the video?

"What do you want?" Her voice was quiet in a way she didn't like, but she'd chalk that up to not wanting to disturb her neighbors in the RV park.

Steven slumped. "I need your help. I want to, like, hire you."

"You think I can find Jessica?"

He took half a step toward her. "You know where she is."

She started to argue.

"Your business card was at my house. You know—"

"Hands!" Jaxton closed in. "Keep them up." He paused a second. "Kenna, call Ryson. Tell him to send a unit to pick up Mr. Pierce."

Steven angled his distraught expression at Jax. "I need her help. She can find Jess. I know she can."

Bile rose in Kenna's throat.

"The police and FBI are working this case. Kenna, get your phone."

"I didn't bring it out."

Jax tossed her his, already unlocked.

She dialed Ryson's number.

"Lieutenant Ryson."

"You answer his calls, but not mine?"

"I'm hanging up now."

"Steven Pierce is at my place. I need officers to come get him."

"You're with Special Agent Jaxton?"

"Are you sending a patrol car, or should I call the non-emergency line?"

He went quiet for a minute. "I'll get a unit on their way."

"Thanks." Kenna hung up on him.

If her former friend had no intention of talking to her, that was hardly something she needed to worry about. She was fine by herself. Ryson suddenly didn't believe she had anything to contribute? She'd just have to prove him wrong when she handed over a result on this case.

"You must know where she is."

She winced. "I know it seems like I'm involved, but I'm not. I don't know where your wife is. I'm sorry things don't look good." *But it's not my fault.*

The last thing she wanted was to break down. No one could be completely cold to the pain in other people without becoming so distant they felt nothing. And then what differ-

ence was there between that person and one who considered
it their right to have power over life or death? Or a person who
thought nothing at all of taking life away.

After all, it was just a life.

"Please." Steve swung around with his arms still raised.

Kenna flinched and took a step back. The side of her head
slammed the awning bar. She went down on one knee with a
grunt and pressed a hand to her temple. "Ouch."

Steven grunted.

Jax had him against the side of her motorhome. He held
Steven with one hand and pulled cuffs from his belt with the
other.

Kenna stood to cover him with her weapon. Just in case.
Her head spun, but it was her arms she was worried about.
She could certainly cover an agent for a few minutes, but any
more than that might be pushing it. She'd been actively
working to strengthen her arm muscles to hold a gun aimed
for extended periods, but some days they still didn't want to
cooperate.

Jax patted him down and found a gun. "Care to explain
this?"

"I have a license to carry concealed. It's for protection."
He sounded like what he was—a grieving man.

Kenna bit the inside of her lip again.

Jax said, "What are you really doing here?"

Kenna frowned. Steven shifted, still pinned against her
home. "I need help. No one knows where Jess is but her!"

"You brought a gun to ask her for help?" Jax shoved the
weapon in the back of his own belt, under his jacket. A patrol
car pulled up as he secured Steven in cuffs. "You okay,
Kenna?"

She lowered her fingers from her temple and spotted
blood. "Ouch."

"Sit down."

When she realized Jax wasn't talking to Steven, she plopped her behind into one of her pharmacy store Adirondack-style plastic chairs. Her head thumped.

Jax handed Steven over to the two officers and explained. At length, given how long it took. She pushed out of the chair and headed for her front door. What was she waiting for anyway?

He blocked her way and opened the door for her. "Let's get you a bandage."

"I'm going inside. Because I live here."

"I'm helping. Because you're hurt, and I'm a nice..." His voice trailed off and his fingers curled around hers. Why was he so warm?

He lifted her hand, a hard stare on the skin of her forearms.

"Nice one, Champ." She yanked her hand from his grasp. "Super subtle."

Kenna trotted up the steps and headed for her bedroom. When she came back out, pulling a sweater on, he was inside. "You didn't need to come in."

He winced. "You need a washcloth, and a bandage."

"Both of which I can find myself."

Jax didn't hide his survey of her home. The single bookshelf that stretched around three walls of her living space packed with journals from her father, beat-up thrillers from the eighties and nineties, and old paperbacks of Lewis and Chesterton her father had dog-eared. She loved the way her father's handwriting flicked and curled. She'd even added some pencil notes of her own.

He moved to the table, where her laptop screen still showed the picture of Officer Pierce. "Go grab the stuff."

Kenna pulled the partition across the bedroom and

ducked in the tiny bathroom. Big enough for one person to turn around—just not with their arms anywhere but by their sides. She looked in the cabinet mirror above the sink and winced. She'd broken the skin a tiny bit, and there was an alien-looking lump close to her ear.

She pressed a wet washcloth to it, cleaned it off, and taped a big bandage on.

When she came back out, Jax had the cupboard under the kitchen sink open. Crouched, he rummaged through, now holding a dog bowl with the leash curled up inside it.

She wanted to kick him. "Are you snooping?"

"Good, you found a bandage." He shut the cupboard and straightened, far too tall in the space. "Do you have a dog?" He looked around as though one might appear.

It didn't.

"It wasn't right, but I understand why Steven Pierce would come to you for answers."

"At one in the morning with a gun, creeping up on my front door." She folded her arms. "Kind of like the way you were."

"You're welcome. I'm glad I was here." He glanced around. "How did you know he was outside? Were you outside?"

"Thanks for your help." She motioned to the door. "I should get back to work. You can get back to...whatever it was you were doing that meant you clocked an intruder outside my rig in the middle of the night. Probably important FBI work."

The skin around his eyes flexed.

"Get out, Jax."

Chapter Fourteen

Tuesday, 9:13am.

A collection of framed photos hung on the wall and the smell of cigar smoke lingered in the air.

"The warden will just be another minute." The pink-cashmered receptionist waddled out of the room and closed the door behind her.

Kenna had already looked at the spine of every book on the shelf, but then something else caught her attention when she turned towards a whole wall of framed photos—two faces, in particular. She stepped closer and zeroed in on the warden standing beside Governor Pacer—Bradley's father.

She closed her eyes. *Bradley.* Though they didn't look a whole lot alike, there was a resemblance that made her heart ache. Must be his smile.

His dad had to know by now that she was back in Salt Lake City.

She'd expected some kind of response. Nothing almost worse, given it made her worry over what was yet to happen.

She shifted in the uncomfortable wingback chair, phone loose in her hand, waiting for the occupant of this office to grace her with his presence. Since he wasn't here yet, Kenna got up out of her chair to move closer to the wall.

She was only here because the police and FBI were busy trying to find Jessica Pierce. Gerald Rickshire might have information for her about Daniel Vaynes, or whoever wanted her attention, so she had to ask the question whether she liked it or not.

One photo depicted the warden and his family—he and his wife dressed in T-shirts and shorts, the kids in swimsuits. Beside it hung another photo of Governor Pacer and the state First Lady, Angeline Pacer, alongside three younger sons Kenna had never met. Same place. Same season. Taken most definitely within the last two years. *Bradley, you should be here.* A family friendship solid enough they'd vacationed together. Even when life got hard.

Great.

It wasn't enough that the entire FBI acted suspiciously with her, now the police department wouldn't even return her calls, and she had to deal with the prison system acting similarly? Kenna gritted her teeth.

No wonder her father worked alone practically his whole life. Sure, she'd been there every step of the way. Now she had only herself to rely on. The way he had.

Put a case together.

Run down leads.

Get a result.

Whether that meant she would find Pierce, Kenna didn't know. She'd gone after enough innocent victims. She knew the odds weren't good. Jessica Pierce didn't deserve this, but Kenna's emotions weren't about to get involved. All that would do was cloud her judgment and cause her to make a mistake.

She still had the FBI to contend with.

Jax had been totally weird. She wasn't over the fact he'd been *in* her RV. No one came in her space. Not to mention how fast he'd reacted to there being an intruder outside her place. It was clear he'd been sitting in his car across the RV Park surveilling her. Stairns had to have ordered him to do it. She couldn't know for sure unless he called and asked—which wasn't going to happen.

The only conversation they'd had in two years and her former boss wanted her to sign on as a consultant. If he needed her skills, then he shouldn't have let her go. Then again, it was probably just so he could keep an eye on her— officially. She was less of a loose cannon if he could control the variables.

As if she would allow that to happen.

"Makenna Banbury."

She spun from the wall of photos, not fast enough to portray guilt. Instead of moving from the spot, she opted to stand here like she had every right to be in this office today. She stuck her hand out as he crossed the room and met her beside the wall of people who, by their association alone, were responsible for making him more important.

"Warden Benton. Thank you for meeting with me."

He gave her hand a lingering shake and rounded his desk, making a production out of removing his suit jacket and fixing the tuck in his shirt.

Kenna continued to study the photos out the corner of her eye as he settled himself in his high-backed leather chair.

"Do have a seat, Ms. Banbury."

She settled on the edge of the bureau below the photos and folded her arms. "I'd like to speak with Gerald Rickshire."

"I met your father. A long time ago." His gaze drifted over her. "He was a legend of a man. It must be hard to live up to that kind of legacy."

"My father always said you have to walk the road in front of you, not the one in front of someone else."

"His was a whole lot more lucrative, though." Warden Benton chuckled. "Not a lot of people go that far."

Her father's picture wasn't on his wall. Perhaps a level this man hadn't managed to achieve thus far. He'd only gotten to the heights of vacationing with the governor and his family. Not the realm where he could make millions from book and movie deals, embellishing ordinary details into fantastical tales that sounded far grittier—and somehow also glamorous— than they really were.

The kind of life some people only dream of.

Meanwhile, she'd eaten at practically every truck stop between Lexington and Reno, got her first period in a gas station bathroom in Ohio, and celebrated more birthdays at the Applebee's of whatever city they'd been passing through than with an actual party with cake and candles. Or friends.

"I'm really only here to speak with Gerald Rickshire. Then I'll be out of your hair."

She wasn't going to make nice. That wasn't how she worked, and the faster he realized it, the faster she'd be out of here. He could call his buddy, the governor, and tell him all about her visit.

The governor would call Stairns.

Stairns would call her.

Kenna would either have a permanent detail of Special Agent babysitters or she'd be marched to the state line and shoved across.

"Right." He pulled over a notepad and stared at a scribble on the top sheet. "That's what my assistant said."

"It's part of an ongoing case of mine."

"As a private investigator."

She nodded.

"I read all about it in the newspaper this morning. Business cards." He hissed in a breath between his teeth. "Exciting stuff."

"I'd like to ask Mr. Rickshire a few additional questions regarding the cases."

Warden Benton's eyes flashed. "Do you really think he's involved? Or he had some prior connection to whoever is doing this?"

Kenna needed to read the paper. Then she'd know if the public had been given all the information, or just part of it. She didn't think Stairns would've handed it all over. The police could have done so in an effort to find Pierce. Surely there'd been a press release about the missing officer. It probably didn't include all the particulars of the video, or the fact Pierce might not be the only victim if Kenna's hunch was correct and this continued to play out.

"That's what I plan to ask." She pressed her lips together and smiled.

"Assuming the FBI agent Rickshire is talking to now doesn't ask first." Benton picked up his desk phone. "Tina, could you have an officer walk Ms. Banbury to the interview area."

Kenna blinked. "The FBI..."

She was still reeling—and trying to disguise it—when the officer walked her close enough she could hear the murmur of conversation. "Thanks." She made sure to keep her voice low, then moved to where she could peer around a corner into the holding cell and observe.

Of course. *Of course* it was Jax sitting there.

Kenna's hands curled into fists at her sides. She lifted

them and stretched her fingers against each other, then shook them out. This wasn't the life she wanted anyway, so there was zero point getting sucked into it. Who cared what the FBI did?

She was going to do her job, alone, and then leave.

Jax sat with his back to her across from Gerald Rickshire. The Seventh Day Killer had a uniformed Sergeant at his shoulder. He looked older than he had last Friday night, but considering Ellayna Feathers was back home with her mom, who honestly cared? This guy could rot here.

He wasn't going to hurt anyone else.

Jax flipped a paper file open on the table and spun a photo so Rickshire could see it. "Do you know this man?"

She figured it was their victim, the as-yet-unidentified older gentleman. Daniel Vaynes was the fake name of a serial killer. Kenna wanted to know what he'd already asked Rickshire while Warden Benton waylaid her in the office, keeping her from participating in this conversation.

Whether his behavior had been about letting the FBI do their job, or about putting out feelers with her, she didn't know. Probably he wanted the daughter of a legendary investigator on his wall, as if she would pose for a picture just so Benton could tell people he knew her.

If that was the case, he hadn't yet put together the connection between her and the Governor. Had he been smart enough to do that, he'd have delayed her out of spite.

Kenna blew out a breath.

"Should I know who this is?" Rickshire leaned forward to peer at the file photo.

Jax had to be trying to figure why her business card was dropped the night she happened to be here in Salt Lake. She wanted to know as well. Someone was aware of her movements during Ellayna's captivity—outside the circle of the child's mother and the desk guy at the RV park. Which meant she had eyes on her. A tap on her phone, or some kind of stalker fan.

All of which made the back of her neck itch and the muscles in her legs contract. Preparing to run. Figuratively, of course, because she didn't have the right shoes on to exercise.

"Just tell me if you recognize him."

Rickshire leaned back in his chair and shrugged. "Never seen him before."

"Guy like this? I figure he runs in your circle." Jax sounded equally nonchalant. "But he's probably above your pay grade."

Rickshire didn't like that.

The whole conversation was a dance. She'd done it many times, and clearly Jax had also. The power struggle had to be managed. Rickshire thought he had the upper hand since Jax needed information. But he was also cuffed and in prison, while Jax upheld the law and walked free.

Therefore, a bargain had to be struck, and it had to be done in a way they'd both feel they got what they wanted without sacrificing too much. The victory came in the give-and-take. Garnering a win that felt satisfying even after the concessions.

"He's dead, so I don't suppose you need to worry what he's been saying about you if that's your concern."

There was a tiny shift in the muscles around Gerald's eyes. Curiosity. Maybe not fully realized, but certainly in its nascence.

"Either you know this guy, or you don't." Jax motioned to the photo.

"What if I do?"

"You get around in killer circles? That it?" Jax paused. "Maybe you're active in the online community."

"You *don't* follow me on Insta-Tok, or whatever? I'm crushed."

"I'm not exactly a fan of the work you do."

Kenna would have played it the same way. Acting like a sycophant wasn't something she would ever do, no matter her motivation or desired outcome. The fact Jax also wasn't going to do that actually made her respect him a little bit.

He towed the party line, upholding the sanctity of the FBI —the way she had, once—and she couldn't exactly fault him for that either. Some people simply believed in the honor of the work they did.

Lately, Kenna upheld it just to survive.

Rickshire stared at Jax. "Maybe you should call *her* here. I'll talk to her about this guy."

"Makenna Banbury?" He chuckled. "She isn't an FBI agent, and she's not working with the FBI on this case."

Something about the way he said it gave her pause. His voice held a disquieting tone. *What are you up to, Mr. FBI?* Because he certainly wasn't making it seem like they were working this case together.

Rickshire lifted his chin. Just a fraction, but enough she spotted it from the hall. "I'll talk to her. But, you—I don't know yet."

"What's the difference?" Jax shrugged one shoulder. "Either way you give the same information. You care so much who you give it to, or is there a reason you want to see her?"

"Get her here, and we'll find out."

"That's not how this works."

"You guys aren't friends? Thought she used to be a fed like you."

Jax didn't move. "Makenna Banbury and I are not friends."

"Why not? Seems like you'd want her as a friend to help you take down dangerous criminals like me."

Kenna winced. Jax was losing the upper hand and needed to get it back quickly.

"You really don't know who this is?" Jax jabbed at the photo with his index finger. "Big time serial killer like this. I'd think he would be famous in your circles."

"You think killers have a club? Or, what? You think there is a secret group on social media? Maybe we get together once a month and network about who we took out recently."

"That's how the world works now, right?" Jax chuckled, but it sounded hollow. "Online groups, forums, and newsletters. You're a subscriber. Or you like to go on Death Files and brag about what you've done. Even if they don't believe it's true, probably still feels good right?" He paused. "You tell them your specialty is little girls? They like that stuff?"

A muscle flexed in Rickshire's jaw.

"Naw, you probably don't. Otherwise you'd have learned how to do what you do without getting caught." He tapped the photo again. "Like this guy, living under our noses for years. He murdered nine women we never even knew were missing. Killed them. Disposed of their bodies with no trace. Then again, he didn't have Makenna Banbury on his trail."

Rickshire said nothing.

"An investigator like her, whose father brought so many criminals in—have you seen those movies?" Jax leaned back in the chair. "Exciting stuff. Especially the one about how he worked with Interpol in Germany. That one's my favorite. Makenna's father took down that whole smuggling ring and brought all those guys to justice. You see that?" He whistled.

Kenna braced a hand on the wall.

"She was right there in the middle of it all. Learning from the master all those years. He taught her everything, right?

How could you have known she'd come after you last Friday? It's not really your fault she caught you."

Rickshire stared at him. "You like her so much, why'd the FBI push her out?"

"She retired."

Rickshire huffed.

From her vantage point, Kenna saw the shift in Jax's shoulders. "Two years now, catching killers with that single-minded purpose she used to bring to the FBI. A guy like you is probably nothing to an investigator like her. You can't really blame yourself for getting caught. All this is just another day on the job for her. Meanwhile, she took away your plaything and two beat cops brought you in while Kenna walks away anonymous. But someone knew she was in Salt Lake."

"There a question in there somewhere, or are you just blowing smoke like a fed?"

"When was the first time you saw or spoke with Makenna Banbury?"

"Am I supposed to say something other than Friday night at the theater?"

"You tell me. Had you ever seen her before she entered that theater and got Ellayna back?"

"Never had the pleasure."

Kenna shivered.

"How'd she know where you were holding the child?"

Rickshire shook his head, a miniscule movement. "Am I supposed to know? She never told me."

"But she didn't seem to have trouble finding you. Maybe you talked too much online and gave it away. Or it was all a setup. You get famous for all that stuff you supposedly did. She gets her name in the paper again after a two-year hiatus in which everyone had forgotten about her."

"You think I haven't killed before?"

"I know the rumors. Doesn't mean I buy them."

Meanwhile, Kenna had seen the Seventh Day Killer's work firsthand. She'd unearthed the bodies.

Rickshire reddened. Tendons in his neck stuck out. He couldn't give it all away, or the things he said would arise in the court case, and he'd be convicted of so many more things than just the evidence she had given the police. She knew there had to be more victims.

But Kenna needed Jax to keep talking, or she wouldn't find out why he was really here.

"Who else was there on Friday night? Or, who else knew about it." Jax motioned to the photo. "This guy was murdered. All wrapped up like a gift, supposedly for Kenna."

"Why do I care?"

"You were set up. No one's gonna give a fig about you when they find out you were nothing but a springboard to get Kenna's name back in the limelight so she can be famous like her daddy. Follow in the old man's footsteps, taking down killers all over the world like he did. Now they've kidnapped and probably killed a police officer. Online, for the whole community to see. Maximum exposure. And it won't stop there, I'm guessing. There's a whole plan in place that all started when you supposedly lured her back to the city so that she just so happens to be here the night this guy is murdered."

Jax flipped the file shut. "Kenna is behind this whole thing, and you foolishly played right into her hands."

Chapter Fifteen

Kenna put her back to the wall and forced her knees to lock. No way was she going to react the way she had outside the morgue. Not only did she not want the seat of her pants to touch the floor in here—gross—she also didn't need anyone seeing her lose it in a prison. She didn't need her own reactions to unwittingly incriminate herself.

She could still hear the murmur of their voices, and tried to hold on to that, but reality settled in. *Of course* the FBI was here to find out from Rickshire whether she was somehow part of what was going on. Not only part of it, but a mastermind. As though anonymity wasn't something she wanted, she had to get her name back in the limelight after two years of blessed solitude.

Kenna hung her head and stared at the toes of her boots.

Maximum exposure.

She knew what that kind of attention felt like. It had been the most awful few days of her life, her name splashed all over the news. Reporters calling. Bloggers. Emails. Texts. She'd shut her phone off in the hospital, but then they'd tried visiting her. Saying they were friends. Colleagues.

Bile rose in her throat, and she squeezed her eyes shut. Sickness churned in her stomach as the façade she'd so carefully presented to the world bled away and that old fear crept back in. *No.* She couldn't go back there.

Not even when her forearms started to ache.

She sucked in a long breath through her nose, trying to settle her stomach, and rubbed the top of one forearm. Then the other. Her cell phone rang in her pocket, but she ignored it, doubting she'd even be able to get any words choked out right now.

She had to get ahold of herself. Maybe try and recall one of the earlier memories of Bradley—before she'd woken up with the tendons in both her arms severed and her hands hanging useless, sticky with blood. Before their future was erased.

Kenna sucked in a long breath of cold air. *It's done. He can't hurt you anymore.* She pushed off the wall and paced across to the other side of the hall, turned, and came back. The motion forced her blood to move around her body the same way life relentlessly moved on after tragedy, and she kept breathing. It might not be many people's definition of what life should be, but it was hers. Her choice. No one could take that autonomy away from her.

Not when it was all she had left.

She peered around to where Jax still sat. Rickshire was on his feet. The FBI agent motioned the other man back to his chair. "We're not done yet."

Rickshire kicked the chair back from the table and plopped into it.

"I don't care about you. I care about this guy who called himself Daniel Vaynes." Jax pointed a finger at the photo. A still image of their dead career killer, back when he was very much alive, taken from his driver's license.

"You said he's dead." Rickshire shrugged with a scrunch of his nose.

"I'm planning my memoirs as an FBI agent and this guy will probably be a good entry, right? He looks like he has a story to tell."

"How'd he die?"

"He was murdered."

"Wasn't me."

"Yes, I know that." Jax didn't move one muscle. "You only kill children. You also like to brag about your achievements online." He paused. "In fact, our technician got permission to access your home computer."

Kenna studied Rickshire for his reaction. Definitely not pleased. She wanted to interject and tell Jax to add 'attempted murder of a private investigator' to the list of charges, but she was still reeling from the entire interview. It was probably enough that he'd been found with Ellayna Feathers, anyway. A victim who fit his profile. The charge was a shoo-in.

Jax continued, "Want to know the interesting things he found?"

Rickshire said nothing.

"You accessed the same website that streamed the video of Officer Pierce. You're a member, in fact. Part of the secret group—which we now have full access to. Thanks to you."

"You're lying."

"If I hadn't seen it, how would I even know it existed?"

Jax kind of had a point, but if Kenna had been at the wheel, she would have questioned Rickshire about the chat rooms and forums that were most certainly a part of the site. Her hunches were almost always spot on.

A muscle in Rickshire's jaw shifted and he sat back. "I wanna talk to her."

"You'll have to tell me who you're referring to. Ellayna Feathers?"

She muffled a gasp. The guy was brazen, that was for sure. No serial murderer would ask for that kind of concession. No way.

"The investigator. Kenna Banbury. I wanna speak to her."

Kenna blew out a breath. *Not gonna happen, buddy.*

"You'll first have to tell me who killed this guy and kidnapped a cop. Who wants to broadcast a murder class online? Then, if I'm satisfied, I might call her in and let you have a moment with her." Jax shrugged one shoulder, like it didn't matter either way to him. And after he'd practically accused her of kidnapping Pierce herself. "Maybe she'll agree to see you."

Rickshire looked ready to explode out of his chair.

She knew how he felt. Jax spoke like she'd have a choice, meanwhile the FBI planned to pin this on her. Okay, maybe right now it was only a theory, but if they didn't come up with anything else, it would wind up their primary one.

Obviously they must have played out the whole scenario in some covert meeting in order to think she was behind this whole thing. There's no way she could have carried this out without an accomplice. How could they explain her being in two places at once? *Clearly,* she was desperate for the fame her father had. She rolled her eyes.

Kenna bit the inside of her lip. If she went to the end on this case, determined to find Pierce and the person responsible for the crimes against her, Kenna could very well end up in prison herself. The FBI could collect all the evidence in favor of their theory and charges could be filed.

Her life would be over.

All because she had the audacity to step somewhere other than the narrative they'd laid out for her.

"Just ask the rest of your questions so we can be done with this."

"You ever watch a video where they're talking about killing? Maybe they're doing it. Post it so all the fans can see the...art?"

She saw a flash of teeth and heard the low rumble born in his chest. "You think I require tutelage."

Jax shrugged. "You got caught, didn't you?"

Jax fingered the photo like he was interested in learning more without the FBI catching on. Making Rickshire wonder if he wasn't here officially. Maybe fishing for more information about the community. "You ever see anything like that?"

"How do you know I didn't start the whole thing? Maybe *I'm* the mastermind."

"Maybe you are." Jax shifted in his chair. Kenna didn't believe Rickshire. She figured the fed didn't either, despite his agreement. Jax shrugged. "Or maybe ... you know who is."

Not it. Kenna waited.

Rickshire looked down at the photo and muttered to himself.

Jax leaned forward, "What was that?"

Rickshire looked up, and his lips shifted. "I don't believe you. I'm getting nothing out of this, so maybe I have nothing."

"This was a waste of time, then?"

He flashed clenched teeth while Jax sat there, stoic. As though this man, and the sickness of evil he'd succumbed to, had no effect on him. In reality, Jax probably wanted to be anywhere but here. And yet he waited, unwilling to be the first one to speak.

Rickshire's gaze shifted across Jax's face. Then he looked down at the picture of the old man on the table. "You say he's dead?"

Jax said nothing.

"Then he's been replaced." Rickshire's lips twitched in a sinister facsimile of a smile. "And if they're calling out Kenna, then I want to speak to her."

"Why?"

"Fame. Why else?"

"So, you're saying she is going after this to get her name in the limelight?"

Rickshire tipped his head back and laughed. "Not hers. Mine."

"You'll have to explain that."

"Mmm. I'm not surprised." Rickshire stared at Jax. "Let me make this simple so you'll be sure to understand, Mr. FBI Agent. Whoever killed the old man is taking over. They're the new king, set to inherit the kingdom."

"Authority over people's lives."

"No." Rickshire shook his head. "The chance to best Makenna Banbury."

"Serial killers don't work together like that."

Rickshire chuckled low.

"Enlighten me." Jax turned his head. He lifted his chin in the direction of the hall, as though indicating she was out there waiting. "Then we can both get what we want."

"I don't know who killed him, but he said Malcom Banbury was his nemesis. When Malcom died, he didn't really care anymore. Started branching out online."

They were going to have to go back over his computer.

"So someone is determined to take over and reign in his stead. They'll post videos that teach people to murder with no evidence and get away with it." Jax shook his head. "Like some kind of ... *online murder class*?"

Use of the actual name from the website didn't register with Rickshire. Jax had been fishing to see how much up-to-date information the Seventh Day Killer actually had. While he seemed to understand the plan, or thought he did, he probably wasn't aware it was happening.

"Guess you didn't want to wait and watch. Now you're here, and you're never getting out."

"The best of us fall," Rickshire spoke slowly. "Eventually."

"What I don't get is this." He leaned back in the chair. "He was like...old and stuff, right? I mean, the guy's got to be pushing seventy at least. Look at him. How come he knew how to do all this chat room, uploading vlogger business? If someone took over the empire, then this guy had to have hired someone else to set it all up."

A computer tech, or website guy. Jax might be onto something. Though, he was way off base with the rest of what he'd said.

Rickshire shrugged. "There's people who do that."

"You pay, and they keep your information secure?"

"I wouldn't know." He stared down his nose at Jax. "But maybe it's what I heard."

"I want to know who this guy ran with. Someone he mentored or trained. A protégé."

Rickshire scoffed. "How about *all of us*?"

"Through this website?"

"We all followed him. The guy was a legend." His face brightened, animated now. "The Professor."

"Gotta find your tribe, right?"

Rickshire laughed.

Kenna figured most of what he'd just said was a lie. There might be a grain of truth there, but Rickshire seemed happy to embellish. Still, it was possible this was all legit.

"All those cases to solve." Jax sighed. "We have a shoebox of mementos. No one ever knew it was him. He got away with murdering for *years*. Could have kept going forever, right?

Instead, he decides to disclose his secrets. Teach others to do what he did *and* get away with it."

"He was the master."

"And yet someone killed him. Kind of like how you were caught."

Kenna stared at the back of Jax's head. She had no doubt now that he suspected her as being part of this.

"He left a legacy." Rickshire looked over Jax's shoulder. "Like her father did. Catching killers like me is in her blood. Why would I be upset or angry that she chose me to come after? It actually kind of energizes me."

Kenna swallowed against a lump in her throat. She'd tried to save a child, and in a way save a pregnant mother. Not to mention herself. The fact all this saving also involved Gerald Rickshire didn't matter much to her other than the satisfaction he was off the streets now.

Meanwhile, it sounded to her like he was in awe of her.

There was a tiny huff. Maybe a laugh, maybe more scoffing. Kenna couldn't tell from this distance, already straining to hear all the words they spoke to each other. Jax would come out soon, and she'd have to figure out fast whether to lie to him or admit she heard everything and knew the FBI had her on their suspect list.

She should stay in town and help Steven Pierce save his wife.

She could admit she wanted the satisfaction of proving herself to them, but it was more than that. Closing cases hit like a rush of dopamine. These days it took more and more each time to get that hit. One day, catching killers and rescuing their victims wouldn't affect her at all. That was the day she would move to her Montana cabin and shut out the world. Live the rest of her days in peace, reading her father's notebooks, and probably poorly trying to write a book of her own. At least she would have something to do, because retirement sounded terrible and incredibly boring—except for her plan to get a hot tub for the back porch.

No more killers. She couldn't even imagine such a life.

"I'll tie his DNA to a pile of open cases, tell the families the sicko who destroyed their lives is dead, then clock out and go home." Jax shoved the chair back from the table.

"That's the thing about a legend." Rickshire leaned forward slightly. "They never really die. You can't kill destiny."

"I don't know about that. He looked pretty cold when I saw him at the morgue."

A muscle flexed at his jaw. "There are things to be done."

"But you won't get to watch them, because guys like you don't have computer privileges."

One of the correctional officers snorted. Rickshire ignored him. "I told you what I know. Now tell her I want to see her."

"You think she takes my orders?" Jax pushed the chair under the table and moved toward the door. "Seeing you, or not, is her choice."

"We had an agreement."

"But I don't have to uphold it," Jax said. "Because you are far from a gentleman."

He walked down the hall while Rickshire raged.

Kenna twisted and leaned against the wall, hiding herself from view by the swinging door. Jax walked through, clearing the mouth of the hall. She followed him from a safe distance and clocked the second he realized someone was behind him. She lifted her chin as he spun.

"Kenna."

"Jax." She used his same tone. "Fancy meeting you here."

He had no idea what she'd heard. She could tell him whatever she wanted.

Jax narrowed his eyes. "Did you want to talk with Rickshire?"

"Seems to me like you covered most of it." What he had said made her want to go ballistic, as her dad would've said. Except what would slapping him in his boy scout face do other than give her the temporary satisfaction of revenge. How could he even *think* she was behind this in any way? Jerk. Just because the suspicion was probably kindled by Stairns, or even the Governor, didn't mean he had to get on the bandwagon.

Unless he was the kind of agent who followed orders and did what he was told to. As if that was the only option.

"Are you okay? You look miles away."

She headed for the door. "Did you know your initials are 'O.J.' like the juice?" Making a joke was much more satisfying than dwelling on her life and the fact the FBI thought she was behind this. Or punching him for believing such garbage.

Jax walked with her, saying nothing. Bradley would have joked around and drawn her out of her melancholy. Not that there were any similarities between the two men. Beyond the badge, at least.

Kenna relished in the awkward silence. It was oddly gratifying to watch him squirm. Maybe that made her a bad person, but she wasn't ready to make nice.

He went to his vehicle, where he paused like he wanted to say something.

She got in her car without a goodbye and exited the parking lot, putting her blinker on to turn left to home sweet trailer life.

Up the street, she saw a diner. *Nothing a caramel milk-shake won't fix.*

Kenna pulled into a parking space just as Jax did the same right beside her. She glanced over from her front seat and stared. Or glared. It was a stare-glare. Long enough he opened the door for her.

She didn't get out. "Keep your friends close, is that it?"

His head jerked. "What?"

"Nothing."

A scraggly looking mutt had been tied with a rope to the bike rack outside. Kenna eyed the dog as she passed, then went straight for a booth where she could face the room. Jax didn't mind having his back to the front door—or the other patrons, apparently. Not that she wanted him to sit beside her.

From between the ketchup and sugar packets, Jax grabbed a menu for himself and eyed her. "Are you actually okay?"

"I'm a free woman, and I'm getting a milkshake. He's in jail because I put him there." Kenna shrugged, though it occurred to her at some point she might *not* be free if she stuck around long enough for the FBI to somehow pin this on her. "Rickshire thinks he's smarter than anyone, but I'm still here and Ellayna is safe." She glanced at the window, where light streamed in.

"Makes the darkness feel a little farther away."

Kenna didn't know how to answer that. Thankfully, the waitress wandered over. She ordered her milkshake with a side of fries. "Also...how long has that dog been there?"

"Couple hours, I think." The waitress shrugged.

Jax got the breakfast scramble.

She studied him as the waitress left. "Officer Pierce is still out there."

Was he really going to bark up this tree of her alleged involvement? The idea she was working with an accomplice just to be famous again seemed ludicrous.

"What about living your life?" He frowned. "You can't enjoy a moment like this without making it about work?"

"Because it can all be snatched away?" She shrugged. "All I've done for the last two years is work. I find people no one else is looking for. Now that a cop is missing? That's hardly going to change."

No way would she stoop to pleading her innocence. If he wanted to believe she was guilty of this, he would have to prove it.

"Do you think you'll find Pierce?"

She sipped her milkshake and watched the dog through the window. It was cold outside. "Because I don't already know where she is?"

He started. "You do?"

"Yes." She leaned forward. "In the clutches of a killer."

He didn't seem amused. "At least I got something from Rickshire. Now we have mention of a professor. Could be the same as the benefactor mentioned in the video, or maybe not."

"A killer who took over for the legend."

"You realize that could be the reason he's intent on drawing you out, right? Because you did the same." Jax checked his phone. "Stairs isn't happy."

Kenna unhooked the base layer from her thumbs so she could eat her fries. She dipped them in the mediocre fry sauce —didn't they know mustard was the secret ingredient to killer sauce—and watched the dog shiver outside. Jax might think her work was all about taking over where her dad left off—no matter that she would be closer to making that happen if she hadn't been forced to retire.

Now she was just trying to move on.

His phone buzzed again.

For a hot second, she wondered if it was the governor.

"It's just an email report from the coroner. Collins says the old man's real name was Christopher Halpert. He was seventy-three, but there isn't much record of him."

"He had those three aliases, including Daniel Vaynes. Probably knew how to hide to keep people from tracking him."

Jax nodded. "The techs are looking for any property he owned in any alias where he might have buried some of the nine women."

Kenna slurped up the rest of her milkshake. "I still think he used the construction work to hide bodies."

"Does he ring a bell? Christopher Halpert."

She shrugged. "He looked familiar when I saw him, but I still haven't placed him."

"Maybe he's from one of your father's cases. An old man who killed so many and was never caught. Rickshire said he knew your father, so this Halpert guy might have as well."

It did seem like the kind of thing Malcom Banbury would have sunk his teeth into...until he captured the guy. Kenna shifted in her chair. "I can email my dad's old agent. Have him search all the files and see if my father mentioned him in one of his books."

"You haven't read them?" Before she could respond, his phone buzzed across the table. Jax flipped it over. "Stairns."

Her phone rang as well. Ryson. She answered it. "Banbury."

"Officer Pierce has been found." He sounded choked.

Kenna gripped the phone. "Is she dead?"

"I'll text you the address." Ryson hung up.

Jax said, "Understood. I'm on my way."

She pulled some bills from her back pocket and folded them under her glass. Her stomach roiled at the thought of seeing Officer Pierce. What had the killer done to her?

Jaxton had a couple of sausage links on his plate.

"Are you going to finish those?"

He shrugged on his suit jacket. "Go right ahead."

She strode outside, breaking the sausage into pieces as she cautiously approached the dog. Kenna crouched a few feet away. Close enough the dog should be able to reach her.

She angled her body sideways to present less of a threat.

The animal sniffed. A girl. She shifted, wariness in every muscle of her furry body.

Kenna held out a piece of sausage. "If you want it—" She spoke softly. "—you'll have to come over here and get it."

The dog sniffed but didn't move.

"You've gotta be brave and take that step."

Jax stood over her. "We should go."

The dog backed up two steps and whined.

Kenna glanced up at him. "Seriously?"

He glanced at the dog. "That's what the sausage is for?"

"Look at her." Malnourished. No collar, just a rope tied around the matted fur of her neck. The animal had been here for hours, and it was barely forty-five degrees. Kenna wasn't going to leave her.

"We have a murder scene to get to."

"So go, Mr. FBI. I'll meet you there."

Jax stared at her, then shook his head and wandered off.

Kenna looked at the dog. "Want some sausage, girl?"

Chapter Sixteen

Tuesday, 1:42pm.

Kenna pulled up to an empty lot on the west side of the city, the sun bright in a blue sky. She sat in the driver's seat and zipped her jacket to ward off the chilled temperature. It wouldn't be so cold if it wasn't so windy. Kenna shivered. They'd have to exercise care to ensure no evidence blew away.

A wet nose touched the side of her neck. She twisted to ruffle her fingers through the fur on the dog's chin. "I guess you'll need a name."

Two patrol cars were parked in front of an empty lot along with two unmarked police cars, their lights flashing. An ambulance drove away from the scene, headed in the opposite direction. The space between two old brick buildings was nothing but a sea of rubble. Concrete pieces, and rebar sticking out. The remnant of what had once been there.

A shell.

Lieutenant Ryson stood on top of a slab in the center,

along with Detective Wilkern. They peered down, past where Kenna could see.

Ryson crouched.

Knuckles rapped on her window. She spun around and saw Jax peer in, a frown on his face. She shoved him back with the door and climbed out.

"Is that the dog from the diner?"

"I left my number with the waitress. If the owner comes back, they can call me."

The dog hopped onto the front seat. Kenna rummaged in the center console and found what she was looking for. She clipped the collar around the dog's neck and scratched her behind her ears. Then she held up a hand, "Stay," and shut the door.

Jax had that FBI disapproval on his face. "So, you just happen to have an extra dog collar in your car? What happened to your dog?"

Headlights flashed. She winced, almost bringing her hand up to shield her eyes. Until she realized the haunting image was only in her mind. A flashback. While her mind warred with her piqued senses, she could hear the screech of tires like she was still standing there. Caught unaware. Hours later she'd woken up with limp, bloody hands.

She jolted out of her terrible reverie. "Are you kidding me? As if you don't already know the answer to that."

She headed for Ryson, moving at a fast clip. So, she couldn't bear to get rid of Bear's collar. So what? Too bad for Jax her life had nothing to do with this case, and therefore, he had no business to it. He should just stay out of it.

His shoes clipped the asphalt behind her. "What did I say?"

As if he hadn't read what had been in the report. Not only was he out to discredit her and land her in prison, now he had to twist that knife in all the way. Bring up every little thing she'd lost.

"Kenna."

She glanced over her shoulder. "Don't pretend you care. I don't like liars."

They moved to the tape, and he gave their names to the officer. Detective Wilkern strode toward them, pulling off a pair of latex gloves. Agony washed over the female detective's face as she angled toward Jax. Suzanne Wilkern didn't stop until she was practically flush with the outside of his arm, as though she wanted to lay her head on his shoulder.

Jax shifted. "Officer Pierce?"

"It's bad."

Kenna left the two of them—the detective and her wordless plea for the special agent to comfort her, and Jax not knowing what to do with her offer—and walked towards the body. Dead people made far more sense to her. They didn't ask stupid questions or make demands.

She clambered over rubble stacked against rubble. A path someone had already marked out for her to traverse.

Halfway to where Pierce's lifeless body lay, she stopped and took in the scene. Not where the body had been placed, but the whole area itself. She needed the perspective before she got into the minutiae of the scene.

"What is it?"

She found Jax beside her, again. "I haven't touched anything, and I'm not about to disturb evidence. I'm just looking."

"Did I warn you not to contaminate the scene? I know you wouldn't."

Regardless of the answer to that question, he was watching to see if she knew her way around. One thing was for sure, Kenna couldn't have placed the body here if she was part of it. After all, she'd either been with him or he'd been watching her rig. That would mean she had an accomplice. If she was working with someone, then she would know details. Jax would be on her the second he thought she showed familiarity with any of this.

Wilkern stood beside him. "He carried her to the middle, rather than just leaving her hidden at the edge."

"A strong guy. Most people can't easily haul a hundred plus pounds too far." Certainly not all the way across this debris to the very center.

"The crime scene unit measured. He laid her dead center."

Kenna murmured. "An offering."

"What was that?" Jax asked.

Wilkern nodded. "She's right. There are some similarities to the old man, though I couldn't tell you exactly what. More like a feeling. This still feels like...I can't put my finger on it."

"It's more than just how her hands were placed." Kenna agreed and glanced back at her car. The dog was sitting up, her butt in Kenna's front seat. Watching. Waiting. She lifted her keys and clicked the lock button to engage her alarm.

"Are you really worried someone will steal the dog you stole?"

She turned to look at the street from this angle. Probably not a whole lot of traffic out here at this time of the afternoon, between lunch and when the final school bell rings to signal the end of day. "It's like a hodge podge of evidence." The kidnapping, the video, the murder scene. "A bunch of random stuff, thrown together. Probably to confuse us with his cleverness."

No one said anything.

"Maybe a delivery driver saw something." She turned back to them. "Someone who works in the area. We'll need to know who owns the property. Who reported discovery of the body?"

Wilkern and Jax just stared.

"What?"

"I have point." Wilkern glanced at Jax. "I'd welcome any assistance from the FBI."

Jax cleared his throat. "Regrettably, my case load—"

"Is far too swamped with the fact you're trying to figure out if *I* did this. You haven't even identified the women from the shoe box yet." Meanwhile, Kenna had discovered where one might've been buried. So why'd he welcome her to the scene when he didn't want her help? Probably just to prove she'd done this so he could arrest her and everyone could go home.

Ryson's booming voice echoed across the concrete debris. "Let's get her covered and out of here. The crows are circling."

Kenna closed the distance until she stood right beside him, the outside of her arm touching his. She discretely slid her hand in his and held on tight. He didn't move, just attempted to break all the bones in her hand.

The medical examiner crouched beside Jessica Pierce. Her hair had been brushed, arranged so it swept over one shoulder. There was a reverence to how she'd been placed. Simple black pants and a pink T-shirt Kenna wasn't sure the woman would ever have worn. Bare feet. No makeup. Both pant legs had been pulled down to her ankles, unlike the old man.

Whatever wounds she'd suffered had long since run dry and been cleaned. They were now covered by clothing.

"He says she's been dead a day at least."

"So right after the video." She let go of his hand and turned to him. "When was she found?"

Ryson looked at his watch. "Three hours ago." He started to step away. "I need to go and see Steven."

She wanted to offer to go with him, but the words stuck in her throat.

A news van pulled up down the street. People gathered behind the police tape to watch what was going on. "Are we recording the crowd?"

It was more customary with arson. However, a case like this was about notoriety. It could give them a shot of the killer.

Ryson nodded.

"Make sure the FBI gets a clear shot of my face from the camera."

He caught her tone. "They think you're involved?"

She wanted to shrug it off but couldn't. Not when a woman was dead.

Ryson squeezed her arm hard, and they stood like that—clinging to each other—for a minute before Kenna turned to Wilkern. "Those people need to be moved back."

The detective glanced at the looky-loos with their cell phones. They wanted to record video of a dead cop? Kenna wanted to slap those phones out of their hands and smash them under the heel of her boot.

A wave of grief rolled through her. Kenna had to shove it down. It wasn't like she'd even really known Officer Pierce. There was no reason for her to feel like this, but she did. She'd always grieved the lost lives of people, whether she knew them or not. Kenna could work through a case and not take it personally, getting emotionally involved, but at some point she did have to process those emotions in order to set them aside and be able to focus.

Ryson swiped at his cheeks and turned to leave.

She called out after him. "Later?"

He nodded, not looking back as he walked away from his

officer's body. Kenna had waited outside the house in Provo while they carried Bradley from the scene, but she still hadn't been able to look at him. Kenna didn't think less of Ryson that he also hadn't been able to take one last look.

Kenna climbed down and closed in on the body while people eyed her. Jax even called down, "She's with me." Probably flashed his badge as well. She just ignored them all.

Collins looked up. "Gloves?"

She shook her head. Kenna didn't plan on touching anything.

"What is it?"

"The clothes." She studied the pants and shirt.

"I agree." Collins said, "Not exactly my purview, but these pants don't fit Officer Pierce the way her clothes usually did. I don't think they belonged to her. Maybe put on after?" He swallowed. "Like I said, not my purview."

"Did you know her personally?"

Collins nodded. "We attended the same book club. As our schedules allowed."

Wilkern entered Kenna's peripheral. "Any reason we're discussing her fashion choices right now?"

Kenna kept her attention on the medical examiner. The old man had also been dressed. "You think..?"

"I already checked." Collins nodded, a look of approval on his face. "The clothes have the same dot of sharpie on the tags. Just like with Daniel Vaynes."

"His real name is Christopher Halpert. These clothes were purchased from the same place as the clothes the old man was wearing."

"That would be a logical conclusion."

"We can check into it." That was Jax.

Wilkern said, "Whoever our vlogger is, you think he killed the old man as well as Officer Pierce?"

"That's for you to find out. Don't you think, Detective?" Collins stood. "I'd like to get her back to my office now."

"Copy that." Wilkern pulled out her phone.

Kenna straightened. "Anything else of significance found?"

Wilkern shook her head. "Not yet, but we're far from done here." She walked off, traversing the concrete on her heeled boots far better than Kenna would have been able to in the same shoes.

Jax said, "Any idea what store the clothes came from?"

"No idea. But it's something."

The idea the killer had dressed his victims in pants and shirts that had been bought from the same place was enough. Or, for right now it was. In the next second, she was going to need more than that.

"Maybe they shopped at the same place?"

It seemed like an invitation to begin an impromptu brainstorming session, so she said, "Or he goes out and buys clothes to dress them in after, so they're clean of evidence."

That fit with the rest of the scene.

Jax said, "Or he has a collection of clothes, and dresses them in something that works well enough." He waved in the direction of Pierce's body. "Which explains the fit."

"He could've just guessed her size and gone shopping." Now wasn't that a great thought? "Probably a second-hand, or consignment store, if they're making a mark on the tag. Their low-tech way of tracking what they have in stock, or perhaps sale items."

Jax nodded. "Let's run with this. Call around, see who does that with their inventory."

"Maybe he even works at one of them."

"That would be a serious win."

She agreed. "Especially if he really is calling the other

viewers out and starting an empire of his own. The social media king of death."

Collins and a couple of the technicians around them shifted. Someone gasped.

Kenna winced. Too long alone without a badge and she was losing her professionalism. "We should regroup, get what we have together and loop in the police department. They need to know what we do."

"So you believe Rickshire."

"Until we can be certain he's lying, I'd like to consider the possibility it's true. At least as one option. If we dismiss it, we open this up for a world of hurt and the only ones to blame will be us."

Jax nodded.

How many people had been watching that video? If each one turned into a killer, it would result in multiple bodies. Whether the victims were local or showed up across the country, or across the world, the fallout could be catastrophic.

Kenna didn't want to bring the big guns, since they were pointed at her right now. But it couldn't be denied this was serious enough to warrant it.

"While we're there, we should have Stairns look at the whole scope of the case. Talk to the DA. We could be looking at a rash of murders based off this guy calling out his viewers."

Jax shot her a look. "Depending on how it shakes out."

Multiple co-conspirators could be tried together and the leader held responsible for what they'd ordered others to do, even if they didn't commit the crimes themselves. If there really was a "benefactor" it could come in handy for the prosecutor. But that was only if the group of killers could be tied together.

"I'll note that in my report."

Kenna turned to Collins. "What was the cause of death?"

"Multiple stab wounds to her torso."

"Different than the old man." Still, it jived with what they'd seen before the feed shut off. "It fits with the persona he was going for on the video."

"You think he was playing a part?"

Kenna shrugged one shoulder. "Aren't we all?"

She walked away, feeling Collins's stare like an itch between her shoulder blades. She clambered over concrete back to the police tape while Jax spoke with the officer on duty. If she headed to the car quick enough, she might be able to lose him.

The dog had fogged up the driver's window and licked a spot clear to see out of.

Over the roof of her car, Kenna watched the stragglers in the crowd with a careful eye. Jax was checking his email, or whatever it was that occupied him on his phone. He was busy enough she could stop and indulge what she was feeling. Unpack it and figure it out.

Though the medical examiner had scrutinized her, Kenna began to think the itch between her shoulder blades may not have been Collins after all. It flickered to life again as she walked back over to her car. She'd been feeling it since she got here.

Was the killer watching her?

A man after notoriety the way this one was wouldn't be content to remain in the shadows for long. She didn't want to paint a bullseye on her back. However, the likelihood was that it was already there. This guy knew who she was.

It would take weeks of sifting through fine details of this case to discern how it had all shaken out. That first business card, the night she'd taken down the Seventh Day Killer. Connections and patterns. Leaving it on the first man's body had been akin to calling her out. The second, left in Pierce's kitchen, was nothing but a taunt.

He had the power. She did not.

Kenna turned to look at the buildings around her. The ones across the street. Windows. The roof. She wasn't going to assume no one watched her. Doing so disrespected her instincts—the ones honed through training and the ones she'd been born into.

Being her father's daughter had kept her alive. He'd essentially trained her to be an investigator, though that may not have been his plan. A lot of the time, she'd had the impression he hadn't liked his job and wanted her to have nothing to do with it. But then he'd haul her along with him to another case.

Another city. Another bad guy.

A compulsion to continue. Addicted to the rush of a result.

They'd gone to live in Miami her junior year of high school. He'd been investigating a case with the DEA as part of a taskforce. A new friend of hers had invited her to a party. Kenna went but left early because the whole situation felt... off. She'd been unable to persuade her new friend to leave both the party and her boyfriend and go with her. The next morning, the news reported that four kids had OD'd at the party, her friend included. Thankfully her friend had received quick medical treatment and survived, but the boyfriend hadn't been so lucky.

Kenna learned the hard way not to ignore her instincts.

Movement across the street caught her attention. She traversed the pavement at a sprint, went to a side door, and ascended concrete steps. The stairwell echoed. Kenna unsnapped the latch on her gun holstered at the small of her back but didn't remove it as she pushed out a door onto the third floor.

Abandoned mid-renovation by the look of it. Now the windows were broken and leaves covered the floor. Brick walls. Busted out windows. Someone should have converted this into a microbrewery already. The whole place was just going to waste.

She walked through every room on the floor looking for whatever—or whoever—she'd seen move in the window.

There was no one here.

"Kenna."

She spun. Jax lifted both hands, his own gun in his right palm. "Just me."

Breath rushed from her lungs, and she realized she'd been holding it.

She turned in a circle, but there was nothing here.

Chapter Seventeen

Tuesday, 7:47pm.

K enna parked next to the van in the driveway, got out, took a deep breath, and marched up the sidewalk. She lifted her hand and rapped her fist on the front door of the thousand-square-foot, single-level, starter family home. Two huge plastic flowerpots sat empty on the stoop beside a snow shovel.

The woman who answered the door had long, straight black hair and a new mom figure. A baby on her hip. Behind her, the TV played a cooking show drowned out by the persistent squeal of the baby crying. Red cheeks, tears falling.

The woman flushed, exhaustion in her eyes. "Kenna."

"Blah, blah, it's been two years. I'm happy to see you, too." Kenna stepped inside. "And meeting you finally, sweet baby. Oh, Luci." Kenna crooned the name a couple more times as she reached out and took the baby from Valentina Ryson. "Oh, baby. It can't be that bad."

Personally, she didn't agree with people who said, "you're fine, you're okay" to babies in that annoying high-pitched voice, trying to get them to quit crying. They didn't think it was fine, or they wouldn't be crying. And Kenna wasn't a liar.

"What's the matter, baby?" She stepped inside and settled the squalling child on her shoulder, turning Luci so the baby's forehead was against the skin of her neck.

The cries quieted.

Kenna almost wanted to apologize. "You just needed a fresh face, that's all," she told the baby. "Because you're a people person."

Valentina sagged against the wall of the entryway. "She's been crying for an hour."

"Go sit down." She took bouncing steps through the living room, strategically avoiding looking too closely at the piles of laundry on the couch. Or the dishes in the sink.

"Can't." Ryson's wife shook her head. "There's too much to do."

"Five minutes, Teens. None of this is going anywhere while you rest."

Valentina looked like she wanted to cry.

"Come on, baby." Kenna patted little Luci's diaper. "Let's go do dishes."

She pulled open the dishwasher. Valentina settled on a bar stool at the counter, put her elbows on the mail and hung her head.

Kenna worked quietly. Turned out the dishwasher was dirty, so she finished filling it, then got a soap tablet from under the sink and started the cycle. She squatted in front of the cabinet under the sink again and found a rag and counter spray and wiped down the counters.

"Please tell me you offer housekeeping services along with being a private investigator."

"I can definitely ask around if you want a recommendation."

"I need one," Valentina said. "What I *want* is different."

Kenna leaned her hips against the counter, patting the baby on the back. She should take the trash out. "Where is he?"

She was about to ask again when Valentina said, "Garage. He won't listen to me. He'll barely even talk to me."

Kenna pushed out a breath. "You want me to try?"

"Isn't that why you're here?" She had to have seen the look on Kenna's face—whatever she was broadcasting. That mom intuition nailed it right on the head. "I have a baby. There's no time to watch the news, and you know he doesn't talk about it." Her eyes filled with tears. "How am I supposed to know what's wrong?"

The baby let out a tiny mew. Kenna rubbed up and down her back. "They found Jessica Pierce's body today."

Valentina paled. "You're on this, right? Finding out who killed her."

Kenna nodded.

"Good."

"I'll put her down for a nap and go talk to him."

"I shouldn't let you. I should be the one to do it, but I'm so grateful I could cry that you're helping me."

Kenna walked over to Valentina and kissed her forehead. "I got this."

Ryson's wife laughed, but it sort of also sounded like she was crying. Kenna found the nursery down the hall, put the baby down, and turned on the monitor. She left the door cracked and grabbed the trash bag from the kitchen before stepping through the doorway that led to the attached garage while Tina stayed behind to attack the laundry volcano that had erupted on the couch.

A single bulb hung from the ceiling, illuminating the way. Kenna tied off the bag and dumped it into the big rolling can.

Ryson sat in the driver's seat of his compact. Kenna climbed in the passenger side. Blank stare. It was like he didn't even notice her come in, which maybe had something to do with the half empty bottle in one hand.

He was drinking again? "Is that just for you?"

"You don't like whiskey."

"Is that the issue?"

"Why are you here?" Ryson shot her a look.

Kenna eased down in the seat and crossed one leg over the other.

"You're gonna tell me to get myself together. Take care of my family."

Saying it was one thing. He had to actually do it, which could only be up to him. "It's your family. You either treat them right, or you don't. Not sure it has anything to do with me."

He huffed out a breath and she expected the smell of his drink to waft through the car, but it didn't.

"Can't have been easy for you. Seeing Pierce like that." When he said nothing, she asked, "How's Meacham?"

He swished the liquid around in the bottom of the bottle.

"It wasn't your fault. Either of yours."

"Tell that to Steven."

"Is he okay?"

"His wife was murdered. What do you think?"

Kenna pressed her lips together. "You know what I mean."

"Lost it. Lost his job. Came around to scream at me. I gave him five thousand. Because throwing money at someone feels better than doing nothing. Haven't seen him since. Wilkern's the one who went to tell him we found her."

"Five thousand? Your side business must have taken off."

He shrugged, then blew out a breath. "I wish. I had it saved from a big flooring job last month. It was supposed to go on the credit card bill." He swirled the liquid again. "He's probably already blown it all trying to forget."

"Like you're doing?"

"Nah. I'm just sitting here figuring out next month's budget."

Kenna winced.

"Definitely not thinking about my dead officer. How she got kidnapped right under my nose, and how I couldn't find her."

"None of that is on you." It was early. Too early for a result, short of the killer turning himself in. Forensics from the first crime scene weren't even back in.

Kenna took the bourbon bottle from him, grabbed the cap out the cup holder and screwed the lid back on. She put it on the floor between her feet. "You don't need this trash, even to convince yourself you're strong enough to not need it. Drinking doesn't bring her back, and it doesn't help Valentina with Luci. Heck, it doesn't even make *you* feel better."

"Why you gotta be like that?"

"Wise?"

"Nah, that's not it." He was quiet for a moment. "I'm sorry."

"Don't go soft on me now. Go to church."

"So we're good?"

As if he needed to ask that. "What came of the scene?"

"There was next to no physical evidence, which is crazy. But we'll work with what we have." Ryson huffed. "I won't hold my breath." He sounded obstinate, but she heard the fear underneath. The pain and guilt of being powerless while his colleague—his friend and fellow cop—had been hurt and killed.

She wanted to be grateful that at least her business card hadn't been left at the crime scene again, but this didn't seem like the time. "I'll need a copy of the file. I want to compare it to the first guy."

"Look for correlations." He nodded. "Good idea."

"I could use your help."

And his passion. Not to mention, it would give him something to do other than wallow in what he couldn't change. Problem was, he'd never ask for her help. She had to make it sound like she was the one who needed him.

"You knew Pierce. I've had one conversation with her. That's an edge I don't have."

He folded his arms across his chest, the seat pushed all the way back. At least he hadn't been planning on going somewhere in this emotional state. Not that facing Valentina and their crying baby would be any better.

"Whether we find anything or not, we owe it to Pierce to at least try. Or you could turn the car on. Just start the engine. We'll drift off, and it will all be over." She knew what she had just suggested. "Maybe I'll be able to go through with it." Even though her stomach flipped over just thinking about it.

Ryson shifted in his seat. He started to say something, caught himself, and said, "Is this your messed up version of reverse psychology?"

He hadn't touched her comment. Realizing that made the knot in her stomach loosen a bit. "Why else would you sit in your car with the garage door down?"

"It mutes the sound of the baby crying." He scrubbed his hands down his face. "The keys are in the house. I'm not going to kill myself, Makenna." He muttered again.

"You need a therapist or an appointment with your pastor. Probably both."

"Ken—"

"Don't argue."

At least he wasn't out here thinking about how to kill himself. She'd had enough of that for a lifetime. Kenna needed to redirect the conversation in a serious way. Get him working the problem instead of wallowing.

"Who knows," she said. "Maybe it'll even be true what the counselor—who also happens to be your best friend—writes in the report about you. Maybe it won't be just a junk piece that has no basis in reality that gets you fired *and* gives them the ammo to set you up afterwards. Just in case they want to argue later that you're crazy enough to kill two people and conspire to do it again."

"You can't possibly think—"

She glanced at him.

Ryson closed his mouth.

"It doesn't matter." She stared out the window at the dryer. "This isn't about me, right?" It was about getting Ryson to fight, instead of quitting like Bradley had.

Her phone started to vibrate in her pocket. Whoever it was, they could leave a message. "Find someone who has nothing to do with the police department and talk to them."

"I'll have to explain the way we do things."

"Find someone who deals with veterans, and PTSS."

"If you tell me to find a group meeting, I'm gonna disown you."

"I thought you already had."

"We were good, then you disowned *me* for two years. My baby doesn't even know you."

"Luci and I met."

He glanced over. "I'm not going to kill myself."

"No, you're just out here going over your budget."

Silence filled the car.

"It hurts." He rubbed his chest.

"Then you need to see more than one medical professional. Because your family in there—" She pointed at the closed door that led to the house. "—are hurting too. And all you have to do is tidy up a bit and give everyone a hug. No murderers, no dead bodies. No death. Just people who care about you and want to know you're okay, even if you can't say you are. Yet."

"That go for you, too? You need a hug?"

Kenna lifted one hand. "No touchy."

Ryson actually might've laughed.

She lifted the bottle from the floor. "I'm pouring this out."

"Thanks."

"I don't want to hear it. How many times have you saved my life, or my sanity?"

"You know I hate what they did to you."

Kenna bit the inside of her lip.

"There's no way I'm going to let them do it again."

Kenna shoved out of the car.

On the way to the door, Kenna retrieved the check she kept folded in her wallet. She wrote it out to Valentina Ryson for two thousand dollars with a note that said *pay the mortgage.* It should cover a couple of months, at least. She hoped. She left it beside the coffee pot.

Tina was asleep on the couch.

A blue Taurus had parked at the curb behind her little car while she'd been inside. The occupant climbed out when she hit the front walk. Dark hair, dark jacket. Probably early forties. Glasses. He moved like someone who sat too much.

The guy met her at the end of the drive, one hand

outstretched for her to shake. *Be careful little hands what you touch.* He started to speak.

"Whoever you are, they have no comment."

He pulled his hand back like she'd tried to bite it off. "I'll let Lieutenant Ryson speak for himself."

"No, you won't." She shifted her arms. The movement made her coat open. Far enough he would've been able to see the badge on her belt if she'd been an FBI agent still. Grief rolled through her, but she shoved it down. She couldn't even flash her gun, given it was behind her back.

He studied her face and his brows lifted. "I know you." It took him a second, but he got there. In a way she knew he wasn't acting. He really hadn't recognized her at first. Now it dawned on him. "Makenna Banbury."

The awe rubbed her the wrong way, but two could play at this game of his. "And you're with the Times? The Post?" She knew he wasn't. People gave up more information when they were defending themselves.

He swallowed. "Uh, no. Utah True Crime. It's a...well, it's a blog and a podcast. I added that recently." His chest expanded and he handed over his business card. "Already got a hundred subscribers on iTunes."

She smiled. The one Stairns told her not to use because it made her look like she wanted to commit murder. "That's great."

He blinked, still holding out the card. She took it, but only so she could hand it to Jaxton later.

"Now turn around and get lost. You see that sign on the door? Means the baby is sleeping, so run along." The sign was in chalk, a little gilded blackboard she figured stayed flipped to the *Baby Sleeping* side just so Valentina wasn't bothered by solicitors knocking on her door. "There's no need for you to come back."

"I want to do a show on what happened to Officer Pierce. Get the word out, you know? Maybe someone will come forward with information and the police can catch her killer."

It actually wasn't an awful idea, except that he probably only wanted to do it so he could be famous. "They don't want to talk to you."

"But if I can—"

"Call the Police Department information line. Ask for Detective Wilkern."

"She shut me down." The guy looked genuinely cut up about it. "Wouldn't even talk to me. She just passed on a message that she didn't have time."

Kenna shrugged, like "what are you gonna do."

"But now you're here. You can tell me all about your father and all those cases he solved. A hometown feel to an international crime fighting story." He needed a breath so he could continue, "He was a legend."

"I know. I was there."

He gasped, eyes wide. "It'll be amazing."

"Turn around and get in your car."

"You'll call me?"

"Sure."

"I need this." He pointed at her, switching up his approach all of a sudden. "I need you to come on the show. It'll be my big break! You have to say yes. You have to come on and tell me all about your father. You can talk about Officer Pierce and how the police don't have any leads on the killer."

Her stomach flipped over. He was entirely too close. Too excited.

She was almost tempted to tell him she'd been in the room when the video of Pierce and the kidnapper had played, just to watch him have a medical emergency.

"Don't bother these people. Don't come here. Don't call and *definitely* don't go poking around in their lives."

He moved toward her instead of away. "Say you'll come on the show." His hands flexed like he wanted to grab her.

She looked at the card, hoping he was distracted by her feigned interest and didn't notice that she'd taken half a step back so she was out of reach. Kenna didn't plan to shoot him, but she also refused to take her safety for granted. "Mr. Eric Wilson, this isn't the time to get pushy. It's late. These people need to be left alone."

"I understand." He clapped. "Say you'll come on the show."

"I'll call you. Now leave."

Chapter Eighteen

Wednesday, 5:13am.

"We got played."

The dog sniffed around the living space of the motorhome and found a crumb by the front passenger seat.

"It's just a theory." Kenna sat at the table and took a sip of her milky hot tea. "He dangled his greatness in front of us and proved what he can do. He tried to put a virus in the FBI computer system, right? Then he cut us off so we had no idea if Pierce was dead or alive. Then they dumped her body in an isolated area with little physical evidence and no way of finding the killer. It's one massive power trip."

She needed a name for the dog, who now wore a new collar Kenna had bought from the pet store. *Emily*. No, that was too similar to one of the victims of the Seventh Day Killer. *Sandy*. That fit with her coloring but was also the name of a famous TV show squirrel. *Bridget*.

Kenna shook her head and did a quick web search. "Cabot." She pronounced it with an "Oh" at the end since it was French. "And it means, 'mutt.' Which is what you are, unless you think that's derogatory, *ma cherie*."

Cabot sniffed her way back to Kenna and got a head scratch. "Now I just need to teach you that Cabot is your name. And then I need to look up do-it-yourself doggie wash places because you stink." She rubbed the sides of Cabot's face. "Yes, you do."

She let go and Cabot moved on. Looking for more crumbs.

Kenna leaned back against the window, her legs along the seat. "Whoever it was, they didn't take any shortcuts. What they did took planning and coordination." She looked over at the dog. "That means he's smart enough to cover his tracks, in case you didn't know."

Cabot sniffed along the baseboard below the kitchen cabinets.

"We're supposed to be smarter than he is," Kenna said. "Or at least craftier."

Cabot stopped at the cupboard under the sink.

The dog sniffed, then pawed at the door.

Kenna scooted to the edge of the seat.

"No." The things in there didn't belong to her. "None of your business, dog." Cabot glanced over so Kenna said, "Go lay down," and pointed at the dog bed she'd bought. "Your nose isn't going to distract me from catching this guy. Although, your stink might."

A familiar pain needled at her heart—having a dog in her home with her once again. She couldn't allow herself to be distracted by that either, not when she was doing what she'd been born to do.

The FBI might be convinced she was pursuing fame like some kind of birthright, despite the fact she'd given years of her life in service to their brand of justice. They didn't know her at all. They hadn't bothered to learn the first thing about her.

She'd been raised to find killers.

Kenna figured that was what the killer thought as well. That he was born with this power over life or death and that power was his for the taking. To be wielded and enjoyed.

Kenna fisted her hands on her lap. "I need *something* I can use. A way to find this guy. Like an undercover investigation where we infiltrate the 'class' or whatever it is."

Cabot laid her head on her paws.

There was a group who'd split the website and gone elsewhere when the feed shut off. The new site was where she needed to be. But how did she find the web address? Kenna blew out a breath. Someone who could pose as a regular visitor and gain their trust might be able to find out where they're congregating.

She thought about the blogger guy, Eric Wilson. Maybe. If she actually trusted him as far as she could throw him, which was not at all.

So far, the cops and feds had nothing about this class or the killer determined to take the police department for a ride they never wanted to go on—because of her. The cases related to the mementos they'd found would be all wrapped up soon enough. The first of the families would be informed once the bodies were unearthed. If a club of murder enthusiasts existed online, there had been nothing that came up through the course of the investigation so far to point in that direction.

Nor had there been in her own search.

Not a single thing she could pass to them that might help find Pierce's killer.

An undercover operation, though...

"They'd probably see that coming a mile away, given what's happened so far. They basically played us."

Blood rushed to her head and spread to the tip of her ears. It probably shouldn't feel like a slight that they'd been bested, but it did.

If it helped her find this guy, who cared? No one who knew about the death—which was basically everyone, given the media coverage—was okay with this guy getting away with what he'd done. She could put aside her pride for the sake of finding him.

Kenna wiggled the mouse and fired up her laptop. No one else needed to be the bait that was dangled out there to catch this guy. Not when she was here and he was intent on involving her in it.

The 'why' hardly mattered.

A sting was a good idea.

She commented on a couple of threads, the subject of which made her want to gag. Part of her wondered if the killer was even online. Maybe he was watching her through the laptop camera, which would get him nothing but a view of the sticky side of the foam circle she'd covered it with. Or he was across the RV Park, watching like Jax. The way she was sure the killer had been watching them process the scene where Jessica Pierce had been left.

The coffee pot sputtered and dribbled as Kenna read through a few pages of the website. People went after what they wanted for lots of different reasons. Some were content to only get online and talk about it. She doubted half the people who frequented a site like this would ever actually follow through in real life.

A chat window flashed in the corner of her screen.

I see you.

.   .   .

Her fingers reached for the keys, but she hesitated. Kenna had to think this through. She didn't know if he meant literally, or if he was in her computer. He could be watching on his end for her comments. Accessing what she did on her laptop.

FBI devices had protections on. Kenna had been swung out into the world with no protection, so she'd had to contact people who were experts in information security and have them install the safeguards. She had a guy she knew who might be able to tell her how this person had access. After the fact, at least.

She took a breath and typed.

WHAT ARE YOU GOING TO DO ABOUT IT?

The window indicated he was typing. Then not. Then typing. Not. Normally that irritated her when she had to sit and watch the thread for a response. Right now it amused her that he had to figure out what to say. *Not so self-assured now, are you?*

Her phone buzzed with a text. The sudden noise in the dim light of her motorhome made her jump. But only a little. She blew out a breath and hit the X to sign out of the web page—and its chat feature. If he hadn't replied yet, maybe he wasn't going to. She wasn't about to wait all day for him to figure out what he wanted to say.

The text on her phone was from a potential client, an appointment requested through filling out a form on her website.

Kenna got up and paced the length of her home. It wasn't enough. She needed to talk to Thomas, the lab tech at the FBI, and find out if he could glean anything from this chat.

She sent an email asking him to call her when he woke up. It wasn't even six in the morning, but she was going to find Jax.

The FBI wanted her in prison. Not just out of the bureau, but convicted of murder. Or confined to a mental facility. It had to be the governor—in retaliation for the fact she was back. There was no other explanation she was willing to entertain. Then again, if this entire thing was a revenge plot, maybe it was deeper than that.

She was better off alone.

Kenna had everything she needed right here. The FBI could do what they wanted. Or try, at least. She would find the killer intent on dragging her back into the light...and then she'd be gone again. The way they wanted her to be. In the meantime, she'd have to keep a close eye.

She pulled up a web page she shouldn't have access to but did. *Thanks, Dad.* Hopefully the person she'd been chatting with hadn't gotten access to her laptop, or he'd see this. But if he had, he'd be disappointed over what he found. She typed in Jax's phone number and waited for the map to load.

She sent the location to her phone and grabbed her keys.

Cabot didn't get up.

"Don't want to come?" The dog didn't lift her head from her paws. "Suit yourself."

Kenna locked up and drove to the south end of Salt Lake City. Didn't matter what time of day it was, the freeway that cut north to south through the hive was always packed. Rush hour, there'd be wall-to-wall vehicles buzzing around in droves. But the view of mountains beyond the town made it a bit more bearable.

She'd spent more time in Colorado as a kid, and down as far as Florida. Even Maryland for a while. London. Oslo. Amsterdam. Wherever her dad had a case working with some local department as a freelance investigator. He'd been in the military before that, but she'd never been able to dig up anything on what he did or even what branch he'd served in.

Utah had been a new thing for Kenna, an FBI assigned posting. She didn't ski, but the idea of it was enough she could feel outdoorsy. The hiking here was insane any time of year, but especially to escape an inversion and get some elevation. Skies were blue above the cloud line and stretched for miles. There were only a few places over the northwest states that she liked better.

Fifteen minutes later, after detouring past her favorite donut shop, she pulled over. This was where GPS had him? A community center, the lights from inside glowed yellow against the cloud-covered night sky.

It was after six-thirty and his car sat outside. He was still here.

Kenna grabbed her coffee and a raspberry-filled sugared donut. She juggled both to get the front door open and followed the lights to find an expansive room where soft music drifted into the foyer.

Kenna stopped in the middle of the empty hall. "Oliver Jaxton!" Her voice echoed in the cavernous space. He had a ridiculous name.

She peered in the room to see him stride toward her with a thunderous look on his face. Sweats. A tight T-shirt. Bare feet.

"You are disturbing—"

Around his shoulder she saw a room full of women and a couple of men, all bent over on long mats. Most looked up at her, not at the floor under them. One of the women fell over. Another one stood to stare at her.

In the background, familiar instrumental music played from a stereo. It sounded like a song she'd heard on the radio on Sunday morning.

Kenna frowned. Before she could say anything, Jax grabbed above her elbow and tugged her away from the door. "I'm trying to teach a class!"

Yeah, if she'd had any uncertainty, this erased them. Being alone was much better. "Yoga?"

She took a bite of her donut. Probably too big of a mouthful, but she would deal the same way she did with everything else. "Isn't it supposed to make you all mellow, or whatever?" It didn't seem to be working.

"What do you have against yoga?"

"Nothing." She spoke around the blob of donut. "I don't Chaturanga."

He studied her. Even barefooted he was taller. "Shame." Before she could respond to that, he said, "Can this wait ten minutes? I need to finish."

She swallowed her bite, aware there was likely a blob of raspberry jam at the corner of her mouth. "I'll be here."

He kicked the doorstopper out with his big toe and strode back to his class as the door swung shut. The woman still stood there watching Kenna.

Doctor Landstadt.

Of course, Taylor took Jax's yoga class.

Never mind that the idea of him teaching was...maybe not so strange. After all, she didn't know anything about the guy other than he was a special agent with the FBI. Maybe it wasn't that surprising.

The world made a whole lot more sense from inside her motorhome.

Especially when the door was tugged open and the doctor stepped out with a tote bag and a rolled up mat. "Kenna." The FBI psychologist who'd written a report that destroyed Kenna's career, the one who also happened to have been her best friend. Former best friend. "How are you?"

Kenna shrugged. As if she was going to let Taylor know just how badly she wanted to toss the rest of her donut in the doctor's face?

"I'd love to talk. If you have time." Taylor shifted her grip on the tote strap by her shoulder. "There's a lot going on for you right now."

"You think you can help me through it?" Kenna tossed the half-drunk paper cup in a huge trash can with a black bag curled over the rim. She dropped the rest of the donut in after the cup and slapped her hands together to brush off the crumbs from her fingers and the ends of her sleeves.

When she turned back, a line of women in yoga pants and tight tank tops scurried out with their hair up and their foreheads damp. Who knew laying on a mat and sticking your behind in the air could make you break such a sweat?

Jax emerged with a backpack over one shoulder and beat up sneakers on his feet. "I got a call from Stairns. We need to—"

"Do you want me to tell you that I'm sorry?" Taylor shifted. "That I had no choice?"

Kenna pulled the sleeves of her shirt over her thumbs and pushed her fingers in her jeans pockets. "There's nothing you have to say that I wanna hear."

Jax glanced from her to Taylor, and back. "Another woman has been kidnapped."

Nausea rolled through her stomach.

"Your business card was left at the scene."

She pushed out the front door of the community center while Taylor called after her, "Kenna!"

Chapter Nineteen

Wednesday, 9:07am.

"You wanna talk about what that was?" Kenna glanced over at Jax as he followed her up the front walk to a tiny two bedroom close to the college. "You mean, you, teaching yoga?"

He shook his head. Before he could respond, Ryson strode from the house. He glanced between them. "Kenna?"

"Jax teaches yoga."

"Kenna eats donuts. Voluntarily." Jax shuddered.

Ryson's lips twitched. "I'm afraid I'm with her on this one."

"Because you're good people, Lieutenant." She gave him a quick hug as she passed. Or tried to. Ryson's arms wrapped around her before she could get any farther, and she felt her feet leave the ground.

"Owe you."

"Probably makes us even."

His chest rumbled under her cheek. "Thank you."

She gave him a quick squeeze. "Always."

When she drew back, Kenna spotted Jax staring at her with a whole new brand of confused expression. She sighed inwardly. As if she was going to explain anything. Not when the FBI was chomping on the bit to entrap her into confirming their suspicion that she was behind this whole thing. Leaving her business cards laying around right when she "happened" to be in town. Just so she could "happen" to be drawn in and save the day. Then she could just "happen" to give an exclusive interview and become famous all over again. *Vomit.*

"What's going on?" Ryson glanced between them.

She shook her head. "Nothing. So, what's this about a missing girl?"

Ryson didn't look convinced. "Meg Parabuchio, a student at the local college. Wilkern went to talk with her mother."

Jax made a note in his phone.

"If you guys could look around, maybe we can find out if there's anything that ties this missing woman to Officer Pierce. In any way other than Kenna's business card."

"No maybes." Kenna stepped inside the house where the victim lived with three other girls.

Her business card lay on the floor of the entryway, beside an evidence marker.

Jax touched the spot between her shoulder blades.

Kenna spun out of reach.

He kept his hand raised, palm out. "Whoa. Sorry."

He should be, but she didn't figure he was apologizing for what he'd actually done wrong. While he was at it, he should also ask for her forgiveness for bringing her into this just so he could see how she reacted to this second disappearance. If she slipped up here—like he'd anticipated she might do at Pierce's crime scene by showing familiarity with the layout, or the

missing girl and details of her life—that would show culpability in his eyes.

Instead of finding the killer, the FBI was waiting for her to
mess up.

"Okay?"

She lifted her chin. "Why wouldn't I be?"

Ryson pointed them to a puffy-faced co-ed with a damp
tissue in her hand. "This is FBI Special Agent Jaxton." The
co-ed perked up, but the mascara tracks on her cheeks kind
of ruined the whole effort. Ryson motioned to her next.
"This is Kenna. She's a private investigator working with us
on this."

Kenna waited for the reaction to her name. Her business
card said *Makenna Banbury*, but this college-educated girl
had every advantage. She could put it together.

Jax sat beside her on the couch, though he kept two feet of
space between him and the girl. Probably accustomed to
witnesses and police detectives falling all over him. And yoga
class attendees. And FBI psychologists.

He and Taylor were probably in league together.
Instructed by Stairns to—

Jax said, "Can you tell us what happened?"

"I just got home." The girl looked at her Apple watch.
"An hour ago, I think."

"And what did you find?"

"The front door was open, and that card was on the floor
in the hall. Meg wasn't here, and she said she would be. We
were going to go out for smoothies." More tears tracked down
her face. "She's not here, but her phone is. I just know something is wrong."

Jax nodded. Then he showed her his phone screen. "Have
you ever seen this man before?"

Kenna figured it was a picture of Charles Halpert.

The young woman shook her head. "Is he the one who took Meg?"

"He's deceased, so you don't need to worry about him." Jax turned his phone around, swiped to another photo. Jessica Pierce. "How about this woman? Is she familiar?"

"That's the cop who was murdered." Her mouth dropped open and she covered it with the hand holding the balled-up tissue. "Does this have to do with her?"

"Have you or your friend ever met this cop?"

Her face scrunched up. "I doubt it, unless they've been to a game recently. Meg and I are cheerleaders." She brushed hair back from her forehead and batted her eyes at Jax.

Much like with Detective Wilkern, it was like he didn't even notice.

Jax wrapped up the initial questioning and excused them both. Kenna walked beside Ryson up the stairs. "What else is new this morning?"

"Autopsy on Pierce." He swallowed.

"Anything?"

"We'll know by end of day."

She squeezed his hand.

The bed had a purple comforter. A silver frame hung on the wall with photos of groups of girls displayed on a string with clothes pins. Kenna walked up to the photo in the middle. The missing young woman and a man. "Boyfriend?"

"They broke up two weeks ago," Ryson said. "Which is apparently about a year in college-girl time."

Kenna nodded. "That's true."

Ryson pressed his lips together. He wasn't okay, but he put good effort into pretending.

Jax said, "None of us are impartial on this, but we know it hits especially close to home for the Salt Lake PD. We need to work together, which includes interviewing the professor..."

He looked at the collection of papers in his hand. "Salvatore. The one who assigned his psychology class the task of getting into a killer's mind."

"You serious?" She read over his shoulder. "Wow, this girl sure had a flair for the dramatic. She also doesn't know the difference between y-o-u-r and y-o-u-r-e."

Jax mock sighed. "The state of the education system these days."

"We should bag everything." Ryson glanced around.

Kenna nodded. "You take care of this. Have your techs go over the room. We'll chat with this professor guy."

Ryson made a face. "You really think some college professor is our killer? He's so good we have two dead, one missing, and no leads?"

Jax waved the papers. "We have to work the case like we'll find this young woman alive."

"We will."

Ryson ignored her statement. "So, this Salvatore professor guy takes her—right after he assigns that? Like we weren't going to go through her things and poke into every part of her life?"

"I agree, it's too easy, but he might know something. Which we won't know unless we ask." Kenna pulled on a pair of gloves. "At least he might've heard a rumor about a community online. It's worth a shot."

Ryson sighed. His expression flashed a look of exhaustion and grief at the same time. "Fine." He sucked in a breath, and it was gone.

"I'll call your captain. Get crime scene out here to collect everything." Jax left her alone in the missing girl's room with Ryson.

"You really okay?"

Ryson shot her a look. "What do you think?"

She closed the space between them. "If we tag team this, we can share information and move the case along quicker and try to shake something loose." He was already shaking his head before she was even done. "We *can*. This professor thing is good stuff, considering we've heard that term before." She explained about Jax's conversation with Gerald Rickshire. "Good work will lead to a result. We're going to catch this guy."

"You didn't think so before."

"He's going to make a mistake. No one can be perfect forever."

Ryson winced. "I don't want to know how many bodies that's going to take. I want him brought in now."

"I'll go talk to this professor. Get the computer looked at by your guys."

"Why?"

She wasn't all hot to tell him about what'd happened when she'd been at that crime scene just hours ago, feeling like she was being watched. She hadn't even had the chance to mention it to Jax yet. "Just trust me, okay? There's someone mixed up in this who knows all about that stuff."

Jax walked in, donning his gloves and quickly picking up on the atmosphere in the room. He pulled open the closet door and stepped inside to look around. Giving them space. "It looks like American Eagle exploded in here."

Ryson pulled out his phone. "Wilkern says that, according to the Mom, our vic takes college classes downtown and hasn't picked a major yet. Cheerleader, which confirms what the friend said. Works part time at some hipster coffee shop Jax has probably heard of, but she apparently comes home every Sunday for lunch and brings her laundry with her."

"If the phone hadn't been left, I wonder if anyone would have realized she went missing."

"Her friends probably all figured she hooked up with some guy and went home with him." Jax pulled open a drawer and closed it quickly, his cheeks flushing. "Like the roommate did."

Kenna crossed to the pink laptop on the desk and lifted the lid. She could log in and pull up the girl's web search history. Nothing worrying, most likely. Kenna didn't think Meg Parabuchio would have frequented Death Files, but it was certainly possible. Still, she guessed it would be a whole lot of online stores, clothes, and food delivery. People could be unpredictable, but that was usually the exception rather than the rule. Most followed a similar pattern.

Kenna looked at spots where the vic had rubbed the letter off a key. It might only be a small sign of how this life had touched the world, but she left her mark just like everyone did. "So no one tried to get ahold of her last night, or worried when she didn't reply?"

"She did her own thing."

Kenna twisted around. The same long-armed co-ed with black hair from downstairs stared at her with hollow eyes.

"We all did."

"You've hooked up before and not told your friend? That's a basic safety measure. One that keeps girls like you alive." This one hadn't checked in, and her friend was missing now.

"She wasn't like that." The girl gasped. "Meg did her own thing. She had her own rules, and she didn't ask permission."

Kenna glanced at Ryson. He gave her a slight side-nod. The mom had confirmed similarly. "You guys didn't care about staying safe?"

"Where's the fun in that? Half her Instagram followers are guys she gave it to, the other half are guys who wanted it."

"So you just figured she met someone. Just like you've done?"

"I didn't *figure* she'd get killed!" A tear rolled down her face. "You aren't gonna find anything in here."

"Because she was wild, but she wasn't reckless."

"Exactly!"

Kenna had different ideas about that. Wild and reckless were neighbors. She also wanted to tell this young woman there wasn't any reason to yell at cops trying to get to the bottom of who took her friend. Instead, she turned away and looked through the computer's browsing history, specifically the social media sites. The girl really should have password protected it. The browser automatically logged her onto every social media account saved in her history.

"You can't read that stuff. It's private."

"What about the name of her killer?" Kenna asked. "Should that be private, too?"

The girl just whimpered.

Ryson ushered her to the hall. "Your friend is missing, and you're scared. It's a horrible thing, but we need to investigate her life so we can figure out who took her."

"Everyone loved Meg."

Kenna pressed her lips together and turned away. She poked around on the computer some more. It didn't seem that the victim had ever gone to the killer-worshipping website Kenna had visited last night.

The camera on the top edge of the screen had a cover that slid over it for privacy. It was partially open. Kenna logged onto a popular social media site and saw that the last few posts the victim had made were from right where Kenna sat, at her desk. The last one was a rant about her psych professor.

Worth checking out.

She pulled out her phone and dialed Thomas's number,

which she'd added back into her contacts after she saw him last. While it rang, she opened the email program and shot him a quick message.

"Kenna?"

"I just sent you an email. Can you get from that email and back to this laptop, remotely?"

"What are you looking for?"

In a word? "Spyware."

Jax shifted close to her side. "You think he was watching her?"

"I know there's no indication of that with Pierce, but—"

Thomas cut her off. "That's not actually true."

"I'm putting you on speaker." She lowered the phone and set it on the desk. "Explain."

"The police department tech who oversees crime scene investigation is a friend of mine. She's an expert in cyber security, and we bounce ideas back and forth sometimes."

"Yeah?" She glanced at Jax. He almost cracked a smile, even though her question should have. Kenna sighed. If Thomas didn't want to share about his friend, then...whatever. "She found something on Pierce's phone?"

"Tracking software. They didn't have access to everything, just enough to know where she was. Follow from a distance. Take her." Thomas sounded sick.

"And this laptop? If there's something similar on it, that's a lead."

Jax nodded. "It is."

Kenna needed to act dumber about technology, or they'd blame that on her too. Back in the day, the way her father had taught her to investigate, it had been old school. She couldn't count the number of times she'd seen him rough up a suspect to shake out a lead or get a confession. These days, everyone was held to a higher standard. Criminals were adept at shifts in technology, and the police were generally one step behind. It meant constant motion, always working hard to fight against the tide of pain and suffering. Selfish people perpetrating violence against those they considered less than them—or nothing at all.

Technology was like money. Neither good nor evil, it could be used in ways that benefited people. But in the hands of the wrong person, it was a deadly weapon. The common denominator? People. Even with the best of intentions, people were still basically selfish.

"Oh."

Kenna straightened at his voice. "What is it?"

"The laptop needs to be brought in, but I'm downloading everything. You'll want to see this."

Jax shifted. "Please tell me you have an image of the kidnapper's face."

"He wore a hood, like with Pierce, so it won't help."

Kenna heard something in his tone. "What is it, Thomas?"

"Someone watched her get taken."

Kenna took the call off speaker and put the phone to her ear. "If I bring you my laptop, can you check it for the same spyware?"

There was a beat of silence then, "Of course, Kenna. And I don't care what Stairns said. I know you're not responsible for this. If he doesn't want me helping you—"

"Don't get in trouble over this."

"I'll punt it to the PD. Their forensic technician will make sure you're safe."

"Thanks, Thomas." Kenna tapped the phone and hung up. She wanted to give in to the urge to shiver but didn't feel free to let Jax know her feelings. Or even that she felt grateful to Thomas for his belief in her innocence. Too much water under the bridge with the FBI. The way they'd tossed a grenade towards her and blown the bridge up.

She walked out of the room, his gaze hot on her back. Powerful enough to kill that sense of being watched from the street. For a second, at least.

Ryson was at the front door, talking to the roommate who only sniffed and nodded. Then she wandered off.

Kenna stopped by his elbow. "Anything?"

"She's going to let the police do what they need to do."

"Good." Kenna opened the front door. A familiar blue Taurus sat at the curb. Mr. Eric Wilson headed toward them. She called out, "How is The Utah True Crime doing this morning?"

Jax glanced at her. "You know this guy?"

"He's a blogger. Podcaster. A murder nerd."

Wilson looked hopeful. "Still waiting for your call."

Jax snorted under his breath. Then he grabbed Eric's arm and shifted him around.

Ryson said, "Jaxton."

He ignored the lieutenant's attempt at a reprimand and shoved the reporter against his car. "How did you know the victim's identity and where she lived?"

"The local news station ran a story this morning about a missing girl."

Kenna said, "Not including her name." Wilkern had only just now notified the mother. "How'd you know it was her?"

"I listened to the police band."

Jax said, "And?"

He grunted. "Ow. That hurts."

"*How?*"

"Fine." He looked at Kenna. "I put a GPS tracker on your car outside the lieutenant's house. I've been following you ever since."

Jax let him lean his backside against the hood. "Talk."

"I'm doing a story. This is the most interesting thing that's happened in *months*. A murder case the police can't solve. The FBI can't solve. The daughter of legendary killer catcher Malcom Banbury can't solve. This stuff is story gold. I'm gonna go national."

Kenna got between them. Behind her back, she shoved at Jax. He didn't budge. "You've been following me?"

Sweat on his brow. Face red. Eric wasn't the guilty party.

"Anyone else you see following me?"

He shook his head. "I have some dog food in the car. I noticed you haven't bought any yet."

Kenna forced herself not to react. Her father had fans of all kinds, and some wrote her letters even now. She knew his type. This guy was harmless—so long as she could keep tabs on him. "Just a GPS tracker?"

Jax said, "You're gonna go soft on this guy?"

She turned to him. "You wanna interrogate him?"

"Uh, *yeah*."

"Not very mellow of you. But then, neither is trying to frame me for all of this just because you think I can't live without my name in lights."

"I'd love an exclusive interview. You could come on my blog."

She didn't turn around. "Shut up, Eric."

A muscle in Jax's chin flexed. "That's not what this is."

"No? Care to share what Stairns has been saying about me?" When he didn't, she continued, "I'm guessing he met with the governor since the discovery of Christopher Halpert's body—when the FBI realized I was back here."

"The governor is out of town right now."

Kenna lifted her chin. "Why don't you run along back to your boss and let him know Eric Wilson and I are going to chat. I'll be sure to tell him—live on the podcast—how the FBI retired me without my consent because the governor leaned on them to get rid of me. All to shut me up so I didn't tell anyone the truth about how my partner died."

"Are you talking about Bradley Pacer?" Wilson sucked in an audible breath. "The governor's son, the one you got kidnapped with? What do you mean the truth about how he died?"

She didn't move her gaze from Jax, trying to assess what he knew and what he didn't.

"I'm still taking Eric in for a chat."

Chapter Twenty

Wednesday, 11:23am.

Her arrival at the FBI office had been delayed due to the fact she'd run home to grab her laptop—and let Cabot outside for a minute. She'd texted Jax twice, but he hadn't answered. Probably in interrogation already, his phone and gun in his desk drawer.

Once she got cleared through security, she headed up the elevator and straight for the interrogation rooms. As soon as the doors opened on the sixth floor, she bit the inside of her cheek. "Special Agent in Charge Stairns. It's so good to see you."

"Really." He stood guard in the hallway.

"If you'll excuse me, I'm late. Consulting business."

"I didn't buy that stuff back when you worked for me, and I don't buy it now."

She stepped off the elevator and strode past him without missing a stride.

"Kenna."

She glanced over her shoulder. "Jax is with Wilson, right?"

If he wasn't going to tell her which interview room they were in, she'd just have to open every door.

"Three. We need to talk."

She smiled to herself and picked up her pace as she headed for it. Never mind the fact he'd used *the tone*. Obviously, she wasn't getting out of here without being forced into a confrontation with him. Again. It'd happened plenty of times before. Kenna would just roll with it, though he probably wouldn't like the outcome. But after what he'd done to her, she was through pulling punches or towing the party line. If they wanted to get a conviction, they'd have to work for it.

And deal with the fact they were sending an innocent person to jail.

Not to mention letting a killer go free.

Kenna shoved open the door to the interview room. "You started without me?" She stuck a hand on her hip. "That's just rude."

Jax leaned back in his chair. "Kenna."

Wilson sat across from him. She waved. "Hey, Eric. How's it going?"

He should've asked for his lawyer. Instead, he grinned. "Fine. Thanks. It's very exciting, you know?"

"Sure." She pointed at Jax. "You're either on that side of the table doing your regular ole day job—" She pointed at Eric. "—or you're on this side and in serious trouble." Then shrugged. "What's not to love?"

"Please stand in the viewing room."

She ignored Jax and touched her palm to the table so she could lean over at Eric. He stared up at her, wide eyed and captivated. Jax was going to eat him alive. "You're really sure you don't want to *refuse* to talk to the FBI? Maybe just walk right out of here—which is your right, you know. Or you could call a lawyer and get counsel, just so you don't say more than necessary?"

There was a lot there, but he needed to think.

Instead, he blinked up at her.

"Eric..."

"I'm helping the FBI with their case."

"And they think you have something to do with it. That you're either involved, or you know who the killer is."

He swallowed. "I'm helping."

Kenna supposed it was possible Eric Wilson wasn't innocent. She straightened. "Ask for a lawyer, Eric."

"The viewing room," Jax repeated. "Ms. Banbury."

The room next door had a giant window, beside which was a speaker on the wall.

Stairns was already inside the room.

She flipped the dial so she could hear them. Next to the speaker was another console that allowed those in the interrogation room to hear anything she said from in here.

Kenna folded her arms across her chest and watched the window. "He should've called for a lawyer."

Stairns grunted.

"We were talking about this." Jax's voice filled the room. She reached over and turned the volume down. Jax tapped a paper between him and Eric—a photo.

She glanced aside. "Jessica Pierce?"

Stairns nodded. He seemed to be watching her more than Jax and Eric in the interrogation room. Trying to figure out if she was part of this? Maybe in cahoots with Wilson. Could be *she* was the one with the protégé, taking women and murdering them in online videos.

That might be their answer—Kenna and Wilson in league to get famous.

She rubbed her palm down the top of her forearm, then repeated the motion with the opposite hand and arm. Despite the fact two years had passed, they still hurt once in a while.

"Did you get full use of your hands back?"

"Good as ever." She'd clocked in around ninety percent with her range of motion, and over seventy with her ability to hold heavy things for prolonged periods. She'd gone through physical therapy. Tests. Another round of surgery. More physical therapy.

"That's good."

Yet despite what she'd told Stairns, she hadn't healed all the way. And that shortfall bothered her. Two years was enough time she knew her limitations. What she could and couldn't manage. But that didn't mean she had to like it.

She guessed she wouldn't qualify for the FBI, even if she wanted to come back. Which she did not. Though the fact her choice was taken from her burned acid in her stomach.

The bitter taste in her mouth prevented words from forming. Did he really care how she was? If he did, he'd have called once in the last two years. Just once. Maybe on her birthday. Instead, Stairns had left her in the hospital and walked away.

That was what it felt like, even if the reality was more akin to excommunication.

The PI license meant she could do the work. Be who she was. Just...elsewhere, so the governor and his family didn't have to suffer. They might run into her and have to relive the pain of losing their golden child.

Through the window, Jax leaned forward in his chair. "You seem to know an awful lot about what's happening."

"I put things together and make connections. The way you guys do when you investigate."

"That's what you're gonna go with?" Jax leaned back in his chair. "I'm not a..." His head dipped to the file. "Blogger, or a podcaster, so you'll have to enlighten me."

Enough to fan club about murder online, Jax was probably thinking. That Wilson couldn't simply be a reporter of events but had to be a fanatic, along with a group of others. Had Eric watched Pierce get killed, the way they had? The feed shut off before the death blow, but the video host had followed through. He'd finished the job.

Eric shrugged one shoulder. "I haven't done anything."

Jax flipped over another photo.

Eric's eyes flared.

He tapped the image. "Knife against the throat, about to kill her in a live feed. I can see why you like to talk about it."

"I thought it was prerecorded."

"Where'd you hear that?"

Eric shrugged.

"Did you watch her die?" Jax pulled the file toward himself and looked at the typed page on top. "What if I were to get a warrant for your home computer and your phone? Would it show that you were online at the time the video was running? It was probably pretty exciting, seeing a woman gasp her last breath."

Kenna wanted to close her eyes against the flashing images in her mind. She stared at a spot on the wall of the interview room and sucked in a long breath. If she rubbed her arms again, Stairns would know. He'd think he was right to have let her go. That she wasn't fit to be an investigator anymore.

Instead of seeing proof she was working with Wilson to get her fame back, he'd see the depth of her fear. No matter how he saw things, she wouldn't win either way.

"We watched the whole thing until he cut us off right

before the finale." Jax let out a frustrated sound. As if irritated the killer had denied him the chance to see the death blow. "It's been a while since I saw that light disappear in someone's eyes."

"You killed someone?"

"It's part of the job. I've spent a lot of bullets, and sometimes things happen. You don't mean it to end like that, but not much you can do when all that hot, sticky blood runs over your hands and, no matter how hard you apply pressure, it pumps out between your fingers. And then there's nothing. Just stillness."

Wilson swallowed. He'd never killed anyone. Kenna was almost certain Eric Wilson hadn't taken a life before. She knew the signs. She couldn't prove it, of course, but he seemed a whole lot more like a harmless guy who maybe wanted to know that feeling. Enough to be obsessed with talking about it. Some kind of weird compulsion he'd built up, maybe based on a traumatic experience.

She'd have talked to Taylor about Eric, if she didn't hate everything her former best friend was, and all she apparently stood for.

"How connected are you with the online community?" Jax was like a puma in the wild, teasing its prey. A little injury. Some blood spilled.

She muttered, "He's good."

Stairns said, "You were better."

She glanced at him. "And yet you caved to the governor and kicked me out."

"I have a lot of fans. Followers." Through the window, Eric sniffed. "People who want to know what I have to say."

"A man like you, connected like that, you'd have to be in the know," Jax mused. "Probably watched that video. Maybe you were even personally invited to view it."

Eric lifted his chin. *So what if I was.*

"Then you'd be able to talk all about it on your podcast."

"I know people."

Jax shrugged. "Sure. That's probably how you find out what's happening, what's new in the life."

Kenna sucked in a long breath. The life of murderers and killers. She tried to shove the bile back down.

Eric said, "I bet there are a lotta cops who'd be interested. They see dead people all the time. They *have* to want to see how they got that way."

He wanted to believe he was understood. Like anyone, he wanted to belong to something. Death in the face of life was a powerful thing to experience. Like the rush of adrenaline. She wondered how far he would go to chase it.

"I'm sure they do," Jax said. "If it's good stuff. But he's drawn our attention now. We're looking for him."

"Doesn't matter. No one can find him." Eric twisted his fingers together. "Even I don't know where he is."

"It'd be seriously cool, getting him on your podcast."

"I tried." Eric blew out a breath. "He sent me a virus that wiped out my whole computer."

"And you still got the video link?"

"That was before."

"When did you get the virus?"

He mushed his lips together. "Yesterday."

"Guy like that. I bet you were angry he didn't give you the time of day. Then he goes and gives you a virus?" Jax shook his head empathetically. "How did you contact him?"

"Through the website. But before you get all worked up about me giving you his information, it was just a generic address. Like a contact form. It probably wasn't even him, but whoever's posting it."

"You don't think he does all that himself?"

"Maybe he shoots the footage, but someone else uploads it. The guy is like...the director or whatever."

"So the killer works with other people to make this happen."

"You'd have to," Eric said. "Otherwise, he'd have no time to concentrate on teaching. On the *art*."

"Maybe."

"Doesn't matter if you don't believe me."

"I don't have to believe you." Jax sat back. "It's the judge you'll need to convince. He or she is the one who has to take your word, not me. Unless you'd care to prove right here and now that you have nothing to do with those two murders, one of whom was a police officer."

"I didn't kill that cop or take the girl. I don't do that."

"You just watch it online." When Eric said nothing in response, Jax continued, "Got yourself in as part of the club. You think I can't find a way to bring charges to everyone who viewed those videos? You're all accessories to murder as far as I'm concerned. He posted that to show off his skills and get you guys stirred up. Ready to go out and commit your own murders."

"It's not like that." Eric shook his head. "I'm not going to kill anyone."

Jax spread his hands. "If you don't want to spend decades in prison with no cell phone, no computer, no social media, no followers except the ones that come around sniffing after you, then you're gonna need to give me what you've got on this guy."

"I don't—"

"Enough lies. Did you get a link for the second video? Is he going to post this woman's death online as well?"

"It was all on my computer. I got a virus. It's gone."

"So, remember." Jax leaned forward. "Or I pin these murders on *you*."

The way he was doing with her? She felt defensiveness rise up in her chest. And it really had no bearing on whether she knew this Eric guy well or not. This was a stand for the way she had been treated when everything went bad. For her, restitution may be too late. But there was no way she would tolerate someone else being treated the same way.

Eric shook his head. "But I didn't do them."

"Doesn't matter. You'll go down as an accessory anyway, and everyone in prison will know that you're the guy who only watched the murder. Because you didn't have the guts to do it yourself."

"I could!" Eric's face reddened. "I almost *did*."

"Yeah?"

"Yeah." The word sputtered from his mouth.

Kenna waited for more, but he didn't choose to incriminate himself in this instance. Or ask for his lawyer when he really needed legal counsel.

Jax said, "Couldn't finish the job?"

Eric shifted in his chair like a three year old throwing a tantrum. "It's not... I could do it if I wanted to."

Jax folded his arms. "Give me the name of the guy who actually managed it. What's he called?"

"I don't know his name."

"Guy like that. He has to have a handle. What is it?"

Whether a handle could actually lead them to him was another question entirely. But they needed at least a shot at catching this guy.

"How did he tell you where to go to see this new girl get killed?"

Eric flushed again. "Just a message. There, and then gone."

"But you clicked on the pop-up."

"Well, yeah."

Kind of like the pop-up that had appeared on her screen. And they wanted to pin this on Eric Wilson? He was nothing but a fanatic with dreams of becoming a famous reporter. An influencer.

Was she the only person in the world who *didn't* want to be famous?

Jax got up. He shook his head and glanced at the ceiling.

Then, suddenly, Jax pushed off the wall. "I don't think you saw the video of the girl at all. I think he shut you out, then he ghosted you. Sent you a virus instead of agreeing to be on your podcast." He planted his fists on the table and leaned forward. "Because he thinks what we do—that you're nothing but a joke."

Eric didn't like that much. He sputtered. "I could've made him even more famous."

"Quid pro quo, right? He scratches your back, you scratch his."

"We could have *done something*."

"Like kill even more people? Get famous?" He shrugged one shoulder and brushed Eric off as he stepped away. "It's not like he needs your help. Seems to me like you need his, though." Jax waved with a hand. "Can't kill anyone. Can't even get famous. One app, and the police scanner. Then you put a tracker on Ms. Banbury's car and follow her around just to be in the know. I bet you never even saw that girl get killed on the live stream."

"I did!" Eric almost exploded out of his chair. "I saw the whole thing. Even the extra footage at the end for gold members."

Jax stilled. "What did he do after she died?"

Eric shook his head. "It was a message. A call to action. Like an update."

"What did he say?"

"It's the viewer's turn to do it now." He glanced between Jax and the window. "Kill someone and get away with it."

Kenna paced away. A call to action, a mission to do what the killer had done. Not just locally, but maybe even all over the world. A tribe of murderers who thought they could get away with whatever they did just because this guy had.

Jax said, "How many people were watching?"

Eric shook his head. "I don't know."

"You'd better start telling us everything you *do* know, or every single murder committed by someone who follows this guy will be on you. And I'll make sure no one *ever* knows your name."

Stairns pushed out of the viewing room into the hall.

Kenna followed. "I thought we were going to talk before I left."

He turned. It hit her then that he looked older now. Two years had passed. He had more gray. More lines.

He sighed. "So talk."

"You set Jax on me, determined to get evidence that I'm somehow behind this. Now you want to sweep Eric Wilson in and make it look like he's my accomplice. First person to show up, and I've met him? Has to be my protégé." She swallowed back the bile that rose in her throat. "Of course, I'm kidnapping and murdering, all to get my name in the papers again."

"Kenna—"

"Don't bother. I won't believe a word of whatever justification you want to offer me." She was vaguely aware of Jax exiting the interview room. "It wasn't enough that Almatter took the use of my hands from me. Or that he cut the tendons in Bradley's legs *and* stole his hope. No. That wasn't enough for you. Between you, Governor Pacer, and Doctor Landstadt, you had to take *everything* I built for myself."

It hadn't been her inheritance, the legacy she was born into.

It had been her life. She hadn't been spoon-fed. She'd worked for it all herself.

And they took all of it away.

Stairns winced. "It didn't need to get out that he..." One glance, toward Jax. The SAC didn't finish.

"Destroying me *again* is justifiable? You guys can't just leave me alone. No. I have to be nothing. No badge. No credibility. No sanity. Because the governor wants to make it so I can't ever tell anyone the truth. That's just great." She took a step away. "If he wanted to be rid of me, he should have just paid someone to put a bullet in my head."

Chapter Twenty-One

Wednesday, 8:42pm.

Kenna lifted the glass and took a sip through the straw. "Is that cherry cola?"

"Real cherries." She set the glass on the bar and stared at the ice cubes rather than the bartender, or the guy settling onto the stool beside her. Certainly not the bowling alley full of people behind her. "It's the only way to drink it."

Jax lifted a finger and ordered a soda water. "Took me a while to track you down."

"I'd prefer to finish my drink before you arrest me."

He took a sip of his own. "Part of me figured you'd be long gone, out of town, by the time I caught up."

"I'm not in the mood for a manhunt." Especially not if she was the one being hunted.

"Or, this is where you go when you run."

"A bowling alley." She snorted. "As if."

"Mmm."

Maybe he knew more than she'd realized. If he'd put that together then he'd been doing his homework on her. Hoping for an arrest? "I'm still going to finish my drink."

"I'm not here to arrest you." He shifted toward her. "I just want to talk."

"Said the spider to the fly."

Friend or foe? She wasn't sure which Jax would turn out to be. Either way, leaving town—especially right now—would only cause more problems for her. A warrant out for her arrest in connection with murder charges would go viral. The daughter of a famous investigator turned killer.

She could see the headlines now.

"Kenna—"

"You seriously think Eric Wilson had anything to do with this?"

"He gave us valuable intel."

"You mean the FBI. He gave *the FBI* valuable intel." She glanced over. "Because I know you don't mean 'us.'" She waved a finger between them.

"Why not?"

She stared at him.

"Isn't this the best way to prove you had nothing to do with this? Clear your name. Restore your reputation. Give a few exclusive interviews, and then write a book about how you were wrongly accused."

She shifted on the stool, uncomfortable with mere thought of talking to a reporter. They generally had all kinds of ulterior motives she couldn't anticipate. Surely, there'd be questions about Bradley. About her father.

"Why are you still here?"

She stared at the empty bottom of her soda glass instead of answering. "My dad used to buy me a cherry cola at the end of every case he worked. No matter the outcome, we got a drink and toasted the close of the case. He died three weeks before I graduated from college. The director of the FBI flew out to Baltimore to tell me himself. Figured it should come from him. I went out and got a cherry cola that night. Seemed fitting to commemorate the end. Until I did the same thing a week later, and again. And again."

Of course, there was rum in the glass as well back then. That first night was a blur and she'd woken up on a stranger's couch. After that, her father only got more famous. She drank more rum. The movies aired over and over on cable TV. She drank more rum. The books surged back up the bestseller lists. She'd managed to finish college, quit the rum, and eventually applied to the FBI. Kenna had found a path of her own that worked—one she actually liked walking.

"I threw off the mojo of closing a case with a celebratory drink. I ruined it." She pushed the glass away. "Doesn't mean anything now."

"That might not be the problem."

"No?"

Before she could say more than that, he said, "What happened to your partner that Stairns and the governor don't want you talking about—enough they used Doctor Landstadt to force you out?"

"No lead in. You just go for the money shot?"

"Landstadt's report indicates you weren't mentally fit to be an FBI agent. Coupled with the injuries sustained that meant surgery and physical therapy, you were in a rough position. But you could've done the work, right? You could have come back."

"Maybe I didn't care to."

"So you lost your partner and walked away from your job."

"You saw the paperwork, so you know Bradley and I were

in a relationship." She glanced over. "Or did they amend that part of the file as well?"

He stared at her, his expression unreadable. If he thought she was going to cry in a bowling alley, he'd be incorrect. "Something Stairns said. It didn't need to get out that he...what?"

Kenna glanced over her shoulder around the room. He thought she'd say it out loud in a place where a group of FBI agents and support staff participated in a bowling league tournament? "Doesn't matter. Doesn't change anything, and it doesn't bring him back."

"You're still here because you're angling for your job?"

"As if. And that's not just bluster. I'm not an agent, and I don't wanna be."

"So why stay?"

His question hit a little too close to home. Salt Lake was where her memories of Bradley lived, and she needed her fix. Though, she would never admit that was the reason she still came home sometimes.

"Maybe because another young woman is in the hands of a sadistic killer, and I happen to know exactly what that feels like? Enough to want to stick around and at least try to help find her." Even if that meant watching her phone just in case she got another link via text. "Someone wants me to be part of this."

"But not you."

"You know those old westerns where they tell the guy to 'never show his face in this town again'?" She waited a beat for him to nod. "They didn't word it exactly like that, but it was close."

"Because your partner's father is the governor of Utah."

"Can't have a scandal get out. Sully the hero golden boy's

reputation and put a stain on the whole family." She leaned over slightly. "Appearance is *everything*, you know?"

"My mother would agree with you."

"Mine is dead, or I'd ask."

He was quiet a minute. "It just washes over you? No feeling. No fear."

"You think I'm not scared, or that I don't feel anything, or you just expect me to be an emotional wreck all the time?" When he said nothing, she continued, "I don't know you, I don't trust you, and I certainly don't owe you my emotions. My feelings are none of your business."

"I'm sorry."

"Why, what did you do?"

"It wasn't an admission of guilt. It was an expression of sympathy. You lost a lot."

"More like stolen, but who's keeping track?"

The skin around his eyes flexed.

"I don't need the emotional weight of your sympathy on top of everything I'm already carrying. I have enough of my own."

"That wasn't my intention." He paused a second, as though making a decision. "I was a quarterback in college. Middle of the fourth quarter, homecoming game." His words stalled.

"What happened?"

"I'm running, and I trip. Simple as that." He paused again. "Then I land, and *snap*."

Kenna winced.

"Six months later and I'm addicted to painkillers, barely hanging on to my grades, and I can't tell anyone. Because, you know, *appearance is everything*."

"What did you do?"

"I found a group, got a sponsor. Got a referral to a physical therapist who got me doing yoga to work through the pain and get my strength back. Not to mention it helped me get out of my head enough to find answers. But I messed up." He shrugged. "I don't think my mother has ever forgiven me for being human."

She realized her gaze had strayed to the wall of framed photos by the bar and shifted back toward Jax. "Have there been any updates?"

He shook his head. "Thomas is still working on the video and the website, trying to get an IP address for the upload."

That wasn't likely to produce much. "It's too easy to mask your IP address so it looks like you're somewhere else. But I'm sure Thomas will come up with something."

"I don't like sitting around waiting." He took a sip from his glass. "We have no way to find Meg, and no leads on who it was. Just a bare-bones profile."

"Of someone with either a grudge against me, or a need to be infamous. Maybe both."

"We should work together. You're good at what you do, and I have the resources of the FBI."

She turned her head slowly toward him.

"Geez, it isn't that bad of an idea."

"You think I'm gonna report to Stairns? I'm waiting for the governor to find out I'm in Salt Lake City and send a patrol of National Guard guys to escort me to the Idaho border."

"I'm not going to let them bully you. And for the record, the governor is at a conference all week down in St. George."

Pacer wasn't even here. Though, if someone wanted to make a point badly enough, distance, or being at a conference out of town, wouldn't get in the way of that.

The stool creaked under her. Kenna had to get ahold of

herself, or she'd betray her feelings to a man who was not her ally.

"All of a sudden you're on my side?" As if she was going to believe that. He worked for Stairns. For the federal government. The Utah governor was a separate entity, but that just meant she had two enemies.

Jax probably didn't want to make her mad by telling her he felt sorry for her.

"I don't want a partner."

"Good." Jax took another sip. "Neither do I."

"Good."

He smiled around the rim of his glass. "It's settled." His attention strayed to the wall of photos.

"Leave it alone."

"Let's get to work then. Figure out who here wants to drag you into something against your will and get famous doing it."

"That is literally the worst reason to kill someone."

"And yet, people kill for far less than notoriety."

Someone stepped between them and leaned close. Kenna got a whiff of body odor and cologne. Special Agent Miller summoned the bartender with a raise of his finger. "Beer." Then his breath whispered across her cheek. "You've finished your little kid drink. Now it's time to go."

"Pretty sure I get to decide for myself when it's time to go." She hopped off the seat. "I think I'll bowl a round. Jax?"

"Kenna." His tone was low, but the other cops still caught it.

The group behind her consisted of Miller and her former colleagues, still mad two years later that she'd cost them their friend's life. So much potential, and they thought he'd sacrificed himself to save her. That was the worst of it.

Miller sneered. "Yeah, *Kenna.*"

She waited for the rest of it, but there was nothing else. "Excuse me." She could be polite.

Miller's gaze drifted over her face.

"Move out of the way, Special Agent Miller."

"Why don't you make me?"

Kenna rolled her eyes. "Why do men always act like they're out at recess with their brains left behind in the classroom?"

Jax didn't respond. "Miller, let her past."

"Sure." He reacted to Jax's order immediately. She clocked the shift of his muscles and saw it coming. "I'll just let her do whatever she wants, even though I'm thinking she's the one behind all of this. Sending us on wild expeditions, like talking to that professor. What a waste of time."

She was able to see the intention in his eyes. Miller was going to try and arrest her.

She stared him down. "You don't remember what happened last time you let your emotions get the better of you?"

He flinched, coming at her like he was going to start a fight.

Kenna caught his forearm before it could swing out in her direction. Her other hand grasped a handful of his shirt. She twisted and slammed his face against the bar like it was the hood of a car.

The room erupted.

"You're guilty." His words were muffled, his cheek pressed against the bar. "We all know it."

Kenna didn't let him up. She leaned in and spoke low in Miller's ear. "You see that picture at the end of the bar, the big one in the middle?"

Miller gritted his teeth. "Let me up. I won't arrest you."

"One sec, I'm not done yet. See that guy between the FBI

Director and the former Salt Lake City Police Commissioner?" She gave him a second to look. "That's my father, wearing that medal they pinned on him."

Another second, to absorb the information. "So if I want to come in here at the end of a bad day, at the end of what's been a really bad week *for all of us,* and I want to have a drink while I spend some time with him, well, it's a free country isn't it? At least that's what I've heard."

He hissed a breath between his teeth.

"Kenna."

She realized the whole crowd of agents stared at her. Bradley was in the middle of them all, staring at her and shaking his head. Like he thought she was nuts. She called his name and took a step towards him. No, not Bradley.

She looked down at her hands. She didn't have Miller pinned against the counter. She never had.

How long had she been standing here talking to herself?

It was time to call it a night. Obviously, she was letting this case and their blame get the best of her.

"Earth to Kenna." He waved a hand in front of her face. "They're right, you know. You have lost it."

She launched at him, but Jax caught her arm just in time. "I think we should go now."

Miller sucked in a breath, not prepared to back down. "I know you're part of this."

She should knock him out, but she visualized herself getting arrested and held back.

Kenna reached into her pocket and grabbed all the bills she had and laid them on the bar. "A round of little kid drinks for my friends."

She walked out of the completely silent bowling alley, not acknowledging anyone or anything. If she did, the place would probably erupt again.

"You could always just tell them the truth of what happened."

She pushed out the front doors into the frozen night air.

"And maybe me, too," Jax suggested.

Since that would involve trusting him, and she didn't, Kenna said nothing.

He sighed. "I'll see you tomorrow?"

"Depends." She turned. Neon bowling alley glow lit his face. "Are you going to sit outside the RV park all night?"

"If I say yes, would you invite me in to sleep on your couch?" His face was doing that blank thing again, not knowing how much to reveal or what to say in order to convince her to give him the answer he wanted.

"I have a dog now." Not to mention a gun and a security system. "I don't need companionship." She didn't think he was playing a game. But he was playing her. Or, at least, managing her while he tried to control the fallout. For the FBI's benefit, or on his own?

"You still have that mutt?"

"Her name is Cabot, and I should go let her out to pee." The noise of a vehicle prompted her to take two steps so she could cross before having to wait for it. "Bye."

He was already headed for his own vehicle. "Call me if you hear anything. I want to know." The way he said it was like he thought they were partners. A team.

The engine of the approaching car revved.

Kenna glanced over at the silver compact headed toward her. They would see her and slow down.

Instead, it sped up.

She hopped back onto the curb and backed up three steps, stumbling on uneven concrete.

The car jumped the curb and came at her. No license

plate. She took half a step more and her shoe caught on the edge of a cut-out planter in the sidewalk.

Someone yelled, "Kenna!"

She twisted as she fell, turning to see the driver. Hoodie. She caught a glimpse of his face. They locked eyes before Kenna rolled out of the way, just in time, across the frozen ground. The engine roared right beside her.

The corner of the bumper swung up, dangerously close.

Closing in.

Chapter Twenty-Two

J ax raced over and stowed his weapon. "Easy. Hey."

Kenna blinked up at the cloudy night sky. "Ow."

His brow had furrowed, creasing the area between his eyes in a way that made him look both concerned and disapproving at the same time. She batted his hands away, which took energy she didn't have right now. He reached for her again.

"What..." Her head swam.

"Like I said, easy."

The world quit spinning and settled. "He hit me."

"Did he?" Jax held out a hand.

She grasped his wrist as though she might use it for leverage to stand but didn't get up. She stared at the jacket over her forearm and held on while her head swam. She already had one bandage on her face.

He crouched. "I'm calling an ambulance." Kenna shut her eyes and held on.

"No. I'm okay."

"I don't think you are."

She looked at him. "I'm *fine*. I don't need a doctor."

The crinkle between his eyes deepened.

"I don't need a doctor." She studied his face. "I'm not going to pass out, and that'd be your only shot at getting me to a hospital. If I was unconscious. Or dead."

"If you're dead you won't need a hospital." He shifted in his crouch. "Feel like getting off the ground? It's freezing out here."

"I like the cold. It's easier." Once she was on her feet, he let go and glanced around.

No crowd had gathered outside the front door, which was good. She was so relieved it was just her and Jax. She didn't need her former colleagues seeing her like this. After spacing out like she had, they already thought she was crazy.

Jax seemed to read her mind. "No one saw but me."

He shouldn't ignore reality. "They'll never accept you if you throw in with me."

"Because the agents you worked with don't know what Stairns made you hide." He pulled out his phone. "You never told them what really happened either, right?"

"Like they'd have cared." She brushed her hands together. They stung, but she managed to hide her reaction. There was antiseptic cream in her motorhome, but she needed to make a stop before she could get back there.

"You think they wouldn't want to know?" He frowned down at her. "That they might act a little more kindly to you if they did?"

"Considering I'm the one they take out their grief on? No. I think they'd feel the same way. That I should have stopped it. That everything I did wasn't enough, or Bradley would still be alive."

She set off toward her car, working out the aches and painful kinks as she walked. Jax didn't move right away. He just stayed where he was. Probably to observe her gait. Assess the damage. See if she really was as crazy as she'd appeared in the bowling alley. He jogged to catch up to her, catching the last part of what she'd been saying. "...anyway, people will think what they want to. They're less inclined to question the narrative when it lines up with what they believe. That a hero was cut down in his prime. So much potential for greatness. The best of us. Gone, because of Sabastian Almatter." She swallowed against the lump in her throat. "Because I wasn't enough to keep Bradley alive."

"I'll call Ryson so you can file a police report."

She shook her head, which turned out to be a bad idea, and angled toward her car. "I'll go find him. Do it in person. Valentina's a nurse so she can check me out. Is that good enough for you?"

She didn't tell him she might need a minute before she could drive without her hands shaking, but she was fine.

He tugged on her elbow and steered her to his car. "I'll drive you over there. How's your head?" Jax pulled open the passenger door for her.

She eyed him and got in. "I just need quiet." The more she talked, the more she'd be inclined to say something she wouldn't have otherwise. The way she already had.

He made a noncommittal noise and shut the door for her. The impact moved through her head like someone hitting a tympani. She tried not to let her head sway with the motion of the car, but that effort only made it hurt worse. Then she let go of the tension and that was worse still.

"Did you see his face?"

"I hit my head pretty hard. Mostly it's all a blur." That sounded pretty good. She was going to go with that. She tried to sound nonchalant, but the truth was she couldn't get his desolate eyes out of her head.

"Maybe you'll remember something later." He tapped the

steering wheel with one index finger. "We can get you a sketch artist."

"You think it's our kidnapper? Pretty sure he's busy with Meg. His latest victim."

He winced. "It could be the same guy. The killer."

"Or someone who thinks he can be one. Or someone else entirely. An accident. Random. A person we aren't able to identify." She touched her forehead. Good thing he was driving. She wasn't sure she'd have made it where she wanted to go. Of course, she wasn't going to admit that to Jax.

"I can't believe the killer would try to hit you with his car."

She looked out the window. "*Maybe* the killer. And me either."

"But if he did, then he's switched, and he's now coming after you."

She would have to figure out how to finesse the whole sketch artist thing. Then there was the issue of the car, and the fact Jax had seen it as well. "Did it have plates?"

"Not that I saw." His voice was tight. "I think this killer has you in his sights."

"Ok, so let's just say it was the killer. We've known he was drawing me in. Why try to kill me? It doesn't fit if he wants me to go up against him head-to-head."

"Unless he wants to make things harder for us."

"He didn't need to do that. Not when he won with Jessica." She rubbed the top of each forearm. "Besides, we have basically no leads anyway."

"He wants the challenge. Clearly the cops can't catch him, but maybe he already knew that. He gets you looped in and takes two women, because he's finally met a worthy adversary."

"Wow, that sounds *awe*some."

Jax gripped the wheel and turned a corner, shooting her a look. "The dead serial killer, Christopher Halpert, was all part of a greater plan to intrigue you into coming after him. Then he follows you so he can keep tabs on you."

There was a flaw in that logic. "If he wants to see if I can catch him, why would he decide now to run me down?"

"He could want you on your toes, unsure of when he's going to strike next. Or where." He sighed. "I should have walked you to your car. I'd have seen him approach."

"It wasn't your fault."

"I might not have caused it, but I should have prevented it."

Her head hurt too much to continue arguing. She pulled in a breath and sighed it out, long and loud.

He made a noise under his breath that sounded suspiciously like he was amused.

"It's not funny to laugh at someone that's hurt."

"How about explaining to someone who won't listen that they're in denial?"

"I'm not in denial. I have healthy reinforcement techniques." She shifted her whole body to look at him. It hurt less than twisting her neck, that was for sure. He really did seem worried about her. "I might throw up."

"Close your eyes."

She glared at him first.

"I'm going to the pharmacy. Otherwise, we won't make it to your place before you bite my head all the way off and chew it up."

"I need food." Before he could comment on her statement she said, "The Greek place on Castaneda Boulevard."

"That is so out of the way, it's not even—"

"There's no time to argue. We need to file a police report with Ryson." She folded her arms. If he wanted to throw in with her, he was going to have to prove himself. And if he didn't? Then she'd know this fake concern was all about keeping tabs on her for Stairns.

Jax flicked the blinker the same second he switched lanes. "At least you don't have a concussion."

"Amen to that."

Ten minutes later he pulled up outside the hole-in-the-wall Greek place. It was bustling despite the late hour, a crowd in one corner. People buzzing around. A waitress looked her up and down and made a face.

Kenna turned to Jax. "I have to pee. Get me a number four."

He looked at her and winced. "Don't take forever. We need to hit the pharmacy next door and then get to Ryson's." Jax pulled out his phone. "I'll let him know we're coming."

Kenna gave him as much of a nod as she could and trailed away to the back hall. Taking a quick look behind her to make sure Jax was occupied with ordering, she bypassed the bathroom door and hit the EXIT at the end, where she pushed outside.

At the corner of the building, she turned to the alley and set a brisk pace, inhaling fresh air like it was full of medicinal qualities, and not smog and pollution. Some places had it, like every state or national park she'd ever been to. Basically, anyplace outside with trees and open sky. Here, downtown? Not so much.

The apartment building was two blocks away.

She rode the elevator up and knocked on the door, then stood to the side so she wouldn't be seen out the peep hole.

The handle twisted and the door opened an inch. Kenna kicked it in. She heard a yelp and pushed her way inside. "What were you thinking?"

Steven Pierce, whose wife had just been brutally

murdered, stumbled back. She grabbed his shirt and shoved him against the wall. "Talk."

He gasped.

"You could have killed me. For all I know, you were trying to." His eyes filled. She realized then they were red rimmed, and she could smell alcohol on his breath. "You went on a rampage that wound up with me on my backside on the sidewalk with road rash."

He said nothing. A grieving husband who'd made a poor choice she didn't exactly fault him for.

Kenna shoved off him and paced away from his tears. Her head pounded. She was doing the same thing he was—taking her pain out on someone else. Only, he was the cause of hers.

Today's pain, anyway.

There was entirely too much of the past close to the surface. She could almost see Bradley's face in her mind's eye. *Thank You*. Only, it *hurt* to remember. It hurt so much to think about those last moments with him, when there was nothing but pain and despair.

Steven sagged to the floor and laid his forearms on his knees.

"Explain what you were trying to accomplish."

He hung his head.

"I should tell the police about this. It's a DUI, Steven."

"I didn't start drinking until I got home."

So he was *sober* when he almost ran her down? That almost made it worse. He hadn't gotten a significant head start, but it was enough. "I don't have much time. I need to get back to work, and your little stunt cost me a couple hours trying to find the man that killed your wife."

"Fat lot of good that's doing. You aren't any closer to catching the guy, and it's been *days*." His voice broke at the end. "Another woman was taken, and you've got nothing!"

"And killing me is going to help?"

"I was just so frustrated. You're the cause of all this, with that business card stuff. On the news they said it happened again, so I read a bunch of articles. Everyone knows you're the real target. But you aren't hurting. At all. You don't even know what this feels like."

She squeezed the bridge of her nose. "So you're the one that's been following me, right?" Aside from Eric Wilson and his GPS tracker. And the FBI.

No wonder that spot between her shoulder blades still itched.

He said nothing.

"Watching. Waiting for me to bring him in so you can hit him with your car while I'm walking him to his arraignment."

His mouth shifted. She saw in his expression the gaping hole that was now his life. Work that was meaningless, and he'd lost his job anyway. All his friends walking on eggshells, not knowing what to say. Hours alone in the apartment his wife had been ripped from. Empty, like his life.

Yeah, she didn't know what that felt like at all.

"Couldn't wait for the arrest, so you went for me." She gazed into his face. Despair, an old acquaintance of hers, looked back. "I'm sorry."

What else was she supposed to say? Catching the killer wasn't going to cure that anger—even if it did help, at least some. Relief wasn't going to be found by hurting someone else.

She leaned back against the opposite wall and stared at him. "You could've killed me."

He said nothing.

"I should tell the police it was you who tried to run me down tonight. Get them to arrest you. Watch you go to prison, so you can spend the next few years of your life in close quarters with the very person you hate. So when I *do* catch him, and I *will*, you'll get to be all up close and personal like you want to be. Might not go your way, though."

Judging by the way her phone vibrated in her back pocket, Jax had finally figured out she wasn't in the bathroom. He probably thought she'd been abducted by their suspect. She pulled out her phone and sent a text.

I'M FINE.

She waited for the indication he'd read it. Her phone started ringing again. *Jax.* She sent him to voicemail and stowed the phone in her back pocket again.

Steven looked sick. "I wasn't trying to kill you."

She wanted to mouth off. Instead, she shut her lips and tried to establish that balance between acknowledging his grief and her need to not be run over. Not to mention her being angry he'd tried. That was fully valid as far as reactions went.

Kenna held it in.

"She's..." Steven's expression dissolved into hiccupping sobs. "...gone. She's gone, and I can't get her back. She's not coming back. Her killer is still out there. Laughing at me. Watching me and laughing at me."

She couldn't promise she'd find this guy. After all, it might be a lie.

And she didn't want to discount his feelings by suggesting that the killer had likely moved on from the Pierces and was more likely watching her. Laughing at her. But what was she supposed to do with grief-induced paranoia?

Kenna hit the bathroom for a second of space and a

moment to think. She balled up a bunch of tissue in her hand and brought it back to give to Steven.

Instead of taking the tissue, Steven pulled on her arm. She tumbled forward, and he caught her in his arms, wrapped them around her, and held her against his chest.

Kenna shifted so her jacket fully covered her gun, her cheek pressed against a man shuddering through a steady stream of sobs. Pressure built in her sinuses. Her head hurt worse now.

She didn't know how long they sat like that. Locked in a kind of despair that never went away. Loneliness so bad it left icicles on her skin. Food didn't taste good. The sun wasn't warm. Laughter never came. Everything was lost, as though it had slipped away and vanished.

Someone cleared their throat. Kenna twisted, keeping her neck as straight as possible.

Jax stood in the doorway.

"Give me a second."

He disappeared again. She didn't figure he was out of earshot.

Steven shifted, tears still wet on his face. "Are you going to tell the police?"

"Are you ever going to do that again?"

He shook his head.

"The slack you get on that rope is not long."

"Don't want me to hang myself with it?"

She was glad he understood since she didn't have the mental capacity to explain her thought process. "You won't get the chance. I'd shoot you first."

On a whim of craziness, Kenna pressed a kiss to his cheek. Everything she wanted to say, she tried to put in her expression.

He nodded.

She clambered to her feet, ignoring how much it hurt. "Sober up. Find someone to talk to."

"Does that actually work?"

"I hope so." After all, it was what she'd told Ryson to do.

Kenna strode out to the hallway. Jax followed her to the elevator, where she jabbed at the button. "Don't."

He held up both hands. But the second the doors shut, he said, "Tell me the truth. Is Steven Pierce on a vigilante mission to find his wife's killer?"

"You think I'd lie to you?" After all, he'd felt the need to ensure she told him the truth.

"Answer the question. Do I need to worry about him?"

"Let's just work on finding Meg, okay?"

"Copy that."

If she caught the murderer and Steven intercepted and killed him, she would have to hand him over to the FBI. She wouldn't want to, but she would do it. Plenty of people lost loved ones in all kinds of tragic circumstances and they didn't react like this, even if they wanted to.

She couldn't take the risk he would harm an innocent person. Someone caught in the crossfire, or the wrong suspect. Anyone she stood with at any moment until this was over could get tagged with a bullet in the heat of the moment.

"Earth to Kenna."

She spun to him, and her phone buzzed in her pocket.

"I asked if you've gotten any links like last time."

She looked at her phone notification. "This is something else unrelated."

He nodded.

"You don't think I'd have told you if I got another link?"

It was the last thing she wanted, and yet another video was what everyone expected. Another woman murdered online. But Kenna hadn't had anything like what she'd been sent before, with Officer Pierce.

And that was what worried her.

That, and the fact her motorhome security system had just been tripped—and then quickly disabled.

Chapter Twenty-Three

Wednesday, 10:17pm.

K enna slid her gun from its holster and crept toward her motorhome. She passed a shiny RV. The TV flashed in the window where the inhabitant watched a late-night cop show. She was bone tired, and yet adrenaline rushed through her like a dam had burst and water issued forth in a torrent.

Jax had dropped her back at her car. She didn't doubt he'd followed—except for the fact he wasn't behind her.

She moved to her little white, picket-fenced patio area. A body lay sprawled on the faux grass beside the walkway between her outdoor living area and the door to her motorhome.

A man. Dark jacket. Jeans. His chest rose and fell slowly.

She could hear Cabot's dull bark.

The front door of her rig was open.

Kenna kicked the man's boot. He groaned and stirred.

Eric Wilson moaned. "Ugh. Ow." He started to sit, and she got a glance at his forehead.

"You look like you've been pistol whipped."

He worked his jaw. "Ow." Then touched the back of his head. "Where were you?"

Kenna's brows rose. "Excuse me?"

"He clocked me." Wilson twisted far enough to see her front door. "He broke in?"

"Assuming that isn't what *you* were trying to do."

"I didn't—"

"What did he look like? Did you get a good look at him?"

He shook his head, looking disappointed.

She sighed and stepped over his legs. "Don't move. If you leave, I'll track you down and finish what he started." Whatever that was. Kenna didn't figure he could put up much of a fight.

Someone had surprised him and broken in. But that didn't mean Wilson was here for benign reasons. Probably snooping for a story still. As if she would be his exclusive. Or tell him anything about her father.

Kenna listened at the bottom of her front step.

Inside was clear. She strode to the bedroom area. Cabot had gone quiet.

The bedroom area was empty. She checked the closet, though it wasn't big enough for an adult. No one ran for the front door.

The bathroom was the only place left.

She twisted the handle down.

Cabot sat in the shower, head low. Cowering. Whining.

Kenna crouched and held out her free hand. "Oh, baby."

The dog approached slowly. Each paw at a time, body shaking. Kenna ran her hand from the dog's cheek, back past her shoulder as Cabot walked almost into a hug and set her chin on Kenna's shoulder. "I know. It's okay." She rubbed the dog's side and found a sore spot. Cabot whined.

"Someone kicked you? And stuffed you in the bathroom?" She rubbed Cabot's face. "I've shot people for less than that before."

"Hey—"

Cabot barked, body braced. Kenna turned and stared along the top of her gun.

Wilson lifted his hands and took a half step back. "Don't shoot." He frowned. "Is your dog okay?"

"Don't expect her to be your best friend anytime soon." She stood and motioned to the front of the RV impatiently. "Now back up to the door." She needed him out of her space. More than one person—and a dog—was too many in the tight hall between the bedroom and living area. It had been bad enough with just Jax.

"Should I shut the door?"

Kenna grabbed a bacon-flavored treat from under the sink and let Cabot sniff it. "Go lay down."

The dog took her treat to her bed and held it between her paws to chew on the end.

"She seems okay."

Kenna wasn't going to make that assessment so quickly. Who knew what the dog had already been through before Kenna took her in, or how she would react to this?

She studied her living space. Something niggled at the back of her mind. The bedroom. She strode back to her closet and looked at the shelf. She must not have registered the blank space on the shelf as she'd headed for the bathroom.

Now it was clear what they'd been here for.

Kenna slid out her phone and dialed Ryson. When he answered, he sounded like she'd woken him.

"Someone broke into my motorhome and took a lockbox from the closet that had my father's gun inside."

"Does it work?" Rustling in the background punctuated his words. Getting dressed?

"It's old, but it works. I use it once in a while at the range."

"I'll send a unit, and I'll be there in ten to get a report filed."

"I don't need cops tromping around my home. Just you." She did need that report filed, plus she figured Jax had already told him about Steven. If the gun was used in commission of a crime, she would be responsible unless she could back up the fact it'd been taken. "But we can do this in the morning."

The rustling stopped. "Why'd you call if you don't want me to come over?"

"Because the FBI will want corroboration that my father's gun was taken, and the time stamp on the call will help."

"Then you should've called someone they know for certain wouldn't lie for you."

Kenna stared at the texturing on the wall.

"Don't get all sappy on me now. It's just the truth."

"I'm covering myself," she said. "For when all this inevitably comes back to bite me."

"Easier to cover yourself if you're a thousand miles away when something happens and they want to pin it on you."

Like she hadn't thought about doing that? "It's what they wanted two years ago."

"Now they want you here—" Ryson fired back. "—to pin this on you?"

"I don't get it any more than you. But it is what it is and I'm not living with a warrant out, on the run from a grudge because of something I *might* do but have no intention of doing. They can't be bothered to even ask me how I feel about it all, or what I want. It's all about covering themselves either way."

Her father might've wanted to tell his story, along with plenty of embellishing. She didn't. In fact, she'd go so far as to admit to anyone who asked that the FBI had actually done her a favor, kicking her out. Life as a PI was preferable to that of an FBI agent. She could go where she wanted, work whatever case she wanted. Paperwork was minimal. Regulations were minimal.

She hadn't been under anyone's thumb until she came back here.

"I'll come see you at work tomorrow. Get the report done in writing."

"I hope you know what you're doing." Ryson hung up.

"You think this will bite you?"

Kenna shoved her phone in her back pocket. "What do you want, Eric?"

He studied her.

"It's late." She prodded.

"That's the only time he'll meet with anyone."

"Who?"

"The computer guy who runs the website."

"Death Files. The Murder Class."

Eric nodded. "He's the one who got me in. He said he'll talk to you, but no cops."

There was more to it than that. She was pretty sure. "Right now?"

He looked at the time on the oven display. "An hour ago. But I'll explain to him why we got held up."

"You need a doctor? He clocked you pretty good and you were unconscious." Kind of like she'd been earlier, after Steven Pierce and his car. Kenna needed eighteen hours of sleep.

"I'm okay." Still, he winced.

"Let me know if you're not." She pulled a can of diet soda from the fridge and offered it. He accepted. "Don't mess with a head injury. You need that noggin for crime reporting."

His expression softened with amusement. "Like you need yours to catch bad guys."

"Don't go soft." She grabbed another soda for herself. It would keep her awake. "They'll eat you alive."

He turned for the door. "Follow me there?"

She nodded. Cabot came with her in the car, and she brought the dog up to the front door on a leash.

"I sent him a text that we're here." Eric stopped beside her at the door.

Cabot sat by her left leg. Kenna looked down. "Perhaps there's hope for you yet. I'm thinking search and rescue training."

Even though training Cabot as a cadaver dog was probably a better fit for Kenna's career, she'd still rather find living people.

The door opened. The man inside was at least six-three, with Christmas hats decorating his pajama pants, above which he wore a black T-shirt that featured My Little Pony characters on a periodic table. Kenna blinked.

"This her?" He shoved a fall of black hair off his forehead and took a step back, opening the door all the way.

"Kenna Banbury, this is Arnie Heraldson." Eric stepped in ahead of her.

She followed. "Nice to meet you, Arnie."

"I thought you'd be shorter."

She eyed him until Cabot tugged on the leash, so she gave the dog a little slack to sniff around the entryway. "What did you want to tell me?"

Arnie said nothing about an animal in his space, so she figured it was good with him. "I'll show you."

Furniture in the living room consisted of a dark blue couch and a well-worn recliner. A few empty beer bottles on the coffee table, along with shoe scuff marks. Lamp on, the shade had been torn by something. Blinds closed in the windows. A bike had been propped against the hallway wall. One bedroom had been converted into an office of sorts, and the room at the end, she assumed, was the bedroom.

Odor emanating from the bathroom didn't make her want to take a look-see in there. She wasn't one to judge. It was just that in the close quarters of a motorhome, odors weren't what you wanted hanging around. She and her father had a pact involving a metal tin of matches she kept in her bathroom to this day. Still, lemon scented bathroom cleaner was a far favorable scent.

The office at the end of the hall had a wall of computer monitors along with two TVs hung above. Multiple fans worked hard to combat the warmth of electronics. The contents of a network closet were stacked on plastic storage shelves in one corner, a hodgepodge of systems equipment this guy had probably hardwired into the best internet connection he could get in his neighborhood. With a backup just in case that went down.

"Nice setup."

Arnie settled into a gamer chair he probably spent more time in than his bed. There was also a couch in here. She wondered if he used the bedroom much at all.

Cabot got bored of sniffing around and lay down against the wall. Kenna dropped the leash so she didn't pull on it inadvertently. If the dog was willing to relax, it was probably a good indication there wasn't imminent danger. Or she'd had a rough night and was exhausted. Kind of like Kenna.

She didn't want to rush the guy, but he typed for several minutes before she said, "Is this going to take long?"

Eric shot her a look. She didn't much care to apologize. The two of them both looked like they'd been through an altercation, and it was late. Arnie had to at least be aware of one of them. Kenna needed sleep if she wanted any hope of not snapping at everyone she met tomorrow.

"There." Arnie pointed to the TV on the wall, the one on the right. The left displayed a paused YouTube video of someone playing a particularly gruesome video game. On the right were lines of code.

"You'll have to translate that into English for us non-native speakers."

"It's code for the website."

"Death Files."

Arnie nodded.

"Which you run."

"I'm paid to maintain it. What *that* shows me, is someone got into the underlying code and made some changes. They can alter whatever they want, and not just because they gave themselves admin rights. It's deeper than that."

"If they're so sneaky, how'd you notice?"

"The first video. That police officer?" He swallowed, finally expressing some emotion. He said nothing else.

"Her name was Jessica Pierce. What was your involvement in that?"

"They sent over the video, and I posted it. But they interrupted the feed part way through and took over. I wasn't even watching it. I got an alert when it happened, and by the time I checked, it was gone from the main site, shifted to another one I don't have credentials for."

"And you didn't report this to the police or FBI? You had to have seen her face on the news."

"Give the cops access to my system?" He looked disgusted.

"Why tell me now?"

"You're a PI, right? Eric said it'd help. Assuming you don't turn me in."

"Tell me the rest."

"The other woman that went missing? They were supposed to send me a video for that one, too. I had planned to send you the link when I posted it. But they never sent it to me."

"You're the one who sent the first link?"

He nodded.

"The FBI will consider you an accessory."

"I didn't know what it was!"

"Yet you were content to profit from it." She didn't have to tell him what that made him. It was doubtful he'd suddenly start feeling remorse now. "How did they send the money?"

"To my bitcoin account."

Thomas could probably trace it but that meant giving the FBI access to Arnie's financials. It would mean the killer would discover there was a case against him. However, it could also be key in finding the missing young woman.

"How do they contact you?"

Arnie motioned to his phone.

"Burner?"

"They gave it to me."

The FBI computer tech would love to get his hands on that. Kenna would as well, she just had limited ability to comb through it and find evidence. "Who are 'they'?"

He hadn't indicated it was one person. Or was it simply easier to refer to them as the unknown.

"I have no idea."

"You're gonna want to come up with one fast. They kidnapped a young woman, and if you know anything—"

"I don't!"

"When they find out you're connected, the FBI is going to ask. It'll be better for you if you can give them something more solid than, 'I have no idea.'"

He groaned. "Death Files was just for fun, you know? A fetish thing. Who cares if no one gets hurt?"

"Now it's not fun. It's being used to broadcast murder."

"I'm gonna shut the whole thing down."

"Not yet you aren't."

Leaving it live could help the case, the way she'd attempted to do when she went on the chat page.

"Did anyone come to you about surveillance and security on a motorhome?"

He shook his head.

"How about opening a lockbox with biometric security?" They'd have had to get her fingerprint. Or bypass the lock somehow. When he shook his head again, she said, "You just jumped on this because they offered you money to post on your site."

"Are you kidding? I've had *thousands* of new hits the last week. The website is *blowing up* like you wouldn't believe." He groaned. "Shutting it down is gonna suck."

"Yeah, that's probably why they picked you."

Duped by money and the promise of "hits," he'd played right into their hands...right up until he got himself arrested for his part in this. Then they wouldn't have to pay the rest of what they'd promised him. "Meanwhile they've covered their tracks well enough the FBI might not be able to figure out who they are. Which leaves you holding the bag."

This wasn't a garden variety killer just in it for the rush of ending a life. This was someone with technical skills enough to manipulate a website-streaming video. Enough to mask their identity on the feed. This was a person who wanted the rush of having the power of life over death, but also wanted fame with it. They wanted to best her. To give the FBI the runaround.

It was personal. Directed at her.

It was skilled.

That, at least in part, explained the choice of the second victim—Jessica Pierce. They'd met almost as soon as Kenna got to town. A cop, so they could prove themselves. Kenna had never met Meg Parabuchio, and her computer program still hadn't finished digging into the young woman's life. When it did, she might find a connection that tied all four of them together—Kenna and the three victims—or she might not.

Even if the two women and the dead old man taken were connected to Kenna, that still didn't clue her in as to who was behind this. The FBI needed access to everything that might be useful in identifying their suspect.

"One woman is already dead, and another is missing. You're sitting on information that could help find Meg and bring those who killed a cop to justice."

His eyes flared when she'd said, "Meg."

Arnie said, "Why do you think you're here?"

The fact he was purveyor of a website all about killing people, one that drew fanatics, gave her serious pause. "I think you know exactly who these people are. Even if you don't know that you know."

She stared him down, sitting in his computer master throne. He was probably head wizard or whatever in some gamer crowd. "Give everything to me. I'll pass it on and tell the FBI I got it from an anonymous source."

She wanted to go through the website registry and figure out which visitor was her most likely suspect.

He started to hedge.

"This person has a goal, and whatever that is involves you being destroyed. When this is done, you're either dead or in jail. Same as me." Before he could argue, she continued, "I figure that puts us somewhere on the same side in this. And when we're done, Eric can tell the world the truth. Maybe someone will listen."

Arnie glanced at his friend. Eric shrugged, but he didn't manage to hide his excitement. Arnie was hiding things from her, but the simple fact he might hand over evidence that could help was worth the risk. She didn't have to worry about kick back from the FBI unless that was for the purpose of arresting her. The feds would probably arrest Arnie and Eric as her accomplices.

This could turn into a mess quickly, but if they got Meg back and brought Jessica's killers to justice, it didn't matter.

Arnie pulled a flash drive from a drawer and stuck it into a port on the tower by his leg. "You won't tell the cops this came from me?"

"What if you were in danger and doing so was going to save your life?"

He didn't like that idea much.

"I know you're trusting me with this. The same way Meg is trusting us to find her before she's killed." She needed to ask one more question. "Couple days ago, I got into your chat room. Was that you talking to me?"

"Part of the deal." At least he looked apologetic. Just not about his website or his part in murder. "Keep giving you the runaround."

Kenna pressed her lips together. She needed to get onto another topic.

His name would come out eventually, and he'd be in trouble. She just didn't know exactly how bad that would be for him. She tried to have a live-and-let-live policy, for the most part. Keeping herself accountable—and stable and sane—was a fulltime job. Other people had to be responsible for their own words and actions.

"They were supposed to send you a new video to post?"

He nodded. "Nothing yet."

"That's longer than it took with Officer Pierce."

"What does that mean?" Eric asked.

"I'm not sure." Kenna glanced at Cabot while she thought about it. The dog looked rested, but her eyes were alert and on Kenna. Her phone rang in her pocket.

"I'm going to figure it out." She pulled out her phone, which said *Jaxton Calling.* "I have to take this."

Arnie handed her the flash drive. Before he let go, he said, "I don't need the feds busting down my door at two in the morning."

She nodded, clicked her fingers and stowed the flash drive in her pocket while Cabot padded beside her to the front door.

She took the leash and answered the phone on the front step. "Banbury."

After a second of silence, Jax spoke. "There's another body."

She stopped beside her car door. "Meg?"

"No. This one is male."

"So how—"

"Your business card."

On a man's body, like Christopher Halpert.

She let Cabot in the backseat and stood beside the car. "Any idea who he is?" Another serial killer left for her, maybe. That didn't fit with a missing woman still out there.

"We're running his prints and the serial number of the revolver left with the body."

Kenna's voice caught, "A revolver?"

"Yep. It's old, too."

Kenna rattled off a series of numbers.

"How did you—"

"Just tell me where you are."

Chapter Twenty Four

Thursday, 12:19am.

"I 'll text you the address. When you get here, you can tell me how you know this weapon." Jax hung up.

Kenna stood beside her car and stared down the street.

"What's going on?"

She spun to Wilson. "Another dead person with my business card, killed with the gun that was stolen from my motorhome.

He looked ready to bolt for his car. "Is it Meg?"

She shook her head, hesitated, and then simply said, "A guy. Empty lot. Similar to Jessica Pierce."

"That's what they hit me for?" He rubbed the back of his head. "So they could commit murder with your gun?"

"They stole a lockbox with biometric security containing an heirloom gun that belonged to my father, then managed to break into it and use the gun to murder a man in the last—what?" She glanced at her phone screen. "Couple hours?"

"Your gun. Your card as well, you say?"

She nodded. Her privacy invaded—and for what? A murder weapon, when any knife or gun off the street would do. It wasn't like getting ahold of a gun was hard these days. Especially for someone with motive and criminal connections.

But they'd chosen her father's. And it, without question, linked her to the crime.

If they'd wanted to implicate her with a weapon, they could have chosen to take the one at the small of her back, but they chose the gun she kept on a shelf in the closet. Locked up.

Who even knew it was there? She only got it out a couple times a year, shot with it at the range, cleaned it, and put it back in the lockbox. Usually on her dad's birthday. Or thanksgiving. Both. Motivated by nostalgia, or a desire to feel connected to him.

The surveillance had to have stretched back weeks for anyone to have known she had the weapon.

There weren't many parts of her past she was in the habit of recalling without being drenched in buckets of guilt. Guilt that led to days of despair, thinking of what she could've, or should've, done differently.

No, this wasn't about an invasion of privacy. It was more than that. It was about the world stealing what little she had left that meant something to her. A mind game.

That old song played in her mind. *You can have this whole world...* A lovely sentiment, but it was so hard to lose those pieces of who she was. Of those she'd lost.

Eric frowned. "They want to make it look like you're the one who killed him."

She might be able to trust Eric, but she also didn't. She'd only met him a few days ago. She hadn't even done a full background check yet.

"And left your business card."

"So, it's a statement." She forced her brain to let go of the emotion—mostly by shoving it aside—to process the facts. "Ok, so I kill him with my father's gun and leave my card. Like I'm on some vigilante revenge plan, same as with the old man, Christopher Halpert. Dropping bad guys with my throwback weapon. A legacy my father would be proud of."

"It's a theory." His eyes flashed.

She caught it. "More than that."

"Fine." His cheeks flushed red. "It's also a great story."

"In my experience, great stories are usually far from the truth of what actually happened. No one wants to remember how things were. They'll tell a story that sounds good because it's safer than reality."

"But if it gets hits, then who cares?" Eric said.

"My father would've liked you."

His flush deepened. He didn't know that wasn't a compliment.

Her phone buzzed with the text from Jax. "The FBI is there now, at the murder scene."

"And you're going, when you're a suspect?" He would probably follow so he could document everything for his podcast.

When she showed up, they would haul her down to the office and question her for hours about her whereabouts at the time of the murder.

Kenna just shrugged.

"You've been with me the whole time."

She had to concede that point. If the time of death was after she'd arrived at the RV park, he could stand for her alibi.

"Unless the dead guy was killed between the time you were hit, and the time I showed up at my place to find you." She leaned back against the car and folded her arms. Had whoever it was broken into her safe that fast? "Either way, the cops and FBI aren't busy finding that missing woman and neither am I if we're all running around because there's a dead man. Pointing fingers at each other and getting distracted by extraneous information that might lead to his killer but won't find the victim."

Wilson's expression darkened. "The missing girl is probably already dead. Something happened that wasn't according to plan and they couldn't make the video. This guy had to die because of it."

It was speculation, but she decided to run with his version. Truth be told, part of her did miss bouncing ideas off another person and not the walls of her motorhome. "They killed this guy for some reason, because of Meg. Or in spite of her, maybe?"

But how did the dead man fit into all of it? She had no idea. Another victim left with her business card. A gift, like Christopher Halpert had been? A serial murderer killed by a vigilante, single-handedly bringing down violent criminals.

Why go to the trouble of stealing her father's gun to do the deed? That didn't make sense at all, given it was cropping up now and not from the start. If it had been used to kill Christopher Halpert, then maybe. But it wasn't.

A copycat killing. Someone incited by the first video and called to action. A viewer who'd taken up the call to kill and try to get away with it. But again, why take her gun to do the deed? The fact she'd been drawn in initially seemed like a poor attempt to implicate her now. Why change the narrative?

At the least, it was a way to distract the feds—and Kenna —from finding Meg. Was the killer scrambling for more time? Off the plan. Reacting on the fly. Good. That was how suspects make mistakes.

"How are you going to find her?"

Kenna fingered the flash drive in her hand. If she went to her motorhome for her laptop, it wouldn't be long before the FBI showed up. After that, she'd be unable to sift through the information and try to figure out who these people were.

"I need to get on a computer." The public library wouldn't open for hours, though. She needed space with no distractions. "If the FBI is going to drag me in, then I need to comb through this stuff and find something on whoever is doing this." She waved the flash drive.

The alternative was to sit and do nothing, waiting for everything to crash down on her again. At least this time the fallout would be considerably smaller—her life had barely any scope to it these days, and that was how she liked it. She wouldn't be caught unaware, injured and in the hospital. Grieving. Her back would never be up against a wall ever again.

Kenna had to maintain the wherewithal to fight. She didn't have a relationship to lose this time, well, except for Cabot. And she was not going to lose another dog. That meant finding a quiet, safe place to look into this website and whoever had contacted Arnie to post the first video.

"My house." He winced, despite the offer. "You should go to my house."

"Worried I'll see your underwear on the floor?" Kenna studied him. No, that wasn't what he was worried about.

Eric desperately wanted to be a part of this. Whether that was for good, or ill, she didn't yet know. He was after inside information, but he'd have to prove to her that he was trustworthy in order to get it.

She would totally feel like she was snooping even if she wasn't. But she did want to know if she could trust him. A peek into his home would give her a better indication if she could, at least to an extent.

Jax expected her to show up at the crime scene. He was probably waiting for her right now. When he realized she wasn't coming, the FBI was going to start looking for her. Assuming her no-show was a display of guilt, couching it in terms like "person of interest" and "material witness." As if she would ever believe they didn't have it out for her.

Sooner or later the governor would find out she was back in Salt Lake City. Then she would be approached by someone who worked for him. Marched all the way to his mansion, and politely—very politely—asked what she thought she was doing here.

The FBI might look for her at Eric Wilson's house. Eventually. It just wouldn't be the first place they went.

"They'll think you really are working with me. If I'm at your house, the FBI will be sure we're cohorts." She wasn't partnering with him, but if she wanted his help, she was going to have to give him at least some part of what he wanted. "I'll give you an exclusive." She swallowed and forced the rest of the words out. "I'll come on the podcast and talk about this case, or my father, but not my last case as an FBI agent—"

His eyes lit. He probably thought he could persuade her to talk about everything.

"—if it finds this girl…" She saw in his face that he understood her. This wasn't about them. It was about the victim caught up in this. "I'll need your address, and I've got to use your computer for a while."

"If it finds that girl." He shrugged. "You're right. How can I argue with that? She's got to be terrified. Being tortured. You can find her, right?"

"That's the plan."

Kenna knew he had to be right about Meg's current situation. Unless he'd been right earlier, and Meg was already dead. Something had to have gone wrong, otherwise there would've been another video by now. Another chance to rub his prowess in their faces.

"I have to get going."

Eric stepped back. "I'll talk to Arnie." He rattled off an address, then glanced at Cabot. "Don't let your dog bother my cat. She'll probably just hide under the bed, so keep the mutt out of the bedroom and away from her."

"Thanks." She figured he was only doing this for the exclusive. Not many people would allow a stranger free rein in their home. "I won't snoop."

"Yeah, you will. But I don't have much to hide." He walked back to the house.

Kenna threaded her car through the grid of city streets while humanity buzzed around her. As it turned out, Eric's house wasn't too far from Arnie's. A square, white structure with a concrete front step and chain link fence around the yard of sparse grass. A dead tree hung frozen branches over the front walk, reaching out like dead fingers.

Kenna sat in her car and watched the front of the house. Cabot could run around out here while she was inside. At least until the temperature dropped much more.

She twisted and ruffled the dog's chin. "Promise you won't eat Eric's cat. I don't think he'd like it."

Before she could get out, Ryson called.

She answered, "Hey."

"The FBI is looking for you and all you can say is, 'hey'?"

Kenna eased back in the seat and continued her study of the house. "*Looking*-looking, or just looking?"

"Am I supposed to know what that even means?"

"Valentina would."

"Probably." He paused. "And she's good, by the way. We're...better."

"Did you talk to someone?"

"Uh, yeah. I talked to you."

She rolled her eyes. "You know what I mean."

"I will." His voice softened. "Appreciate it."

"So you said. Now help me evade the feds long enough to find that missing girl."

There was a long pause on Ryson's end. "What've you got?"

"Nothing but a flash drive. Yet."

Eric had already sent her details for the spot where he kept a hidden key. As she got out of the car, she explained to Ryson about the email address and whoever had sent Arnie the video to post online. Before he'd sent the link to her phone.

"So Eric's friend is in the thick of this?"

"I'm not going to tell you his name."

"You already know that's withholding evidence. Puts you in touching distance of accessory after the fact. Gonna tell me now?"

"Later."

"This who you are now?"

"Yes." She slammed her door shut. "It is who I am now. Sorry to disappoint you." She rounded the car and let Cabot into the front yard. "All I've got is me and all I trust is me, so I investigate by myself and find the victim because no one else is looking hard enough or in the right places."

Kind of like the way she'd found Sarah Bestman.

"Well, this time you've got help."

"The FBI is pointing their finger at me. Do you think they care like you do about catching Jessica Pierce's killer? If you're all caught up in this new development, then nobody is looking for Meg."

More silence.

"You know I'm right."

"So you're gonna do this alone, or do you want my help?"

Kenna thought about the door to her motorhome being open and Eric lying on the ground unconscious. Then she thought about Valentina, and baby Luci. "I don't need your help."

"Doesn't mean I won't be there."

"What I want doesn't factor? Sorry, but I've had enough of that the past few years. I do what I want now." She almost hung up. The fact it was Ryson on the other end made her hesitate.

"That's how it was supposed to be all along. They kicked you out, and you just walked away with no fight."

"I didn't just walk away." She looked at the cloud cover, lit from above by the afternoon sun.

"No, you crawled. Licking your wounds."

"You don't—"

"Tell me."

Her chest ached at his tone.

"It's been two years. Will you please tell me?"

She squeezed her eyes shut against the gathering moisture. The days she'd spent in the hospital after Bradley's death, following the first surgery. She'd refused to see Ryson and Valentina.

After Stairns, and then Collins, and then Stairns again, she hadn't been able to face anyone. Not with all the tests and procedures. Poked. Prodded and scraped. Even a friendly face belonging to a trusted friend was much too much for the fragile state she'd been in. She'd told the nurse to make him leave.

"Why did you let them do it to you?"

"Bradley wasn't killed by Almatter." She sucked in half a

breath, all the air she could get. "He couldn't handle the fear, thinking about what was going to happen. He couldn't walk. He thought he'd be the reason I was killed. I tried to convince him to stay with me, but he..." She couldn't even say it.

"He what?"

Kenna's stomach roiled. "He lost hope."

"Your partner killed himself."

"The governor didn't want the story to get out. They wanted Bradley to go into politics after the FBI." They couldn't handle anyone thinking he would've quit. "Pacer and Stairns leaned on Taylor to say whatever it is she ended up writing to prove I couldn't handle the job anymore."

"So you accepted it all and walked away."

"The day Stairns..." The lump in her throat cut her off.

"Tell me."

The soft tone of his voice drew a lump up to her throat. "...he said I was done. And that Doctor Landstadt agreed I wasn't fit to be an agent anymore. And then..." She couldn't get the words out.

"Tell me, Kenna."

"I lost the baby I was carrying. In the hospital, recovering from what happened with Almatter, losing everything. I lost my baby, too. Six weeks along. I'll never know if it was a girl or a boy."

"You don't move. You stay exactly where you are and I'll be there in three minutes, but you've gotta give me the address."

She swiped at her cheeks. "I'm fine, Ryson."

A black SUV pulled onto the street and headed for her car.

She swiped harder, using her sleeve. The ever-present twinge in her forearms reminded her of the worst week of her life. Her boyfriend. Her partner. Her job. Her baby. Her life, and her future. All of it.

Gone.

"Kenna. You're not fine."

The driver's door opened. "Jax is here." She turned for the hidden key spot and let herself in while Cabot barked.

Kenna hung up the phone, not even sure what she was doing. Retreating. Searching for a spot where she could have solitude and pretend the world wasn't looking to take what she had built for the last two years.

Her breath came in gasps as she moved through the hall. Living room. Dining room. Old carpet, mediocre furniture. Masculine décor. Not much on the walls but some old newspaper front pages he'd framed. *Serial Murderer Caught* and *Famous Investigator Solves Cold Case.* Bookshelves lined the hall, stuffed full of tattered paperbacks.

"Kenna!" His voice bellowed to her.

She kept walking.

A sensation settled in her bones like a flash of premonition. What—? And then it hit her. The atmosphere, and that heavy feeling in the air. The smell.

"Jax!" She stopped at the bedroom door.

He thundered down the hall. "Running away, really? Do you realize how that looks, when I'm trying to convince Stairns this is all too easy?"

His eyes scanned her face, and then his head jerked back.

Great. He knew she'd been crying.

There was a lot there, in what he'd said, and they'd have to address it later. But for now, she had to mention the pressing issue. "That's not our biggest problem."

"A man is dead, and I don't think—"

Kenna nudged the bedroom door open with her elbow and was immediately assailed by the color red. The bedcovers.

The walls. Above the bed hung a canvas print that depicted a bound woman. Red paint sprayed from an inflicted wound. The photo taken between heartbeats.

But that wasn't what had her attention.

Their missing young woman lay on the bed below the print.

Chapter Twenty Five

Thursday, 12:46am.

"Y ou can't be here." Jax sounded exasperated. Any other time she'd be amused at the ruffling of his feathers. "We need to have a conversation about the dead guy. I'll call this in. Don't touch anything and don't go anywhere."

Kenna studied the body while Jax made his calls behind her. She checked that the carpet was clear and then took a couple of steps. Several business cards lay on the bloody corpse. No clothing. Multiple knife wounds. This woman's end had included moments of terror and fighting for her life.

"You let her in there?" That was Miller. *Great.*

"I'm done." Kenna flipped her hands in the air and rolled her eyes. She strode past him to the hall, where Jax had his phone to his ear.

"Understood." He hung up. "Care to explain why you're here, and so is our missing young woman?"

If she pushed it, he'd haul her down to the office for a chat in interrogation. Kenna didn't want to be on the opposite side of that table, where Eric Wilson had been. Not when Meg's murderer was still out there, and she had nothing to do with it.

"I know why I'm here. As for Meg—" She motioned over her shoulder. "—I have no idea."

"Not good enough, considering I just came from a scene where a man was shot with a gun that belongs to you."

"You only know that because I all *but* told you the gun was mine," Kenna said. "And why would I do that if it incriminated me?"

"Some might be inclined to believe it's because you want to be famous again."

Miller leaned in. "Yeah, me."

She shivered. Not just at the idea of being in the spotlight. "Can you back off?"

He didn't. Not until Jax made it clear he should.

She put her hands in her pockets. Right. Two bodies, and all she had was a flash drive from Arnie Heraldson that she wouldn't be looking at anytime soon. "I didn't know she'd be here. And if I did that to her—" She motioned over her shoulder. "—there would be blood on me."

"So you took a shower. Cleaned up."

She turned to Miller. "Do I look cleaned up to you? Or am I wearing the same clothes I was wearing at the bowling alley? The ones I was nearly *run over in.*"

Kenna blew out a breath. She needed to get a handle on herself or they would take her in.

Miller's eyes narrowed. "Who ran you over?"

"I said nearly."

"What are you talking about? What happened?"

"Because now you care?"

He leaned in. "If you're killed, we'll never figure out what exactly you did to all these people now, will we?"

Kenna bit the inside of her lip. She asked Jax, "Is CSU coming?"

"Of course."

"Stairns?"

Jax frowned. "He wants you brought in for questioning about the dead guy and your gun. He doesn't even know about this yet."

Miller said, "He's no contact until seven tomorrow morning."

This hallway was getting entirely too crowded. "I need to go outside."

Jax nodded and followed her out. "Miller, stay here."

More agents had congregated outside, as had several residents. Kenna looked around to see where Cabot had gone, probably hiding in a shadowed corner because of all the people out here. "You can't think I did that, Jax."

What was it he'd said before? That he was trying to convince Stairns this was too easy.

"Right now I don't know what to think about any of— what are you doing?"

"Looking for my dog."

"You don't need to be worried about the mutt. Right now you need to be worried about you. This is serious, Kenna."

"You think I don't know that?" She folded her arms. The tension helped her think past the ache. "Christopher Halpert was killed. Then Jessica Pierce. Then a guy gets shot with my gun, completely breaking whatever pattern this was becoming, and now this woman is dumped here. It makes no sense."

"What do you mean dumped?"

"She wasn't killed here. Blood would've pooled on the comforter underneath her. She also wasn't cleaned up and re-dressed like Pierce. I'd be inclined to think it was someone else entirely." She winced. "Someone angry."

"The old man—Halpert—was killed somewhere else."

"What about the man shot with my father's gun, the one I reported stolen?" Unfortunately, Eric Wilson was her alibi on that. A man now suspected of murdering a woman.

She pulled out her phone and sent him a text telling him to stay away from his house for a couple of days. Maybe stay with Arnie. But also to keep her apprised of his whereabouts —just in case she needed to find him.

He replied with a question followed by two more texts, also both questions.

She replied only with, "Later." And stowed the phone. "Where is my dog?" Kenna passed Jax and crossed the front yard. "Cabot, where you at?"

Jax walked with her but, given the noises he was making under his breath, he wasn't happy about it.

"I need a flashlight." There was one in the trunk of her car. "Was she out here when you showed up?"

"Maybe." He frowned. "I think so."

"And now the gate is open?" No, Cabot hadn't run off. She wouldn't. She had to be here somewhere hiding. "Cabot. Come here, girl."

"Jaxton."

She didn't care what Miller had to say. She checked the dark alley on the side of the house in case Cabot was hiding by the trash cans. When she didn't find the dog, Kenna headed back to the front to check the other side of the house.

As she passed Jax, he said, "Do you have any business cards on you—"

She nearly tripped, then spun around to face him.

"—for Utah True Crime."

Kenna pulled the small billfold from the inside pocket of her coat and slid out the card. "Just one."

Jax put it in an evidence bag.

Wait. "The business cards on the body?"

He nodded, assessing her with that disapproving expression.

She'd assumed those were hers as well. Though, why leave multiple? That wasn't a calling card. Tossing down several seemed more like a move of frustration and to make a point, kind of like the way that young woman had been killed.

Which made no sense except to implicate Eric as involved, and frustrated because he was getting no attention.

She walked to the other side of the house. Whoever killed Jessica Pierce had been a whole lot more methodical. It was meant to have been precise. A killer, proving to everyone he could get away with whatever he wanted.

Then a man was killed with her dad's gun. That could be unrelated, someone who'd been watching the news and learned of her name through her business cards, leaving a body for the cops. Doing the world a favor.

Now someone kills a young woman in a rage.

Pierce's killer, but now he'd snapped?

Kenna had reached the other side of the house. Still no Cabot. She turned to the gathered crowd of agents she used to work with. "Okay, listen up. Who here saw my dog when you pulled up?"

Someone must have. The alternative was that they were careless and oblivious, not exactly the kind of FBI agents you wanted working your case.

A couple of people shrugged.

"Someone saw her. She was out here." Frustration burned in her stomach. "Where did she go? One of you must've left the gate open."

Cabot might have run out after the feds ran in.

She swallowed the lump of emotion in her throat and strode through the gate with Jax still on her tail.

"Tell me where Eric Wilson is."

"I will. After we find Cabot."

"She's a stray—"

She spun to him. "She's *not* a stray." She wasn't entirely Kenna's dog. Not yet. Loyalty took time. "We need to find her. She might be hurt." Alone, in the dark.

"Where is Eric Wilson?"

She kept moving. "Not here."

"You need to tell me. He needs to be locked down so we can get to the bottom of this, not running around who-knows-where."

"He's fine." Eric had been with her. Which meant Kenna could potentially be his alibi. And how would that help him when she had zero credibility with the FBI? They'd think he was as guilty as her. "He's with a friend."

One who'd given her evidence she should turn over to the FBI. Which she would, *after* she looked it over herself. She was a private investigator, and this was her case. If that young woman hadn't been in Eric's bed in his murder-fan bedroom—not that she wanted to even think about that freaky decor any longer—she'd already have gone through the flash drive.

She'd have copied everything to Jax so the FBI could use their resources to track down the person behind the web videos.

A police unit pulled up behind the farthest black SUV and Ryson got out.

"Lieutenant! Thank you for coming. I'm not sure..."

He ignored Jax and came right for her.

Kenna remembered what she'd told him on the phone. "Don't."

Ryson shook his head. "I told you I was coming. I said stay where you were."

"Maybe if I had I wouldn't have found our missing woman."

"Nope. You're not going to distract me. This isn't about that." He walked all the way up into her space. "This is about what you told me on the phone."

Kenna shook her head. "Just help me find my dog!" A couple of tears began their descent. She swiped them away with the hem of her sleeves. She realized Ryson hadn't even met her dog, yet. Didn't even know about Cabot. "She's an abandoned dog I rescued."

He looked at her with pity. "Kenna, Bear isn't—"

"I'm not talking about Bear!" She checked under one of the SUVs, in case the dog was hiding. "Where are you, girl? Cabot!"

As she continued to search, she could heard the two of them murmuring behind her and whirled around. "This is none of his business." If Ryson told Jax... "Don't tell him."

"Kenna—"

"I'm trying to find my dog."

"Your dog ran off." Ryson's tone was too gentle. "He's gone, Kenna. Just like Bradley." He shook his head.

"No, not Bear. I rescued Cabot. Ask Jax." She couldn't believe this. "You really think I'm having a mental breakdown?"

"It would be understandable, given what you told me." Ryson moved to her. "No one would blame you."

She leaned in and yelled out her frustration in his face. "*I rescued a dog on Tuesday. I'm not crazy.*"

Ryson winced. She went back to calling for Cabot.

"You can't run from this, Kenna. You have to talk to me."

"She did rescue a dog," Jax kept his voice low. "We were at a diner."

Ryson said something she couldn't hear.

She was *not* having an emotional breakdown. Never mind that she'd been raised to believe tears were a sign of weakness. If she had tears, they were legitimate and she would cry if she wanted to, whether she was angry, or sad, or frustrated. She could do whatever she wanted. They would think she'd lost it finally and Taylor Landstadt's report would seem all the more plausible. Kenna was unstable. She wasn't fit to be an FBI agent. Now she was probably a killer, too.

She could only imagine what the bureau psychologist had written about her two years ago. And her *child*. Her partner. Her dog. Her career. Her life in Salt Lake City. Everything she'd built that was hers. And now Ryson had jumped on the bandwagon, too.

Landstadt probably hadn't mentioned that the night she and Bradley had been abducted her dog had run off. They'd often gone for a run to chew on the details of the case. Jogging and talking. Bear had never complained about the exercise.

Then they'd been taken. Tranquilized and stuffed in that van, tendons sliced. She'd never seen Bear again.

Kenna crouched to look under a parked car. No dog. Behind it was her car, and Kenna immediately found what she'd been looking for. "Hey." She scooted to the bottom edge of the rear door. "Cabot."

The dog whined.

"I know." She kept her voice low and soft. "And I don't have sausage this time, so you're going to have to brave it and come here."

The dog whined.

"I know. All these people." Kenna settled on the ground. "I don't like them either. I prefer the motorhome, so it's okay if you do, too."

She didn't care what the FBI thought, or what they planned to do next.

Arrest her and bring in Wilson as well. Probably Arnie, and Steven too. Why not sweep them all up and claim a conspiracy was underway? They should check her phone records because they'd discover she'd spoken to exactly one person in the three weeks before she showed back up in Salt Lake City. Ellayna's mother.

Hardly enough communication to set up an entire plot and have everything organized the night she hit town.

"Banbury!"

She flinched. "Miller needs to quiet down." She held out her fingers for Cabot. "Yes, he does."

The dog whined.

"Not now." That was Jax. "Give her a minute."

He was defending her. He'd tried to convince Stairns this was "too easy." Which she figured meant their theory she was behind all of this.

"Come on, girl."

Kenna was tired. She couldn't fight them. But despite the lack of gumption to take on the entire FBI—to prove to them all she was innocent—she could work this case.

She would speak the truth publicly if that was what it came down to. Maybe with evidence that Bradley's wounds had been self-inflicted.

A tear rolled down her face. "Come here," she whispered.

The last thing Kenna wanted to do was tell the world he'd lost hope and opted instead to abandon her. It wouldn't prove she didn't want fame, though.

Ryson crouched. "Uh, there really is a dog under there."

She shot him a dirty look and saw him pull a packet out of his pocket. Not jerky, but similar. A healthy meat snack. Her gaze softened. "Thanks."

"Don't worry about it. You know I owe you."

"I'm not crazy." She held a piece of the meat out to Cabot. "I didn't come home for this. I don't even want to be here."

"You know life sometimes happens, and we have no control."

"I have to have some semblance of control."

Cabot sniffed, then started to inch forward. Kenna used the treat to get her to come all the way out from under the car until the dog was in her lap. "There we go. That's it."

"You need to tell them everything."

She shook her head and buried her face in Cabot's fur. "They aren't getting that from me, because they don't care. It won't mean anything, and it doesn't even prove what I've been saying."

"This isn't pity."

"No, it's more like emotional manipulation."

"Kenna—"

"I'm not using my loss to bolster my story just so they give me a break long enough to find the real killer. Two women and two men are dead. This whole thing is a giant mess and, instead of investigating, I'm getting sucked into peripheral stuff every time. We all are."

Jax frowned down at her and looked at Ryson expectantly. The crowd of agents headed up by Miller stood beside him.

"Special-Agent-in-Charge-Stairs doesn't want the truth to come out." Ryson stood. "He and the governor want Kenna to keep what really happened to Bradley under wraps. Or they want her to have no credibility because everyone thinks she's either crazy or lying."

Kenna lifted her chin. "Both, actually."

Miller started to speak.

She shook her head. "You only know what they told you."

Jax said, "What happened to your partner, Kenna?"

If they'd been alone, she'd have told him for the look on his face alone, and Oliver Jaxton might have actually believed her. The others didn't deserve her explanation.

Instead, she pointed at Miller and the other agents. "Tell them to leave me alone." She was going to get to the bottom of this herself, and that meant looking at the flash drive.

Kenna let the dog into the car.

"You're leaving? You can't leave." Miller strode toward her.

"Hey." Jax tossed Miller his keys. "I'll get her statement. You guys process the scene here. We'll reconvene later."

She wasn't sure how she felt about that. Jax and his knowing gaze—and that FBI disapproval—didn't need to be in her space. But considering her motorhome had been broken into, maybe it wasn't a terrible idea to have someone with her...even to help watch Cabot. The dog didn't need to suffer any more that she already had.

Too bad there would be a price to pay.

Jax stared at her. "I'm going to need you to explain all of this."

Chapter Twenty Six

Friday, 7:02am.

"He knew he couldn't walk. Almatter had severed his Achilles tendons, the way he severed my forearms." Her full coffee cup sat on the table, cold now.

Kenna absently scratched under Cabot's chin while Jax sat quietly.

"He left us in the basement. We knew he would come back, so it was just a question of when. But he didn't. It was hours, and Bradley was convinced Almatter would leave us there to die.

"I'd twisted my ankle when we fell down the basement stairs. But I was just happy that the baby seemed to be okay." Her voice hitched and she swallowed. "No cramps. Nothing. I tried to convince Bradley that was a good thing. That someone was looking out for us." She pointed at the ceiling.

Jax nodded.

"Aren't you supposed to be at Eric's house, working the girl's murder? Or trying to prove I killed that man with my father's gun."

"Finish the story, Kenna."

She closed her eyes, but not from tiredness. They'd both slept after Jax followed her back to her motorhome. She'd wrapped herself in her dad's quilt and watched Jax recline the driver's seat wrapped in her duvet. He'd succumbed to sleep, dressed in his gym clothes. Much better for her than lying there alone, wondering if someone would break in again.

Neither of them had mentioned the fear. And yet, he'd stayed. As though he knew this was something she couldn't—or shouldn't—do alone.

Dawn had broken far too early, and now she had to face the day. The truth. The past.

"It didn't work. Bradley wanted me to make a run for it, since it was only my hands that weren't working. But Almatter had pulled the stairs up. They were too high to pull down and my hands didn't work anyway. I couldn't get through any of the windows. He thought I was just staying because of him. Then Bradley had a different idea. He wanted me to wait for Almatter to come in and, when he was distracted, make a run for it.

"I told him I wouldn't leave him there like that. We could have overpowered Almatter together, but he wouldn't listen. He just kept saying, 'Go, Kenna. Leave me here and go.' He wouldn't even *try*. He thought me leaving him was the best idea, but I could see the fear. He didn't want to face what was coming. While I was rummaging through a closet in the base-ment, looking in the dark for anything—a weapon, or some-thing to help us with a way out—he pulled off his undershirt and ripped it."

She blew out a breath. "I thought he was just mad. Or

working on a way out. But he rolled it up and managed to tie it to a hook that jutted out from an alcove. He was strong."

She took a breath. Even Cabot had stilled. "He leveraged himself up enough his body weight did the rest. By the time I found something useful, which was a tire iron, I turned around, finally ready with my speech to get him to listen to me, and he was already jerking. I ran over and tried to untie the shirt but there was blood everywhere from the cuts on my forearms, and I couldn't untie it. My hands were slick, and my fingers wouldn't work because of the severed tendons. I was screaming. He whispered that he loved me. I didn't stop trying, even when I knew it was too late. And in the end, he was right because I did escape. Almatter came down. He was laughing. That's what I remember. The sound of him laughing."

"The file says they found you in the woods."

She nodded. "I used what I had and managed to get the best of Almatter. Then I ran. Stairns followed my blood trail back to him. When he got there, Almatter was still knocked clean out. I'd hit him over the head with the tire iron. The blow sent him back onto the stairs, and his head bounced off one of the steps. A double whammy. Stairns cuffed him and ordered a couple agents to take him in, while I sat outside with another agent to wait. When he came back up, I knew. I could see it in his eyes that he'd found Bradley down there."

Kenna closed her eyes to compose herself.

"He crouched by me to ask a question, and it all just came pouring out. It's a wonder he could understand anything I was saying between the sobbing and sniffing. But he radioed in. Had an agent stay with me and ordered the rest to hold."

"And the others never saw the shirt around Bradley's neck? Miller and the guys, they never realized?"

"It was covered in my blood. Stairns asked me if I did it."

"He really thought you might have?"

"Taylor asked me the same thing." Her supposed best friend.

"And the governor?"

She shrugged. "There's a reason they kept it quiet and said Almatter killed him. They even produced a garotte, and he pled guilty to all killings so there wasn't a long, drawn-out trial. I didn't have to testify. They set me up, forced me to leave the FBI, and told me not to come back. Ever. I figured our esteemed governor didn't want it to get out that his only son killed himself. And I got the impression that if I ever tried to tell anyone what really happened, they would produce evidence to show I'm not in my right mind. Like I made it all up just to discredit the governor."

"Did Governor Pacer know about the baby?"

She shook her head. "I didn't tell him. But I did go see him."

Jax's expression remained unreadable.

"If he wanted me out, he was going to have to sign off on a private investigator license. And not just for Utah. I figured with friends all over the place, I could ask for multiple states and he delivered. In exchange, I stayed away. Two years."

"And the second you came back, all this began."

"I don't understand it any more than you do. I've been back before to get my mail. Why this time?"

"Because you were here on a case?"

She shrugged.

"We will figure it out."

Jax assumed she believed it was possible to find answers. "You should get to work."

"Good idea." He took her coffee and dumped it in the sink. "You're coming with me." He looked at the screen of his watch. "First stop is the morgue."

"Because that went so well last time?"

Chapter Twenty-Seven

He stopped outside the door to the medical examiner's office and turned to her.

Kenna said, "Are you gonna offer to hold my hand?"

He'd been quiet the whole way here. Probably processing her story and how he was planning to deal with it. If Stairns ordered him to arrest her, Jax would have no choice but to do it. Didn't matter if he felt sorry for what she'd been through.

"Thank you for trusting me."

She needed more sleep because she had to be on her A-game to deal with Oliver Jaxton. I mean, what was she supposed to say to that? "I know you don't owe me anything, so thanks. And you're welcome. I'm working on that trust part."

His phone rang for the first time all morning. He'd been on it, sending emails or texts. He'd probably told the FBI he would get her to talk so they could finally arrest her. As if that would stop all this. Ugh, that trust issue again. "Stairns?"

He shook his head. "My mother. Apparently, I'm supposed to attend a gala in Denver next month. With my ex-wife."

The ME's office door opened. Probably for the best, since whatever she'd been about to say probably should not come out of her mouth. She definitely needed a nap.

"Doctor Collins."

"Ms. Banbury." The older gentleman raised his brows and glanced between them.

"Jax was about to fill me in on the details of his sordid romantic past. Unfortunately, that will have to wait."

"Shame." Collins stepped back and held the door.

"Yes, it is." She strode in. At least they didn't have to be with the dead bodies. "But only because a coffee date would seem daring to me at this point."

"My dear."

Kenna nearly laughed. "Tell me about it. But there's no time for that, either." She dropped into a wingback chair and asked Jax, "Did the FBI check my father's gun for fingerprints?"

"Wiped clean." He sat in the chair beside her.

"If they wanted to implicate me, they should've left mine on there."

"That would have made sense."

Collins typed on his keyboard. "The deceased was Clive Burnette, thirty-seven. I'm sure the FBI can avail you of his lengthy criminal history."

"Oh yeah?"

Jax nodded. "That's next."

"Healthy, except for the scratch marks on his face and neck, the abrasions on his hands and the gunshot. Close enough to leave a burn mark around the entry wound. Right to the heart." Collins turned his computer screen so they could get a look at it.

Kenna caught her breath and stared at the image. "That's the guy?"

He was someone who didn't get second glances. He seemed ordinary. She remembered thinking that many years ago, the first time she'd met him. This was a guy who flew under the radar, never standing out enough to make anyone remember him.

"What is it?" A wealth of caution undercut Jax's tone.

He'd caught on that she'd seen him before. After all, consensus leaned toward her guilt, so it made sense she would recognize this guy.

"It was about six years ago. Maybe five. It was winter—I remember because he wore a scarf so that woman didn't get the chance to scratch him...the way someone was obviously able to do this time around. Still, her testimony meant he was convicted. Aggravated assault. I think."

Jax had his phone out. "He had a charge for that five years ago."

"Look at the arresting officer."

He looked up, eyebrows raised. "Bradley Pacer."

"Now I'm wondering if Bradley had arrested Christopher Halpert at one time. Maybe that's why he looked familiar to me."

"I'll check into it," Jax said. "What happened to Burnette?"

"He got a few years. No more than a slap on the wrist and then parole." Kenna shook her head. She'd forgotten all about this guy. "And now he's back to his old tricks. Or he was until this."

If someone intended to posit a theory that *she* was the vigilante here, cleaning up the mean streets of Salt Lake City, this guy certainly fit the bill. The kind of person she'd want taken out before he hurt anyone else.

What she needed was proof to back up her story. Even if she

did want to tell anyone how Bradley really died, which she did not. The fact was, whether she liked it or not, Kenna might have to circumvent what was happening by telling the truth the governor had tried to hide. Governor Pacer thought it was a weakness that Bradley had died the way he did, but she'd chosen to believe he'd done what he thought was right. Even if that meant leaving her alone with Sebastian Almatter. Anything could have happened, but in the end maybe he did save her life.

Now Kenna was going to have to save herself.

"I should call Stairns. Fill him in." Jax excused himself.

Before Collins could start the small talk, she said, "You weren't the Medical Examiner I recall from two years ago."

"I've only been here fourteen months."

"And before you?"

"Everett Manforth."

Kenna nodded. "That's right. Did he retire?"

Collins said, "Florida, I think."

"Thanks."

"Would you like me to email you the contact information for him?"

"Yes, thanks again." It wasn't a plan, but at least it was the start of an idea. They needed to get back on the topic of the dead guy, though. "Anything else I should know about how Clive Burnette died?"

"I've been looking at all four victims as a unit, as well as individually. Just in case there are correlations."

"You found some?"

Collins tipped his head to the side. "Yes, and no. Clive was left-handed. Whoever killed Jessica Pierce was left-handed."

Before she could say what popped into her head, Collins continued, "Whoever killed Meg Parabuchio was also left-handed, and I found some of Clive's DNA under her fingernails."

"The old man, Christopher Halpert, was drugged, right?"

"Which caused a heart attack."

"The man in the video with Jessica was right-handed, so it wasn't Clive. Or maybe the guy recorded the video, and Clive is the one who killed her." Kenna needed a blank piece of paper. This was getting complicated. "So the old man is drugged. Then Jessica gets taken, but whoever was in the video isn't the one who killed her. And it might've been Clive who did it, but there was no DNA on her. Then he takes Meg and kills her. But he gets shot, supposedly by me." She thought some more and said, "The old man's death was calculated, a means to an end. Jessica's death was staged to look like something else. Meg's death—"

"That was passion. And anger." Collins winced. "On occasion the two are indistinguishable."

"And Clive had to be taken out, maybe because he lost control with Meg, and they couldn't abide that. He'd become a liability not to be trusted."

"But your father's gun?"

"Another way to tie me to this. Muddy the waters."

"What about Eric Wilson, and the fact Meg was left at his house? I'm sure Eric is one of the suspects in the case." Jax leaned against the door frame. How long had he been there? The guy might be uptight, but he wasn't hard to look at. She preferred the yoga sweats, though. "Kenna?"

She cleared her throat and thought she heard Collins chuckle. She tried to keep her cheeks from flushing. Like that was possible. "Eric isn't part of this." She thought of the artwork on Eric's wall. "Despite his proclivities. Kind of like me, he's being dragged in and implicated by association."

"We need to find the man from the video. He's more

likely to be the mastermind behind this rather than any of our victims." He motioned to the hall. "Let's head to the office and find out what they've got so far on Clive Burnette. Known associates, that kind of thing."

Kenna stood. Collins met her at the door. She stuck out her hand. "Thank you for your time."

He nodded, sincerity in his eyes. "I'll send you that information."

In the hall, Jax said, "What information?"

Kenna hit the button to call the elevator down. "Nothing that relates to this."

He might not believe her, and Kenna didn't really blame him, but she also wasn't going to explain. Right now she didn't even know if the previous medical examiner knew anything about the truth of Bradley's death, let alone if he'd stand up for her when she told the truth.

If she told the truth.

"Am I going to be arrested the second I go into the FBI office?"

Jax shook his head. "I need a couple more statements from you."

"So this is official."

"Officially, I need your help." The elevator doors opened, and he strode out.

Kenna caught up at the revolving door. "You think I was on to something?"

He scanned the street outside.

"Steven promised he wasn't going to try and run me over again."

"It's a shame I can't arrest you for being annoying."

"Yeah. Shame."

His eyes flared. The way they had when she'd told him

she didn't Chaturanga. That was just the way he was, though. Some people were magnetic.

She wasn't anything close to being a magnet. Kenna was more like cardboard someone had flattened and thrown out for the recycling truck. Only Bradley had ever bothered to look beneath the surface.

"Come on. The day's wasting."

Chapter Twenty Eight

She'd expected some kind of reception at the FBI office, but not Taylor. "I don't want to talk to you. I'm not sure I can make that any clearer, Doctor Landstadt."

Kenna tried to walk around her, but Taylor sidestepped in front of her.

Before Taylor could say anything, Kenna jumped in again. "Four people are dead. There's work to do."

Taylor's eyes filled with tears. "Four?"

"Don't do that."

"Feel something?" She practically wailed the words, then leaned in. "After what I did to you?" Her attempt at whispering sucked.

"Would you two like to talk privately?"

She shot Jax a look.

Taylor clasped her hands together. "Yes. Kenna, *please*."

She strode to the conference room and let Taylor shut the door behind her. "Ambushing me was not cool."

"We were friends once."

"And you tossed it aside. For what? This prestigious position?"

Taylor pressed her lips together. "I'm sorry. You can probably guess I was pressured to write the report the way they wanted me to. I'm not proud of it, but I had a lot of student loan debt. Ian and I were drowning, and we'd just had Bethany. I saw a way out and I took it."

"How do you not see that as a complete betrayal of someone who was supposed to be your *friend*?"

"I'm sorry." Taylor shook her head, the tears falling.

"Yeah, me too." Sorry she'd wasted time and energy caring about Taylor and her family. She'd spent time with her daughter and made conversation with the husband, even when she thought he was kind of uptight. Still, what was the point in dragging up the past and going over it all again? That wouldn't heal the wounds these people had left her with.

"Are you...doing okay, with everything?" Taylor had switched to therapist mode.

"Oh, I get it. Stairns sent you in here to get me to open up. Find out where I'm at with all this before they find the evidence they need to arrest me for four murders."

"Did you kill them?"

"Are you seriously asking me that?"

"It's been two years, you're a different person."

Kenna folded her arms, even though it made her look defensive. "If I am, don't you think it's because that's what you all made me into? Someone who has to keep things close to the vest, suspecting the worst of people she used to call friends? Because no one is outside suspicion right now. Not when my freedom is on the line." She took a step closer. "And considering that's the only thing I have left? I'm not going to let anyone take it away from me."

"I know you'd never do something like this."

"Am I supposed to be glad that you believe in me? Ryson's

never questioned my innocence because he's a true friend." She saw that her words hit home. "That's all I need."

Jax might believe her as well. He'd listened to her story, and she got the feeling he didn't share much about his personal life with his colleagues. But he had with her. At the bowling alley he'd told her about his struggles.

"As far as all this murder business? I want to see it through. Not to prove I had no part in it. The person responsible should be found."

"That's what the FBI wants, too."

"But Stairns's personal feelings are a different story. If he signs off on my arrest, Jax will have to read me my rights. Or one of the others will." Miller would probably take pleasure in it. She would be tempted to fight them, and that wasn't going to end well. "I'm damned if I do, and damned if I don't."

"Feeling powerless isn't comfortable for anyone." Psychologist mode was back. Taylor even had that professional, slightly aloof stare going on. She seemed distracted. "And I can honestly say I understand the fear of unwanted attention now."

Something in her voice made Kenna's ears perk. "What is it? What do you mean by that?"

Taylor scrunched up her nose. "I'm dealing with it. But this isn't about me." She waved her hand to dismiss their train of conversation. "Anyway, I guess what I am saying is that it's understandable you'd want to solve this mystery. But would it be so bad if you left town? Until this all blows over?"

"So they can hunt me?" Kenna brushed hair off her face and saw Taylor's gaze slip to her forearms. "Besides, I'd have to steal my father's gun from the evidence locker first. I'm not leaving town without it."

"It's my understanding that gun is a murder weapon. It's evidence."

Kenna stuck her hands in her coat pockets and sighed. Her fingers found the flash drive Eric's friend Arnie had given her. She needed to call them both, make sure they were okay. Get them here to give statements, now that this situation had ballooned out of control.

Evidence she hadn't even looked at yet because she'd been distracted with finding the young woman's body, losing her dog, and then telling Jax everything.

"This whole thing is getting more and more bizarre as it goes on."

"There's a logic to everything, even if it can't be explained."

Kenna shrugged. "Sometimes there are no answers. We can't know what's in people's minds that propel them to do what they do."

"You are different now."

"That happens when everything you thought you wanted is taken away from you."

"Kenna—"

"This chat is over." She strode over and pulled the door open. "I'd like to say it was good to see you."

Taylor stopped in front of her. "It actually is good to see you. You look...well."

Kenna remained silent and stared after her as Taylor walked to the elevators.

"Everything okay?"

"I need a computer." She turned to Jax and pulled the flash drive from her pocket. The more people who saw what was on it, the better. Any evidence they found couldn't be "lost" or explained away if half the office had seen it. "This is from the website guy who set up Death Files. He's the one who sent me the link to the video."

Jax looked about to explode. "It's—"

"You should go meditate on a Psalm or something. After you get me a laptop."

His fingers twitched by his sides.

"If you throttle me, everyone will see."

He made a sound of frustration and walked off. Kenna leaned against the doorframe and looked around. It was still weird being here, but less so than last time. Maybe one day she'd be able to walk around these rooms and not think of Bradley. Of course, that meant she'd keep coming back here.

That was not the plan.

Right now, instead of regret and loss, she was more concerned that they thought she was their chief suspect. She half expected to find a murder board somewhere with her name at the top.

The door to Stairns's office opened and Angeline Pacer stepped out. Perfect lilac skirt suit, curled hair, and pearls. Bradley's mother spotted her immediately. Her serene smile faltered at the edges. Kenna wondered if the woman hated her as much as she imagined, or if it was more.

There was a quiet exchange of words and the suited security detail guy moved to the elevator while Mrs. Pacer headed over. Kenna wasn't going to get out of this. She met the First Lady of Utah halfway.

Angeline held her hands out, tipped with those perfectly manicured fingernails. Her skin was almost too soft. The smile not quite believable.

Kenna tried to smile back. "Hello, Mrs. Pacer."

"Sweetheart." Angeline's eyes filled with tears. Even up close she looked younger than she was.

Angelina knew Kenna and Bradley had been more than partners.

Bradley's mother tugged on Kenna's hands, then enveloped her in a hug. One second, just a foot away and the very next second, her bosom slammed into Kenna's. A cloud rushed at her face and perfume stung the inside of Kenna's nose. "Oh, sweetheart."

She coughed.

"It's okay." Angeline patted Kenna's back. "Everything's going to be okay now. No one's going to hurt you."

Chapter Twenty-Nine

Friday, 10:34am.

"Feel like telling me what that was?"

Kenna shut the door to the conference room. She set her coffee on the table. "Maybe she needed a hug." But Angeline Pacer hadn't come solely to speak to her. There were a limited number of other reasons the state's First Lady might have been talking to Stairns. The fact Kenna had caught her attention was nothing but a coincidence. Maybe. Probably.

"Do you really believe that?"

Kenna settled in the chair. "Can we not talk about this?"

Two emotional reunions in one day were two too many. She didn't want to dissect her conversation with Taylor any more than she did the two minutes spent awkwardly trying to peel a weepy woman from her shoulder, even though the woman would've been the grandmother of Kenna's baby. That didn't mean she owed her anything now.

Jax studied her. "You push people away."

She started to argue.

He cut her off. "But only because they pushed you away first. It's a way of protecting yourself."

"I have healthy boundaries."

"And you hide behind them whether there's a war raging or not. Hunkered down, just in case."

"Good thing for me there *is* a war raging, otherwise it'd just be paranoia. Turns out they really are out to get me."

He didn't return her smile.

She didn't blame him. "If you tell me to read a Brené Brown book..."

"I'll send you a link. It's a short video."

Maybe it was everyone else who should operate differently from now on—or fix their mindset, or whatever. Could be Kenna wasn't the one with the problem. "You're assuming I even want to change."

"I think life changes us whether we want it to or not."

"Knock, knock." Thomas stepped in.

"Good timing." Kenna lifted her coffee cup in salute.

"Yeah, things were just getting personal."

She was about to fire a quip back but caught Jax's wink. Just this morning she'd laid out the darkest part of her. Now he was bringing things back to a place of light banter. He was so well adjusted it was irritating. He knew how to bring everyone around him to that mellow spot where he lived, all cool and calm.

She fought the urge to be lulled in by him by reminding herself he was basically micromanaging her until he had probable cause, and then he'd turn around and arrest her.

She ignored that figuring-her-out stare and turned to the tech. "The flash drive?" She'd handed it over an hour ago.

"There's a lot to sort through, but the main thing is it gave us the company name behind the site. Even though it's not exactly the same on the dark web, money still changes hands. If you want to set up shop, there's a paper trail."

Jax sat forward in his chair. "You have a physical address for this company?"

"We're getting close."

"Is the site still up and running?" Kenna asked. "I know the video we saw for Murder Files was moved and their connection is done on a different site, but the main web page is still operational, right?" She'd been on there. Arnie had said he was the one who'd communicated with her. Maybe whoever was behind the video didn't use the site like the rest of its patrons.

"The page is different now. Death Files is still there with its regular visitors. Murder Class was deep web, though. We'll never find where it's gone. We'd have to be given another link."

"What does that mean?" For two years she'd lived mostly analogue, except for research she'd done on clients over social media. People put everything online. It was a treasure trove of personal information. "You said deep web and dark web. What's the difference?"

"The deep web is like the magma layer beneath the earth's surface. The dark web is the core. All we see is above ground, and your browser search will return results that are all above ground. Under the surface, nothing is indexed or searchable. Even with the right browser you can't just search for something. You get a referral and you're given a security certificate that grants you access to a server."

"But you monitor some sites?"

Thomas bounced on the balls of his feet. "It's my own undercover operation. I have a username I've established, and I regularly make transactions on the deep web. I've made a name for myself. So far it's going pretty well." He motioned to the tablet under his arm. "This guy, though? He's bigtime. His username is one that gets whispered about. He's Sargeras."

"His real name is Arnold."

Jax looked at her like she'd grown another head. "Thomas, you said you're following the money?"

"It's the fastest way to find out who's funding Murder Class. We can't just get a location from his IP address." Thomas snorted. "Sargeras uses a browser that bounces your IP through proxy servers around the world. The only way we were able to access it before was because the link Kenna received contained a proxy that could access the site. But not for long. We lost access."

"Pretty sure Kenna knows where he lives."

Thomas gasped. "You do?!"

"He was paid to set up Death Files and send me the video, but he's not behind it. He's just their web contractor."

Jax eyed her again.

Yes, she was going to tell him who Arnold was and where to find him. But only if he asked nicely.

She reminded him of an important fact. "Without the flash drive of information he gave us, we would never even know they were based here in town. They could be anywhere in the world if it's all done online."

Thomas settled on the edge of the table. "The company is a shell corporation, and I'm sure that at the bottom of the well we'll find real people with real bank accounts. Then you can go kick their door down and haul them in. It'll take time, since the transactions all happened in—"

"Bitcoin." Kenna and Jax both said it at the same time.

Kenna shrugged. "It's always bitcoin these days." At least, that was how it seemed. "Is it traceable?"

"Soon as I have something, I'll let you know."

Kenna was willing to hedge her bets a little. "Get me names, and I'll introduce you to Sargeras."

Thomas flushed. "That would be..."

"You should tell the FBI his name regardless," Jax said. "I want him and all his equipment brought in."

"You'd be better off using him as a confidential informant." She figured Thomas might be able to convince the boss Arnie could be useful in his professional capacity—as Sargeras, the dark web broker. That would be a win for the FBI.

Jax folded his arms. "When we find the person who killed Jessica Pierce, are you going to recommend something other than arresting them? That seems to be your trend."

"Uh...I'll leave you guys to your work."

"Thanks, Thomas." Kenna waved as the tech left. The second the door clicked shut, she turned to Jax. "The person who killed Jessica? Really?"

"You seem pretty anti-justice right now. What am I supposed to think?"

"That I'd be okay letting a murderer go free when I've spent the last two years—and all the years before that—working for exactly one thing. Bringing them to justice. Sure. That's exactly it." She shoved her chair back and went to stare out the window.

"So why let Eric Wilson skate out from under suspicion? Can you be perfectly sure he hasn't done anything illegal, whether it's part of this or not?"

"No." She folded her arms and found her car in the parking lot.

"What about this guy, Arnold? Shouldn't he come in and answer some questions since he's the closest we've got to the people who took Officer Pierce?"

She sighed.

"What about you? Should I not report back to Stairns

everything you say? Your mindset and my thoughts about your involvement. Should I ignore suspicion?"

"I think you should do your job, which I'm trusting is what you're doing. Not playing politics. Just your job."

It's what she would have done before the FBI betrayed her. The bureau was too big for one agent not to get crushed as the machine lumbered on. There wasn't anything Jax could do about it. She was never going to get her reputation back.

"I'm going to talk to Stairns." She headed for the door.

Jax stalled her. "Not a good idea right now."

"Because he's busy politicking with the governor's wife? That's what landed me jobless in the first place. Maybe I deserve an explanation as to precisely how deep into the pockets of state government he is."

"You're here to solve this case. Unraveling everything that put four people in the morgue is higher priority."

"I think I've put the greater good ahead of what I needed for long enough. Keeping everyone from the truth of Bradley's death—that he took his own life—just so they can't herald him as a martyr was never a good enough reason to destroy my career. I don't care that he's the memorialized poster boy for justice. How he died was *tragic*."

"Because he lost hope."

He'd died in silence while her back was turned. "We can't talk about that. It doesn't fit the narrative they want, so the truth gets buried while we're all supposed go on thinking, 'so sad. Poor Bradley Pacer, son of the governor. His whole life ahead of him, and he's cut down in his prime by a vicious killer.' Because that's what they want us to think."

"I understand."

"Do you?"

"More than you know." His expression softened. "Not what it's like to lose so much, but how it can feel when you're told what to believe. How to be. That your experience, and the pain you feel, is not the point."

"I didn't ask to be dragged back here. I wanted to be left alone. Why now, two years later?"

Two dead women. Two dead men. All murdered differently.

It was an elaborate plan, but not perfect. Then again, they never were.

"Why can't everyone just leave me alone?" She didn't want to see the pity in his eyes. "I trusted you, but I'm not going to be betrayed again. And that's not me just having healthy boundaries, that's me keeping my sanity. What if I build something here, with this—" She waved at the room, the window. The city outside. "—and it gets taken away again?"

"So you're staying?"

"Only until the case is done." The rest of it? She couldn't do it again.

"Then work with me."

"I don't take orders."

His lips twitched. "Trust me. I noticed."

Her phone buzzed across the table.

"Eric?"

She looked at the screen and shook her head. "Ryson." Did she want to answer the text when her involvement pulled people into her orbit whether she safeguarded them or not? Kenna wasn't willing to risk that happening with him, or Valentina, and especially not Luci. "I need to check in with Eric and his friend. And I need to get out of here."

If he wanted her to stay put in the office, he was going to have a fight on his hands.

"Road trip."

She narrowed her gaze on him. "Where?"

"Clive Burnette's house. I want your take on what we found there."

Kenna swiped up her coat. "Well, why didn't you say so —" Pain sliced through her forearm and her coat dropped to the floor. Kenna let out a hiss through clenched teeth.

Jax picked up her coat.

She breathed through the pain and straightened to find him holding out her coat, as though he intended to help her put it on. She grabbed the collar with her other hand. "Let's go."

"Not before you tell me what that was."

"I jarred my arm on the ground when I fell."

"When Steven tried to kill you." His tone sounded flat. "I'm surprised you didn't get a concussion."

"My dad always said I had a hard head."

"I figure it's kept you alive this long. He was probably right."

She wanted to smile but couldn't. "Sometimes I wonder if that's even a good thing."

Chapter Thirty

T he front door of Clive Burnette's house had been kicked in. By whoever shot him with her father's gun, or the FBI? "He lived alone?"

Jax had been quiet since her declaration. "Single. Lived alone. This is a one-bedroom. He has a grandmother in St. George who disowned him years ago and had him removed from church membership."

Kenna pulled on a pair of blue gloves and stared at the front living area. Couch cushions had been shredded. The coffee table—she assumed—was now nothing but a stack of broken shards of wood. On the surfaces that weren't covered with scraps of books hacked to pieces, fingerprint powder remained.

So, not the cops. Someone wanted Clive's life in tatters. Total destruction. Nothing left. He might turn out to be a murderer, but that didn't keep her emotions from accepting him as a kindred spirit.

"Forensics already went through here?"

"Yes. He had no phone on him, and it wasn't found anywhere here. I'm wondering if whoever killed him took it."

Kenna could see that being the case. She wandered around the room, avoiding the debris of Burnette's life, but looking at each piece. "He messed up and they had to eliminate him, which involved keeping his phone."

"He messed up?"

"It's a theory. I mean, presumably there was supposed to be another Murder Class video. But it was never sent."

"So they're cleaning up a mess. The one he made with Meg?"

"Regrouping and figuring out what the plan is now, which means they'll be harder to find because they're laying low after this whole disaster."

"Just wish I knew what that plan was."

Kenna felt the same. She wandered through the kitchen and bedroom with the feeling the place hadn't been all that tidy even before everything had been tossed around. "Did anyone check this?" She pointed to the monitor on the dresser.

"The TV?"

"It's a computer. One of those all-in-one units." She found the mouse in Burnette's sock drawer right below it and slid the device across the surface beside the screen. Nothing happened. She checked the underside. The wireless mouse had a switch. She flipped it to on and repeated the swipe on the dresser top.

A fan inside whirred and the computer booted up.

"Probably passworded."

She shot Jax a look for that unhelpful comment. "Thomas can work his magic with..." Her comment trailed off as she got a look at the image that loaded on screen. "That's Meg's bedroom."

"But we took her computer after you figured out someone got into it."

"Then this is old video because it's the right angle, and I don't think it's a live feed."

"Clive was watching prerecorded footage." Jax moved to stand beside her. "The highlight reel?"

"Someone fed his habit. Then they took Meg, and he got to play with her."

"Payment for a job well done." Jax stilled. "Officer Pierce. And maybe Christopher Halpert. Not his scene, but he did those anyway. His reward was he got his toy."

"And Meg paid the price."

Jax nodded.

"Then he went too far with her and didn't follow the plan, so he had to be taken out." Kenna scratched her jaw, her forearm still sore from earlier. "They knew about my father's gun. They didn't make this kind of mess in my rig." She motioned to the stuff everywhere with a chin lift.

"They were here looking for something and, unlike your gun, they didn't know where it was."

Kenna blew out a breath, creeped out by that idea. "It's all just speculation until we know who they are." She navigated with the mouse back to the home screen and into the file menus. "Maybe he uploaded here what went missing on his phone. Worth a try, though these people seemed to be on top of electronics.

Maybe they'd paid Arnie to hack Clive Burnette's life, and the guy hadn't told her that.

She found a couple of hidden folders full of photos. Kenna opened his desktop email app and sent the whole collection to an email address Thomas had set up. She wrote in all caps in the body of the email. Just in case there was spyware on this computer as well.

Two more emails were sent with the other folders, one

compressed to reduce the size of all the videos. More footage of Meg?

Jax's phone rang. "Special Agent Jaxton." He turned away but didn't leave the room.

Kenna lifted the mattress even though the agents in forensics would've done that. She winced at the belongings pushed underneath. A pair of old sneakers caked with mud. Clothing. Books and papers. Magazines. Bills. Even a moldy sandwich.

She lowered the mattress carefully to prevent it from dropping back into place and wafting all that back up. Then she opened the app on her phone that swept for bugs.

Probably couldn't hurt, and it was something forensics likely hadn't done. She figured it wasn't going to ruffle any feathers. Especially if nothing—

The meter raced to the red zone, and her phone emitted a high tone.

Jax hung up. "Thomas found an office registered to the same business that funded the website. Now tell me what that was."

Kenna tracked the sound to its source. The alarm clock. She lifted it and stared at the digital display for long enough to be sure. She turned so her back was to it. Maybe they could see, but not hear. It was worth being safe.

"The alarm clock has a bug in it."

Jax looked from it to the computer monitor. "They could see what he was watching."

"And blackmail him into doing whatever they needed."

"We need a warrant to access his bank accounts. I'll call Stairns from the car." He tossed her his keys. "You can drive."

Chapter Thirty One

J ax hung up his phone. "He's going to put the paperwork through." He grabbed a bulletproof vest from the trunk and handed it to her.

Kenna slipped it over her head. "How did he sound?"

Jax secured his own vest over his shirt. "He's as eager to unravel all this as you are. Remember, he wanted to sign you on as a consultant."

"He should've just filled everything out for me like he did with my retirement paperwork."

"Because the governor didn't want the story getting out." Jax spoke as though he was still trying to figure it all out in his head. She didn't blame him. It was a lot to process.

She nodded, "Like I said before, together they leaned on Doctor Landstadt and got me to walk away quietly. Because no one could know that Bradley took his own life."

"*That's* what happened?"

She spun to find Miller behind her, a thunderous expression on his face.

"I knew that didn't add up," Miller said. "Stairns wouldn't let anyone but himself process the scene, which was weird for an operation. No one's supposed to go at it alone. It's supposed to guard against liability issues. I didn't figure he did it to manipulate the situation." He shook his head and then looked back up at her. "You're saying Bradley took his own life?"

"He wanted me to run." She leaned against the car and stared at her sneakers. *He lost hope, and I wasn't enough to make him stay.* "He wanted one of us to live."

"And you never told any of us?"

Why did Miller still sound so skeptical? She wanted to hate him for it, but deep down she knew he was hurting over this news.

Across the parking lot, the HRT commander yelled for the team to go.

Kenna pushed off the car so she could enter the building behind them. On the way past Miller she said, "Hard to do that when you wouldn't even talk to me."

"Kenna—"

She shook her head and glanced back over her shoulder. "Don't."

Now wasn't the time to talk about it. If she wanted to, which she didn't. They could ask Stairns if they had more questions.

Jax caught up to her as HRT breached the office space. Kenna's mind swirled with theories. Could be this whole thing was nothing but a sensational attempt to get the FBI to think this was something bigger than a simple revenge plot against her. A website. Videos. A benefactor they'd all but implied could be Kenna. Viewership and an instructor. A call to action.

Turned out it was all a ploy. A way to make the FBI believe Kenna wanted the limelight. Or so her primary theory went.

These were the people who had taken Jessica and Meg. The ones responsible for their deaths.

She didn't care what they had in mind for her. Nor did she consider what they planned to do next, or if she would end up in jail because of it.

Her own well-being was not important to her. People were dying.

Kenna had called Eric and Arnie a couple more times and sent texts but had gotten no replies. Whatever they were doing had better be good. She definitely agreed they should be laying low until she figured out why Meg's body had been left in Eric's bed, but not responding? What was that all about? She didn't think Eric had anything to do with the young woman's death, and it would be a waste of the FBI's time to chase down that rabbit hole. She was going to have to get him to understand he was on a very short leash.

Was she now manipulating the investigation, the way Stairns had manipulated her? It wasn't good practice to only follow one theory, but that's what the feds had done. Is that what she was doing, too? No. Unlike her former boss, she wanted to find the truth. She was a PI. This wasn't obstruction of justice. Not when the truth would come out eventually.

"Okay?" Jax leaned against the wall beside her while the HRT guys kicked the doors in and ran inside, yelling.

There was a familiar comfort in the sound of a building being breached to serve a warrant. Call her crazy. "I've missed that."

His lips curled up at the corners.

"Yeah, yeah. But it's true. The authority they have and how they exercise it. Not a lot of that in my line of work now."

She'd always figured she would be part of all this until she retired...years from now. But it wasn't how her life had worked out.

She couldn't arrest anyone.

She wasn't part of the justice system.

It was easier to forget she'd ever worn the badge when she was alone and far from this city. There were times it seemed like it had all been a dream. A strain, even, to pick out the details. And then, suddenly, all the memories of those years would flood her mind and make that separation of thought difficult. Being alone was far simpler than having to deal with other people or their expectations.

Jax's radio crackled. "It's clear, Special Agent Jaxton. The place is empty."

He lifted it. "Copy that. Thanks."

They headed inside where HRT men and women had crowded in the lobby. Beyond that was an area with partitioned desks, like a small call center. Rooms branched off around the perimeter. A side room with a desk, the sign on the door read MANAGER. The kitchen and the hallway beyond, where the bathrooms probably were.

Jax slowed and surveyed the call center. "Wires and cords, but all the computers and monitors are gone. Even the phones."

She headed for the final room, where one of the HRT guys stood with a grim look on his face. "What is it?"

He motioned in the room with a nod.

She looked inside and sucked in a huge breath. "Jax!"

He rushed over. What is...oh."

"This is where the video was shot." The wall was the same—the background from the video of Jessica Pierce. "She was here."

"She wasn't killed here."

"Special Agent Jaxton."

They both ignored the HRT guy. This was it. It was where they'd brought Jessica to make the video.

Kenna fought back the burn of tears in her eyes. She wasn't going to cry in front of her old colleagues and Jax. They wouldn't blame her for it, but they would still walk away thinking she was right to have left the FBI. That she couldn't handle the work anymore.

The fact they might be right was hardly the point.

Kenna stared at the room. "Maybe there's blood."

"Forensics will go through this place but, if she wasn't killed here, then we'll still need to find out where it did happen."

"Special Agent Jaxton." The HRT agent was a little more irritated now.

Kenna stared at the tripod that had been left. No camera. "We need to do a search for fingerprints. Though, why leave anything at all if there's a chance we might find prints? Unless they know we won't get a result in any database, or they figure they'll be long gone before we get any kind of match."

"That would be careless, even if they did leave in a hurry. It wouldn't fly with their meticulous processes so far. We've found no trace of these people or who they are."

After the break-in at her house, she hadn't dusted anything for prints. Why make a mess when it was clear they were professionals? They'd disabled her security system and stolen a lockbox with biometric security. The kind of person who could do that didn't leave prints behind.

But did professionals target a private investigator with extreme prejudice? That hardly made sense.

Could be they'd been hired to do the job. Maybe it wasn't personal on their end at all.

The break-in. The website and video. The business cards.

Meanwhile, the actual murder was subcontracted to Clive Burnette.

"Special Agent Jaxton."

They both spun to the agent, irritated. Kenna said, "What?"

The HRT agent said, "You're going to want to look at the women's bathroom." He turned away, dismissing them after delivering his statement.

The ladies' room was at the end of the hall, just before the EXIT door at the end. Two stalls, plus the handicapped, splattered with blood spray. One sink. The floor had a drain in the center. Blood had pooled on the floor and had dried while in the process of trickling down.

"Jessica's blood." She probably should've asked it as a question, though Jax didn't know the answer either. "Maybe Meg's too."

"Forensics will find out."

She pulled out her phone and already had it unlocked before she realized what she was doing. "Maybe I shouldn't tell Ryson we found where she was killed." Even as she pondered whether to tell him, she knew she'd never keep something like this from her friend.

"We *think* we found it."

"This could be Jessica's blood and Meg's. Or one, but not the other."

Jax nodded, a dark expression on his face. "They made the video, then brought her in here and killed her. They didn't do that while the livestream was running. And they made sure the mess would happen someplace it could be cleaned."

He was right. The murder had occurred in a bathroom where the tile was a lot easier to clean than carpet. Not to mention the drain in the center of the room. "But they didn't tidy in here before they left, the way they did with the office."

"So they don't care that we found the blood. Evidence."

"Maybe that's not it. Maybe they had orders to clean up. But didn't."

She said, "I wonder if we'll find Clive's DNA, or a fingerprint. Meanwhile, we've got nothing in terms of a paper trail, physical or electronic."

"You think Clive was shot here?"

"Maybe. But that's not what I meant."

"You think he killed Jessica."

"And Meg. But maybe they couldn't make the second video." Kenna went back out into the hall. She didn't need to stare at the blood anymore. "I think they were hired to make a spectacle of all this with the business cards and murder."

To get back at me.

After all, this had been personal since Christopher Halpert's body showed up with her business card on it. There must be someone else with a grudge besides the governor.

Jax folded his arms. "But they never made a video of Meg."

"I still think Clive screwed up, and that's why they shot him. It's a different M.O. than the other deaths. He was disposed of."

"And the old man?"

"Poison is a lot less hands-on. You can hand over a coffee laced with something and walk away. Or break into a house and switch out someone's meds." They'd already broken into her home, so why not? "In order to get rid of him, they had to know who he was. Maybe through the website."

"Now they've cleared out."

"Maybe the plan is over."

She wasn't going to count on it. Kenna would continue as though the threat was very real. That, and not her hardheadedness, was what had kept her alive. "Clive Burnette might have killed Meg, and maybe also Jessica and Halpert, but he wasn't the mastermind behind this."

Jax nodded. "He's small time. This was organized. Did Clive have a grudge? Was he blackmailed because of his obsession with Meg, or was there a reason he might've wanted to get back at you?"

Kenna didn't know. "Maybe both."

She'd thought this was all about setting her up to look like a vigilante who dispensed justice with her gun—or by any other means necessary. Someone who wanted to be in the limelight like her father.

The FBI, or at least Stairns, had bought the story.

Did the fact this office had been abandoned mean the plan was over?

"We need to find the guy from the video." She thought it through. "He's the one who can tell us who was involved, and why."

"We'll dust this whole place for prints." Jax winced. "We might find one that leads us in the right direction."

Kenna pulled out her phone and called Eric again. While it rang, she thought about Arnie. He might claim he had no idea who these people were, but was that true? He might know who it was that'd starred with Jessica in the video. The cool head who narrated her death before she was handed over to Clive to finish off.

Thomas might know, if all the information was on the flash drive.

"And if we find a print of mine here?"

Jax scratched at his jaw. "Then we'll know for sure you're being framed. Right?"

A concerted effort to destroy her. "Right."

Whoever was behind this might be someone who didn't have the stomach for that kind of work. A person she could lean on and make talk. They wouldn't want a long jail sentence. Nor would they want anyone to think they were that kind of monster. Just a smart guy who made good business decisions, not a killer. If she was right, that person would cave when faced with the FBI.

"No answer. Again." She bit her lip. "We need to go check on Eric and Arnie."

Never mind that she was supposed to keep their names out of it. She didn't want the FBI to find Eric yet, but Kenna was worried now. Something might've happened.

Jax drove. She directed him to the house where she'd left Eric. Had he stayed? She didn't want to believe either was involved, but the people who'd paid Arnie were professionals. They had cleaned up after themselves so far. Could be they intended to tie up all the loose ends.

"Uh-oh." Jax pulled onto Arnie's street.

"Yeah, no kidding." Kenna surveyed the emergency vehicles crowded on the street in front of the house. Fire truck. Ambulance. Even a police car. "Let's find out what happened."

Jax found the scene commander and explained who they were. Before the fire chief could say anything, Kenna asked, "Was anyone inside?"

He nodded, a grim-faced expression on his face. "Two bodies, I'm sorry to say."

"Can we take a look, or is it still too hot to get in?"

"Give it a few hours to cool. Then the bodies will be on their way to the morgue. You can coordinate with the fire investigator if you're on this case."

Jax said, "Was it arson?"

"Like I said, you can coordinate with the fire investigator. I'll get you his card." The chief strode away, toward his men.

"Two bodies?"

Kenna swallowed. "Eric Wilson and Arnie Heraldson."

He stared at her.

"You know this was no accident, right?"

He put a hand between her shoulder blades and walked her back to the car. Until she shook him off and paced away, trying to breathe through it. *Two bodies.* Because she had told Eric to stay here. Had they been killed in the house fire, or murdered before the flames even started?

Either way, the result was the same. They were dead. "It's my fault."

Jax said nothing.

"I told him to hole up here with Arnie. They were friends, that's how Eric introduced me."

"Arnie is who?"

"The one who set up the website and sent me the video link. Thomas won't get to meet him now." As if that was the pertinent point. She shook her head and tried to get a handle on her roiling emotions.

She needed to be alone.

She needed the road.

Jax's fingers folded around hers. "Stick with me."

"People are *dead.*" And he couldn't say it wasn't going to happen again before they found these people. "This is crazy. We don't even have a suspect. It could be a group, or a team. Someone could've hired them, and then they hired sub-contractors. It could be a whole company!"

"The more people involved, the higher the chance we find a way into the group. The more people there are to find, the more likely we are to ID one and work our way to getting them all."

"I did! That was Arnie. And now he's burned to a crisp in there because he talked to me."

"This isn't your fault."

"Only my back was turned. Again." Figuratively. "This time, two people are gone. Before I even got a chance to realize that was what was happening."

"You're not responsible."

"They're gone, and I did nothing to stop it." Just like with Bradley. She hadn't even known they were headed for death, and that neglect was as bad as if she'd stood aside and watched it happen.

"This is organized. They're cleaning up after themselves, disposing of loose ends."

She turned to him. "Because that will make us stop hunting them?"

Something crossed his eyes, like a shadow cast when a cloud crossed in front of the sun. He didn't explain.

"We're not going to. Right?"

"I'm with you until this case ends," he said. "But not if you're going to blame yourself."

"Well *excuse* me for feeling responsible. They left my business cards. They did this because I'm back in town. Tell me how I'm not right in the middle of it?"

"I'm not going to."

Because she was. "I have some culpability."

"That's something I'd debate with you. But not if it means standing around here doing nothing or reasoning around in circles. That doesn't move this thing along."

She preferred motion. "Fine. Where do we go?"

It could take days to get a report on Eric and Arnie's deaths, as well as forensic results from the office they'd found. The place where at least Jessica had been murdered—or so she figured. Until then, what was she supposed to do? Thomas could come up with something else. The other FBI agents working this could get a lead.

Kenna needed something to do so she wasn't just waiting around.

That might have been part of the job as an FBI agent, but as a PI, she ran down anything and everything just in case. It kept her moving. The way she'd been since Bradley died. Since she was released from the hospital.

Why slow down, or stop, when it would force her to realize all she'd lost? Then she'd have to face it.

"Let's go to the office."

"Good." She got her phone out, but not to make a call. "I want to look some more at Christopher Halpert's victims. See if we can identify another."

Eventually, she wanted to have names for each so she could visit the next of kin and tell them what had happened to their loved one. Make sure they could be put to rest—the way she'd done with Sarah Bateman once her body had been found. Then at least she'd know something good had come out of this when she woke in the middle of the night with Jessica's face lingering from her nightmare.

Kenna checked the security on her motorhome. It hadn't been disturbed. She logged in and remotely activated the camera on her laptop so she could see Cabot. The dog, pixelated through the camera, lay on her side, her head off the dog bed. Belly rising and falling.

"Everything okay?" Jax looked over her shoulder.

"She's fine." Kenna barely got the words out.

"Can I ask..?" He paused. "What happened to the dog you had before?"

She nodded in answer to his first question. "Bradley and I used to go for runs when we needed to talk through a case. We would run until we'd worked it out. We would take Bear with us." She pulled in a long breath and blew it out slowly. "The night Almatter tracked and kidnapped us, we were on the trail. He shot us both with his dart gun, and I heard him kick Bear. My dog whimpered, and I couldn't do anything, I just passed out. A witness said he ran off into the woods."

"No one ever found him."

She shook her head.

"I'm sorry for your loss."

"You know, no one's ever said that to me." She stared at the white-peaked mountains. "Not for Bradley. Or our baby. And not for Bear."

He shifted toward her and was about to say something when his phone rang. He answered, "Jaxton." He listened for a moment. "We're on our way."

He hung up. "Doctor Landstadt has been kidnapped."

Chapter Thirty-Two

Friday, 2:17pm.

The burgundy Toyota at the curb belonged to the FBI motorpool. Kenna bumped the lock and was out of the car before Jax could even put it in park.

She let herself in the front door. "Hello?"

The downstairs was an open plan. Both FBI agents flinched for their guns, then realized who it was. Ian looked up from his seat on the edge of his recliner. Relief washed over his puffy face. "Kenna." He stood and moved to her. "I was hoping you'd come."

"Hey, Ian."

"Mommy!" A six-year-old tornado tore out of the kitchen area and skidded to a halt. She'd left the babysitter behind with the half-eaten sandwich on the breakfast bar.

"Baby—" Ian didn't get to finish.

The little girl skidded to a stop. "Who are you?" The girl's cheeks said she'd barely finished crying, and there was still that little hitch in her breath.

"I'm Makenna." She crouched to eye level. "I find people who are missing."

"Did you find my mommy?"

"Not yet, but I will." Kenna heard Miller hiss. Jax was inside now, and Sanchez was over in the FBI huddle, too.

The little girl padded back to the babysitter with her thumb in her mouth. Ian held out his hand. Kenna clasped his wrist and he helped her stand back up. "Ian, she's beautiful."

He nodded, understandably too distracted by his wife's disappearance to admire the child they'd made. "Thank you for coming." He leaned in and kissed her on the cheek.

Kenna squeezed his hand. "I'm going to do everything I can. I didn't lie to Bethany, I find people."

"Taylor said you're a private investigator now."

Kenna led him back to the couch. "Tell me what happened."

Sanchez got a notification. Whatever it was, he showed his phone to Miller. When his partner read the email, his eyebrows rose. Miller glanced up to look sharply at Ian. Neither let Kenna in on whatever it was.

"Ian?"

"Okay." He took a long breath. "Her work called just before one. I'm not due in until later today, so I was here with Bethany and the babysitter was coming after lunch. They said Taylor hadn't come back from an early lunch meeting and asked if I knew where she was." Ian swallowed. "I called but she didn't answer. Her location is turned off. I think her whole phone is off."

Kenna glanced at Sanchez, who shook his head. They hadn't found the phone. Given the way GPS worked, even if a phone was turned off, that meant it had either been destroyed or the battery had been removed somehow.

"I called the gym since she sometimes goes at lunch. She checked in at noon, but they hadn't seen her leave or anything. They don't watch the door. She only stays thirty minutes."

"Which gym?"

Kenna answered Miller's question, "Freedom Fitness."

Ian nodded.

Jax said, "The one on Central, or on Magdalaney?"

"Central." Ian's chin quivered. "Was it that cop killer from the video?"

"She told you about that?" Kenna's stomach flipped over, and she had to swallow back bile.

"We talked about you being back, and that's when she told me." He took another tissue from the box on the coffee table. "Is it connected?"

Two years ago, Kenna hadn't really liked Ian, truth be told. They just hadn't jived in any way, despite her and Taylor being friends. She wanted to say no. That this abduction—if that's what it was—didn't relate at all to the murder of four people. "We just don't know, not yet."

The idea Taylor had been targeted because of their association—their former friendship—crossed her mind. She couldn't let that occupy her head space, though. It would drag her down into a spiral that wasn't going to find Taylor.

Ian looked like he was going to be sick.

"I'll get her back." She squeezed his hand. "I am going to find her and bring her back to you."

Someone made a noise. Kenna didn't much care if they didn't like that she was saying this. She wanted to get in Ian's face and make him believe her, but they'd never had much beyond an acquaintanceship that had Taylor squarely in the middle.

"I will find her."

"And if it's the serial killer?"

"Then I'll deal." The way she'd done before. "It won't change the plan. I'll find her."

"Was it because of you and her?"

Kenna frowned. "What do you mean?"

"She's been trying to speak with you since you got home, and it finally happened?"

Kenna nodded.

"She was preparing a statement. Did she tell you that? Figuring out what to say, and how she would get it all out."

"Did she tell you what it was about?" Kenna didn't want to be accused of suggesting anything in front of three FBI agents versus allowing Ian to speak unhindered.

"She felt so bad about what she did to you. It practically destroyed her, the guilt. The past few months she's been trying to figure out how to get the truth out so people would know what really happened."

A few months?

"It was hard for her to face what she'd done. But writing it down seemed so much easier. She was thinking about posting it online or contacting news outlets. Telling the truth about how the governor had put pressure on her to lie about what you said happened."

Kenna had suffered a whole lot more than a difficult conversation. Meanwhile, Taylor had lied about her. And for what? Student loan payoffs? That debt wasn't going to come back if she told the truth, but she could lose her job and her license.

Kenna had lost a whole lot more than that. "Did she tell anyone other than you about this?"

Ian shook his head.

She wanted to ask a million more questions about Taylor but now wasn't the time. She stood so she could go find her friend. She could ask those questions directly once Taylor was safe again.

Not because she wanted her to be able to tell everyone the truth.

That couldn't be the reason she was doing this, and yet it would likely come across that way regardless. Didn't matter, though. Kenna would find Taylor before whoever took her enacted their plan.

Did that mean another video, or would she wind up dead before they could follow any clues, like Meg, Christopher, and Clive? There was no way to tell since none of this made sense beyond her collection of dissonant theories. She had little in the way of hard proof unless she could ID whoever had taken Taylor.

If that was even what'd happened. With her whole heart she wished that Taylor just decided she had been in need of a break and left town.

Kenna walked to the front door. Jax stood on the porch on his phone.

"That could've gone a lot differently." Sanchez.

She reached between him and Miller to close the front door.

"If I was him—" Miller lifted his chin at her. "—you'd be at the top of my list of people responsible."

Kenna faced off both men. "Then it's a good thing you're not him. I don't know how many times I'm going to have to tell you guys I had nothing to do with this."

"Not entirely true now, is it?" Sanchez lifted his chin.

Miller said, "The husband knows more than he's saying about what might've happened to Doctor Landstadt."

"Can we not—"

He cut her off. "Sanchez found out Mr. Landstadt's been taking lump sum payouts into an account his wife has no access to. Probably on the take. Dirty dealings with contractors, or the county building inspector. They either took the wife to put pressure on him or he arranged it so he can get a payout from her life insurance to settle the debt."

"You think he's going to have her killed, blame it on the cop killer, and cash in?" She hadn't gotten that vibe from Ian at all, but wouldn't rule out being surprised by something she never saw coming. It wouldn't pay to assume she'd figured this out.

"I'll add that to the bottom of my long list of theories." In truth, Kenna wasn't even going to entertain the idea until she'd ruled out everything else. "Do we know for sure that she was abducted?"

Sanchez said. "Maybe she ran off with a boyfriend."

"And leave Bethany?" Kenna shook her head.

"Believe what you want to believe," Sanchez said. "The truth is the truth."

Kenna sighed. She had to keep her cool. They were only being like this to get a rise out of her. "I'll be investigating the disappearance of the FBI office psychologist while you guys squabble like two pigeons over a scrap of moldy bread." Too bad she was the moldy bread. "But thanks for coming. I appreciate your being here first." The little girl, Bethany, didn't need to wait longer than necessary to get her mother back.

"You'll appreciate it a whole lot less when we sit you down for questioning." It looked like Miller enjoyed that thought. "Find out exactly how responsible you are for this."

And here she thought Miller finding out the truth about what really happened to Bradley would have given him a new perspective on her involvement in the case. Cleary she'd given him too much credit.

She whipped around and locked eyes with him. "Was she kidnapped? Do we have video I don't know about?" These people seemed to be cleaning up loose ends, burning down that house with Eric and Arnie in it. Now they'd taken Taylor? Maybe she was dead already—all because she'd wanted to tell the truth about Bradley's death. If that was true, it was probable there would be no video.

Miller shrugged. "You tell me."

Kenna turned to Jax so they didn't see the look on her face. He lifted one finger for her to hold on. *Ugh.* What was he even doing?

Sanchez said, "We'll set up in case Mr. Lanstadt receives a ransom call."

She figured that was a waste of time, but considering it was procedure they'd argue nothing was a waste of time. She left the two of them and walked over to Jax.

He looked over, the phone to his ear. "Because we'll be there in ten." He paused. "A friend of mine that I'm working this with." He sighed. "No, it isn't. You'll like this one."

He hung up.

"Let's go." Jax walked her to his car.

Suddenly, Kenna didn't feel so steady. "Where are we going?" She tried not to stumble and fall on her face.

"As well as teaching yoga at the community center, I also teach kickboxing at Freedom Fitness. Mostly just to fill in when they need a sub, but it's regular." He spoke over the roof of the car. "I might have a CI who knows something about Doctor Lanstadt."

Everything she'd held back and pushed down while talking to Ian—in order to keep him calm and hopeful—rushed in now. Rushed through and around her. Relentless.

Unyielding. *Go, Kenna. Run.* Kenna stumbled off the curb and fell onto the passenger seat. She shut the door with a shaky hand while a wave of fear rolled over her.

She must have made a noise in her throat because Jax twisted to her.

"Head between your knees."

She shook her head. Hands on her lap, fingers twisted together. Nothing she could do but ride the wave to the inevitable wipe-out that always came.

Jessica Pierce.

The college girl, Meg.

Both dead now.

The old man. The younger man. Christopher and Clive. Her friend Taylor—former friend—the woman who'd betrayed her. She pictured Meg, spread out on Eric's bed. Covered in blood.

Now Eric was dead, along with his friend Arnie. People who knew something. Or were involved. This thing had spread like a virus, now infecting unsuspecting victims.

Kenna gulped a breath. Would she find Taylor like the others?

"Easy." His warm fingers touched the back of her neck. He crooned nonsense words as if she was about to blow and he wouldn't know how to handle the fallout. Like she was the "Ryson" in this situation, and he was the one having to talk *her* off the ledge before she did something that hurt not only herself but others as well. She resented him for treating her that way but deep down knew it wasn't Jax she resented. He was just trying to help. She resented herself for not being in control when a human life hung in the balance.

"Taylor." Kenna sucked in a breath.

"We'll find her. My guy is squirrely. He won't wait long."

"So, go."

He drove. Kenna gripped the handle on the door. *Go.* In her other hand, she had her phone squeezed so tight she was probably about to crack the screen in half. Jax wouldn't try to hold her hand. She wouldn't accept anyway. As much as she didn't want to admit needing anyone, it wasn't always true.

Sometimes she didn't want to be alone.

"Miller might be right. This could be my fault." Because she'd spoken with Taylor yesterday? "Someone found out Taylor was going to tell the truth about Bradley."

That meant this was a conspiracy to keep it quiet. But with the governor away at that conference, it didn't make a whole lot of sense.

"Don't do that. You don't know her abduction had anything to do with you." Jax turned a corner. "We don't even know she's been taken."

"If she was, it's because of me." She wasn't about to let this go. Her friend was the one missing now. Not just an acquaintance, or a name on a police report. "I was there when Bethany was born. I told her nothing would ever happen to either of them. That there wasn't anything to worry about." Kenna squeezed her eyes shut.

He squeezed her wrist for a second. "We'll do everything we know to do, and then we'll do more."

"I don't want to just try. I want to find her. I *need* to find her."

"I know."

"You're much easier to deal with when you're accusing me of being behind all this."

"Because then you'd have proof that I'm not worth trusting, so you can write me off as a jerk so you don't have to be vulnerable." He didn't wait much more than a beat before he said, "Your friend is missing. I'm not gonna be mean to you."

"See. Annoying."

He drove to the Freedom Fitness location where Taylor worked out and pulled into a pharmacy lot across the street. A van had been parked in the corner of the lot. Beside it was a sign advertising smog checks.

She figured if the owner even attempted to drive that thing out of this lot, it would disintegrate before they even got off the cracked concrete and onto the asphalt.

"Wait here."

She didn't, but she did hang back.

"Barney, my man." Jax held out his hand to greet the mountainous shape that rose up to meet him. "How you doin'?"

The mountain might not be a huge purple dinosaur, but he fit the moniker. His red hair made him significantly taller than he was, and his slender body in oversized clothes made her wonder if he made money from these smog checks, or off the stuff he sold alongside that. He probably figured both was a public service.

"Not bad." The mountain shrugged.

Jax waved her over. "Tell her what you told me on the phone."

"I been here all morning."

"You were here when a woman was abducted from that parking lot over there?" She motioned in the direction of the gym.

Barney didn't want to admit whatever it was he knew.

"Don't lie to me, Barn."

He shot a glance in Jax's direction. "You know me. Any chance to do my civic duty."

"What did you see?"

"Who says I saw anything?"

"Then why am I wasting my time?"

Kenna tipped her head to the side. "I'm sure this responsible citizen won't mind at all if we look around his trailer."

"It's a motorhome."

"Whatever."

He looked affronted.

"I'm thinking that's a good idea." Jax took two steps toward the van.

Barney intercepted him. "Hold up. Hold up. Okay?"

Jax took another step.

"Fine." Barney heaved out a breath that seemed too big for his chest. "I park here on purpose. Prime view of all those gym honeys coming and going. Best part is when they bend over."

Kenna gauged the distance. "Binoculars?"

"Nah, I got a sweet camera setup."

At that, Jax nearly took the door off the hinges to get access to it.

"Dude!"

Before Barney could stop Jax, Kenna grabbed a fistful of his collar and slammed him against the outside of his van. "Did you see a woman get abducted this morning while you were creeping on unsuspecting women? Tell me!"

His eyes flickered. She added pressure to her forearm, against his neck.

"I will shoot you if I find out you ever flex one photo-triggering-finger in my direction. Do you hear me?" She gritted her teeth. "Talk. Or you won't be looking at anyone ever again."

"I saw her."

"Someone took her?"

He nodded, eyes glinting. Skin clammy now. "Black van. Before you ask, there were no license plates."

"Any other markings?"

He shook his head.

"What about the guy? What did he look like? Any distinctive features? Tattoos. The way he walked. Clothes. Hair color." Barney needed to give her something.

She couldn't be this close to a lead and watch it slip through her fingers.

Jax stepped back out. "He got a shot."

She backed up and held out a finger. "Don't move."

"T-there's a killer out there," Barney stammered. "People are turning up dead. You think I don't know that? I told you I'm a responsible citizen doing my civic duty." He sucked in a breath that puffed up his chest to about half the normal size. "No way I wasn't going to get him on camera."

"But you didn't stop it?"

"Are you crazy? He'd've killed me too!"

"You saw him kill her?"

"Nah, man. It's an expression."

"You called 9-1-1 straight away instead?"

"I was just about to call my buddy Jax here when he called me first."

Jax showed her the camera's tiny display screen. "Face and everything." The image was high resolution. Taylor, clearly unconscious, on a man's shoulder. He had his hood up, but there was enough face showing that Kenna had to fight back the need to grab the camera and jump in Jax's car. To get this back to the office ASAP so it could be run.

Was this the day they would get an ID?

Finally find out who this guy was?

Find her friend, the woman who'd betrayed her but didn't need to die simply because she'd decided it was time to tell the truth.

"Has anyone broken into your van recently?"

Barney shook his head.

"What about someone coming around, asking about you or interested in your pictures?"

He just shrugged.

"Anyone ever bought any from you? Maybe they leaned on you about your…proclivities."

"Like for a free smog check?"

It was her turn to shrug.

Jax had apparently had enough. "This camera alone costs more than your van is worth. Never mind that big TV you've got in there." Jax shook his head. "But I'm actually glad you're a perv right now. We're taking this."

Barney's face fell. "You can't take—" Jax was already walking away. "—my camera!"

Kenna said, "Thanks for doing your civic duty. Not making us get a warrant."

"Just take the sim card!"

"We'll take the whole thing. Thanks." She pulled open the door on her side. "Who knows, if this leads to the rescue of an FBI employee, there could be a reward."

"Uniforms are on their way." Jax handed over the camera and started the engine. "They'll bring him in and question him about being a total perv." His jaw flexed. "Some of those pictures." He shook his head.

Great.

She wanted to feel relief, but she didn't. The photo alone didn't get Taylor back.

Chapter Thirty-Three

K enna shoved past an agent in full tactical gear and stepped inside the house. Thanks to the FBI's facial recognition database, they'd ID'd the kidnapper. "Taylor!"

Someone said, "Easy." But she didn't listen. Even when he said, "Dead guy in the living room."

She was momentarily relieved to hear that the dead body was male and not her friend. But any dead body was bad. She continued, avoiding the living room, but moving through the rest of the house, checking every room. Every closet. Every dark corner. *Where is she?* Taylor had to be here.

"Slow down."

She was almost to the kitchen when a door opened in her path. The agent who came out nearly collided with her. "Someone needs to see this."

"What is it?" Her stomach dropped. *Please not Taylor's dead body.*

He led her downstairs. The second she stepped off the bottom of the wood staircase, she got a look at the basement and immediately twisted back around to the open doorway at the top. "Jaxton!"

"What's going..." He trotted down the steps and stopped short. "Oh."

The entire basement was one giant clean room. A torture chamber. A place to murder and leave no evidence. "He's got the whole setup here." She knew what she sounded like. The fear probably reflected on her face. "He had plans to kill someone."

"Kenna."

She moved toward the plastic sheeting and pulled it aside. A metal bed, pristine, was inside. Surrounded by more plastic on all sides. Even the ceiling.

"He never got the chance to use it." Hung on the wall at the end was an array of tools. Weapons. Sheers. Clippers. Chef's knives. Hunting gear.

"Let's go outside. Get some air." Jax got between her and the sheet and tried to lead her out. It was a valiant effort, but there was no way she would be herded like an errant sheep.

"He was going to bring Taylor here." She pointed again, her finger shaky. "To this." She pressed her lips together.

"Let's go up," Jax said. "You don't need to be down here."

Jax gently guided Kenna up the stairs.

Under the archway between the living room and kitchen, a man lay in a pool of his own blood. "Is that the guy from the photo?"

No one said anything.

"I should call his ex-wife. Tell her she doesn't have to worry about forwarding his magazines anymore." Kenna stared at him. It was the kidnapper they'd just ID'd as Elijah Hammersmith. After first visiting the address on his driver's license, his ex-wife had told them he lived here now. "How did he die?"

Jax moved toward the body and crouched.

A tactical agent stepped up beside her. "There's no one else here."

Kenna stared at the dead man who'd abducted her friend. "Why couldn't she have been here?"

The tactical agent squeezed her shoulder. "We're all worried about Doctor Landstadt." His voice broke, and he cleared his throat before walking off quickly.

Elijah Hammersmith lay on his side.

"Single gunshot. This is the exit wound." Jax put one knee down beside the blood pool. "He hasn't been dead long."

"He's the first person we've found all week who was actually killed in the exact place we found him."

He turned to her and nodded.

"So the killer could still be in the area?"

Jax motioned to the window. "We can go look, but who are we looking for? Taylor, or someone else?"

"He takes Taylor. Now he's dead." Kenna had to figure this out. "Did she kill him? If she did, where is she? If someone else did, then *where is she*?"

"Only one we've got on camera so far has been Elijah and look where that got him. Unless this guy had a camera doorbell or some other kind of surveillance, there's no way to find out who else was here." He waved over an agent. "Canvas the neighborhood. See if anyone saw anything."

The agent nodded.

"Someone killed him and took Taylor from her kidnapper."

Jax said, "So he was a means to an end?"

"His car is still here. We have no idea who has Taylor and what they're doing." She squeezed her hands into fists. "Unpacking this guy's life to find out who told him to snatch her will take too long."

The fastest way to get information would be to find his

phone.

Kenna walked through the house again, even though trying to locate such an obvious piece of evidence like a phone was likely futile. They hadn't garnered a result like that yet, so why did she think they would now? This guy had taken Taylor, and then he'd been killed. Because of it? She thought of Ian, but immediately dismissed it. He still had a detail of agents at his house so she would know if he'd left.

Then there was Steven, who'd been following her. So frustrated with their lack of progress that he'd tried to run her over with his car.

Right now she could almost say she understood what that felt like. This was her former friend, but the feeling of power-lessness was about the limit of what she could handle—and only because she refused to give in to the fear. The second she let herself think about what was happening to Taylor? She'd lose it. Like, any second now.

Elijah Hammersmith could have been a viewer on the original website.

"He takes her to kill her," Jax said. "Then he's killed, and she's again taken, this time by another killer?"

"That would be my guess. Elijah was a killer, if the base-ment is anything to go by."

Jax nodded. "The old man is poisoned. One guy takes Jessica, probably Clive. He hands her over for the video, and then he's responsible for killing her after that. Clive takes Meg next but loses control, so they scramble. Dump her and kill him. Now they need someone else, so they hire this guy—Elijah—to take Taylor. No slip ups are allowed, so they kill him and now he's not a problem cause he can't talk. Leaves them free to do...whatever they want."

"But why Taylor? My business card wasn't left outside the gym. It was a simple snatch and grab."

The answer to that was, "Kenna."

She ignored him and pulled out her phone, just in case. Called the number Elijah's ex-wife had given them.

A muffled ringing abruptly ended all conversation in the room.

"Where is that coming from?" Jax crossed to the couch and started pulling out the cushions. The ringing got louder.

Kenna hung up as Jax lifted the phone.

He stared at the screen. "There are messages."

Kenna sent a text to the ex-wife, asking what his phone passcode might be. She replied a few seconds later, and Kenna read the numbers aloud.

"Bingo." Jax swiped his thumb across the screen. "I've got a string of texts that start with, I have her. Reply: I'm coming to you. Elijah—" He motioned to the dead man. "—says back, Okay, how long? Reply: Just sit tight."

"The killer had him bring her here, and then took her from him?"

"Elijah didn't take her for himself," Jax said.

Kenna nodded. Again the idea this was her fault rolled through her mind. She knew Jax would disagree, so she didn't voice it aloud. No matter how vehemently he argued, it wouldn't change what had happened. Passion didn't mean truth. It could just mean passion, even if the person was also completely wrong.

Kenna preferred to be realistic.

Bethany could be left motherless, and it would be because of Kenna. She wasn't going to kid herself about what was at stake here. Kenna liked facts too much for that.

"So, he arranges a meet," Jax said. "Whoever Elijah was talking to came and got her and killed Elijah in the process. We can dump the phone and find out everything there is to know about whoever was on the other end of this number, and where they are now." Jax grinned. "He finally screwed up. Not realizing the phone was still here left us a huge clue."

"This guy doesn't make mistakes. If he left the phone here, it was for a reason."

"It was buried in the couch cushions."

"He could've forgotten it, sure." Kenna shrugged. "But I don't think so. I think we aren't going to find out anything about him. Unless..."

What if he still had his?

Kenna swiped the phone out of his hands. If she was to blame, then the answer to this clearly landed with her.

She hit the little phone icon and listened to it ring. Kenna moved to the window so she could pretend everyone she'd worked with and respected two years ago wasn't here in the room with her. Plus Jax.

The ringing stopped. Heavy breathing.

"Well, well, well."

She forced herself not to jump right on him. Nor did she intend to acknowledge the way his voice slithered over her like clammy hands. Kenna took a deep breath. "Where's Taylor?"

She heard him chuckle.

"Wow, you're a bona fide cliché. Twirling your mustache much?"

"Hardly." His voice was sharp and hard.

"Oh, forgive me. I spoke too soon," her tone bled with sarcasm.

"Your friend's life is on the line."

"You're right. It is. In light of that, I should endeavor to befriend you, right? Try to get you to trust me. Maybe establish a rapport. Then I'll have to see what you want—make some kind of trade for my friend who you know I'll do just about anything to get back."

"Mmm."

In the background she heard Jax groan. The other agents shifted. She didn't care. What were they going to do, write a report about her?

"We could cut to the chase. You kill her, I'll kill you. It's that simple. No trade. Now where is she?"

He chuckled again.

"I'm so glad you find this amusing. I plan on being amused when I put a bullet in you."

"You'll never save her."

She gripped the phone and stared, unseeing, out the window.

"You'll never find her. You'll never win. You'll never beat me."

"No one lives forever," she said. "Not even you."

Jax moved in beside her, a frown canyon on his forehead. He made a circular motion with his index finger and mouthed, *Keep him talking.* Like she didn't know that? But it was good to know they were tracing the call.

"Sentiment?" The suspect huffed. "That's unexpected since Taylor tells me you haven't spoken in two years. Until yesterday."

She said, "You haven't killed my friend *yet.* Just a police officer, a college girl, and two men."

"I fail to see what concession I might need from you, Ms. Banbury. There will be no bargain."

"So, you did kill all four of them?"

Quiet.

"Or just Christopher Halpert and Clive Burnette. I don't think you killed the women." However, she did think he was the one from the video. The spokesperson. The guy who faced the camera while others did the dirty work.

"You think I won't kill your frenemy, Taylor?"

Kenna rolled her eyes, only because he couldn't see her. "How about I just hand you to the FBI instead of shooting you? As much as I might want to do otherwise."

"As if I will be sent to prison. You'll make sure of that. Won't you, Kenna?"

What was that supposed to mean? "You're looking for a different outcome?"

"I'm sure you and I can work something out. Like we did before."

She stilled. "Before?"

"That's why I answered the phone. So I could inform you. Let you know that everything is going according to plan."

Kenna froze.

"Nothing to worry about."

"Where is she?"

He said nothing. Around her, the atmosphere in the room went electric. She didn't blame them, considering he'd just insinuated what Stairns still believed—that she was behind this.

Kenna said, "Where is she?"

"Ask me one more time, maybe I'll tell you."

"This isn't a game, and I'm not playing."

"All of life is a game."

"And you're going to be the winner?"

Jax appeared again. He shook his head.

Great. Nothing on the trace. "Tell me where she is."

"Having trouble getting a bead on me?"

"Who said anything about that?"

He said nothing.

"TELL ME WHERE SHE IS."

The line went dead.

Chapter Thirty Four

Friday, 11:12pm.

"This how you plan to find Taylor?" Jax shut the door to the interview room. "It's a formality."

"Oh, I get it. Because the guy I spoke to on the phone insinuated he and I have had prior dealings. That I'm in league with him, or something. Well, guess what. He lied."

Kenna was getting tired of coming to her own defense. Over and over and over again. She might as well be talking to a brick wall.

"So I should allow you to continue to operate with no oversight. Because he *lied*. Kenna—don't do this to me. You know there are checks and balances."

"And the reason you had me surrender my weapon on the way in?" She'd have left it in the car otherwise, but he'd insisted.

Jax flipped open the file he'd brought in with him. "Arnold Heraldson and Eric Wilson were shot before the fire was set."

Kenna flinched. "Executions?"

"Arnold was shot in the front, Eric in the back."

"So he saw his friend die and ran."

Jax studied her.

"Stairns thinks I did it? Fine. Keep me here and not out on the streets. Where I can help look for Taylor."

"Stairns is working something else right now. All we've got is an insinuation you're part of this. We don't even know if Taylor is still alive."

Because she hadn't asked for proof of life. "She's alive."

"Maybe."

Kenna leaned forward. "Of course she's alive. I'd know if she wasn't. That's why we have to figure out who these guys are and where they're holding her."

"The guy you spoke to, why would he even answer the phone when he knew Elijah was dead? He had what he wanted."

"Taylor."

"So why pick up?"

"To cast suspicion on me as his accomplice." Kenna wasn't going to let herself get tied to the railroad tracks so the FBI could run over her. Not when a woman was in danger. "But answer this...if I was his accomplice, why break into my motorhome and steal my father's gun?"

"If that's what happened. The only person who could've corroborated that story is now dead. Executed, as you suggested. Shot in the back. Trying to get away."

Kenna shook her head. "The FBI sure has gone downhill in the last two years."

"Like I said, this is a formality."

"No, it's called myopia. It's because Stairns is being leaned on by the governor to play along with the narrative that

I'm some kind of accomplice. That I want my name in lights, or that I'm looking for a movie deal."

"Isn't everyone trying to get famous these days?"

"I've spent the last two years basically alone. If I wanted fame, I'd have gone after it then instead of waiting until everyone has forgotten about me. The only good thing that's happened since I've been back is that I remember why I enjoyed the solitude. Because people suck." She blew out a breath. "Make sure someone feeds my dog while I'm in here. And let her out to pee, because if I have to clean up a mess when I get to go back, then I'm hiring someone and the FBI is paying the bill."

"That's what you're concerned about right now?"

"The life under my care? Yes."

"Not Taylor?"

"She betrayed me two years ago. Does it bother me that she's probably scared, or already dead? Of course. Bethany shouldn't grow up without a mother. I know how that feels, and it sucks."

"Her betrayal gives you motive to want her taken out."

"The way you think I'm motivated to take out every serial killer I come across? Because I already told you I haven't killed anyone. Not in two years. But sure, I've got a revenge plan all worked out. Almatter is dead. Who am I supposed to take out my frustration on?"

"The people who cut you loose."

He had it all figured out, didn't he? "Shame you didn't find a journal detailing my plans."

"As if you'd be sloppy enough to keep one."

"Mmm that's the reason." She'd never understood journaling. "Just so I can't be implicated."

He flipped over a page and slid the one beneath it across the table. "This is a warrant to search your motorhome and everything inside. Your car and any other property under your name."

"Hopefully Thomas can tell the difference between what's mine on my laptop and what was planted there to add to the evidence necessary to sell their story."

"Seems like something a true crime blogger might do, don't you think? Padding the story with coincidence."

"He's dead."

"Still, he'd have helped get the word out. Maybe someone should carry on the torch. Get access to the platform and all those followers."

"Like a person who happened to be in his house at the time a dead young woman was found in his bed?" So this was a theory of theirs, too? Kenna had involved Eric to implicate him and steal his following? It wasn't an awful idea, just completely off the mark.

Too bad the alternative meant she was either clueless or no better than an innocent bystander in all this. Someone along for the ride.

She didn't like being either of those any more than she liked being a victim.

"I'm sure my laptop will prove that, until two days ago, I'd never visited the Utah True Crime website, the blog, or the podcast. I never so much as even searched for Eric Wilson online. I'd never heard of him."

"You've never received an email request for an interview?"

"Those go in my spam folder. You think I read or even respond every time I get asked to come on some show?" She shook her head. "You and I don't know each other all that well, but that's a big no."

"Good to know, given much of what you experienced as

an FBI agent binds you to the confidentiality rules to keep it from being public."

"You ever get sick of all the rules?"

He shrugged one shoulder. "Can't say it's ever happened before."

"I feel like people have this view of private investigators. Like we're all renegades with no respect for the law, but I still have to follow the rules. I couldn't, say, go around killing whoever I want. Leaving bodies all over the Northwest, maybe with a note so whoever found them learned what that person did to deserve a bullet."

"Gotta be tempting."

He probably thought she'd been playing them all from the start. Every word she said, everything she did. Every inch of trust they'd built between them. All of it nothing but subterfuge to cover her agenda.

"Care to share?"

"Revenge is a much better story than fame." She shrugged. "If you've got to pick one, that's what I'd go with."

"So why haven't you touched the governor? You could've driven down to St. George at any time. Put this all to bed."

"Probably because I had no idea any of this was going to happen. I caught the Seventh Day Killer, handed him to the police, and got Ellayna Feathers to safety. The plan was to check my mail and then leave. I wasn't even going to go and see Ryson."

"So, you being on a revenge kick isn't a plausible motive."

"I kept my end of the bargain where I stayed quiet about how Bradley died, and the governor and First Lady never saw me again."

"If it was a bargain, what did they give you in exchange?"

"I already told you about the private investigator licenses. Other than that, they're supposed to leave me alone." She tapped her index finger on the table. "This doesn't feel like being left alone. This feels like being targeted. I just haven't figured out why."

"It might not even have to do with Special Agent Pacer. It could be someone else you've made an enemy of." Jax picked up his pen. "Anyone you can think of? Someone out on parole with a grudge."

"I probably cut them off in traffic."

"And in response, they kill a bunch of people? If they're trying to implicate you as the culprit, they're doing a poor job. So far all we have is suspicion."

"This is about Bradley." She just couldn't figure out why, now, after two years. "It's about dragging up the past to cause problems for me. I'll either end up dead, in jail, or confined to some psychiatric facility because they've convinced everyone I'm crazy. They won't be investigated. I'll have been completely discredited. No one will ever believe a word I say again, let alone any wild conspiracy theories."

"Who, other than the governor, is angry enough at you to go to all this trouble?"

"Who says they're angry? It might not be grief. Maybe I'm just a giant pain in someone's behind, and they need to get rid of me."

"Again. They've gone to a lot of trouble."

"So whatever it is, the trouble is worth it." She shrugged. "Is the governor talking about running for president? He could be cleaning the skeletons from his closet. I think he hired the guys who did the video at that office."

"Not to my knowledge. And if he hired anyone, there would be a money trail."

"So get a warrant for that. When you're done tearing through my life, you can look at his financial records." She had to believe he would find the truth. Otherwise, what hope did she have? The last thing Kenna wanted was to reach the place Bradley had been—no way out except one.

And wouldn't that be incredibly convenient for the governor?

She'd planned on being a pain in his behind for *years* to come. Only, with all this happening, it seemed like there would be an end sooner or later. The truth would out, or she would find herself imprisoned. Again.

Kenna shivered.

She'd been content to know the governor would always wonder where she was, and what trouble she might cause him. Especially when he had no idea where she was. That was how she'd ordered her life—so he couldn't track her.

Unless the spyware had been on her phone for two years.

He could've been keeping tabs on her since the day she left. That would mean they'd known the second she came back to Salt Lake City—the night this had all kicked off.

"Should I be writing this down? Maybe you could lay out the whole investigation for me. I'll take notes."

She almost smiled. "That was good work with your confidential informant, by the way. It got us an ID on Elijah when it could've taken days to find his body." At which point, Taylor would be dead.

"Seems strange they'd bring on someone new at this point."

"They forced Clive to kill for them because of his obsession with Meg, but he lost it. At least, that's what I assume." She'd been thinking of nothing else for days. "What's the connection between Elijah Hammersmith and Doctor Landstadt?"

Jax stared, as though deciding whether to trust her with the information. "He was her patient. She did pro bono hours in a unit for the criminally insane."

"And he was released? A man declared criminally insane?"

"She treated him years ago, early on in her career. He was let out sixteen months ago. He completed his treatment."

That brought on another shiver. "Evidently not, given his basement."

"I can get you a cup of coffee."

Kenna shook her head. "I've accepted enough from the FBI. I don't want anything else from you." She'd thought she could keep the two separate—her past and Jax's badge. But he was part of the machine. He did as he was told regardless of his personal feelings. That wasn't a failing. It was the job.

But that didn't mean she had to like it.

Yes, she was bound by the law as a private investigator. But the only procedure she adhered to was what she assigned herself. There were ways of doing things. If she came across a suspect who didn't fit the mold, someone possibly being set up, Kenna wouldn't accept anything at face value. She tried to always give people the benefit of the doubt.

Why lay awake at night worrying that she'd missed something? There was plenty in her head to achieve that goal already. She didn't need to add regret to all the loss and nightmare images.

Jax said, "If Elijah Hammersmith was obsessed with Doctor Landstadt, I'm surprised she didn't tell her husband or her boss how much he was contacting her."

"She mentioned something to me about unwanted attention. But not his name or what was happening."

Jax sighed.

"Some things can't be prevented, no matter the precautions we take. People who think they have the right to power in a situation still just do whatever they want."

She of all people knew that was true. Signing up for the

FBI, she'd been happy with the trade-off. She got to carry their badge and live out what the bureau stood for. In return, they were supposed to have her back. Safeguard her. One phone call from the governor to SAC Stairns and that had all gone out the window. Because one man decided his agenda was more important than her career.

"Speaking of..." Jax settled back into detective mode. "You decided to get back at the governor. You hired Elijah Hammersmith because you knew he had a thing for the doctor." He flipped over another page. "I'm guessing you knew about Clive and his obsession. About the serial killer with his shoe box of mementos. I can't figure out Jessica Pierce, though. Maybe she looked at you wrong the night you handed over the Seventh Day Killer. Pretty good way of establishing your commitment to the cause of justice. Hand over a serial killer, then we don't look at you when the first person is taken. You probably even hired Steven Pierce to try and run you over."

Jax pushed the page across the table. A printout of the visitor log for a psychiatric facility. Her name had been highlighted in the middle. Date and time of visit.

Kenna did the math in her head and smiled. "Finally, you actually have proof I'm being set up."

"Excuse me?"

The date she was supposed to have visited this guy was three months after she left Salt Lake City. Three months from the day she walked away from her entire life. "Did you put in a request for the security footage?"

"Your build. Your hairstyle."

Okay, that could be a problem. Instead of it being clear she was never there, it was a lookalike? Still, it wasn't impossible to refute. "But it doesn't show my face."

He shook his head.

"Because I was in Reno. Find the copy of my taxes on my laptop. I scan in all my receipts, and those will prove I was nowhere near that psychiatric facility on that day." She smiled. "Looks like their plan isn't foolproof after all."

"Is that right?"

"Yes, because Reno is where my physical therapist lives. The one who helped me after the third surgery to repair the damage Sebastian Almatter did to my forearms." She pulled back her sleeves to the elbows. He'd seen the scars, but that night had been dark. "If they want to prove I'm the suspect here, they'll have to do better than a woman pretending to be me on a day I was a state away receiving medical treatment."

Fear rolled through her. This plan had been in the works for so long.

Ever since she'd left, someone had been laying the groundwork to get back at her. But they hadn't tracked her movements. Or not well, at least.

Alone, Kenna might not be able to prove her innocence. Jax didn't seem likely to help. Taylor had been snatched off the street by a man obsessed with her and was now in the hands of a completely different man. One with a cold voice who laughed far too easily. Or was that yet more subterfuge? Eric and Arnie were dead. She didn't believe the FBI would accept the truth, even if they found it.

"All this is a waste of time," she said. "We're just going around and around the same things and getting nowhere. Meanwhile, Taylor is out there." She pointed at the door, even though she had no idea where her former friend was. "If I was her, I'd be praying for rescue any second. But it isn't coming. Because we're sitting here wasting time. Just like with Bradley and I, help will come far too late. After the worst has happened."

"How do you suggest we go about finding her? The phone

number you called was a burner. It's either had the battery or the SIM card removed. Either way, we can't track them."

"And Hammersmith's neighbors didn't see anything? We have no idea what vehicle she was taken in? The full force of the FBI, and you have nothing."

She would be out on the streets, pounding her fists on doors until she came up with something. Considering the fact she seemed to be the focus of so much of this, why not set herself up as bait? Surely they'd grab her too, if they got the chance.

She doubted there could be yet another obsessed crazy out there with a grudge, willing to kidnap her.

Then again, what did she know?

"I have an idea."

Jax shook his head. "What you need to do is to contact a lawyer."

"Get Stairns. I want to talk to him."

Jax did nothing.

"Call him. Right now. I think I know how to end this."

Everything in her rebelled at the idea of walking into a trap. But for six-year-old Bethany, and the risk that she might grow up without a mother, Kenna would do it. For Jessica. For Meg.

Jax stood. "I'll ask if he'll speak to you."

"If you want Doctor Landstadt back, do better than that."

The door opened before he got to it. The agent poked his head in and spoke quietly so she couldn't hear. Jax nodded. "Please tell SAC Stairns I need to speak to him immediately."

The agent nodded. The door clicked shut.

"Has Taylor been found?"

Jax shook his head and sighed, "There was a clerical mix-up at the courthouse. Gerald Rickshire was just released."

Chapter Thirty Five

Friday, 11:52pm.

"Just sit tight, Ms. Feathers. Two agents are on their way, and they're not leaving until he's back in prison. Okay?"

Kenna held the phone to her ear. She felt Jax shift closer to her. Showing solidarity, being here for her even though it was just a phone call. "I'll stay on the phone until they show. Did you tell Ellayna?"

"No. I don't want to add to the anxiety she already has. It doesn't matter though. She'll figure out something's wrong, and she'll know it's about her."

"I need you to let the agents protect you. Don't worry about Rickshire. He isn't going to get near you."

"I'd feel better if you were here. I know Laynie would too."

Kenna squeezed her eyes shut. "I need to be out here looking for him."

It would be more of an attempt to draw out the Seventh Day Killer, but Ellayna's mother didn't need to know that. They had enough going on. Including her high-risk pregnancy. She didn't need to go into labor early because she was stressed.

"Will you come and see us after? I think Ellayna would like that."

"I would, too."

"Thanks, Kenna." In the background, a mature, soprano voice spoke—too far away to hear. Ellayna's mother's alto tone came through the line. "My mom said the agents are here." She whispered, "Now she can go back to rearranging my kitchen."

Kenna smiled. "Can you put one on the phone?"

A few seconds later the agent came on the line. "It's Sanchez. We'll secure the house and make sure Rickshire doesn't get anywhere near this family."

"Good." Their conversation lasted long enough she could ensure it was really him. "Thanks."

After spending a little more time reassuring Ellayna's mother, Kenna managed to hang up, and then, as if on cue, her vision blurred.

"Are you okay?"

She waved off Jax, breathing hard to gather her composure. "Where's Cabot?"

Instead of speaking, he pointed. Across the bullpen and through the glass door to the break room, her dog stared at her. She hadn't even noticed until now, but Cabot seemed to keep constant tabs on Kenna these days.

Kenna hauled open the door and her dog jumped. Kenna attempted to brace herself but was too late and landed on her behind instead, Cabot on her lap. Laughter overcame her as her dog licked her tears until there were no more. It was nice to laugh. There hadn't been any reason to in too long. No matter how brief.

Jax handed her a bundle of tissue. She wiped her face. "Thanks."

"Nothing is going to happen to Ellayna Feathers."

"What about Taylor?"

There was so much more to worry about. Ryson and Valentina, and baby Luci. What if something happened to them as well?

Kenna clasped his wrist, and he helped her to her feet. Cabot followed, until she slumped into a chair in the conference room and the dog lay down with her head on Kenna's boot. Despite telling Ellayna's mother she would be out looking for Rickshire, Stairns wanted to be briefed first. And she was more than happy to accommodate him.

After all, she was a private investigator now. Not one of his agents.

She'd also received four texts from Ryson, in a thread that included Valentina. They were safe and together. Ryson was taking the day off to stay with them. He would probably rather be aiding the search for their escaped prisoner, and helping her, but agreed it was the best place for him right now.

Kenna closed her eyes for a second.

"Okay?"

She looked at Jax and nodded. "Stairns?"

Her former boss turned from watching the screen on the wall. Given the look on his face, he read her tone precisely. "Something to say?"

Uh, yeah. "It's not like you can fire me. So yeah, I have something to say."

"The governor?"

"Why do you insist on standing up for him, even now?

Are you seriously telling me you *don't* suspect him as being part of this?"

Stairns said nothing.

"How could he be a part of any of this?" Jax asked. "He's down in St. George. He has a full schedule of speaking all week. There's no way he'd even have time to coordinate anything, let alone all the side-steps and reactions that had to happen."

Stairns sat on the edge of the table. "I called him. He said the same thing. He's been swamped all week with conference stuff. You know how that is, what with all the training you've been on. You step away from the real world and, by the end of the week, you're overloaded with information and utterly exhausted."

"Which makes it a great cover for taking me down."

Jax shifted. "You think he wants you dead?"

Stairns said, "He has no reason to kill you. Why would he?"

"Not dead, just destroyed. Because I'm a threat. I know something he doesn't want to get out and, instead of sticking to the agreement we made, he's decided randomly that right now is a great time to terrorize me. Not to mention make law enforcement scramble and get us all running in circles. Pointing fingers."

Most of those fingers were pointed at her, but she could be diplomatic and not bring up the fact they'd been about to put her in jail.

"Do either of you really not consider it highly suspicious that Taylor had been about to publicize everything?"

Kenna would never have coordinated a plan that got a cop killed. Even without having taken the oath of an FBI officer, Kenna would never let a child killer free.

Stairns knew that, and it might turn out to be her saving grace. They needed to find Rickshire before he hurt someone.

Neither of them said anything. Kenna lifted her hands palms up and then let them fall back to her lap. "Then who else? Because someone hates me enough to go to all this trouble instead of just burning down my motorhome. Or shooting me."

Jax pulled a breath in between his clenched teeth.

"We need to be on the streets looking for Taylor. But not until we figure this out. Agree on a plan."

Neither of them could argue with that.

Jax said, "You can stay here. The FBI will take care of Rickshire and find Taylor."

"If you were going to find Taylor, you'd have done it already." She was as sure as she could be that if she could just be the bait and let Rickshire take her, she would find Taylor. *She can't be dead. Not yet.* Even if it made more sense that her former friend had been silenced already. "I'm not sitting this one out."

Not when she could be the key to finishing this.

"All you have to do is follow me. When Rickshire grabs me, you follow. Simple enough."

Jax got up and strode to the window, visibly upset with the idea. Stairns watched him walk away. He turned and shot her a look, and she knew what he was asking.

She'd had a relationship with Bradley. Was she having one now with Jax?

She shook her head.

Stairns glanced back and forth like he didn't completely believe her.

Was that the point right now? Kenna cleared her throat and tried to not sound exasperated. "If it's not the governor, it's someone else. They have connections and resources.

They're coordinated and know how to find people, online and in person. Whoever this is, they've managed all the moving parts. When something goes wrong, someone ends up dead. Now they let Rickshire out of prison? No. We have—"

Stairns interrupted with a long, drawn-out sigh. "Fine. Fine. Fine."

Jax turned.

Kenna leaned forward and pointed at Stairns. "You've been withholding."

"I've been managing the situation, thank you very much." He thumped his chest. "That's what I do."

"If you tell me all this was for my own good..." She didn't threaten him. That wasn't a good idea on any day.

She also couldn't demand he explain.

Stairns looked at the floor for a minute. "It isn't like I wanted to do it. Kick you out of the agency. But would you really have been able to come back as an agent anyway, with the damage to your arms?"

Kenna just stared at him, holding everything in her completely still. Or she'd completely blow up. Anything else, and she wouldn't be able to contain her reaction.

"They wanted you gone." His expression flickered with something she couldn't catch. "*She* wanted you gone."

"The First Lady?"

"Yes, but I know what you are suggesting. She wouldn't do all this," Stairns said. "How could she? The woman doesn't have resources. Or smarts."

"Oh yeah...no one ever used their wealth and a position of power to victimize someone." Sarcasm dripped from her voice, and Kenna bit the inside of her lip hard. "That doesn't happen, right?"

Jax came back over. "The First Lady has established a reputation as the grieving mother of a hero. A pristine example of the kind of woman who stands behind her husband in office." He paused. "It's a good cover. No one would believe her capable of kidnapping and murder. Using criminals and hiring people to cover the details. I'd never suspect her."

"If she hired people, she had to pay them." Kenna solved most crimes by following the money. It made the world turn.

Stairns shook his head. "We'd never get a warrant for her financial records without some kind of proof. You're barking up a tree, Kenna."

"It's her. Tell me that doesn't make complete sense to you."

A muscle in his jaw flexed. But he said nothing.

"She was here talking to you. What did she say?"

"You think a woman who spent a lifetime in politics let something slip?" Stairns frowned. "She asked how you were."

"Tracking how things were going in the cause of terrorizing me."

"Why would she do that when she got rid of you two years ago?"

"She's been planning this ever since." Kenna's stomach lurched. "Two years of organization figuring out how to cover her tracks and keep her name clear."

"By hiring people?"

"Experts at subterfuge and kidnapping." She thought about the guy on the video. Was he the one she'd spoken to on the phone? "Coordination. They contacted Arnie and got the website set up and sent me the video of Jessica."

"That seems overly complicated."

"Or just complex enough no one would be in danger of believing me when I say it's all a setup. There's gotta be some compromising email somewhere, in my laptop maybe. Their attempt at proving I was behind it all."

Stairns glanced at Jax.

"If there was," Jax said, "and we could prove it had been planted, that would be a nail in their coffin."

"Like the prison visitor log. Made to look like me. And if the email was written to whoever she hired, it means she intends to double-cross them as well. Make it look like I contacted them and hung them out to dry as accomplices. Unless it says I coerced them. Blackmail, or some other way I forced them to help me."

Another glance between the two men.

"There's an email on my computer? And you weren't going to mention it to me?"

"Thomas said it's in your draft folder."

"It was never sent?"

Jax shrugged one shoulder. "If you give someone else your email login information, trading messages in the draft folder is a great way to communicate without an electronic record. You can write each other messages and never send them."

"But the two of you believe I wasn't behind this, right?" If they did, she'd be in a holding cell right now.

All Stairns said was, "We need proof of what's actually going on. After we find the doctor and get Rickshire back where he belongs."

Kenna wanted to work this out so they could get out of here. This needed to be over already. "The guy on the phone seemed devoted. Not like someone playing a role."

As she spoke, Stairns's expression changed again. A thought.

"What?"

He swallowed. "The First Lady has private security."

"Her nephew." Kenna jumped out of her chair. When she spotted Jax's confused look, she explained, "She has a nephew who was in the...Army, right?" She glanced at Stairns, who nodded. Kenna continued, "That's what I thought Bradley told me. He's been the head of her security team since the governor was elected."

"He owes her." Jax folded his arms.

"And he was here with her when she visited you."

Stairns nodded. "He was."

"Gauging how I was doing." Kenna swallowed the bile in her throat. "How their plan was affecting me."

"That was what she wanted to know." Stairns sighed. "Though, she couched it in a whole load of concern for you. Worry over your mental state."

"What does that mean?"

"She thought you've been through enough."

"She's going to kill me."

Stairns shook his head. "You don't even know if it's her."

She shot him a look. "I don't?"

Jax said, "Wouldn't she worry that coming here would tip her hand?"

"I never would've suspected her." Kenna would regret that lapse in judgment for the rest of her life.

"Sir?"

Stairns didn't answer right away. He scratched at the late-day stubble on his jaw. "She gets what she wants. It's just a way she has about her. You want to do what she needs, and then suddenly you find yourself doing things you never would have otherwise."

Kenna caught his meaning right away. "I can't believe this. You slept with her."

Stairns glared. "It was one time."

"Now you're under her thumb. Like she hypnotized you with her feminine wiles." It would be amusing any other time. Even a guy like Stairns wasn't immune to a beautiful woman.

Too bad that with Angeline Pacer, what was under the surface wasn't attractive at all.

"She was going to tell my wife."

Cabot watched her pace. "You want proof?" She grabbed her phone, searched on the internet for the private security business and came up with a cell phone number under his photo on the contact page. The First Lady's nephew.

She put the phone to her ear and listened to it ring, praying this would work.

"Amhurst Security."

"Yeah," she used her best Georgia accent. "This is Brenda over at First National Bank. I just need to double check an incoming transaction. Given the amount, I thought it best to confirm the details."

"How much is it?"

Kenna resisted the urge to smile. That would be poor sportsmanship. "Fifty thousand dollars, sir."

"I can give you my bank account information right now."

Kenna played it out to the end. It took another internet search on Jax's phone, but she gave him enough he shouldn't be suspicious while he handed over his personal information. Finally, she signed off and hung up.

Both men stared at her.

"Phone scams. No one's immune."

"First National Bank?"

She shrugged. "Sounds legit enough."

"Did he actually just give you his account information?" Jax said, "That won't be admissible in court."

"It's for my files. Not yours." She grinned. "And this gets better."

"How's that?"

"That voice on the phone? It was the same guy I spoke to.

The one who has Taylor." She drew the next words out slowly, enunciating each word carefully. "The First Lady's cousin." Considering she was a witness, that information *was* admissible.

Stairns headed for the door. "I'll get a warrant."

Kenna turned to Jax and set her hand on her hip. She was just about to ask him if he wanted to go catch a killer, when her phone buzzed with a text from Ryson.

SOMEONE IS IN THE HOUSE.

Chapter Thirty-Six

Friday, 12:17am.

J ax had to drive her. Cabot rode on the backseat the whole way while Kenna tried to get Ryson to answer his phone.

Come on, come on.

It felt like an eternity. "I only saw them once." She fought back the urge to give in to her emotions. To break down. "Valentina and Luci." She moaned the baby's name.

Jax reached over and squeezed her hand. "You don't know that anything happened." He checked the rearview. "The cops should be there any minute."

Cabot rested her chin on Kenna's shoulder. She scratched the side of her dog's face. In such a short time, this animal had become part of her life. That probably said more about Kenna's loneliness, and the fact she'd latch onto anyone willing to support her. All the better, it was a dog. They were about complete devotion—no ulterior motives.

She couldn't say the same for people.

Dogs were a safe bet. Humans took longer because it meant learning to trust them and allowing them to learn they could trust her in return.

Aside from Ryson and his family, who she'd already done that with, did she even want that? Jax was an obvious choice, but he was FBI and still convinced she was a suspect.

Jax represented everything she'd walked away from—everyone she'd convinced herself she was done with—and she'd even gone so far as to say she hated the FBI after what they'd done. But was that even true when she couldn't bring herself to even hate Taylor? Aside from the slashing pain of betrayal, all she felt was sadness that her friend hadn't stood up for her.

Fifteen long minutes later, Jax pulled onto the street and she could see the house.

"Lights are on." She watched for movement. Any sign of someone approaching or an altercation going on inside. Nothing. "No car in the drive, so Valentina is out. She always said Ryson might need to leave in an emergency, so she'd be the one to normally scrape ice off her car when needed. Not him." *Thank You, God.* "Ryson might've been alone in the house." But then, where was Luci? Out with her mother running errands, or home with her father?

Jax pulled to the curb and checked his phone notifications. "Detective Wilkern is on her way, but she'll be a few minutes still."

Kenna shoved her door open. "I haven't replied to any of Wilkern's messages since Jessica's body was found. I was afraid she would get taken next." And now this?

"We'll find them."

She moved out.

"Crack the window for your dog."

Kenna slammed the door shut, ignoring his request, and pulled her gun as she ran to the front door. Kenna twisted the handle and skidded across the hardwood floor of the foyer. "Ryson!"

She searched the living area, then the garage. His car was still here. "Ryson!"

A shuffle from the bedroom drew her. She raced for it and found the window in the master pushed up. Cold air gusted in, shaking the blinds against the frame up high where they were gathered. The string dangled to the floor and flapped against the wall. *Clack, clack.*

"Kenna!" Jax was inside.

She took a breath to answer and a cold, damp cloth covered her mouth. Arms banded around her, and she sucked in a breath of surprise. Then she realized what a mistake that was. The cloth smelled and tasted *wrong.* She knew what that meant.

Chloroform.

Kenna swung her gun up, but only managed to bend her arm at the elbow because of the arms like steel bands around her.

The cold worked quickly. The taste coated her tongue and made her head swim. Her feet were lifted off the floor.

Moving.

The outside of her leg bumped the bottom of the window frame.

She hit the ground, face in the bark. Her fingers curled in the grass. *Gun. Where is your gun?* She needed to... She had to...

"Kenna, where are you?" Jax's voice drifted to her.

Someone lifted her and everything went black.

Jax.

Chapter Thirty-Seven

K enna's body swayed. She blinked at the ceiling of a car. Seat under her. Laying down.

Her brain rebooted like an old computer. Slow enough she began to wonder what was wrong.

The smell and the cold were still against her lips and over her nose. The lingering sensation of the chloroform that had knocked her out. She could feel it. Smell it. Like it was still there, even though the cloth was no longer pressed against her face.

She managed to lift her hand. The other came with it, secured together at the wrists with a plastic tie. For a split second, everything inside her screamed as that familiar pain slashed through her. Her stomach dropped—no, no, no, no. Not again. Wait, no blood. She stared at her hands, then tugged them down her face.

The driver's door opened, and someone climbed in.

She was in the backseat.

Kenna rolled. Wait, this was her car. The driver had long dark hair like hers and wore a leather jacket like the one in her closet that she never wore because it was too big for her.

Another item she hadn't realized had been stolen from her motorhome?

A man said, "It's done." Then dropped a phone in the cupholder and tugged off the hair to reveal a flattened cap of dark hair. His eyes caught hers, and he grinned.

Gerald Rickshire.

The engine started. "I knew this would be fun." The car started moving. "You're not my type, but you deserve what I have coming for you. For catching me."

Her mouth opened, but no sound came out. She tried to speak, and all that emerged was a moan.

Where were they going? What was going on, and why had he been dressed like her? None of this made any sense.

Taylor. She wanted to know where her friend was.

Jax.

She managed to moan.

Rickshire chuckled. "Aw...desperate pleas. I never get tired of that." He put the phone to his ear and listened. "Yeah, she's awake. What do you want me to do?" Pause. "Fine." He didn't sound happy about whatever he'd been told. Rickshire hung up. "Working alone is way more fun."

She managed to choke out a single word. "Why?"

"Because they're paying me." He turned a corner too fast, and she nearly rolled onto the floor. "Can't start a new life with no money."

The only part of her that could move, a tear, dripped from the corner of her eye and into her hair.

Last time she'd been in a situation like this, it had been with Bradley. There was nothing of that she wanted to relive, not right now when the fear was fresh and real. When Rickshire sat in front all smug, about to get whatever he wanted. *Ellayna.*

The girl was in FBI protective custody. Nothing would happen to her—she was safe.

She's safe.

Kenna was very much not safe.

No one knew who had her, or where she was. *I'm sorry, Taylor.* Whether she liked it or not, it was Kenna's fault her friend had been taken. If she hadn't come back to Salt Lake City, this wouldn't have happened. If she hadn't become a private investigator. If she'd never followed her father's path in life.

It was supposed to have been about forging her own way, but also honoring who he'd been and what he'd instilled in her.

Too bad she'd ruined it in all the ways.

She could do the job well enough. She had the skills her dad and FBI training had given her. Too bad it had been Kenna's destiny all along to destroy it by dragging everyone she cared about into this corrupt oblivion with her.

The car stopped.

Kenna's body shifted with the movement, and she blinked against the dark. Rickshire got out. She waited, long enough she tried to roll over, but the door opened and two hands hauled her out by her armpits. She was bent over a shoulder and lifted. The swaying motion of his walking made her head swim. She should try to get a weapon. Find something in his pocket—keys, or a tool he forgot he carried. The blood rushing to her head made her eyes burn.

Before she could collect herself enough to get her arms to work, she was tipped back and dumped onto the floor. Her head bounced on linoleum, and someone gasped. A woman.

"Kenna."

She was rolled over—rather kicked—and Taylor's face swam in front of her.

All Kenna could do was lie there and stare up at her friend.

"Hey."

She squeezed her eyes shut and tried to jump-start her brain. "Taylor."

One of Taylor's eyes was swollen shut. She had a cut and a bruise, high on her cheekbone. "Hey." Tears dripped onto her cheeks, and she swiped them away. "You're here."

All Kenna could do was watch.

"They took you, too? I can't believe you're here."

They hadn't told Taylor she would be coming. Maybe she'd been isolated since her capture with no social interaction at all. In the corner of the room was a plastic tray with a bowl and spoon on top, along with a red plastic cup. Cafeteria style. They had at least fed her.

But why did they need Taylor alive?

Kenna glanced around. This looked like some kind of storage room. Where were they? "Help me up."

Taylor lifted her shoulders and helped her lean back against the wall. Kenna looked around while her former friend settled in front of her, legs curled up. "Are you okay?"

Kenna took note of the padlock on the window and the heavy door. Then she looked back at Taylor. "You haven't managed to escape yet?"

Her friend flinched. "If I had, then you'd have no one with you."

"And I enjoy company so much."

She made a sound Kenna wasn't sure was laughter or crying, or both. "Sorry." Taylor motioned to her face. "This happened when I tried to get away from Elijah. I'm afraid I haven't tried to get away since."

Kenna shifted her bound hands and opened her fingers. Taylor held them. "We'll figure it out together."

A dark expression crossed Taylor's face, an unspoken thing between them. Until she nodded. "Together."

Kenna had told her all about what had happened with Bradley. Taylor knew every second of it, and she'd used it as the basis for her statement to the FBI that Kenna was no longer mentally fit to be an agent. She'd wielded it like ammunition to destroy Kenna's life. The loss of her baby could have been due to the stress of that, or all of what'd happened. She would never know. Everything from those few terrible days was all mixed up in her, like someone had blended it together until she couldn't separate one iota from anything else.

Almatter was to blame for all of it, and he was dead, so she had to move on and not hold a grudge. That was what she'd settled on. Everyone else could be blamed as willing participants—but the reality was that if he hadn't started it by kidnapping her and Bradley, then none of it would have happened.

She would've had a family. She would've been a mom.

"You're drifting." Taylor sounded scared. She'd likely been alone since she was taken and didn't want to be alone again with an unconscious Kenna.

She shook off the lingering fog and said, "Chloroform."

Taylor nodded. "That's what they did to me."

"Mine was Gerald Rickshire."

"Elijah Hammersmith."

"The one you told me about—your patient?" When Taylor nodded, Kenna said, "He was obsessed with you, but not me." Kenna knew that didn't make a whole lot of sense. She just didn't know how to get her brain to work long enough to explain. "Gerald wanted Ellayna, not me."

"As near as I can figure, guys like Elijah and Gerald are a means to an end. Someone to do the grunt work. But they killed Elijah. He was so obsessed with me, it just wasn't helpful."

"Like Clive with Meg." But they didn't want Taylor dead. So what did they want?

Taylor frowned. "Gerald Rickshire is a little more...functional. That man—the one in charge—I heard him tell Gerald he'd get the little girl back for him." Taylor gasped. "Please tell me you won't let that happen."

Kenna nodded. Hot tears burned her eyes, making Taylor swim in front of her. She looked at the ceiling and blinked through it. "We'll figure a way out." She shook her head. "Escape."

Taylor squeezed her fingers.

Kenna's short-term memory came back in pieces. Each one fell into place, and she had to wade through it. Put them together one by one until she had the whole picture.

She studied her friend. Dirty clothes, her hair matted and sticky with blood beside her temple. "Tell me what happened since the time you were taken."

Taylor nodded. "Elijah grabbed me outside the gym. He put a cloth over my mouth, and I passed out right as he shoved me in the backseat of his car." She shivered. "I can't believe what you went through with Almatter, and yet you survived. And had to try to have a normal life. Live like everything was okay. That's all I've been able to think about. *Kenna did this. She survived this.* If I can be as strong as you, maybe I can make it too."

"That isn't what it's about." Strength didn't always mean survival. "But you did survive, and that had nothing to do with me." She squeezed Taylor's hand. "Tell me what happened when you woke up."

Taylor swallowed. "Elijah was dead. There was this man standing over him, holding a gun."

"Does he work for Angeline Pacer on her security team?"

Taylor frowned, her mouth open. "He looked familiar after the fact, but at the time I was just so scared. I thought he was going to kill me, too. I screamed my head off, and he hit me with the gun." Her breath came fast now. "He had friends there, dressed like him."

Before Taylor could continue, Kenna said, "How do you mean?"

"Black T-shirts, with a collar and three buttons. Like a polo shirt. Black cargo pants and boots."

"Bulletproof vests? Or any kind of insignia?"

Taylor shook her head. "What does it mean?"

"They wanted to look professional but didn't want to wear any kind of logo that could be traced back to their company. They can spot a teammate as a friendly if need be because they all look the same, and yet they're generic enough to pass for a bunch of guys out doing whatever story they came up with."

"So...untraceable?"

"It's why we didn't find you."

"You did." Taylor squeezed her hand. "You're here."

"I'm here because Gerald Rickshire caught me at Ryson's house. Seems like he had the same arrangement as Elijah."

"I hope they kill him."

Kenna felt her brows rise.

"What? I'm a psychologist so I'm not allowed to say that?"

"Taylor—"

"I have a daughter. I might firmly believe people can be treated, but that man?" She shook her head. "He's just sick. Plain and simple."

Kenna wanted to believe the First Lady's nephew—whatever his name was—would kill Gerald Rickshire the way he'd shot Clive and Elijah. People on both sides were turning up dead, and this guy was in the middle of it all.

He needed to be in cuffs.

Taylor looked at the door. Kenna spotted an expression she'd never seen before.

"What?"

Taylor shook her head. "What?"

"There's more you're not telling me." It was a guess, but when Taylor bristled like a witness across the table in interrogation, she knew she was right. "What is it?"

Taylor looked at their hands, still clasped together. "They have a plan."

"Another video?" Kenna didn't plan on dying live online. She didn't even want to live that way, in the public eye, let alone take her last breath with people watching. People she'd never even met.

"Yes, but that's not the worst part."

Kenna waited.

"I'm supposed to die, and their plan is to blame you for everything. I overheard them talk about how they made it look like you're the one who got Gerald Rickshire out."

Kenna fought the urge to run. There was nowhere to go. "I didn't. I was with Jax at the time."

Taylor perked up. "Oh?"

"It's not like that. He's FBI. And besides, I have a dog. It's proven they're actually woman's best friend, so..."

She had no idea why she felt the need to share that right now. She didn't have to defend her lack of desire for a romantic relationship. Besides, she wasn't going to end a two-year dry spell with the first half-decent guy she met. There was no way, even if she was attracted to him. Which she most definitely was not. *Liar*.

Taylor said, "But—"

"I'm not interested in history repeating itself. Let's just leave it at that."

She'd made plenty of mistakes with Bradley. Ones she needed to heal within herself before she jumped in like that again with someone new. She'd learned a lot since then.

Taylor sighed, disappointed. "Does that mean Jax isn't out looking for you with the rest of the agents? Because if they don't get here quick enough..."

"What's their plan?"

"They're going to make it look like you killed me. Because you're so angry at me for my betrayal, that now you hate me. That's what this has all been about. Getting back at everyone that hurt you."

"Like Jessica Pierce, and a college girl I've never met? That makes no sense. Killing Eric and Arnie was to cover their own tracks, not mine. No one will believe it." She hoped. She prayed. "This isn't on me."

"No?" Taylor held still. "They won't believe you don't hate me after I lied and you lost your job?"

"I'm not going to kill you, Tay. You don't get out of this relationship that easily."

Taylor let out a sob and collapsed against Kenna. She lifted her arms over Taylor's head, and they shared an awkward hug.

"Thank you."

Kenna said, "Thank me when we're out of here. Right now, we're in serious trouble."

"What are we going to do?"

"Are there cameras in here? Do you think they're watching, or listening?"

"Watching. I don't know about listening. I didn't say anything." Taylor frowned. "Why?"

Kenna dropped her voice, lower than a whisper, "I have a

few hidden things. Assuming they were distracted by the two guns I carry, they might've missed something."

Taylor gaped. "You can get us out of here? Do it. Do it now."

Kenna heard a shuffle out in the hall. It drew closer to the door. "I need to know what's going on."

The handle rotated and the door eased open.

Chapter Thirty-Eight

With help from Taylor, Kenna scrambled to her feet. She then moved her friend behind her and faced the entrant.

Gerald Rickshire stepped inside the room.

Everything in Kenna froze at the sight of a criminal like him walking free in the world instead of locked up the way he was supposed to be.

Behind him she spotted one of the black-T-shirt-black-cargo-pants guys Taylor had mentioned but couldn't see his face. The First Lady's nephew? Whatever the case, his intention was obviously to stay away from her. She could see it in the way he hung back, trying to stay in the shadows. Hopefully he'd heard stories of what she was capable of and was at least cautious over what she might do—if not outright scared.

"Hey!"

The door started to close, leaving Gerald Rickshire inside with them.

"I want to talk to your boss!" She knew she was making big assumptions. As if there was no question the guy in the shadows was an underling with orders to deliver the murderer to their room for a boss who was nowhere in sight. Didn't matter. "Hey!"

The door clicked shut. She waited for the sound of the lock turning to seal them in.

It never came.

They could get out, except they'd have to first break past Gerald Rickshire standing between them and the door. Escape felt just out of reach, like a faint specter in a dark room. There, but completely intangible.

Taylor grasped the back of her shirt—for both moral support and to steady herself. Kenna stood as tall as she could and put on her game face, like Gerald was nothing to her and this was just another day on the job. Meanwhile, he stared at the two of them with a tiny, smug smile on his face.

"You're not going to touch either of us." She didn't want to get into a fight with him when she was far from a hundred percent. The effects of being dosed with chloroform still lingered. Her reflexes were as sluggish as her thoughts, and it wouldn't be long until he figured that out and took advantage it.

So maybe he already suspected it but, for now, all he knew was what he saw. She had no weapons, and her hands were bound together. Definitely not what one would consider a worthy opponent.

He didn't move. He only stood there and stared at her and Taylor. Intimidation tactic?

"What is this? What's going on?" She lifted her chin in defiance and tried to sound confident on top of pretending she was in full control of her faculties. Not that she didn't have her hands up in front to ward him off. A defense mechanism.

Figure it out. She needed to gain control and fast.

The door eased open again. Quietly. Not wide enough for a person. Gerald didn't budge—didn't hear it?

Suddenly, a pistol skated across the floor and, based on its trajectory, Kenna understood almost immediately who the intended recipient was.

Her.

She lurched forward. Taylor gasped and her hold on Kenna's shirt loosened. Gerald didn't move as the gun came right at her. Didn't even reach for it.

Kenna grabbed the gun off the floor and palmed it between her bound hands. She took two steps back so she was once again in front of Taylor, held the gun up, and pointed it at Gerald's forehead. "Someone had better explain what this is."

Gerald just stood there.

Taylor said, "Are you going to shoot him?"

Kenna stared down the barrel of her gun. Her eyes bore into the killer in front of her. "He's unarmed."

"But he kills children."

Kenna pressed her lips together. "It doesn't matter. There are rules."

Kenna wasn't going to compromise herself. She needed no more black marks on her soul. Besides, she knew how this worked. Killing Rickshire would only play into these people's hands. It was exactly what they wanted.

"I'm not going to shoot him unless he forces me to do it." She stared at Gerald. "Which he won't, because he's going to stay on that side of the room until we figure out what this is."

"I heard about her kid." Gerald smiled at Taylor, a revolting expression of greed. "They told me all about her." The words rolled off his tongue like the persistent drip of a leaky faucet. "Even showed me pictures." A glint flashed in his eyes.

Taylor whimpered.

Kenna needed information. He knew what was going on

beyond that door, and if she shot him she wouldn't get answers. "She's a little young, even for you."

Her stomach rolled but it was empty, so she wasn't in danger of hurling on his prison canvas shoes. They'd given him street clothes but left those on his feet—or maybe they hadn't found a pair of sneakers or boots that fit him. She found that odd, though. If it wasn't a mistake, then it was on purpose. In order that he didn't forget they'd broken him out, or so the police would spot the odd footwear and realize who he was?

That confirmed her thoughts—Gerald was a means to an end.

"I thought Ellayna Feathers was more your type." Kenna's mind conjured up an image of the little girl huddled in the corner of that basement room under the theater. Suddenly, Kenna's mind switched, and it was her waking up in a child's bed. As though she was Ellayna, even though she'd never even been to Ellayna's house. She became that child, even though she knew it was nothing but a fabrication of her mind where fear filled in the blanks. But the empathy, along with her own encounter with a killer, had served her well as a private investigator, and it wasn't a stretch for her mind to imagine the horror felt by Ellayna.

Then again, maybe she was losing it.

"I'll have Ellayna, too."

The way he said her name. Hot anger washed over her. Kenna bit back sharply, "No. You won't."

Taylor grasped her shirt again. "Just shoot him. Get it over with."

"And deny the justice system the chance to punish him for the rest of his life?"

"He doesn't deserve to live," Taylor said. "I'd rather know he was burning in hell."

"Not my call."

Kenna would shoot him if the situation warranted it. She very much *could* shoot him. She could even understand Taylor's rush to judgment. No one wanted to know a sick man like this walked free. She was thoroughly prepared to kill him, but only if he forced her to do it.

Instead, she said, "You're nothing but a means to an end. To them, you're a pawn. They have a plan that's much bigger than you are. You're a small bit in their little play, destined to die because they've decided your life isn't worth it. You deserve to die, and it serves their aim."

A guy like Gerald, who thought himself above the law and cared little for human standards of morality, wouldn't want to be seen as nothing. That was how he saw everyone else in the world—something to be manipulated, not even worthy of the title "human." Either they were inconsequential, or a means to achieve the rush of pleasure he got when he destroyed life.

"In this scenario, *you're* the one who is nothing."

Gerald sneered. So far, he hadn't moved and only proceeded to taunted her with that vile look in his eyes.

"They want me to kill you, right?"

He would never go along with that willingly. Unless he wore a vest, or some other protective gear. She would have to circumvent the training that had her instinctively aiming at his torso and put a bullet in his brain also. *Bang. Bang.* It would be satisfying to see him drop. She could admit that.

Ellayna would be safe.

Bethany would never have to be afraid of this man.

Kenna and Taylor would be rid of him.

"I'm not going to do that while you're unarmed. So, we get to talk." It was worth a try. Maybe he was capable of being reasonable, and maybe not. She would never know if she didn't at least make the attempt. "We could even come to some kind of agreement."

"No talking."

She couldn't decipher his expression. Before Kenna figured out how to argue this, the door opened again. Another man in black clothes tossed a gun to Rickshire.

Kenna's world coalesced into slow motion as Rickshire caught the weapon and swung it around to her and Taylor.

She fired right at his chest. He stumbled back and the gun in his hand went off. She aimed her second shot at his head. The gun clicked.

Empty. *You've got to be kidding me.* Only one bullet.

He pointed the gun at her chest and prepared to pull the trigger.

She wobbled back into Taylor, but his gun never went off. The slide locked. Empty.

Rickshire was on his feet. As if she never even shot the bullet into his chest.

Taylor started to cry. The hall door opened, and the entrant laughed. She recognized him from his photo on the company website. This was Angeline Pacer's nephew: Andrew Callis. "Thanks for playing."

She stared at him while her mind buzzed. "He's not dead."

She'd been sure they'd been trying to fool her into killing him. Rickshire had to be wearing a vest under that jacket, because she'd hit him square in the chest, and he wasn't bleeding.

So...what was the deal? Maybe she'd been wrong about Rickshire being dispensable.

"I'm not going to play your stupid game and kill Taylor and, for some reason, you obviously didn't want me to kill Rickshire. So what are we doing here?"

Rickshire visibly shook off the giant bruise that was no doubt already forming on his sternum. "I might not have been killed, but I'm gonna be dead."

That was what this was?

"Faking your death." She felt Taylor grab the back of her shirt again. Kenna continued, "They didn't do that with any of the others. Elijah, Clive, and Christopher. What makes you special? Why do you think they'll let you live?"

He had to know this group of private security guys were getting paid for a job they wouldn't deviate from. They had their plan, and it had worked so far.

"I'm not like the others." Rickshire seemed pleased. Of course he'd want to be top dog. "Best to not be confused by that."

"My gun had a bullet in it."

He patted his chest.

"Pretty high stakes on that gamble. So you get a new name, and our friend here—" She motioned with the empty pistol at Andrew Callis. "—he gets to tell everyone how he brought you down? Is that it?" She shook her head. "He gets his name in the papers and suddenly he's famous."

No way was she going to drop the only weapon she had. Even if it had no bullets in it, she could still pistol-whip with the best of them.

Andrew stood listening. Kenna wanted to scream at him for an explanation but refused to lose her cool. He didn't need to know how close to the edge her emotions really were. She was at a serious disadvantage in this situation.

"They'll need a body to turn over to the cops if they want to be heroes and prove you're dead."

Andrew smiled. "You're the only one who knows where you disposed of him. Maybe there's nothing left. Meanwhile

I've got video of you killing Gerald here, and no one can refute it."

"Except he didn't die."

"The magic of editing will take care of that."

"All so I'm blamed?" Kenna asked. "As though I would get him released just to kill him as an escaped fugitive. Wouldn't I have just shot him when I arrested him? Would've been easy enough."

Except that Kenna had gone in there like she always did, armed with non-lethal weapons. No matter what the suspect had done, she would always treat it as a rescue operation first. If she caught the culprit, she would bring him to the police, but that was never her priority. The temptation to take vengeance was also stronger than she might've wanted to admit.

"Who knows why you do what you do? You're crazy. Since you quit the FBI, you haven't done anything. There are no arrests anywhere with your name on them. If you told anyone you've been doing investigative work, taking down dangerous criminals, how can they prove it? There's no evidence of anything but your instability. You've been plotting a way to get back in the spotlight since you left."

"You show a video, and suddenly everyone believes you?"

"Uh...that's how the internet works. If it aligns with people's preconceived narrative, then they'll believe it's true. You're a disgruntled FBI agent. Why wouldn't anyone think you wanted to bring your own brand of justice? Get back in the limelight, like your father did after his career dwindled to nothing."

She started toward him, then caught herself.

Andrew laughed. Gerald flinched, touched a hand to his chest and rubbed the spot where she'd shot him.

This was all exactly what she'd told the FBI. It had been

nothing but a throw away comment, the first thing to pop into her head. A plausible reason she might've killed Christopher Halpert and left her business card. All to get her name back in the press.

She'd hit that nail square on. It had been their entire reasoning after all. "Is she paying you? Is that it?"

Angeline Pacer was behind this. She'd never seen that coming, too focused on the governor and their last conversation. His anger had shone bright enough to eclipse whatever had been going on with Angeline. Two years of grief, planning this extensive revenge plot.

Kenna wanted to cry for her, carrying that much pain inside. Unable to let anyone see it. Too bad Angelina had taken it beyond anyone's ability to help her. So like her son, and yet so different.

Gerald headed out into the hall, and Andrew started to do the same. She couldn't let him leave. She needed him to tell her everything. "I'm not going to kill Taylor and neither are you."

Leaving Gerald to walk free? No. No way would she allow that to happen. How these guys could even think that was a good idea was beyond her comprehension. No matter how corrupt they were.

"Gerald hurts children. *Kills them*," she said. "You want that on your conscience, knowing he's walking around free because *you* let him out?"

"I've got a guy." He shrugged. "He's developed, shall we say, a *taste* for killing people. He can take care of Gerald."

"You have it all figured out?"

"I don't even need you to play a part. I've got what I need."

"Editing? The FBI will prove your videos are fake."

"Doesn't matter. By then, everyone will believe the story

I've told. You'll be dead. And your friend here," he shot a tormenting smile at Taylor, "will be another victim of your crazed mind." He held the edge of the door.

"How much is she paying you?"

He smiled. "You think this is about money."

"So it's about loyalty? You owe her?"

"Interesting."

"Or she's giving you something you can't buy with money." What could that be? Before she could delay him any further, he shut the door.

Taylor sagged against the wall. "He scares me more than Gerald."

"What does he want? You're a psychologist. I need you to diagnose him." She turned to face her friend. "Tell me what will work to convince him to give up this plan. There has to be something he'll take in exchange for walking away."

"Because everyone has a price?"

"I don't know. Do they?" Kenna lifted her bound hands. "All I know is that I need to get us out of here."

Both of them. Together.

Though if Kenna could create some kind of diversion, then Taylor could run for safety. It didn't really matter what happened to her, as long as Bethany got her mother back.

She could take away their power by…

Kenna sagged against the wall and closed her eyes. *Bradley.*

She took a few long breaths, absorbing the very same realization he must have had. In a very similar situation.

That was the moment he'd reached. The knowledge he would willingly suffer anything to see her go free.

Even end his own life.

Taylor groaned. "We're going to die, aren't we?"

Kenna didn't have the energy to try and convince her

otherwise. "I haven't lost hope. Until this ends, neither of us knows what will happen."

"I should just believe it's going to turn out fine? Hope doesn't get me back to my family."

"I've lived on hope for two years since I lost mine. Every morning, wondering if today's the day that things might change and something bright might come along. Until recently, it was the only thing I had left. Don't take the little I have away from me."

Taylor wiped a tear from her cheek.

What Kenna had now wasn't perfect. Parts of it were downright nightmarish since she got back to Salt Lake City. But the good was in there if she was willing to look for it—new and old. A life she might want to build on, grace given in the dark when she'd been too scared to ask and risk losing everything again.

No way was Kenna going to give it up now that there was something in her life to live for again.

Friends. Freedom.

Bradley. She didn't know what had been in his mind the moment he'd taken his life and never would. He hadn't told her the why of it—whatever he'd felt in that moment that had overwhelmed him to action.

I'm sorry. So sorry you thought you had no other way out.

It overwhelmed whatever loyalty he'd had for her, or their baby. The fight in him to stay alive. To survive. She'd thought she and the baby rated highly. Perhaps she'd been wrong, and perhaps he'd made the greatest sacrifice.

The outcome was the same either way. He wasn't here because he had made the choice to leave her.

Kenna stared at Taylor, knowing she wasn't going to do to Taylor what had been done to her. God had given Taylor a friend in this very situation who understood what she'd been through and cared about her, so she didn't have to be alone.

A grace in the darkness.

They would get out of this together, and Kenna knew how.

Chapter Thirty-Nine

She reached underneath her collar with her bound hands and down the front of her shirt.

"Uh..." Taylor shifted.

Kenna said, "It's a gamble whether a captor will check... um...*everywhere*."

"I thought they took your gun."

"And my backup." She lifted her foot and shook it. "Most people don't know how to do it right—a thorough pat-down. So I've got to make it look like I've got an itch somewhere hard to reach."

"You have a weapon?"

"Yes, but intel always comes first. What's the point of escaping if you leave not knowing exactly what it is you're escaping from? It can't all be for nothing."

She wiggled the tiny multitool out but was careful to conceal it tightly between her palms as she turned inconspicuously away from the cameras high on the wall. It was a habit to locate surveillance whenever she was abducted by a madman. Which unfortunately had happened more than once. Twice was way too often.

No, it wasn't big, but it was still big enough to be a weapon—one that wasn't necessarily comfortable to wear all the time. But things had been crazy lately.

Kenna turned to face Taylor once again. "I needed to know if they could hear us," Kenna said. "Seems to me that if they're watching, they're not listening because he'd have made reference to something we said to each other. Andrew must've been by the door to have known I wouldn't shoot Gerald unless he was armed."

She twisted her hand so Taylor would see the edge of the multitool.

"You can cut yourself free?"

"Not yet. Tied up, they'll think I'm helpless. That gives me an edge."

Kenna had purposely avoided thinking about the weapons she still had on her until this point. She had to come across as genuinely downtrodden and full of fear. That only happened in a moment of honesty as she faced the fear. Tied up, with no weapons in reach.

Now they would underestimate her, thinking she was desperate. She knew what they wanted and was already cooking up a plan to get her and Taylor out of here.

Kenna sat down. She felt around her ankle holster. "Yep, they took the gun."

"I could throw the holster at them."

Kenna felt the inside edge and slid out a mini version of the baton she'd used on Gerald Rickshire the night she rescued Ellayna Feathers.

"You have more?" Taylor's voice was brimming with relief.

"What we need is a plan. Because neither are particularly lethal, nor do they pack a lot of punch."

"First, tell me more about the weapons you hide on your

person." Taylor had far too much knowing in her eyes.

"Oh, this is nothing. It's normal for me to have one weapon taped to the top of my bathroom wall. There are two guns in my car, including one in the trunk in case I'm locked inside. There are knives all over my motorhome and in my backpack. I draw the line at one of those pouches you clip around your waist."

"Because?"

The FBI psychologist was often indistinguishable from the friend she'd known for years. "You want to analyze me or spend some time figuring out our escape?"

"Just talk to me. It's only going to take a second."

Kenna sighed. "I know what it feels like to be at the mercy of a psycho. You think for one second I'd let that happen again and not do every possible thing in my power to prepare for it?"

"No, I don't think that."

"But you think I'm reacting because of fear."

"Fear isn't a bad thing."

She started to object.

Taylor cut her off. "Fear gives you enough clarity to exercise some caution which you can use to make better choices. If you can get outside of the fear and use it. Like you are."

Unless she was frozen. "Sometimes it consumes me. There's no way out. It's like being trapped in a block of ice, and I can't break free. I get sucked under the fear, and it's all I can think about. Everything goes into overdrive. Heart pounding, gasping until my head spins. I can't pull a single thought together. It's just the fear, and I'm right back there."

"Where?"

As if she didn't know. "That moment I turn and see Bradley dead. Dangling there with a T-shirt around his neck."

"What happened next?"

"Almatter came back in." Kenna pulled her hands apart

until the ties cut into her skin. She wasn't frozen. She was right there. "I guess I was screaming. He dragged me off Bradley. I turned and attacked him."

"I saw the report. You got out."

"The team found me half a mile away, nearly frozen in the snow. And they only found me because I tripped."

"So now you never leave home without an arsenal of weapons to reach for. Just in case you need them," Taylor said. "That sounds smart to me. Kind of like pretending you're a true victim here, completely incapacitated, so that your responses are genuine. Gathering intel. When the truth is, you are far from helpless."

Kenna wanted to shrug but couldn't quite make her shoulders move like that. "Let's just concentrate on getting out of here."

"I would be grateful." A small smile arched up Taylor's lips, but that was the only concession she gave past her own fear. "Maybe I'll find myself concealing a small weapon from now on."

Kenna stood, shaking off the tension that came from delving too close to the truth of her feelings. The sheer terror she lived with every day. "My partner died because I was unprepared and unable to protect myself. That's not going to happen to you, Taylor."

Taylor shivered, her face pale. Bruises accentuated. Dark circles and smudges of dirt.

She was scared, and with good reason. Probably she wanted to be Doctor Landstadt right now instead of Taylor, kidnap victim. Mother. Wife. Friend. The professional persona was a refuge, a place she could be logical rather than emotional.

"I'm serious, Tay. I'm not going to let you get hurt."

"I know you'd never allow it." The statement sounded a

little too much like Taylor was talking her off some ledge, instead of the other way around.

Kenna lived there on a permanent basis. On some ledge, just about to slip over. She didn't exactly blame Taylor. If anyone in the world had ever been a candidate for a psychologist's aid, it was probably her. Kenna might as well walk around with the word "dysfunctional" on her forehead.

"Maybe I can make an appointment with you. If we get out of this."

"Now you're not so sure we'll get out?"

"We need a plan, Tay. Standing here doesn't get us free."

"And the FBI won't find us?"

"They're looking for you. I doubt I'm a high priority." She held up her hands even though the ties hurt a lot. "And that's not another invitation for a psychological diagnosis. It's just a fact. They'll find you."

"When they do, let's have dinner. Not an appointment. Just dinner."

Kenna nodded. "I'd like that."

She figured Taylor wanted to argue on Kenna's behalf—that there were people who cared for her, too. But the truth was that she didn't want to be close with anyone when it meant they were a liability that could be used against her. If one of her friends was hurt because of her? She shivered, and yet heat rose up inside her.

If anything had happened to Ryson, Valentina, or Luci, Kenna would descend into a place there was no way back from.

She knew enough about herself to know that. The way she knew Bradley's death wasn't her fault.

She squeezed the multitool in her hand. "We need to get one of them in here. Hopefully it's Andrew."

"You're going to try and reason with him again?"

"I have a different idea in mind." She needed Taylor to do something she probably wouldn't be crazy about doing in order to surprise the guy.

"He'll be wary of you," Taylor guessed. "It'll be hard to convince him you're incapacitated given what he knows of you. He's going to expect you to try something."

Kenna nodded.

"Give me the weapon." Taylor swallowed.

"Can you do it?"

"Do I want to see my daughter before they put the two of us in a video and make it look like you killed me? Yes, I can do it."

Kenna crouched by her and twisted out the knife. "If there was another way..."

Taylor just said, "Medical emergency?"

"We need him to turn his back on you. Preferably when he's close enough to be within reach."

Faking serious need for an ambulance was a last ditch effort to turn the tables. Kenna didn't like Taylor making herself vulnerable like this, but they didn't have much choice. These people intended to kill her friend and make it look like Kenna was the one responsible for it.

Some kind of vendetta dished back for Taylor's betrayal, as if they knew what she was thinking. Andrew had been right about that. People believed what they wanted to. Like assuming she was still bitter and wanted revenge instead of working for two years to keep her life moving. The ice didn't have the chance to build up when she did that.

It was when she stopped that the memories crept back in, and if she stayed that way long enough, the ice was then too thick to break free. She forced it to stay dormant inside her, as small as she could make it, so that it never overtook her.

Taylor stared up at her. "And if this doesn't work?"

She was right to consider this might not work. More than one armed man could come in. Or maybe no one would answer Kenna's cry. He might not get close enough to Taylor. Kenna might not be able to get her mini baton out in time to use it.

"Don't think that way. Just adapt. Improvise."

She twisted the biggest knife out from the mechanism. All Taylor had to do was use it.

"Now you're scaring me." Taylor put her hand on Kenna's. "Please...let me cut you free."

Kenna backed up and turned to the door, rushing as though this had happened suddenly. She hammered her fists against the wood. "Help!" She took a couple of quick breaths, so she'd sound freaked out and desperate. Not that that was hard to do. "We need help!" She hammered until the vibrations traveled to her elbows, until she could barely feel her hands. "Someone help!"

She kept pounding until the lock rattled. Kenna stepped back as the door opened and turned to reveal Taylor in the throes of what appeared to be a full-blown seizure. "She needs medical help!"

Andrew's colleague let out a frustrated sound and cursed. "You help her."

He stood by the door. Younger than Andrew, with patchy stubble on his chin and a dusting of orange powder on his T-shirt. Probably from lunch. She almost felt bad doing this to such a young guy.

Almost.

Kenna wailed, "My hands are tied!" Literally, they were tied. And the plastic bit grooves into her skin deep enough she didn't need to fake the tears in her eyes. "She needs an ambulance!"

"Stay back." He held out a palm. "I'd rather just shoot both of you. We can still get what we want if you're dead."

Kenna backed up to the wall. If these guys didn't care whether they were dead or alive, why check on her? He should've ignored the pounding and waited for Taylor to finish her pretend medical emergency—or stop breathing.

Taylor's convulsions had slowed. She still twitched every few seconds, and she made it look like her eyes had rolled back in her head. Kenna couldn't see what she'd done with the multitool and its protruding blade.

The door was still open. Kenna didn't hear anyone in the hall over the sound of her own gasps. Which weren't completely fake. It wasn't too much of a stretch that she was freaked out right now. She wanted this to work. They *needed* it to work.

"You should call an ambulance. She needs help. Look at her." Kenna poured all the desperation she felt into the tone of her voice.

The guy crouched by Taylor and reached out a hand to the skin of her neck.

Taylor's hand whipped up, and she shoved the knife blade into his side.

Kenna raced over, shoved him down, and pinned him there, her shin on his back. She wrestled the gun from his holster and backed up while he coughed. Blood soaked the side of his shirt.

The multitool clattered to the floor, Taylor's fingers bloody.

"You heard them." Kenna stared at the young, uniformed man. "We die, they don't even care. It's not even an inconvenience."

The guy rolled to glare at her, clutching his side.

She held the gun pointed at him. "Taylor, get his radio and then cut me free."

She saw the intention in his eyes, pulled back her foot, and kicked him in the chin.

He slumped to the floor.

Taylor made a noise in the back of her throat. "Can I just say, I'm glad I'm not still on your bad side."

Kenna held still while Taylor cut her free. Her wrists released, and she hissed out a breath. "Yeesh, that hurts a lot."

"What now?"

Kenna turned to the door, twisting the volume dial on the radio. Just static. "You okay?"

"Just get me out of here. That's the only thing I care about."

"Check his pockets for a cell phone." She went to the door and listened for a few long moments to make sure no one was coming. "Maybe he's all alone and the rest of them went to lunch."

"Or they're around the corner waiting to kill us."

Kenna figured it was more likely she'd played right into their hands. That this whole escape scenario was nothing but a setup so they could get rid of both Kenna and Taylor in one fell swoop, telling the FBI they couldn't get here in time to save the doctor.

From Kenna.

"Nothing."

"Come on." Kenna reached back with her left hand. "Hold on to me. We're doing this together."

Taylor grasped her hand.

Chapter Forty

B efore Kenna stepped into the hall, she checked the gun. If this was a setup, and it was their plan that she rob the guard of his gun, there would be zero bullets in this weapon. Or maybe only a single one. More, and she would know the young man came in here in good faith.

She released the magazine so it dropped into her waiting palm. "It's full."

"What does that mean?"

Kenna reinserted the magazine and pulled the slide back halfway, just far enough to confirm there was a round in the chamber. Loaded, safety off. "The kid was on guard duty. This isn't a setup. Which means they left him in charge, but probably only because everyone else is on something more important."

"We're not the most important thing happening here?" Taylor huffed. "I'm almost insulted."

"It makes no sense." He'd believed that they had an actual medical emergency. "Where is his backup? Unless they figured no way would he open the door."

"So, what? We fooled them. Him. Whichever."

Kenna peered out into the hall. "Maybe."

Taylor squeezed her hand. Kenna didn't let go. Solidarity was what she needed right now as she crept down the hall. Gun first.

Rickshire could still be here. Other men, including Andrew, could be as well. She couldn't take them all on alone, and Taylor had nothing to defend herself with. She'd left the bloody multitool beside the unconscious young man.

Kenna pulled out her baton from the holster at her ankle and flicked it to its full length. "Hold this. Just in case."

"Thanks."

Kenna clasped Taylor's free hand again and tugged. "Come on."

They headed for the end of the hall. "Not much we can do about cameras," Kenna whispered. She stopped and peered around the corner. "Just as long as we can find a phone."

"This whole place looks abandoned."

Taylor was right. There was trash on the floor. A couple of empty rooms they passed had those square ceiling tiles hanging down. Bare bulbs. Boxes broken down, stacked in a pile in the corner. Broken window blinds.

"Like a business that went out of business." Wow, she was tired. Kenna shook her head. "We need an office they're using."

If there were security cameras, there would be a security office. Or the front desk—no, too exposed to plant themselves in the lobby and be seen from the window. Unless their whole thing was minimal boots on the ground. Smaller footprint. If they were asked what this place was, they'd say they were just paid security guards. No one else here.

"Or a bathroom." Taylor shivered enough Kenna felt it in their clasped hands.

"Sorry, but that's not high priority." Kenna checked the next open door. "But they did walk you there and then back to the room when you had to use the facilities?"

"They took me the other way, but I didn't see an exit. Just a door for the stairs, I think."

"Elevator?"

"Not that I remember. The toilets didn't even work." Taylor shuddered.

"Maybe we're on the second floor. Or in a basement. Do you see any windows?"

"No."

Kenna nudged a door with her shoe. Open plan office, like a call center with no desks. Just those little cubicles that blocked the noise, all shoved against one wall. Plastic sheets. A camera setup. Laptop on a table.

Kenna kept going, trying not to contemplate what was supposed to happen in there. Looking at a computer could be a waste of time if they weren't hooked up, and she couldn't risk it. Time was something they didn't have a lot of right now.

She reached a closed door at the end of the hall.

"Maybe we should backtrack and find an exit?"

Kenna tugged on Taylor's hand. "Stand against the wall."

"Why are you going in there?"

She pointed to the strip of light at the bottom of the door, watching to make sure there was no visible movement. A shadow, someone walking around in front of the light.

Nothing.

The hall behind her was clear. Kenna twisted the handle and pushed the door open. Empty. Just a bank of computers with multiple monitors. Video images of empty halls. Rooms. A bathroom.

"Gross. They watched me pee."

Kenna looked at the screens again. "The garage." She

pointed it out to Taylor and, as if on cue, both doors opened up, revealing two huge black SUVs.

Kenna grabbed the phone from the desk off its base and called Ryson's number while the SUVs parked in the garage. Doors opened on both sides, both cars. Multiple men climbed out.

"We have to leave." Taylor covered her mouth. "They're coming."

Ryson answered. "This better be you, Kenna."

She was about to make a joke about his car warranty when her eyes filled with tears. "They're coming. We don't have much time."

"Taylor?"

"She's here. You need to send—"

She heard him click his fingers and his voice grew fainter, like he was talking over his shoulder. "Do you have it?"

In the background, someone said, "The number she's calling from is registered to a business. I have the address."

"Okay." She could barely get the word out.

"Sit tight. The cavalry is coming, and you can tell me everything when I get there, but for right now find somewhere secure to hole up."

"Copy that." The words were barely audible.

"Gotta go now."

Kenna didn't want to hang up. "Bye."

"Hide." The line went dead.

"Look at that." Taylor pointed at a screen two monitors away. "Is that Gerald Rickshire?"

Kenna put her palm on the desk and stared at the image. They'd left the young man bleeding out. What was the Seventh Day Killer doing going in there? "Oh yeah...you're right. But all he'll find is that poor kid we left unconscious. He'll probably kill him."

"Those men are *coming*."

"Find somewhere to hide." She touched Taylor's shoulders. "Hide and don't come out."

Taylor nodded. "What are you going to do?"

"My job."

Kenna raced down the hall. She said a prayer for Taylor, that she would find a safe place and be secure there until the police showed up. She had a gun with plenty of bullets this time. These people had shown their true colors when they left a serial child murderer to roam free around this place.

Kenna raced down the hall, back to the room where they'd been held captive. She kicked the door open. "Rickshire!"

He spun around, bloody knife in hand.

Kenna didn't need to look overlong at the guard to know he was dead. "You shouldn't have done that." As if he needed more black marks on his soul.

Rickshire stood holding her multitool. He said nothing.

Maybe Taylor had killed the young man. Or maybe Rickshire had finished the job.

"That's mine." It now had his fingerprints on it. "Drop it." She held her gun aimed at his chest. Did he still have that vest on? She raised the weapon.

He flashed his teeth and dropped the knife. "You'll kill an unarmed man? You don't do that, remember."

"I would make an exception. Just this one time. No one is watching, and I'm out of camera range back here."

The skin around his eyes flexed.

"Yeah, I know about the office. The cops are on their way. There's nowhere to go, so just give it up Rickshire. It's over for you."

"They're not the only ones on their way. Who will get up here first, do you think? Your friends, or our hosts and their *benefactor*?"

Kenna swallowed. "Who is it?" She had her suspicions, but if Rickshire knew then he could verify it for her. No one had actually yet confirmed Angeline Pacer's involvement. "Tell me who's running the show, and I'll let the cops know you cooperated."

"End of the line for me. No deals."

He was likely correct in his estimation. An escaped prisoner helping a group of kidnappers? He wouldn't be allowed to get away with this. "Tell me who the Benefactor is. You have nothing to lose. You could go on to live your life."

"In prison?"

"Better than dead."

"Is it?"

Kenna started to speak. A heavy door down the hall swung open and hit the wall. Men in black cargoes and black T-shirts poured out.

She had nowhere to go, but would rather take her chances with a single man than a whole group. She flung the door shut and held the gun on Rickshire so he didn't try anything while she got the keys from the dead kid.

He laughed when she locked them in and pocketed the keys. "Interesting choice."

The men in the hall pounded the door and tried the handle. "Shoot out the lock!"

Another voice replied, "That never actually works."

An argument ensued, followed by more pounding and yelling. She felt—more than heard—Rickshire move toward her. Kenna tried to fight back the fear. She had a gun, and he was only one man. There was nothing impressive about a killer who targeted helpless children.

She started to lift the gun. Her arms were so heavy the way they'd been in the days after her surgeries. Breath escaped her mouth in a cloud as the ice spread over. Inch by inch, freezing her in its wake until she couldn't move. Couldn't think.

Rickshire swung out with her multitool.

Kenna spun away from him to shield her body from the slash before her mind even registered the fire that whipped across the outside of her arm. She turned back and held the gun up. "Drop the weapon! Drop it now!"

Rickshire came at her again. He screamed, intent on murder. Revenge.

Kenna squeezed off a single round that exploded in the room. Light so bright it blinded her. The sound, a boom that shook her eardrums.

He collapsed, clutching his leg. His face twisted as though to cry out. She couldn't hear it.

Kenna kicked the knife out of his reach.

Her ears registered the sound of pounding on the door. Yelling.

She backed up until she hit the wall, breathing hard. Rickshire lay on the floor, blood on his hands and the leg of his pants and the floor underneath him. He screamed curses her ears couldn't register. She slid down until her knees bent and her behind hit the floor, still clasping the gun in her hands.

Alone, trapped with a serial killer.

The victim. Again.

This time it ends differently.

She didn't know how long it was until the door opened. How long she stared at Rickshire while he bled out from his thigh.

Then the world erupted into movement around her. She saw those blue shell jackets. Yellow letters emblazoned on the back. FBI. An agent rolled Rickshire to his face and put a knee in his back. The released killer was cuffed.

Another agent touched the young man's neck and shook his head.

They moved around her, while Kenna sat staring.

Someone touched her knee.

Kenna started.

"Easy." He took the gun from her hands. Jax.

"Where's Taylor?"

"We found her. She's okay. The men are all either dead or in custody."

"The benefactor is here."

He shook his head. "We'll sort through it all. Can you stand?"

Kenna stared at him.

"Are you okay?"

She tried to speak. No words came.

He holstered his gun and touched her hands, feeling the cuts from the ties on her wrists. He checked her arms. Her legs. Straightening one and then the other. He shone a light in her eyes.

Kenna frowned.

"There you are." He touched her chin, worry and relief on his face.

Kenna bit her lip. Jax started to stand. She grabbed his jacket and pulled him to her the way Jessica Pierce's husband, Steven, had done on the floor of his hallway. A moment of shared pain.

She pulled in a long breath that broke a few times while she buried her face in his collar.

"Come on. Let's get out of here." Jax lifted her into his arms.

"I can walk."

"It's three flights of stairs."

"Where is my dog?"

"In my car. Hopefully it doesn't stink now." His voice rumbled under her cheek.

"Don't take me to the hospital."

"You may not get that choice, but we'll ask the EMTs."

"I'm fine. Just tired."

"Mmm." More rumble.

"This doesn't mean I trust you."

Chapter Forty-One

Jax reached for the door to her motorhome first. "Don't bother arguing."

She didn't even have the energy to ask him what he was talking about. She needed eighteen hours of uninterrupted sleep.

Jax stepped inside, leaving her to wait while he checked to make sure no homicidal types waited for her. At least, that was what she figured he was doing. Considering she'd been the victim of a break-in before she was kidnapped, she didn't mind so much if he wanted to make sure her space was safe.

Cabot jumped up after him and headed for her bed.

Kenna leaned against the door frame. "You're such a good dog. Yes, you are."

Cabot lay down and stared at her, tail wagging.

The knife wound on the outside of her arm stung. In the end, she'd persuaded Jax to take her to the doctor's office where Valentina worked, which served double-duty because Ryson had been able to glare at her the whole time. After telling her that Wilkern was out with Steven explaining everything that had happened, so he'd know the whole story about his wife's death, Ryson had given her a lengthy lecture about putting herself in danger.

The fact he'd been holding a baby all through the diatribe negated the displeasure rolling from him, but Kenna got the message. He was upset because she'd been hurt. Because his phone had been stolen, and they'd used a fake text from him. Because his absence from home—he'd been at the grocery store with Valentina and Luci—had been used to lure her into a trap set by homicidal kidnappers.

Kenna didn't care. Well, that wasn't entirely true. She did care. She knew what it felt like to be worried sick over a loved one. But it hadn't been all bad, getting a lecture from Ryson. She'd been able to see her friends while she got stitched up, and now she was home.

Her phone buzzed in her pocket. Kenna looked at the screen, then stowed it again. Not Ryson this time. Another text from Taylor. One in a long string of photos, GIFs, and messages from her friend. And from Ian. Even a video from Bethany.

Taylor was at the hospital being assessed, safe and with her family.

"It's clear."

She took a step towards Jax before stumbling backward off the step stool. "Whoa."

"Sorry." He held out a hand and tugged her inside. "You okay?"

Cabot stared at her.

"No one is trying to kill me or convince everyone I'm crazy, so I'm thinking *yeah*."

Even if they hadn't found the benefactor, all those guys were in jail. Including Gerald Rickshire. The First Lady was nowhere to be found, but she would turn up eventually.

He closed the door. "I can't tell if you're trying to be funny."

"I'm too tired to be funny." Kenna stared at the closed door. Then she glanced at him.

Whatever he read on her face made him sigh. "I'll make tea. I brought a bag, it's my special blend."

She was too tired to argue.

Kenna slumped into a seat at the table, too exhausted to even try to make a plan about how to clean herself up. How she was going to change her clothes one-handed, she had no idea. She also needed a shower since her arm had been smeared with Betadine. Change the bandage. Wash her hair. It was like the days after her surgeries all over again. Figuring out how to do things alone when she had limited use of her hands. Even unscrewing the cap on the prescription bottle of pain meds had been a chore.

She touched her forehead to the table. The urge to run persisted even now but, until she was healed, there was no point trying to drive long distances. And she wanted to see Taylor tomorrow. And baby Luci.

Then there was the conversation she needed to have with Stairns.

The First Lady was still out there.

Kenna shuddered. This was just lingering adrenaline from the last few days. The need to flee attention was only a reflex.

She heard Jax settle on the opposite side of her table and she lifted her head to meet his gaze. "Tell me where we're at."

"The First Lady was supposedly with the men who arrived in the two SUVs."

"So she *was* the benefactor?"

He shrugged one shoulder. "No one saw her, and no one knows how she slipped away."

"Duh, someone helped her."

He frowned. "We're unpacking the details from their statements, and when we find her we'll get everything figured out. Right now, she's missing."

"But there's a manhunt underway?"

"A low-key one. No one needs this blown out of proportion."

Kenna started to speak.

"Last night, just after eleven in the evening, a group of men attempted to kidnap Governor Pacer. Stairns was there in St. George. He stopped it."

"A kidnapping? That sounds familiar." Stairns was the one who stopped it? Kenna didn't understand her old boss at all. Was he an ally, or not? "Andrew and all his guys were here in Salt Lake City, so who was behind that?"

"There were three of them. Stairns shot one, and the Governor's men took out the other two. Stairns is a hero who foiled an assassination plot."

Kenna took a sip of tea. "Of course he is." The beverage wasn't terrible, considering it kind of tasted like licorice. "The First Lady came to the office and met with Stairns. Whether she told him then, or he learned another way what she had planned, he worked to circumvent it. So she was really going to take her husband out?"

This whole thing was so crazy Kenna could hardly keep it all straight in her mind. Stairns had seen the light. He'd gone against Angeline Pacer to save a life instead of destroying one. Whatever the reason, it had resulted in something good.

For once.

Not to mention the plan to set Kenna up, making it look like she'd killed both Taylor *and* the governor, hadn't been successful. She figured that would've been Angeline's plan.

To make sure everyone thoroughly believed Kenna had done it all just to get back at them.

Revenge.

Jax sipped from his own mug. "And now Stairns is working things out with the governor, getting it all straight. He won't be back in town for a few days. Maybe not until Mrs. Pacer is brought in. Stairns put himself out there to save the governor and bring to light what the First Lady had planned."

That was something, at least. Though Kenna couldn't help but think it might be a case of too little, too late, considering people were dead because of Angeline. The First Lady had it in her head that after everything Kenna had lost, it still wasn't enough. She also needed to be completely discredited.

The woman was a menace. Kenna wanted her brought in before someone else was hurt. Or before Angeline decided Kenna needed to be dead. "Where is she?"

"We'll find her."

She couldn't decipher the look in his eyes. "What about the guys you arrested at the warehouse? What are they saying?"

"You were right."

"That's what they're saying?"

Jax smiled. "You know what I mean." He brushed nonexistent crumbs from the table. "You put it together about the First Lady and her nephew. All of this—the misdirection and the issues they had—you're the one who figured it out."

"And what are *you* saying?"

"Stairns was an idiot to let you go."

Kenna started to object. "You know what? You're right. I was an asset as an agent."

"You still are."

She wondered what was going to come next.

"Stick around. Sign on as a consultant."

Kenna's gut reaction was to tell him no, but she didn't want to do that just because she hadn't let go of all the resentment yet. She might not want revenge, but that didn't mean there wasn't plenty for her to work through.

Instead, Kenna gave herself time to say, "I'll think about it. I want some alone time first. It's been days upon days, and I really need the solitude back for a while so I can get my equilibrium."

It might take a few hours, or a couple of days. It might take weeks, or months. She didn't know.

"I understand that."

"You do?"

He nodded. "What we get isn't always what we want. Even if everyone doesn't understand why we need it. Sometimes you have to walk away. Do a one-eighty and take the risk you'll find something better."

"I feel like there's a story there."

Jax shifted to the edge of the bench and stood. "I'll tell you. Someday. If you stick around." He shot her a smile and the door snapped shut behind him.

Kenna smiled to the empty room. She wanted to wish she'd never come back to Salt Lake City at all, but then Gerald Rickshire would've killed Ellayna Feathers. Kenna could, and did, live with a lot. But she refused to live with that. Even for the sake of revenge, she would never allow a child to die.

Perhaps if she had wanted revenge the way the narrative went, she might not feel so empty all the time. Like the motorhome without a dog. But she just couldn't muster the energy for payback.

Cabot came over and sniffed her hand. Kenna ruffled the fur under her chin. The dog continued on down the hall. She hopped up on the bed and lay down with a groan.

Great.

Kenna was about to call her down when the door opened again. "So much for alone time," she joked. "What'd you forget?" She lifted her gaze.

It wasn't Jax.

"Hey, what—?"

Angeline Pacer stepped inside, a gun in one hand. Clothes disheveled, hair a mess. Makeup smeared on her cheeks. She'd been through the wringer and still managed to look better than Kenna.

Cabot lifted to stand on the bed, the hair on her back raised. She barked twice.

"Shut the door on that dog."

Kenna edged toward the end of the bench seat. Was Angeline going to fire that gun as soon as her back was turned? "Easy. Okay?"

"Just do it."

Exhaustion weighed down her muscles as she took the two steps toward the bedroom and slid the door closed. Cabot jumped down to stick her nose between the door and frame. "No, baby. Out."

The dog backed up half a step. She didn't want to obey, but she would. That was good. Kenna didn't want mindless obedience.

She catalogued every weapon she owned, but there was nothing within reach. Not a single one on her person. The FBI had confiscated everything as evidence, given it had all been used to take down the guys associated with the threat this woman had caused.

There was nothing in the motorhome that she could get to without opening a drawer or cupboard door.

No way to defend herself.

Kenna couldn't even get to her phone. She turned to Angeline and saw the First Lady hadn't moved. Was she going to use that gun, or had she just come here to say what she wanted to say and then leave?

"Coming here was a mistake. You should have run."

The normally serene look on Angeline's face devolved into a sneer that could have cut Kenna's skin it was so vicious. The First Lady's true colors were finally on display. The woman she was, without the mask of civility. "I'm right where I should be."

Kenna spread her hands. Never mind that Angeline had no right to enter Kenna's personal space. Her private property.

The stitches on her arm bit into her skin. She didn't show even an ounce of pain. "What do you want?"

She hadn't taken enough already? She had to come here and try to take even more. *We both grieve for Bradley. For what could have been.*

Behind her, Cabot scratched at the door and whined.

How did she get Angeline to understand?

"I want my son back." The First Lady bit the words out. "Since I'll never get that, you don't get to live free. I'm not running before I kill you."

They had a shared loss, and yet Angeline had apparently never seen it that way. "We're both going to—"

Angeline squeezed the trigger.

The shot hit Kenna right in the middle of her chest. Her body flinched. She cried out at the tearing pain.

The door slammed open. "FBI! Drop the gun! Drop it!" A gun exploded.

Kenna slumped to the ground.

Angeline Pacer also hit the floor in front of her. Dead.

Consciousness swam in and out like the tide. Each roll brought a wave of pain. Her chest was on fire.

"Kenna." He bit out a curse. "Yes, this is FBI Special Agent Jaxton. I need an ambulance. *Now.*"

Chapter Forty-Two

Warmth crowded her. It was too warm.

Kenna squirmed. Pain shot through the numbness that made her limbs feel like she was floating.

"Easy."

Kenna latched onto the familiar voice.

"She's waking up."

"Let her get here in her own time."

She blinked, but the world was too bright. Kenna squeezed her eyes shut and darkness descended.

Sometime later, Kenna blinked again but she didn't know how long it had been. The room came into focus, along with a man who sat beside the bed. The hospital. She was at the hospital. He was here.

"Bradley."

The man lifted his head. It wasn't Bradley, it was Jax. He got up and came to lean against the bed. "Hey."

Fear filled her. Kenna didn't know how to beat it back.

"Hey." He laid a hand on hers and leaned down. "It's okay. You're safe."

Kenna shook her head. "Stairs. Taylor..."

"Everything is fine."

My baby.

"You're safe."

She'd been right here before, in a hospital room just like this, and this was like reliving her worst nightmare. A waking dream. Betrayed. Retired. Hung out to dry. She'd lost her baby, her career, and her partner in one go. And then she had nothing but the pain. The guilt and shame.

It felt like she'd been split open.

"Easy. You'll hurt yourself."

She grasped Jax's arm and felt the familiar ice pick jab in her forearm.

"You aren't alone. Not this time." He knew why she didn't want to be here, where everything had gone wrong. Jax leaned down and kissed her forehead. "Easy, Kenna. Take it easy."

Full circle. She'd come right back to that moment when she'd hit bottom. Why did God want her to relive it? This couldn't be some twisted method to get her to see something she'd missed before. A lesson not yet learned. No. He didn't work that way.

"Why?" She couldn't get a sentence out. Just that one word.

"You got shot." Jax settled on the edge of the bed. "You're okay. They put you back together." He looked like he wanted to be sick.

"Angeline?"

"I killed her." Before she could ask, he continued, "I was in my car, and I saw her approach with a gun. I should have known she'd show up. I'm just grateful to God that I stuck around because if I hadn't..." He didn't finish.

"You saved my life."

"I didn't keep you from getting shot. Your dog freaked out. She's in my car again." He didn't seem so happy about that.

"But you're okay, and that's the point. Ryson and his family were here. They want me to call when you wake up. And he said Ellayna Feathers's mother is here as well, on the fifth floor, having her baby."

Life, moving on.

Kenna had wanted to run again. She would have, except for this. Now she was back here in this place. Waiting for God to give her what He hadn't before.

Was this it? Life.

Friendship.

People she shouldn't push away. People who cared for her.

"Thank you."

He shook his head. "I don't deserve that."

"We don't often get what we deserve."

He looked shaken. Pale, like he hadn't slept in days. "Stairs came by as well. He wants to apologize."

"Don't tell him I woke up. And if he has paperwork he says I signed—" She had to take a breath to get the rest out, but it was important. "—shred it. Or burn it."

"You don't want to sign on as my civilian partner?" He touched a hand to his chest. "I'm distraught."

"You do need my help to solve cases."

The corner of his mouth curled up. "I'm not taking that bait. I'm just going to marvel in the fact Angeline Pacer is dead and you're not. Rickshire is in custody, and so is Angeline's nephew. His guys won't stop talking. Can't get a one of them to shut up. Things are good. Not perfect, that's an impossible standard. But they are good."

"Knock, knock." The unfamiliar voice belonged to an older woman. Holding onto the stylish woman's hand was a girl Kenna knew.

"Ellayna."

She hesitated beside her grandmother and tucked her body close to the older woman's side. She eyed Jax for a second but returned all her attention to Kenna.

"When we heard you were here, she wanted to see you. But we don't want to interrupt."

Jax rounded the bed to her left so they could approach from the door. "Not at all. Please, come in."

"Go ahead, honey." The grandmother ushered Ellayna close. Kenna reached out.

"Hi." *Take my hand.*

Ellayna slid a tiny hand in hers.

Relief rolled through Kenna.

"Bubby is coming."

Kenna smiled. "Is he? That's exciting."

"Grandma said it's kind of icky, and I agree. But Mommy was crying."

Kenna looked at the grandmother, who shook her head very slightly. It didn't seem like anything was wrong. Maybe that was normal.

Before she could say anything to Ellayna, Kenna felt those tiny fingers run across the skin of her forearm. The scars from Sebastian Almatter, and the cuts he'd made to her forearms.

"Now I'll have another one to match." Kenna touched the fingers of her other hand to the hospital gown over her front. "Right here. Just as jagged and ugly as this one."

Ellayna stared up at her.

"Sometimes the inside feels like that, too. You know? You get so scared and then later, when you're alone in your bedroom, it's like you're right back there. It hurts."

Ellayna didn't respond, just looked at Kenna's arm again. Her fingers slid across the raised skin. She nodded, the barest of movements. Eight years old, and she already knew the horrors the world could bring.

"Life is happening all around you. You'll see it, Laynie. When you meet Bubby, or when it's Christmas or your birthday. When you're at the beach and the sun is shining, and you get ice cream in your hair. You won't have to live back there in the dark, where you're scared. Not anymore." Kenna motioned between them with one finger. "You live right here. In the daylight. With people who love you."

Kenna felt a tear drop onto the back of her hand. Behind her, the grandmother mouthed, *thank you.*

Ellayna ducked her head and laid the barest of kisses on the scar on Kenna's forearm. And then they were gone.

Jax sat quietly with her while Kenna pretended to doze for a while. She heard a scuffle and opened her eyes. His back to her, at the door. Barring entry to someone.

Stairns.

"Jax."

He didn't turn. "Papers."

She frowned.

Stairns said, "I need to speak to her. And I'm still your boss, Jaxton."

"It's okay." She might as well get it over with, and Jax was here with her. It wasn't like last time.

Stairns came to her bedside.

Jax took his seat and the SAC looked at him. Jax just folded his arms.

Kenna didn't have the energy to be amused. "What is it?"

Stairns separated the papers into two piles. "These are *my* retirement papers." The ones in his right hand.

"Sir—"

He ignored Jax's objection and waved the ones in his left. "This is an employment contract."

She waited for him to explain.

"The First Lady was going to run for president herself, as

the grieving mother and the strong woman who had weathered the atrocities you'd planned. She had it all figured out, right under my nose, and I didn't see it until it was too late." He shrugged. "I was planning to retire in a couple of years anyway, so I just moved up the timetable."

"Because you think you lost your edge?"

"You and I both know I've lost a lot more than that within the last few years."

"Why tell me now?"

He waved the employment contract.

"You got a new job?"

"Yeah, working for you."

Kenna frowned. She started to object but had no idea where to even start. "There's not... I don't..."

"It's not a terrible idea. Don't dismiss it. Let me tell you what I'm planning."

"I don't need to be a boss."

He shook his head. "Support staff. Research I can do from my deck. Someone you can run a theory by. Like a partner."

"If you think—"

"On a strictly voluntary basis."

"You want to work for me for free?"

Stairns said, "I'll be retired, but I'll need something to do." Like figuring out that the governor's life was in danger and foiling the assassination plot? "I messed up two years ago. Let me make amends."

"I don't need your penance." And yet, she would be getting something for free. Help. Support. Friendship.

Grace to shine in those dark places.

She eyed him. "I'll think about it."

After all, she wasn't just going to say yes without making him grovel at least a little bit more.

Stairns smiled. It was scary. "Excellent."

"I'm going to regret this, aren't I?"

Jax said, "Maybe he can watch your dog until you're out of the hospital."

Kenna laughed. Then she glared at Jax, because laughing *hurt*. He didn't seem too bothered by her ire.

She looked at Stairns. Wasn't he going to leave now that he'd said what he came here to say?

"I'm guessing you already have a case for me."

She realized she did. "Those nine women, Christopher Halpert's victims? Help me find their bodies."

Life moved on, and she walked her path in the light where she could feel the warmth of hope on her face. Where people who cared about her showed up.

Where grace overflowed from those dark places to fill her whole future.

————

I hope you enjoyed *Cold Dead Night,* the first in my new thriller series, *Brand of Justice*. This series is planned to be a long-running series over the next few years! Please know, I'm not forsaking my Romantic Suspense roots. *Benson First Responders*, will be releasing in parallel and will build on the *Downrange* series. Keep an eye out for more information, sign up for my newsletter and follow me on Facebook to stay up-to-date!

Would you consider leaving a review, please? It genuinely helps others to find their next read!

Also by Lisa Phillips

Find out more about Brand of Justice at my website:
https://authorlisaphillips.com/brand-of-justice

Book 1: Cold Dead Night (Aug 2022)

Book 2: Burn the Dawn (Nov 2022)

Book 3: Quick and Dead (Feb 2023)

———

Other series by Lisa:

Last Chance Downrange

Chevalier Protection Specialists

Last Chance County

Northwest Counter-Terrorism Taskforce

Double Down

WITSEC Town (Sanctuary)

———

Numerous other titles including several with *Love Inspired Suspense*, find the complete list here:

https://authorlisaphillips.com/full-book-list

About the Author

Find out more about Lisa Phillips, and other books she has written, by visiting her website: https://authorlisaphillips.com

Would you also share about the book on Social Media, leave a review on Lisa's page and share about your experience? Your review will help others find great clean fiction and decide what to read next!

Visit https://authorlisaphillips.com/subscribe where you can sign up for my NEWSLETTER and get free books!

Printed in Great Britain
by Amazon

38170110R00239